LOST IN THE STARS

Vol. 2 of the Three Worlds Saga

Carol A. Strickland

Other books by Carol A. Strickland

Touch of Danger – vol. 1 of the Three Worlds Saga

Lost in the Stars – vol. 2 of the Three Worlds Saga

Worlds Apart – vol. 4 of the Three Worlds Saga

Mind Shift – vol. 5 of the Three Worlds Saga

Secrets of the Worlds – vol. 6 of the Three Worlds Saga

Applesauce and Moonbeams – wacky soft sci fi

Nothing Personal – ditto but wackier

Burgundy and Lies – sweet historical romance

Star-Spangled Panties – the full nonfiction dish on Wonder Woman!

Published by Carol A. Strickland
www.CarolAStrickland.com

Publisher's Note: This is a work of fiction. Names, characters, places, and incidents are a product of the author's imagination. Locales and public names are sometimes used for atmospheric purposes. Any resemblance to actual people, living or dead, or to businesses, companies, events, institutions, or locales is completely coincidental.

Book Layout © 2017 BookDesignTemplates.com

Interior illustration by the amazing Colleen Doran.

Lost in the Stars / Carol A. Strickland.
ISBN Print edition 978-0-9912688-7-0
ISBN Digital edition 978-0-9912688-6-3
ISBN IngramSpark Print edition 978-1-941318-26-3
ISBN IngramSpark Digital edition 978-1-941318-27-0

WITH THANKS…

…to Colleen Doran for agreeing to do the illustrations for this first four-volume story arc, though I may have stacked the deck when I hinted that Jae might bear a physical resemblance to a certain Tromian she loves.

…to the various HCRW, RWA, and general indie lists/workshop folks who are helping everyone through this brain-twisting transformation in printing we call "Indie." Sarra Cannon, you're right there at the top of the list of Helpful People!

…to David Williamson for Irish dialogue advice.

…to Anselm Audley for edits on the original book.

A Wedding Reception Interrupted

Carolina O'Kelly's stomach clenched. Hundreds of eyes stared at her. Strangers. People she'd never heard of, but who were crazy famous here on this new world of Sarastor: Lon knew them all.

Courage, she reminded herself.

"Lina, we need a reception," Londo Rand told her as they descended the steps from the stage into the computer-generated, grassy amphitheater. "You can port in something from Earzh and we'll all go through quarantine again for three days here in the holosuite, all right? It'll be cozy."

She made a tight sound like a cornered mouse.

The fingers of his left hand pressed into her waist. "Relax, *chérie*," he whispered. "I'm with you. You're safe."

"Luckily for us," he declared in louder tones for the guests' sake, "we're at Affiliated Systems Mega-Legion Headquarters, which just happens to be the most advanced fortress in the sector. Maybe even the entire galaxy. If we can provision an army at the drop of a hat, we can get some supplies for *une soirée*."

The crowd of Mega-Legionnaires and their families pressed in. Despite her determination, Lina clutched at Londo. He held up his free hand and the crowd went silent.

"*Pardonnez-moi un moment, mes amis*," he announced, "but I must arrange for a proper wedding reception. Give me a few minutes and then we can party!"

They ran into problems when the Mega-Legion's nutritional director objected not only to a fancy breakfast with "*termidge hek* proteins," whatever those were, but also to the concept of a frosted cake being served to her charges. Subcommander Andri, one of the few Legionnaires Lina recognized, was nice enough to override some of the rules for them.

Then it took mere minutes for automated tables laden with breakfast to roll in through the holosuite's doors, followed by a squad of white-uniformed service personnel. By then Lon had programmed lawn games. The younger members of the crowd whacked at small, low-floating balls with bats as if they were in a death match version of croquet.

As odd yet familiar music filled the meadow, some of the adults began to form groups in various patterns away from the games in order to hop and step in a line-dance.

"Aren't Kool and his Gang supposed to be singing to this?" Lina whispered to Lon as they watched.

"I had to strip off the vocals and more than half the instruments," Lon whispered back. "They don't go for singing here, *chérie*, but they like the beat.

"*Voyons*." He rubbed his nose thoughtfully as he glanced around the springtime woodland meadow setting. The glorious, sun-filled design had been Jae's work, a reflection of Jae's home world as it had once been when its days had been lush and fecund.

Lon noted that the crowd seemed to be enjoying the entertainment he'd programmed, the food he'd ordered. They might be moving a little slowly because of the earliness of the hour, but the wedding had been invigorating enough. He added a few more recreation areas, some seating, and even a shallow fish pond with a fountain and sound shielding for those more contemplative members to appreciate. Finally he glanced to the suite's CGI sky and nodded. "It doesn't look like rain. This place is perfect."

But the first person to separate from the crowd to greet them was Aiko Fallow, aka the great heroine Orenya.

She hugged Lon and gave him a huge kiss on the cheek, then came over to Lina and did the same. Her gold-tipped hair batted lightly against Lina's cheek, along with an earring that more accompanied her ear than was attached to it. She too had pointed ears like Lon's friend Jae, though hers pointed toward the back.

She certainly seemed an elf princess. She had a bright China-doll smile and dark chocolate complexion. Cheekbones and a svelte figure that any model would die for. And a broken heart hiding behind it all.

Lina didn't know what to say when they were introduced. She could tell that Aiko knew that she knew what Aiko had been to Londo.

Lina looked at Lon.

"I talked to Aiko already," he assured her.

When had he had a chance to–?

"He said you were in the shower," Aiko said quietly. People around them were looking expectant, waiting for a scene. "Don't worry; I'll be fine. *Mazel tov.*"

Lina and Lon both startled at the translation from the marble that floated next to Lina's ear, and had to explain it to Aiko.

"So you're the lucky girl who finally got him." Aiko raised her voice for the immediate crowd to hear. "I've been wondering what you all have been up to, quarantined in the lab. Now we know, hm? Congratulations. And Lina, I've got some embarrassing stories that you'll need to keep him in line. I'll talk to you later, all right?"

Lina did her best to form a genuine smile, and agreed.

"Don't believe anything she tells you," Lon stage-whispered to Lina as Aiko turned to leave. Aiko laughed loudly in disdain, as did others around her.

Poor, brave Aiko. Lina knew she'd never have had the courage to be here if the situation had been reversed. Aiko even made her flight away from the newlyweds seem like a social stroll.

"Who's hiding the drinks?" Lon asked. The merriment had drained from him.

"Neutrino's in charge of ratchets!" someone behind them shouted.

"It's too early for ratchets," Londo protested. "But I know a perfect morning cocktail—"

"No alcohol!" Andri's voice boomed unnaturally across the crowd, punctuated by writing in the sky that Lon confirmed to Lina reiterated what she said. "Ten demerits per glass!"

Two people in those white jumpsuit uniforms entered through the tree-doorway to the holosuite, guiding a table that contained a large, flat green thing to the dining area. It must be the cake. Andri had insisted upon a fruit glaze instead of icing. Guests who had lined up to be served from the breakfast spread, curiously scrutinized the new arrival.

"That was fast," Lina said.

"We're efficient. We are the Legion. STAY AWAY FROM THE CAKE!" Lon dropped her hand and strode toward the cake table, pointing accusation. The server who'd been about to make the first cut dropped his knife with a clang, and everyone within six feet backed away hurriedly.

"The cake is for later," Londo commanded. "Bride and groom have the first slices. It is a ceremony. But first—"

Over Lon's shoulder Lina glimpsed two familiar people halfway across the meadow. The Mega-Legion's commander, Stoan Kinrol, seemed to be questioning Dr. Wilder Mem-Bazer with great agitation. The scholarly Wiley calmly lectured in response but was being interrupted again and again. Of course they must be discussing mind control. And Lina.

Now others came up to the newlyweds, people whose skin ranged up and down the bluish, orangish and brownish spectrums. Most wore tight, tight suits, and not all of them were parahero uniforms, Lina thought.

Minor features varied here and there, but nothing that Industrial Light and Magic couldn't easily do. Then there was the human-sized mantis who greeted Lon and made a joke Lina's translator didn't explain well. Still, she smiled at the thing to be polite.

And there came the short, rangy man who smirked his way up to Londo. It appeared that he'd won on the Legion's betting boards. Oh no. Not that bet.

Londo wound up tossing him into the air as if he'd been a baseball, to a roar of laughter from the crowd. The man had comically shaken his fist at Lon and floated down to disappear behind the others.

These were the people Londo worked with.

Lon nudged her in the ribs. That was all the warning she had before he tipped his head back and bellowed to the heavens, "TERRAN TRADITION!" Then in a more reasonable tone: "My lovely bride is going to throw the bridal bouquet."

He waved the crowd back to create some space, then strode to a rise of the green and orated as they all listened. Lina could tell that he loved being the center of attention.

In his Napoleonic wedding finery, he made a stupendous figure even against the garish colors of the crowd. His voice was rich and powerful as he wove his story.

"This is an ancient Terran custom, dating back – I don't know. Centuries. Millennia, maybe. Back before technology, to the mysterious Dark Ages of Earzh! These were the times between the fall of empires and the struggle to regain the knowledge that was lost. From this era came epics of heroes saving their maidens fair, of battles against fierce monsters using only swords and sheer bravery for defense!"

He began to fight an imaginary creature with an air sword, describing the battle and invoking both Robin Hood and Rapunzel in the same breath. He parried and thrust. The crowd ebbed back before him and followed not too closely behind as the battle raged to a new spot. Finally he cut the – whatever it was – into bloody strips to lie dying on the ground and then cleaned his air sword with an imaginary rag.

"Alas, poor dragon," he sorrowed, "I knew it well."

Some of the people in the group applauded. Lina distinctly heard a "Don't encourage him," from someone behind her, and Londo bowed to all corners, lastly to her.

"Everyone – You'll notice that flowers are used as the bouquet as well as the decorations for a wedding. This is all very traditional. Earzh is a beautiful planet, filled with flowers. Now – All eligible females try to catch the bouquet to see who's going to be the next bride. No exceptions!" Lon wagged his finger at some little girls in the front of the crowd who were watching him goggle-eyed. Apparently he had admirers of many ages across the galaxy. "Gather 'round! Gather 'round!"

Lina joined him and hefted her bouquet. "This won't go very far," she warned everyone. The group of girls and women moved closer. Lina turned her back and gave it a hearty toss over her head. It arced over female hands to land at the back in Aiko's arms.

"Interesting air currents in here," Lina murmured to Londo.

"Dragon wings," he whispered back. "So are you wearing a garter under all that?"

"A garter?" Lina's eyes darted unfocused back and forth as she shifted her legs under her long skirt. "Um. I think I am. Just one, right leg."

"Someone knew I was coming." Lon chortled.

"Just like Someone knows you're French." She fingered the lapel of his French Imperial outfit that was not a fashion out of French-Canadian legend. His mouth opened slightly as he realized the truth of it. An orphan with parents unknown – perhaps this was another hint at his origins from whoever or whatever had orchestrated their clothing?

It took a few minutes to explain the garter custom and get the eligible men gathered. Lon took great delight in divesting her of her garter ("This is not obscene," he yelled at a gossiping clique. "This is wholesome Terran tradition! Get your minds out of the gutter!"), and when he threw it it landed on the top of Jae Rallene's blond head. Jae had not been a part of the receiving crowd. He hadn't even been turned toward them.

"Favoritism!" someone yelled, but Lon just laughed at them. "I don't think I'll tell them the part about how Jae has to put it on Aiko," he told Lina. "Things might get too rowdy for the–"

Without warning, blinking red light flooded the entire meadow. The music stopped in mid-note. For a moment, everyone froze.

"Clear program!" Stoan shouted into the silence.

The temple and meadow vanished. It was just a gray, auditorium-sized room now. The floor leveled out rapidly.

"Monitor!"

A huge screen appeared in midair, showing the tight face of a teenage girl. Her image appeared straight on, no matter what angle she was viewed from.

"Hyperspace accident," she reported tersely. "Territory 103-D. It's Purple-Class flight 324, the *Travern* out of Bragan, and the situation is critical. Over six thousand people trapped. Severe structural damage, environment barely stable. It was all they could do to fire a comm drone into normal space to relay the message. They registered an explosion, maybe a bomb, maybe more than one – hard to tell. I have projected rendezvous coordinates."

"*Crisse*," Londo muttered. "Lina, they're going to need me on this. I can travel faster than the hyperspace ships. With the structural damage – I can deal with that better than most of the people here." He paused to press her hands between his, apology spilling from his eyes. "Six thousand people, *chérie*. Three times the *Titanic* – and there are no lifeboats. They need my help."

"Ohmigod. Are you ready for this? Do you feel up to it?"

"I'm one hundred percent."

She took a breath. "Then of course it's okay, Lon," she said, sick in the pit of her stomach. "How long?"

He nodded at the group of people beginning to congregate around Stoan. "Let me check," he told her and rushed off with the others.

Now you could see the difference: which ones were Legionnaires and which, civilians. The ones with the identifying rings – they wore bands around their wrists and ankles, too, Lina noticed – gathered into a series of large knots, sorting themselves out, calling out to each other and pointing. Five to eight people made up a knot. One from each commanded a computer padd that unscrolled a screen for the group to view. The civilians held back. Parents used their arms as barriers so the little ones couldn't toddle to see what Mommy or Daddy were up to.

Chérie, *can you find my padd for me?*

Lina tried not to let Londo feel her anxiety as she got the image from him: the drawer next to his bed, and ported a little handheld computer to him. So carefully – mustn't scramble the circuits.

It's fine. Don't worry about it, he told her as he ran it through a quick calibration just to make sure.

He and Jae, Stoan, Wiley, Andri, Aiko, and a few others conferred while screens slid into place all around them showing diagrams of some kind of vessel, star maps, columns of writing.

Londo pointed to this one and that while Stoan nodded his approval. Andri gestured at the screens, which changed their writing, as well as the angle of view for the vessel. Wiley made a few comments and then Jae said something and poked at one line, which changed as Londo rubbed the bridge of his nose, concentrating, and then nodded. He reached down to get something from his pocket and must have realized that he wasn't in uniform. Wiley handed him a small matchbox instead and Londo held the box up to one of the screens for a moment.

"Attention all," Stoan said to the room. His voice carried throughout the holosuite, echoing slightly from all the padd screens in use. "This party is officially over. All Legionnaires, late yellowline or better – I don't think we have any injured in HQ anyway, do we? – are in on this except Doctor Mem-Bazer, of course. Everyone else back to their normal sectors. I remind our guests of Security Procedures for this event. Computer, security mark: ten minutes to standard systems again. Everyone have their assignments? Check-in in twenty minutes to lead ship. Right – Go!"

One entire side of the holosuite bloomed open to the hallway outside. In a burst of activity, the crowd surged toward it. Parents herded their children out of the way. Some people took off ceremonial accessories and handed them quickly to their spouses. There were fast embraces, hugs for everyone, a few tears here and there, but no undue emotion. These people had been through it all before.

Lina hadn't.

She had just been married and now Londo was leaving. She blinked hard and set her teeth. Damned if these strangers were going to see her cry! Here he was, hurrying back to her with an apologetic expression on his dearest of faces.

"*Chérie.*" He took her by her shoulders so she'd look straight at him. "I know this is tough. This is going to take four, maybe five days. Territory 103's pretty far away. Most of that is travel time. The actual rescue shouldn't take long, maybe a day and a half at most, with a ship that size."

"Four days." She shook her head and tried to smile. "You can't wear that."

She started to port the two of them back to his quarters, but he shook his head. "Alone," he told her quietly. "I have some things to do first. Give me a few minutes."

"Of course, darling." She took a full minute to get a careful image and the feel of him, and ported him back to his room so he could change. She should have insisted on going with him but if she had, she might not let him go.

She was lost now. The universe pressed down on her, just when life had opened her up. Where was there an empty corner for her to cry in?

With people streaming around him, Wilder walked slowly toward the narrowing exit as he held two of those computer padds in his hands. Stoan remained with Jae, pointing at her. What was going on?

Jae shook his head but Stoan seemed adamant even as Jae frowned at him and then nodded. Stoan clapped him on his back and gave a hand-signal to a small group who'd remained. They moved at his command, integrating Stoan into their midst.

Wilder paused in his computations and Jae walked to him as the breakfast tables and their attendants rolled past. It was just the three of them now in this auditorium, so Lina joined them, not knowing if she should. Before she could ask, Wiley looked up to see Jae still there.

"It seems I'm staying," Jae said, but he didn't look at Lina.

Londo adjusted his belt as he made the message to his adoptive father. "Hal," he told the recording eye, "I'm sorry you had to learn this way. I've been trying to get hold of you for days. You know how it goes. Our signals just missed this time. I was thinking that maybe Lina could port you in and you could attend the wedding in a quarantine suit, but *non*, you couldn't check your damned voice mail." Lon huffed to himself in frustration.

"So now you have a daughter-in-law, and if you're seeing this, I'm gone and she's alone." He smiled crookedly into the camera and paused as he fastened his shirt closed. "I was going to come up with the all-time funniest way to break it to you. Maybe flying wedding cake to the face with reporters lying in wait. It would be a top hit on YouTube for years, you know? But sometimes you don't get what you want."

He took a breath. "She's going to be scared, Hal. She won't show it, but she'll be frightened to death. Take care of her for me. See that the lawyers and the press don't hound her. If they keep bringing up this mind control *marde*, defend her.

"I love her more than anyone I've ever known. Love her for that, if you can't find any other reason. But you will. She's a wonderful girl."

His face went grim and he made the gesture to terminate recording. "Add to end of Last Message to Hal," he said, and the room beeped twice at him. He finished fastening his pants and belt. "New Last Message for Carolina O'Kelly…Rand," he said, and that brought the slight smile back to his lips.

"*Chérie*," he told the eye as it followed him to the kitchenette. He programmed the replicator for travel rations and stuffed them into his duffel along with the extra padd with all the downloads of the judicial history of mind control he had managed over the past day. "I'm making this right before I leave, so it's a lot quicker than these things usually are. I'm leaving a message for Hal about you, and the Mega-Legion can tell anyone who needs to know, too.

"You'll inherit my estate, which means you can devote your life to art and those cats and whatever you want. If you can't handle things, for god's sake, ask for help. This is going to be a hard time for you I know, and you'll want to keep it inside. Don't. Just this once, go to someone.

"Go to Jae; he's the best listener there is. He's had a lot of hard times himself. He'll understand. But be gentle with him, love. He's…" Lon scratched his nose and then ran his hand down to rub his chin. This was difficult. He wasn't prepared to tell her this, not yet. He hadn't figured it all out.

"Ask him to tell you. He'll know what it's about. Show him this and tell him that I said it was okay. I have to go now. You know I love you. From wherever I am out there, I'll love you forever. And… And I know that we're going to meet up again someday. We're soulmates. That means we'll come back together at some point.

"But that doesn't mean that you can't find someone else while I'm gone. You deserve love, *chérie*. I don't want you to be lonely any more. It's my final wish that you find someone who'll love you and that you'll marry him and have lots of kids who'll love you, too. You got that?" He smiled into the eye, picturing her face as she'd slipped the ring onto his finger. "I do love you, with all my heart." He gestured end recording. Two beeps.

Londo sighed. Just one more, very quick. He grabbed his vest. "New recording," he told the eye. "Add to end of Last Message for Jae Rallene. Jae, this is right after the wedding. I want you to look after her. I know that the plans we made have all gone to hell, but you still have your problem and I'm gone now." He sighed and shook his head apologetically. "I didn't tell her yet, you know that. It's all happened too fast to think straight…"

Lina.

She concentrated to bring Londo here. Now he was in full uniform, every inch the parahero Valiant, with a black duffel bag slung over his left shoulder. He clutched her to him and kissed her frenziedly as she hugged him as hard as she could. He couldn't go, not now! Stay with her, forever with her!

"Go. Go!" she urged between kisses. If he didn't go now, she wouldn't let him leave. "I'll be here when you come back, I promise, I'll be here."

"Give me something to take with me," he said quickly. "My lady's favor."

What? She couldn't port anything in from Earth, not without creating another quarantine. Just what she had on. She reached for a flower from her hair and something inside said *no,* so she fumbled instead at the clasp on the back of her necklace. It finally separated in her shaking fingers. She pressed the necklace into Lon's hand. He gazed at it for a second and then carefully secured it into one of his vest pockets.

"Honeymoon," he instructed her in severe tones. "You decide where you want to go, the craziest, most romantic place you can imagine. Think about what kind of furniture you want for here. Buy some new clothes. Don't just sit around and mope."

"I won't mope. I'll sit around and think of you." *Smile for his sake! Don't let him see you with your eyes red and puffy!*

"And I'll be thinking of nothing but you." He embraced her and kissed her, then kissed her again. "Lina, I have to–"

"Go! And be careful!" She watched her husband run out like the others had, taking to the air before he cleared the doorway. **I love you,** she called after him. **I love you so much. Be safe.**

I love you, too, wife. If Hal calls, stall him. I want to be the one to break the news. Let Wiley talk to him instead.

He shouted something she didn't quite catch at someone he was passing. She got the impression that already he was floors and floors away. There was a feeling of sky, as if he'd flown up outside the building…

Get Wiley to show you around. Even he should be sick of the lab by now. If he can't make it, Legion Protocol should assign you a guide. Try to have some fun; you're still on vacation.

It won't be the same without you.

No answer.

"He's gone," she said to no one. She ran to Wilder, trying not to panic. By now the wall had reappeared, leaving one narrow open door. Wiley paused beside it as Lina caught up to him and Jae. "He's gone! No answer on the telepathy circuit. What happened?"

Wiley considered. "By now he's in hyperspace. Telepaths can't communicate between normal space and hyperspace."

No! "Someone could have warned me!" She bit her lip; she was *not* going to cry! Her trailing gown pinned her to this world, weighing her down. "Londo…"

She was all alone, on her own. A week ago that would have been normal for her, cut off from the world, having to rely only on herself for everything.

But now Londo had entered her life. He had become a part of her heart, a part of all her waking thoughts. Now half of her was missing. She wobbled, unsure of what to do, even of who she was any more as the universe spun around her.

Lost.

Jae turned to her slowly, his eyes on the floor, his lips pursed. Finally he looked up, gave Wiley a glance, and then focused on her.

"Carolina O'Kelly Rand," he said in a strange, tight voice, "you are under arrest for suspicion of mind control. You'll have to come with me."

1

"A-arrest?" Lina asked. She stared up at the so-tall Legionnaire with the startlingly beautiful face. Her head was still whirling from the events of this night. Now this?

She clutched the abundant white lace of her wedding dress because she didn't know how else to hide her shaking hands. They'd waited to do this until Londo had gone. She remembered how to survive without him being near, didn't she?

A week ago she hadn't even known Lon. Three hours ago, maybe less, he'd convinced her to accept his proposal. Now even the flower-scented breeze that had wafted through their wedding was gone.

Lina shivered in the emptiness. Did Lon know that they'd planned this arrest?

No, of course not. She trusted Lon. He was the only person that she did trust. He couldn't help it if the universe was spinning out of control and dragging the two of them with it. Lon was used to this kind of thing. Lina wasn't even used to this world.

Jae grimaced as he ran his hand through the mop of sun-gold hair that framed his head and shoulders. For a moment the points of his elf-like ears showed and then were covered again.

"Look, Lina, the commander didn't specify that you were to be put in a holding cell. I'm going to declare you under house arrest, and I'll define what that house is. I'm your confinement officer; that means that whatever I say you take as an order."

She gave a dazed nod at the best friend of her new husband. She should have been expecting something like this the moment the four of them got out of quarantine. Stupid of her not to.

But everything was topsy-turvy now. House arrest? She had a faint idea of what that entailed on Earth, but here – a far-flung world totally unknown to her, with a technology beyond her imagination – what did that mean?

Mind control had to be a major crime, possibly on terrorist level. Did they have lawyers Out Here? And if so, how would she contact one?

Londo would know, but Lon wasn't here.

Leave it to sour Stoan Kinrol, the Mega-Legion's commander, to railroad a charge like this against her. No one Out Here would believe she, the Terran "witch-doctor," was innocent, would they? To them Terrans were barbarians – except for Lon, the most powerful being this side of forever.

Jae lifted the minister's stole that he had worn across his shoulders to officiate at the wedding. He regarded it a moment, then folded it into a black square and tucked it under his arm.

"I suppose this last miracle was asking for too much." Lina tried to smile bravely about her minutes-old marriage, but had to hide her trembling mouth with her hand.

The holosuite's walls echoed Jae's words now that it stood empty and colorless: "Central command is being transferred to Lab 1-A. That's standard procedure with a skeleton staff. Wiley hardly ever goes on missions with the rest of us. He's in charge now."

"Wiley?" Dr. Wilder Mem-Bazer was both a theoretical and practical physicist – with five minds in one body.

"He's not just Wiley; he's a high-ranking Legionnaire. Think of him as a major when it comes to these situations." The marble that floated next to Lina translated the position as well as the rest of Jae's sentences into English.

At Lina's jerky nod Jae added, "All you have to do is stay in the lab under watch until everyone gets back. We'll need to run a few tests, ask you some questions. If we get a quorum in the meantime, don't worry. You won't be going into any cell. If I'm called away, you will stay with Wiley, is that clear?"

"Yes. Thank–" Her voice broke and she whirled from him, tears erupting. She was alone. She wanted Londo! He'd make everything all right again.

Lon was a brand-new telepath. The power had likely catalyzed by her mind-talking with him so much in the past few days. It hadn't occurred to him to warn her about the silence of hyperspace, but when he'd entered it, flying under his own power, it had been as if her insides had been sucked out, trying to follow him to wherever he was bound. She couldn't find him anywhere.

Where had all this helplessness come from? When had she stopped being her own person and started relying on Londo instead? In her entire life she'd made her own way in the world. Now why was she clinging to a husband for what she should be providing herself?

She wasn't going to put that burden on Lon. The famous Valiant had enough problems to deal with.

Embarrassed to weep in front of Londo's friend, she fought for control. A loudly voiced sob – She couldn't choke it down and it echoed in this auditorium. "I'm sorry," she managed to say. She sniffled her way to a semblance of order and held her hands over her face, breathing purposefully to get rid of the redness and puffiness that must be there. "I seem to… My emotions aren't being very–" she sniffed – "logical these days. Give me a minute, please."

"Sure," she thought Jae said.

God, what he must think of her. He'd warned Lon before they got married, hadn't he? He'd told Lon that she was a weakness he didn't need, a target for his enemies. He'd told her that Lon needed to explain the situation to her before they got married. But Lon had convinced Jae to officiate at the wedding. Didn't that mean that Jae approved of her, even a little?

With a shake, she straightened herself. Being wife to the great mega-parahero Valiant meant that she couldn't allow her actions to detract from his reputation. "I'm sorry," she repeated, but now she turned around to face Jae. "It won't happen again. It's just… everything at once."

Now she blinked not to get rid of tears, but because they were back in Wiley's warehouse-sized laboratory – or rather, in the little break room just off the entrance to it. She hadn't ported. They'd accused her of teleporting to arrange the strange things that had been happening lately, but it hadn't been her and her new power of interstellar teleportation. "How–?"

"You knew we had our own intra-planetary transporters," Jae gave her a small smile that might have been meant to be encouraging. Obviously he was uneasy around females on a crying jag. "I just saved us a trip. You okay now? You look all right. A little red around the nose."

"No, I'm fine." A snuffle betrayed her. "How does this house arrest work? Do you need to get my fingerprints or a-anything? Do I get to call a lawyer?"

"No. Come on," Jae told her brusquely. "There might be time to see the last off. Watch the dress."

He strode away from her. Lina grabbed on to the lace train of her wedding gown to make sure that it didn't sweep across machinery or into any of the boxy experiment stations here in the main lab. It was an expansive if dim place, most of the front third gridded with enclosed tables that contained a variety of monitored experiments. In the past few days she and Lon had benefited from a couple medical stations Wiley had rigged. Jae had set up a shooting gallery along the far wall to while away quarantine.

The back of the lab she hadn't had time to explore, but she'd used a spa-sized mini-pool there that was otherwise utilized for marine experiments. A full bathroom was nearby, hidden computer stations occurred at various spots along the walls, and other than that, it looked like *Hoarders* could shoot a long season of episodes with the piles that she could see back there. In the far reaches of the lab, equipment the size of cement trucks sat buried among the stuff.

Unfortunately, Lon's minutes-long death throes two days ago had created an indoor hurricane, from which the warehouse's automatic cleaners were still trying to recover.

She followed Jae to the central data desk where Dr. Wilder Mem-Bazer had already settled.

The aqua-skinned genius with the subdued brush of violet hair was talking to a 3-D screen hanging in the air. "Systems are checking in full blue. I've got you cleared for hyperspace insertion coordinates EF-679-45. Three minutes."

"Right." It was golden Aiko herself, known as the hero Orenya, who filled most of the screen, with the hint of a person or two behind her. She still held her courageous, cover-up smile from the wedding. And there was something odd…

"Coordinates noted," she said as she checked her subscreens. "Time marked. All other Legion passenger ships are clicking out of comm range. There goes the hospital ship, mark. Robot drones are checking in; I'm giving them the go-ahead now. Time for us, I suppose. We'll see you in about four or five days, Wiley. Oh – There's the bride herself."

Aiko nodded to Lina. "Congratulations again. Sorry we have to take him away from you for a while. On my world we have a saying: 'Dark start, bright finish.' We'll continue that party when we all get back. He'll be fine; don't worry."

"Thank you." Lina tried to bring up a genuine smile, but her very bones quaked in horror. "Good luck to you all."

"We don't need luck; we are the Legion. Take care of business, Wiley. Jae. Hyperspace insertion mode commencing. Fallow out." The screen blanked.

Fighting back a scream, Lina turned quickly from the screen. She clapped both hands to her mouth and then realized that Jae was still staring at the space in the air where the screen had been. His almond-brown skin had gone pale.

"You saw it too," she accused him.

Wilder caught the words and turned toward the two of them. "What's the matter with you? I can understand Lina being upset, but you, Jae…" He paused. One of his eyes targeted Jae and the other, Lina. "What the *skurn* is it?"

Jae tried to speak, then tried again. "Aiko… She's not coming back."

"What? What do you mean?"

Lina put her hands on Jae's shoulders, surprised that she could do that much as he stood paralyzed. She said, "He means that she's g-going to be killed. Real soon."

She squeezed her eyes shut, exhaled as much of her fear as she could. Nothing to be done…

Wilder turned to his control board and then back to them. "They're gone; no further direct communications possible until they return to normal space. What's this about?"

Jae choked, "I saw the Mark of Ramseur on her: the Feithi death sign."

Lina nodded, tight-lipped. "I saw her d-dead in Londo's arms in a room filled with flame and smoke," she said. "There was something sticking in her, in her mid-section." Her own guts throbbed in sympathy and she laid a hand on her stomach to calm them. Lon had been all right, hadn't he? She would have noticed if he hadn't.

She felt numb all over, but studied Jae before she turned to Wilder, who obviously didn't believe in death omens. Still she could tell that he was considering it, considering the thought of Aiko dead.

"How many times have you had death visions come true?" he finally asked her.

Lina took another deep breath to collect herself. Thank heaven she didn't really know Aiko. But no one should have to go through… that. "Never," she said. "But I know this one will. I've had gut feelings before, just never ones that concerned someone's death."

"The Mark of Ramseur." Jae glanced around in a daze. "I've never seen it, but I know what it was. It's always true. Always. There's a phrase, 'As true as the Ramseur,' but people didn't say it much because it was… so…"

His gaze met Wiley's. "She's going to die," he told him. "Aiko. Aiko!" He grabbed Wiley by the lapels of his yellow lab coat. "A ship. We'll get another ship and follow them–"

"Because of a psychic event? If it was one?" Wiley asked. "You just said that this Mark of Ramseur was always correct. Have you ever heard of anyone beating it?"

Jae's face fell.

"I take it that's a no. Then what good would it do to follow? We have real work here. You've been in quarantine for days, Jae. You've been off your schedule for too long. The wedding this morning – It's just nerves."

"It's not nerves," Jae said tightly. "I am not insane."

"I didn't say you were. But sometimes you get upset when you've been through too many strange circumstances," Wiley told him in a cooling tone. "All I'm saying is that perhaps, due to the wedding and all the changes it implies, that your imagination or subconscious may have summoned a literal example of what you think has figuratively happened."

"You make it sound so cold," muttered Jae.

"Not cold, just more rational. If you were Tishana, Jae, I could well believe you saw something. But you aren't, so chances are that it was just–"

"I am Feithi. We were far beyond the Tishana."

Wiley pressed his lips together as if he'd almost begun to say, "Maybe you used to be," and decided against it.

"Aiko's going to die," Lina interrupted gently. "I'm sorry if the thought distresses you so much that you can't consider it seriously, Wiley, but it's a fact."

"It is not a fact, Lina."

"Okay, not yet. There is a realm beyond known science. Time and space don't really mean so much there." Lina waved at his black communications board blinking in multi-colors. "You're whiz with all this, but you can't see underneath it."

Both his wandering eyes focused on her. "Let's be realistic with what we have. I could point out that Aiko and Londo were well known to be in a relationship – until you came along. For all I know, it was your imagination that came up with the death-wish image and transferred it telepathically to Jae."

Could she have done that? Was she so threatened by Aiko?

"Plus you've mentioned that your accuracy is not absolute."

"I'm maybe sixty or eighty percent right, most of the time." Lina pursed her lips. "These past few days I've been hitting things out of the park."

"A sports metaphor. You admit your abilities have been abnormal during this crisis. That crisis is over. There's nothing we can do about Aiko in either case," Wiley told them. "Jae, I won't agree to taking another ship out to catch up with them. We're too short-handed here for you going on a *ripe-sulse* chase. I'll make a note of the event on the log, and we'll see what happens."

Jae reached to the communications console and typed a few colors there. "At least I can send the information to them." A small swath of the black surface of the console oozed upward, spinning into a fist-sized globe which rose to eye-level. Jae let it record his crisp and reasoned message of warning, ending with "Rallene out," and the globe darted out of the room.

Wiley didn't say anything for a moment afterward. "That's assuming that the bombed ship's communications are operating at high enough levels to secure the comm globe," he finally said. "With that much damage, the globe might get lost on linkup, too."

"I can only do what I can do." The determination on Jae's face dissolved into weariness. "Aiko. *Grigach*, Aiko…" He took a breath. "We may want to investigate funeral proceedings," he said. "I doubt if many will be in a business state of mind when they return."

Wilder paused. "I'm not sure I want to go that far either."

"Then I'll do it on my responsibility. Just the preliminaries, nothing to alarm anyone on the outside." Jae straightened and shook himself. His features settled into a cool, neutral mask of Legionnaire efficiency.

"All right." Wilder returned to his console as Jae moved to one of the private communications screens against the wall.

"How often does this happen, that a hero dies?" Lina asked Wiley quietly. "I thought your medical science was so advanced?"

He didn't have to search anywhere for the figures. "In the approximately two hundred fifty years the Mega-Legion has been operating, there have been one hundred seventy deaths in the line of duty, including the Omega Night tragedy and the ambush on Doden-3. If indeed Aiko dies, that will make one hundred seventy-one. What we do is dangerous work." He paused. "If you saw that for her, why didn't you warn her?"

"What would I say? 'You're going to die'? If I'd seen the circumstances of how it happened, I would have. If I get a vision of a client getting hit by a car while they're walking across a street, I tell them to make sure they double-check that there's no traffic when they cross streets for a while. I don't tell them that they're going to be injured. They can change the future by being careful; the vision is a warning, not a prediction."

"And Aiko? Can she change her future?"

"I don't think so. How can I explain it to you? It's like the heavens sound some kind of gong to punctuate a decision, and your stomach is between the gong and the mallet. Believe me, you know."

Wiley saw the pain on her face and filed the information and expression into Mind #3, the most clerical of his five minds. "I didn't think you knew Aiko that well."

She shook her head with its bridal crown of flowers, a curl of hair dislodged. "I only met her at the reception. I was just thinking that this is going to hit Londo very hard." Lina held two fingers to her mouth as she considered. "I've never had a death near me, but Lon's watched too many loved ones die. Aiko was… very special to him."

"Yes." Wiley's eyes worked in concert as he watched Jae. "I could help Jae. Just as a precaution."

"Try to calm him down while you're doing it, too." Lina glanced over at the blond Legionnaire who spoke in such even, level-headed tones to a communications screen centered on the wall. "I think he's pretty upset. He doesn't show it."

"He's good at that."

"Since you'll both be busy, would it be all right if I went back to Lon's quarters and got some sleep? I'm sorry. That sounds so callous. But it's been a very long day. And night. Jae said you were in command now. Do I really have to stay here? Jae said–"

"He told you you were under supervised house arrest." Wiley doubted if that's what Stoan had in mind. Solitary confinement was standard for mind controllers, with the options being under force field conditions or in a hyperspace chamber.

Stoan detested mind controllers as much as anyone Wiley had ever seen. Of course the Legion commander had his reasons, but they often made him unreasonable in this one area. That and slavery; Stoan was inclined to over-react there as well. But Stoan had been in a hurry. Perhaps he hadn't specified to Jae exactly what the confinement was supposed to be.

And perhaps Lina was beginning to use mind control to influence Jae.

Another of Wiley's five minds clicked in, reminding himself of the events of the past few days. Lina had brought the mortally injured Londo in from distant Earth when she herself had been dying. She'd risked her life to save his, utilizing strange but effective Terran psychic healing techniques. She'd had access to Legion computers but hadn't come close to breaking security.

A third mind pointed out that preliminary scans showed that she held no trace of artificial telepathy implants that usually signaled a mind controller. All five of his minds conferred.

No, Commander Stoan Kinrol was wrong about Londo's new bride. Probably. Just as Jae and Lina were both wrong about Aiko.

Probably.

One mind – a different one for either situation – disagreed. Each began to collect data to build their cases as the others observed with interest.

Wiley looked at Lina and crooked a smile at her in her strange, erotic wedding gown with all its lace and flowers and bare shoulders. In the holosuite's sunny meadow it had seemed a historical holdover, but here in his state-of-the-art laboratory surrounded by black acrylic and holo-puters, it looked otherworldly. And that was exactly what it was.

"What have you done?" he asked her. "Londo – Valiant – married. I thought I told you two no sex."

A slow smile of her own brightened her face. "He kept quoting you: 'For a while,' you said. And we did wait. You sure are nosy."

"It's my job. But do you really think that you had to get married so quickly?"

"Lon thought so." She looked down at her dress and smoothed it. "And Someone Else thought so, too."

"And you think that none of the–" Wiley waved his hands in the air to include lights, voices, miracles of healing, ceremonial clothing mysteriously appearing a little while ago–"was coming from you, even unconsciously?"

"If it did, it was way, way subconscious."

"So you went along with it all," Wiley said. "A lifetime contracted marriage."

"Sometimes the only way to move is to jump, Wiley, even if you think you aren't ready. We might have been a bit premature, but we would have done it eventually. I don't think Lon likes the concept of 'eventually.'"

He nodded and his left eye began wandering again, utilizing another mind than the one speaking to Lina. "I suppose we'll all see if that's correct. So now you want to sleep it off. I will release you to quarters. Puter, keep door to Rand quarters secured until further notice." Two beeps gave the affirmative response. "Lina, don't port anywhere beside to there and back here. You can take your translator with you." He nodded at the marble that floated next to her.

He held up two fingers to stop her from porting. "Two things first," he said in the voice of Official Legionnaire. She waited expectantly.

Wiley rummaged through a built-in cabinet against the near wall and emerged with a bracelet: flat and white, about an inch wide, with its use clearly labeled in black lettering that was not English. On his way back he stopped by his medical unit and programmed an ampoule of tranks.

The bracelet he fastened onto her wrist over her lace sleeve.

"You will wear this as long as you're under arrest."

"Some kind of locator?" she asked and he nodded. "Okay." She bit her lip. "I guess I'm really under arrest."

"You are."

Wiley held up his ampoule and she made a nasty face but stretched her neck for him to deliver the dose.

"You have twenty-five minutes to prepare for bed. After that, you won't be waking up for a while."

"Yes, sir," she said sourly.

"You may go now."

It took Lina a full minute to gather her concentration so she could utilize this parapower she'd suddenly acquired, the power of teleportation. Startling dimness enveloped her except for blue glows scattered here and there nearby.

"Computer, turn on the lights, please," she instructed, hoping the computer was listening. Sure enough, ceiling lights came on and she was in Lon's spacious Legion apartment. "Puter, cancel those quarantine force fields around the plants now." Two beeps; the blue glows vanished.

Londo's apartment, so big, so empty without him here. She trudged into the bedroom and gazed at the bed, the sheets still rumpled from where she and Lon had made love. Where she had realized that she was a good enough person to accept his proposal, not a muttbutt at all!

Then she caught a glimpse of a bride walking in the back of the room. A full-length mirror stood there. Hesitantly she approached it. For the first time in her life, when she gazed into it she truly saw herself, not the ugliness she'd always imagined. She did look like a real bride. Maybe even like she should be in a wedding magazine. Imagine: Lina Muttbutt a bride!

She turned back and forth, taking in the image as much as she could. This had all happened too fast. It hadn't sunk in yet. Surely when Londo returned it would – unless he'd gotten his sense back by then and wanted to call everything off.

Poor Londo. And even poorer Aiko! Aiko'd been blindsided by the wedding. Why did she have to die on top of it all? Why would the Universe do that to someone?

Trust, her ever-present spirit guides told her. **This is how her incarnation was planned. Her tests are complete.**

Still, a helluva time for this to happen. Lina asked the guides if she could at least complain about that, and she felt their amusement. But it wouldn't be amusing in the least to Londo. He wouldn't be braced for this. He hadn't even had a chance to put some emotional distance between himself and Aiko yet.

He'd need Lina, but she had no idea what to do.

She lifted the crown of blossoms from her hair and wondered what kind of flowers they were. They were sweet little miniature daisies with something like baby's breath filling out the design. She knew they were alive, but couldn't figure out where their root system was. She was about to find them some water when they disappeared.

Ah, it was a rental, she decided, and thanked Whomever for the use of it. Mysterious forces had done some crazy and wonderful things in the past few hours. She thanked Them for the clothes, for the everything that had happened today, and waited for her dress to disappear. Lon's miracle outfit lay neatly folded on a chair, but its buttonhole flower was the only thing to vanish.

Why did she think that the familiar voice of Earth was one of the voices that had gifted her with these? It had sounded so like her, but this world of Sarastor was many light-years – no, they counted the distance in parsecs or something close to that Out Here – from home. Earth couldn't have been there, could she?

Lina reached around to the fastenings on the back of her dress, but she couldn't feel any. She twisted to see, then it occurred to her to check the mirror's 3-D subscreen. Passing her hand in front of that portion rotated the image.

There was nothing to open to get out of the dress. It was as if she'd been sewn in. She smiled to herself. It would have been interesting if Lon had stuck around and then tried to get her out of this. At least it was no problem for her; she just ported it off and draped the gown with all its lace next to Lon's clothing.

Her fingers traced the myriad symbols embroidered into his vest's fabric, smooth thread against the rougher background. They were the same as the symbols forming the lace on her dress. Even Jae's new minister clothing had held these symbols, but those had been knitted in. If these outfits were still around tomorrow morning, she'd take them to the lab and have Wiley figure them out.

She'd also have to make more of a fuss about lawyers and bail. She needed to be loud, so someone would listen. As a rule, being loud was not in her nature. She was more into hiding from the world. She would have to do a lot of research on everything, starting from the very basics of this alien society and working her way up. Ugh. At least they had good computers Out Here, plus that handy translator marble.

Her hose were lace stayups, the shoes a sturdy white lace with a small heel. Bra seemed a standard strapless, although she'd never worn one of those before, and her elegant gold earrings looked the same as any she could have bought on Earth. How strange, after the parade of other-worldly costumes this morning, that she should find herself granted Terran clothing for her miraculous marriage.

Her eyes began to droop, her mind to haze, so quickly she unpinned her hair (regular hair pins) and crawled into bed. She thought she could smell Londo in the sheets. She spread herself out on them as if they were him, and already she dreamed of his caresses. Londo, to have and to hold – forever.

Skurn it all. Jaeson Rallene knew he should have treated Lina like a real suspected mind controller. The commander's orders had been incomplete since he'd been more concerned with the hyperspace emergency at hand. It opened the possibility of bending the rules.

Jae should have clapped her into one of the inner cells of the force field section – but he couldn't. Londo was his best friend and this was his wife. Jae had just presided at the marriage.

It had only been a couple hours ago that he'd been trying to talk the two of them out of this crazy idea. Then Londo had promised him that Jae would get his chance to present the entire problem to Lina, with certain truths that Londo just didn't have the guts to tell her beforehand.

Londo might be Valiant, the most powerful being in the sector next to his adoptive father Maximus, and deservedly renowned for his bravery and cunning, but about a good-sized slice of his life Londo was a coward. Lon didn't trust anyone, not all the way – not even his best friend. And not even his girlfriend – no, his *wife*. Now there'd be no discussion until Lon returned.

Would her being a mind controller begin to explain what had happened in the past few days? A mega telepath appears out of nowhere, with the mighty Valiant completely in her thrall. Equaled mind controller.

Or: Yet another Terran megapara appears, this one a shapely witchdoctor who, because of mysterious psychic techniques, is able to have sex safely with Londo even when he's in full power mode. Londo, the frustrated virgin until now because of his excessive strength. She even brings Lon back from brief death.

Lon then grabs her up before anyone else can, and cements her to himself via a permanent marriage contract without a thought to anyone else whose long-range plans he might have derailed along the way by doing so. Equaled Londo being his normal strategizing, self-absorbed self in rare bastard mode.

Only an hour ago the main holosuite downstairs had been filled with celebrating Legionnaires and their families. Londo had smiled and laughed more than Jae had seen him do in a long time. Maybe this strange Terran girl was good for him.

And maybe she had him under her control.

Over it all loomed Aiko and the Mark of Ramseur. Jae tried to grasp the entirety of it, but part of his mind insisted it was unreal. The other part, the deeper, Feithi part, knew the unshakable truth of it. He would never see his friend Aiko alive again.

He made sure his face was composed in the expression he called his Number Four, the not-quite-interested-but-listening-politely one that served him so well when his emotions seethed. Then he began his inquiries to contractors noted in Legion records as having played a part before in funeral arrangements for the organization. The people he spoke to were dazzled at facing Neutrino, the last surviving Feithi and famed Mega-Legionnaire. "Updating our records," he told some. "Just a drill," he informed others.

In a few days it would not be. Between calls he tapped his left forearm to release the meds that would help him stay calm and in control.

When the list was done, he closed his eyes and took ten deep breaths. He would not think of Aiko again, not until the Legionnaires returned with real-world news. As they would. It was useless to obsess about something he had no control over.

That was a fine theory. Someday he might believe it.

For the next few days he should concentrate on his prisoner. He needed to collect evidence. He would make sure she was kept under control. Physical control, that was, not mind control. How did you accomplish that with a teleporter? It was good that she'd discovered that interplanetary ports brought germs and subsequent quarantines with them. That would keep her on Sarastor at least.

Until she learned how to port cleanly.

For some reason Jae thought that might not take much time. She'd only been porting for a few days now, and on her second day had managed a teleport across eighty parsecs to a world that she'd heard of only from Londo. It had resulted in a quarantine that he and Wiley had been caught in. Sloppiness on her part did not diminish the marvel of the deed.

Great *grigach*, she'd seemed so forlorn when Londo left. This little witchdoctor was precisely the woman that Londo had always wanted. And now that the bruising, cuts and swelling of her injuries had suddenly disappeared this night, she'd turned out to be extremely pretty. She was about four inches shorter than Lon, whose height was less than average. Lina couldn't have stood more than six feet. Lon had told him that on Earth she'd be considered quite tall, but then, he said that of himself. As it was, the top of Lina's head came to the base of Jae's neck.

Lina didn't wear her hair in Affiliated Systems fashion. Lon had always hated the style of shaved heads, especially when it came to women. "Redheads are the hottest," Londo had confided to him many times over the years. Lina's auburn hair did glow with red highlights when the light struck it strongly. Of course Lon would like the hair that hung halfway down Lina's back when she wore it in her usual braid. It was softly curly when it wasn't braided. Jae hadn't seen hair like that since his childhood on Feith, though Imperial fashion came close.

But even without that or the innocent, oval face, without the generous breasts that were precisely what Londo would order, there were the green eyes that seemed to gaze unaccusingly into your soul. There was no way that Londo could have escaped their magic. Or was it mind control? Was that how some controllers did it, to catch their victim unawares? Did Lina present an updated version of a dire threat?

And if so, how safe was Jae from her? He'd been locked in quarantine with her for almost three days now. He had to keep tabs on her for how much longer? She'd channeled spirit – his grandfather – for him, told him that he'd chosen this empty life for a purpose. Was that to get on his good side? Was it his imagination, or was there someone scritch-scratching at his brain, trying to worm their way into his mind?

The last thing Jae wanted was to play watchdog to Lina O'Kelly… Rand. *Grigach*, he'd married her to Londo! That Londo had tricked him. The miracles of the morning had dazzled him so he didn't notice how blatantly Lon had twisted things to make Jae play his way – having him preside at Londo's own wedding. *Kick* and *skurn* Londo anyway!

And sunfire take Lina Rand for completely screwing up their plans. *His* plans.

When Londo came back, Jae would make a few things very, very public. See him try to worm his way out of that! Lon could be cruel. By the orb, Lon could be kind, too. So many times when Jae had been maddest at Londo, it had turned out that Lon had had Jae's best interests at heart. He just had a *kick* of a habit of trying to command circumstances to make them work out his way. Like now.

Poor Lina was caught in all this. For a moment Jae wondered if she knew, and then he shook his head to himself. Of course she didn't. Londo didn't tell people important things; he didn't trust them enough. He didn't trust Jae, his closest friend for so many years. He wouldn't trust this woman he'd just met.

This woman he'd just married.

How in sunfire could Jae get through these next few days when he had to keep secrets from a telepath?

Ah grigach, *Londo, what have you done? What have I helped you do?*

2

Wiley regarded the young woman in Londo's bed and made an annoyed sound.

"Problem, Wiley?" Jae's voice came from all around.

"Terrans sleep in the nude," Wiley said as he began to unpack a satchel.

"Waitasec. I'll be right down to confirm that for you."

"Stay at station, Legionnaire. Computer, no site visual for this record," Wiley told the air and two beeps answered.

"Darn," Jae said.

"Just make a note to have Legion Protocol stress dress code to her." Wiley set up his equipment around the bed. "And Jae, don't let your hormones run wild. She's well-covered with the sheet."

"Darn again. Readings coming in now."

Sensors swarmed around Lina like insects. Wiley gestured for anti-grav units and Lina's body rose in the air a few inches, the sheet hanging around her. The swarm descended upon her from all sides. She stirred.

"That's not right." Wiley checked his readings. "She should be in delta mode."

"Could be a dream," Jae put in. "Or maybe those spirit guides of hers are trying to warn her?"

"Guides," Wiley muttered darkly.

"Yo, guides," Jae said to no one that Wiley could discern, "let's keep her in the dark about this, can we? The less she knows about the testing, the purer the tests and the sooner we can clear her."

Lina sighed and then stilled.

"It was a pre-dream state," Wiley said.

"Of course. Sensors don't show any obvious brain implants, Wile."

"We already knew that; this was just for the official record. Releasing the nano-sensors," Wiley replied.

"Just a sheet, you say? How thick?"

Wiley made a non-committal sound as Jae chattered.

"Londo can really pick 'em, can't he? Of course, so can I. Data coordinating now. I've even tried to aim some of my cast-offs his dreary way when he was between girls."

"I'm sure he appreciated that," Wiley said with some distraction.

"I don't think they ever got up the courage to try him. I mean just imagine: Valiant. The mightiest megapara around. One hug from him and you're mush. My ladies wouldn't have been the kind to appreciate the romance of that, you know, literally dying in Valiant's arms."

"A noble end."

Jae laughed. "What a way for them to go. Speaking of that little problem of Londo's, I am willing to bet that you've got–"

"I've had time to consider the situation further," Wiley said. "And yes, I am scanning to gain insight into this mystery. Her claim of talking to his cells makes no sense."

"If you ever find out how they do it, don't keep it a secret. I'm sure you could make a fortune out of releasing that information to Lon's groupies."

"Lina? Lina!"

Londo was calling her. Where was she?

"Lina?"

Ohmigod, she'd promised him *children!*

The shock of that brought her fully awake. But the voice was Jae's, not Lon's. He must be in the living room. The wedding had been so early this morning; what time was it now? How long had Londo been gone?

She was under arrest.

Lina snatched up the sheet to cover herself as she rose. She ported her robe to herself and slipped it on, afraid that Jae would appear in the bedroom doorway before she could. Then she hurried out to see him, trying to smooth her hair along the way. He'd seen her in worse.

He stood in the spacious living room. The panoramic "windows" there still held the breathtaking view from Starhaven, Lon's in-progress house in Wyoming that would become their home. Legion rooms didn't have real windows. Windows would have been a defensive breach in the secure headquarters.

"Good afternoon," Jae said.

"Afternoon? How in the world do you tell time around here? Are you okay? Have you gotten any sleep?"

"Yes. And unlike some of us, I managed some shuteye last night."

She blushed, remembering why Lon and she hadn't slept.

Jae was now dressed in his full uniform, as the TV had CGI'd him during the interview he'd had the other day. It was light blue with white and leather-looking accessories: over-the-knee boots, two belts crisscrossed and such. Like the doctor, narrow bands wrapped wrists and ankles, of a color and material to blend into the rest. A blue holographic triangle/pyramid emblazoned the front of each shoulder. He wore a blue stud in his left ear lobe.

It all was capped off by a flowing white cape that reminded Lina of Londo's father, Maximus, because it hung the same way on Jae as it did on the Big Blue Max. Maximus's was shorter, just coming down to his thighs, but Jae's came down to his calves. Maximus's was friendly; Jae's looked swashbuckly and tough. Legionnaire-ish, she decided.

But Jae didn't look quite so tough as he plunked himself upon the couch. This involved flipping the cape up a moment before his bottom hit the cushions, so it didn't choke him. "For better or for worse, we're stuck with each other for a few days," he said sourly.

His tone took Lina aback. "I, ah, I hope you don't mind guarding the jail," she told him. "I'm sorry if I'm a nuisance."

"You're not a nuisance," he muttered.

"No, I just married your best friend," she said. "I know things will be different for you two, but I really will try not to get in your way."

He looked up at that from where he'd been playing with a stylus. "What, did Lon – I got the impression that Lon's barely had time to tell you anything about the way things are on Sarastor."

She shook her head. "He hasn't. I just want you to know that I won't come between you and Lon. I'm his wife now and I deserve a portion of his time, but I won't deny you two whatever time you need. Guys need to do guy things. I suppose para-heroes need to do parahero things. Is that okay with you? I mean, I haven't had time to talk with Lon about this, but it seems fair to me."

"Yeah." Jae stared straight ahead. "Yeah, it's fair. He'll go along with it."

"Please don't hate me because I love him," Lina said quietly.

"Who said I hated you?"

"You're acting…" Her voice trailed off as she realized that he'd faced the death of a close friend today. "Oh, I'm sorry. I forgot. That's unforgivable, but honestly, I did."

Jae nodded. "I don't know if I even believe what I saw." He glanced at her. "It's true?" She nodded and for a moment he looked like his breath had left him. "All right, I know it's true, too. But it's not going to be real until they come back and she's not with them. I'm just moody, all right? Let that be my excuse. Everyone says, 'Jae's the moody one.' At least, they do when Lon's not around."

"Lon's moody?"

That made the corner of Jae's mouth quirk. "Yes, Londo Rand is moody. But he ranges from serious to foul. A little black cloud seems to follow him for days at a time. Often it is a big black cloud – with lightning and thunder."

"Oh."

"The woman who just married him says, 'oh.' You're supposed to know who you're marrying, Lina Rand."

"O'Kelly."

He blinked. "You're kidding."

She shook her head.

"Does Lon know?"

Again she shook her head, but this time with a small, nervous smile.

He screwed his mouth this way and that. "I don't know how they do things on Earth, Lina *O'Kelly*, but here, if the marriage is contracted for more than six years, the two spouses take the same last name, that being the name of the spouse with more prestige or rank."

"Which would definitely be 'Rand' in this case," Lina said. "On Earth it's traditional for the woman to take the man's name, to show that she is his property."

"Property?"

Lina could swear that those pointed ears of Jae's perked up. She said, "I'm nobody's property. I worked hard for my own independence. Nobody owns me."

That did bring a smile to his face. "So let me get this straight for my own tired brain to absorb. You marry Lon Rand, son of Hal Rand, which makes 'Rand' the biggest, baddest name this side of 'Yanist-Glory'… and you aren't going to take it on?"

She shook her head quickly and Jae laughed.

"Okay, okay," he said. "Give me a ticket to when you tell Lon. Give me a ticket for when you tell Legion Protocol. That should be good." He eased back on the couch. "All right. In addition to being your confinement officer, it seems I'm your teacher as well. You need an introduction to Sarastor today, don't you? We'll have to start you out from the very beginning. Wiley's lab in no way represents the planet."

He stretched, sat up straighter, and then reached out to touch the coffee table. It lit up like the *U.S.S. Enterprise* comm board, only with hologram screens floating above it as well. He explained that bare legs – like the ones peeking out from under her robe – were verboten, per Legion regs. She'd been okay while they'd been in quarantine, but she had no excuse now.

"Stand over there." He pointed to just beyond the corner of the table. When she obeyed, a blue beam of light shone out of the table to play over her. It disappeared after a few seconds, leaving a miniature 3-D picture of herself hanging above the table. Good golly, her hair was a mess.

"Finished," he announced, and she froze in place.

She should sit on the couch. Ordinarily she'd sit as far from others as she could, to avoid being touched. But she didn't feel any warning twinge from her phobia now. Come to think of it, just before the wedding she'd held Jae by the arm so she and Lon could talk privately with him.

And really, she should have been babbling with terror as all those strangers descended upon them at the reception. She'd been scared, but just stranger-scared, not touch-scared.

Did this have something to do with what Londo had done in her mind last night? Back on that island, he'd managed to break through her fears so that she could touch him – and more. Now he'd done this?

She blinked. Jae hadn't noticed her pause, so she decided to experiment. She sat on the couch about a foot and a half from him.

Nothing. Right now she couldn't recall quite what her fear had been about. Here was Jae, a friend. He didn't want to hurt her. When he patted the couch a little closer to himself, she scooted over so she could better see what he did with the table. How odd. How amazing. People did this kind of thing all the time, and now she could, too. She grinned in wonder at the universe. *Look at me!*

Jae was too busy with the table's controls to notice. He told her he was, in effect, dumbing down the table's reactive mode until she learned how to use electronics the efficient Sarastoran way. Then he showed her how to link to the galactic Web and the shopping nets, which showcased the peculiar fashions Out Here.

Much was a smothering style, like wearing tents and tarps layered in precise drapes. "These–" Lina said of the other style, a thick non-spandex spandex – "look like something paraheroes would wear. Isn't there anything in between? Like what you wore to the wedding, or that man, that…" Names! Lina could never remember names! "That man who made the bet." Lina's mouth curled in embarrassment. "The one Londo threw into the crowd."

Jae rolled back on the couch and laughed. "That was Kuttr." He slapped his knee. "Definitely need to review the tape on that one. Coming up to gloat that he'd won the betting pool–" Kuttr's bet was not only on when Londo would finally lose his virginity, but held a rider that he'd lose it to another virgin. Apparently the pot had been monumental – "but won the rider as well. I can see where Londo thought he deserved a lesson in party etiquette."

"He flew," Lina said in wonder. Lon had jokingly tossed the man into the air, but the man had caught himself and floated down to the ground, no harm done.

"All Legionnaires can fly," Jae said easily, as if he'd just admitted the sky was blue. "Kuttr wears those foo-foo Imperial styles on high occasions. He escaped from the Empire years ago."

Did that mean Jae could fly, too? The question in Lina's mind was drowned out by the hideous implication of Kuttr. "The Empire? Yanist-Glory Empire?" she gasped. Emperor Yanist-Glory was the man who had kidnapped Londo when he was a child. It was his cruel experiments that had given Londo the same powers as Maximus, the man who'd eventually adopted him.

"Kuttr's all right, Lina. He was thoroughly investigated when he showed up in AffSys space. He wouldn't be a Legionnaire unless we could trust him. In fact, his security rating is top of the scale."

"Oh."

"But you shouldn't dress in Imperial styles. Especially since the commander has a theory that you're an Imperial citizen. Are you?"

"Of course not."

Jae snapped his fingers. "And that completes my interrogation." At her hopeful expression, he shook his head. "A joke."

"How about me dressing like a Terran?"

Jae snorted.

"Why would that be so bad?" Lina asked. "I thought people here were supposed to be open to other cultures."

"As long as those cultures fit their definition of civilization," Jae told her. "Earth doesn't. Earth is a barbaric backwater. Remember that. That's how people are going to see you. It took Lon a long time to settle on a uniform that pleased everyone."

"What, he had to get it approved?"

"Of course."

"And here I thought he'd just changed it because, well, he wasn't a kid anymore. Didn't need to be Maximus Junior."

"Maximus Junior," Jae chuckled. "I like that. No, Lon went through a definite de-Terran-ization."

"Who made him do that? This Legion Protocol group?"

"He did it himself." Jae turned to her. "It was his idea from the start. I told you, being Terran is not a positive thing, even if you're Maximus Junior. Or Maximus himself."

"Lon's passing," she realized in amazement.

"Going around? Succeeding?" Jae eyed her translation marble suspiciously.

"Passing. Pretending to be something he's not, passing as Sarastoran. How very odd." Lina chewed her lip as she considered it.

"Oh the joys of marrying someone you don't know."

That brought Lina's concentration back to him. She waved off the comment with her hand. "I'll get to know him. All right. Well, if I've picked what clothing I want – Do they have tee shirts that say 'I married a Legionnaire and all I got was this lousy tee shirt'?"

Jae shook his head no. The left edge of his mouth curled up at the joke.

"How do I get anything? My wallet burned up back on Earth, along with my better credit cards."

"You just said it," Jae prompted.

Lina looked blank.

"The 'I married a Legionnaire' part," he explained.

"Oh? Oh!"

She had to identify herself to the nets by touching the table with two fingertips and her thumb. Apparently no one had yet informed the furniture that Londo Rand had married. The table triggered a spark of electricity that tingled up to her scalp and down to her toes. It wasn't enough to cry out at, but she could still feel it.

Two beeps signaled that she was now a part of the official interstellar financial network. She had no idea how much money Lon had, but probably if she were her usual frugal self it might not be any problem. They had to have a talk about money when he came back. They had to talk about a lot of things.

Jae didn't understand Lina's problem in deciding how to determine fair pricing. "Just order what you need to. Prices are set."

"Okay," she said doubtfully.

"That should start you off." Jae leaned back, satisfied. "You pick your own clothes, though you can ask the puter for help. It understands both society and Legion regs."

"Are all prison guards this friendly?"

"I won't be friendly if you don't follow directions during all this. I am defining your house arrest as you remaining here or in the lab," Jae told her. "I was thinking that once you're cleaned up and dressed, I might just bend that rule. We could go out for lunch or for you, breakfast, but I'd still be watching you. I've got–" and the translator wouldn't handle the word.

"Cabin fever," Lina guessed. Quarantine had not been fun, and the mere idea of imprisonment set her hackles to rise. Freedom might help take her mind off of Lon. "Me, too." Oh boy, an alien world to explore! This was better than being on a *Star Trek* away team. There'd be no monsters here, no expendable red shirts!

Jae told her it was early spring and chilly, to order a "Climalon" jacket, and not to get too excited; she was still very much under arrest. They made general plans for the meal: not too formal, not too casual.

Lina said, "When we get back I want Wiley to teach me how to use those bio-cleaning chambers. I am going to learn how to biofilter. Tonight." She snapped her fingers in her determination. "Goal A-plus: I am going home tonight to feed my cats."

"I don't recall house arrest including trips to Earth," Jae said. Though his manner was pleasant, there was steel in the voice.

"Oh please, Jae. They'll starve! Faf needs her medicine. I think the sitter I hired stopped today. Maybe yesterday. I don't know; I've got my days mixed up. But I promise I'll do everything you tell me to, just let me take care of the cats. They can't live on their own."

His chin jutted as he considered, rolling the decision around in his mouth as if it were a hard candy. "I'll have to go with you. Assess the situation; gather background evidence. Yes, the commander will approve."

Lina let out the breath she'd been holding. "I should be able to handle a passenger. I got Lon here, right? You'll like Earth, even if it is a barbaric backwater."

"From what Lon's told me all these years, maybe I will." He settled back with a contemplative look.

Jae's ring buzzed, and he gestured toward the tabletop. Wilder's face showed on a screen above it. "Yes?"

"Level four planetside emergency," Wiley said briskly.

"I'm on it. Rallene out," Jae said as some words or numbers flashed across the tabletop. Lina wasn't sure which. She'd have to learn Panlingua in both verbal and written form. That was going to be a royal pain.

"I'll be back in about ninety minutes. Computer, keep track of Lina O'Kelly and report any movements outside of these quarters or Lab 1-A to Dr. Mem-Bazer. *Skurnit*, I wish we had a few more members here to do this. Lina, report to Wiley in the lab when you're ready for the day," Jae told her. He reached over to press his fingers against some lit areas of the console, tapping them as if he were entering information, and turned to her. "See, we can do it, too."

He faded from view in a dot pattern.

Transporter effect, Lina decided. It needed shrilly *Star Trek* sound effects to make it seem real.

"Cool." She went to scrounge a little nosh, just enough to tide her over until second breakfast.

She walked around the apartment exploring as she finished Lon's last protein bar. There were cold drawers in the kitchenette instead of a refrigerator, that held lumps of… Well, one was a piece of frosted cake and the others were complete un-knowns. Otherwise she recognized a variety of high-fat salty snacks in a cupboard. The rest of the apartment was not that friendly to her presence. Most drawers and cabinets wouldn't open for her. That electric shock must not have told everyone after all.

That left surfaces. One wall of the living room displayed Lon's nicer CD covers, augmented by a small cube that contained his jukebox. Tables held stashes of Terran printed magazines. Most had articles about either Londo or his father. Some of the covers had stickie reminders to someone named Grace or G to correct this article, or to write a letter to the editor with a complaint, or to thank a journalist about their story.

So that's what Lon's handwriting looked like, kind of scritchy with big caps. Was Grace his secretary? Maybe the person who had made the cake?

Lina found out by accident that some of the awards in Lon's trophy room had a pressure point that you could activate to get a 3-D recording of the award ceremony, plus another point that showed the feats that warranted the award. She watched amazing footage of Londo rescuing space travelers, stopping entire oceans from flooding residential areas, rushing vaccine to all corners of the sector, even flying into the outer atmosphere of a star to retrieve a lost sensor experiment. Sometimes her translator unit, which flew constantly by her side, didn't give her equivalents of some words and the picture didn't help either, so she just left it to her imagination as to what he had done. Lon was wonderful. Give him lots of awards just for that!

The odd thing about the master bath was that there was no shaving paraphernalia at all, but lots of other grooming supplies. Maybe Lon's good looks were a studied skill. Whatever they were, he was certainly doing the right thing. Tall, dark and gor-geous – woof!

Bedroom came next. Dresser drawers opened to her touch. She found underwear but also civilian-type clothing ranging from sweaters knitted with holographic yarn to what she supposed was gym wear. Hanging in the closet next to the backup Val-iant costumes that had ticked off Lon when she'd laughed at the sheer volume of them, were civilian outfits that seemed very dressy and Out There, plus some variations on the Valiant costume that she couldn't see the sense of. Why a uniform all in magenta glitter? Did the Legion observe a Diva Night?

In the cabinet next to the bed was a tall stack of porn magazines she recognized from work and newsstands. She picked up an odd, undecorated box from his bed stand and jumped when a bald-headed but completely solid-seeming woman appeared right in front of her and began to coo in a language she really wished her translator marble wouldn't translate. The woman began to disrobe and Lina hastily cried, "Computer! Please turn this off for me!"

The woman disappeared, and Lina sank onto the bed. So that was what Lon's virginal sex life had been like. She didn't want to look farther for fear that she'd find something worse, but then she realized that she'd examined almost every available nook and cranny of the apartment.

Jae had said ninety minutes; how long had she taken?

She ported into Wiley's lab within a very little while, freshly showered and wearing something quite like a pareo that she'd found on the shopping network with – if you used your imagination – a tropical print. It had a tied top and was supposed to be worn with a shirt underneath, a capelet over, tall boots and tights, but she'd foregone that. Just the dress, please. A belt cinched it, and she'd replicated her stayup hose from the wedding, but now in deep suntan, to cover her legs.

Finding shoes had been a pain. There weren't even sandals. Bare toes would be too shocking, she supposed. Almost everyone wore either boots or a kind of soled tights that looked too uncomfortably much like pantyhose to her.

The ordering process was all kind of cool. She could cross-reference to match the shoes to the fabric of the pareo. The outfit had appeared in an open cabinet as soon as she'd finished ordering it. No box, no tissue paper, no bill of sale. Maybe it had been manufactured in there, like those newfangled 3-D copying machines back home. The bongo beat of Classic *Trek* thrummed through her mind. Welcome to the future, Lina O'Kelly!

The coordinating Climalon jacket she shrugged off after a few minutes in the lab. It would cover her up tidily when she was out in public, but she didn't want to wear it inside. For whatever reason Wiley must have turned up the temperature in here and unlike her time in quarantine, excess clothing wouldn't be needed. She told herself she was still on tropical vacation, not a prisoner on another planet, and she was going to dress that way!

Wiley was handling a call so she didn't disturb him. He had eight large screens displayed in a semi-circle around himself. Jae wasn't back, so she sat down at the station she'd been using to test her biofiltering process. She'd worked here for hours yesterday with Lon cheering her on – he was so sweet – but hadn't managed to port anything in without it becoming a biohazard. The windowed compartment in front of her was sealed germ-tight and came equipped with a system to safely clear her failed experiments.

Something bright flashed over her head, zipping toward Wiley in a red glow. She ducked, but no other flashes followed. Oookay.

She asked the computer to show her how the monitor screens would look if she ported in something with no contamination. Unfortunately that resulted in columns of writing or numbers that she couldn't read, so she got the computer to make a color bar that indicated germ levels. Color, she could read.

With a nod to herself, she set to work doing some serious interstellar porting. She had to get out of here. It wouldn't be an escape, it would just be… going home. Yes. Where she was supposed to be. Winding up on Sarastor had been a mistake – a lucky mistake, in that only that way could Londo have been saved – or herself, come to think of it. But Out Here she was a Terran witchdoctor, plainly unwelcome and made even more so by all this ridiculous, unwarranted and unfair arrest shit.

If she could get to Earth, she'd be out of the Legion's jurisdiction, wouldn't she? She just wouldn't come back here anymore, problem solved.

And yet the things she'd already seen Out Here, the people she'd been introduced to – so exotic, so paraheroish, so *Star Trek*. Jae and Wiley were her friends now. Darn it all, it was exciting just to be here, even if she was under arrest. She wanted to get herself legally free so she could explore without recriminations.

And maybe… No "maybe." It would definitely reflect badly on Londo if she took off to Earth and didn't come back.

She'd think about it after she mastered this porting thing. To make things worse, she had a time limit. Take more than five and a half minutes to separate contagion from an object as she held it just outside of normal space, and the object ceased to exist.

She still had some chess pieces left after all the trials yesterday, so she ported them in one by one from her home. She quickly grew frustrated because it seemed the more she concentrated, the worse she got. Getting small objects from Earth to Sarastor just naturally brought in all kinds of atmospheric and electrical imbalances, as well as a cloud of bacteria. In screening through it all as she held it outside of reality, she was trying to be painstakingly thorough. She wasn't a painstaking kind of person.

Well, she thought, *let's give the opposite a try.* Clearing the chamber and resetting parameters, she merely beamed in another plastic pawn from Earth instantaneously. And jumped clear out of her chair as a blinding electric spark went off inside the chamber, incinerating everything.

Okay, not that way. So. What if she consciously compensated for electromagnetic differential and atmospheric pressure – she didn't want people's ears to pop – and didn't try anything else?

The reading on this next pawn was the lowest in contamination of any of her tests so far.

That was pretty much how she'd brought them in three days ago, wasn't it? What would improve it? She leaned back in the chair, weaving ideas together.

She was porting from Earth to Sarastor. Was there any way she could, maybe, connect to the *feel* of the planet she was porting to, and just go with the flow? See what the planet would comfortably accept? Leave the rest to dissolve in stasis.

She tried it. The computer console in front of her buzzed. The progress bar showed clean blue: no contamination on the pawn. "Yeees!" she cried.

Wilder used his right eye to glance from the conversation he was having with Dubblest authorities. His console monitored Lina's. She'd just successfully biofiltered something she had ported in from Earth. Now she could come and go as she pleased, and there would be nothing they could do to stop her if she wanted to run from house arrest. What would she do?

Lina cleared the chamber and tried it again with a larger object: a fuzzy pillow that Molly loved to sleep on, a pillow chock-full of germs and cat dander and who knew what. Things didn't come more contaminated than that. But the console shone blue again. All clear. She jounced in her chair excitedly.

She ported the pillow into the next chamber so Molly would still have her little bed, and faced the now-empty chamber. Lina ported in a small container of cat grass. It was chewed in places, but still very much alive when it arrived. All clear! Third time's the charm.

Lina took a breath and imagined her house. No, not her house. That would get the cats excited, make them think she was home again. She built up the mental picture of her driveway, gathered in the feel of herself taking up space in the universe, and then ported.

Wiley caught his breath when she disappeared, trying not to let the official on the screen notice. He snapped the audio alarm off before it could sound, then signaled to Jae what had happened and to hurry back, although he couldn't think what they would do to apprehend an interstellar teleporter. Portable force field generators were a possibility, but Earth was a partial day away by Hyperspace Level 3 speed. They would have to enlist the Terran Paranorm Network. He didn't think they'd have projectors. *Grigach* take working short-handed!

Seven minutes passed. He was still trying to get rid of the official when out of the corner of his eye he saw Lina reappear, carrying a pile of white parchment leaves. He turned the screen audio to mute.

"Don't do that again," he told her as he canceled the alert to Jae.

She looked puzzled, and then apologetic. "Oh. I'm sorry. I didn't think. How are contamination levels?"

He glanced at a readout on his console. "Normal."

"Good." She beamed a grin at him before relocating to the table in the break room so she could spread out her newspaper.

When the monitor finally cleared, Wilder joined her. "Sleeves," he told her. "Cover up. I thought Jae was going to give you an orientation lecture?"

"I have a jacket for public wear," she told him. "I've been carefully observing, and I believe everyone present has arms. They won't see anything they haven't seen before."

"That's not the point. No demerits for dress violation this time. I only allotted five demerits for your trip because it was impulsive and it was your first time."

"Demerits?"

"That wasn't included in your orientation lecture?" At her blank look, he said, "Legion demerits are assigned when rules are broken."

"Um, are demerits particularly bad?"

"Spousal demerits appear on the record of their spouse at a one-to-ten ratio."

"I take it that doesn't mean Lon got fifty demerits…"

"He now has half of one."

A half demerit didn't sound too bad for an accident…

"A member gets enough demerits and he goes on suspension. If he garners even more demerits, or a review board rules against him, he must leave the Mega-Legion."

Londo – Oh, what had she done? "How many demerits is that?" she asked, panic rising. "Can I do something to cancel them?"

"Obey the rules of your arrest and you won't have to worry."

"Oh yes! I will!"

"Good." He frowned at her paper, but both his eyes focused on it. "What is this?"

"A newspaper," she said, then pointed at a particular spot. "And I found out what it was."

"What what was?"

She tapped on the page-five story. "Lon and I were running around on Tiawa for days and asking, 'Where the hell is everybody?' It says here that there was a mass scare. Someone – gee, I wonder who – told everyone that they had to evacuate because there was going to be atomic testing."

"Atomic testing?" Wiley squinted at the English print. "Is that usual?"

"I guess there are still a couple nations that do above-ground testing. The Bikini Atoll is close to Tiawa. That's where they did the first big tests back in the Fifties."

"So all the people evacuated."

"There weren't that many people there in the first place, just a small town, a native village, and a few odd homes here and there. It says here that soldiers with guns came to each house and ordered the people out, right then and there. Most of the poor people were crammed on a small fleet of ships whose crews abandoned them after three days. Luckily someone knew how to use their communications equipment and got rescued. Thirteen thousand people."

Lina shook her head. Terry Whatsherface had certainly pulled out all stops to set her trap for Londo. Right now she must be pretty pissed. Wouldn't it be nice to get back to see Lon rub her nose in it? Lina chuckled nastily to herself. See the bitch get what she deserved, yeah. She'd lead the court in a chant of "Guilty! Guilty! Guilty!"

"And you didn't notice any of this?" Wiley asked. "Didn't sense anything wrong?"

"My hotel was pretty far outside the town. There were just a couple of guys who gave me the creeps." Men who had later committed suicide right in front of her, rather than be captured by Valiant.

Lina turned the page, smoothing it out flat. "After everything went crazy, I had to spend a whole day with my antenna up and on full power. I must have blown myself open. Before, I didn't have to use psi just to survive."

Wiley nodded and questioned her about a gamut of newspaper stories. Lina was only too happy to try to answer his questions. Here was something that was familiar to her, the news of Earth. Over this, at least, she had some control. She chatted as she tore out food coupons, another thing that Wiley also didn't understand. He'd probably never had to live on tuna, crackers and three-for-a-dollar canned vegetables for an entire pay period.

"And you get these newspapers every week?" They discussed the benefits of electronic news vs printed news. Wiley was more than a little surprised to find how widespread the Internet and its services were on Earth.

Lina turned a page and smoothed it down. "A Sunday reading ritual is very satisfying," she told him as she carefully tore the page. She sighed. "Although the ritual is not worth killing so many trees. I need to switch to digital."

Wiley perused the ParaNet and political news on the front page. Lina gave him her interpretation of modern American politics. It was obvious that Wiley's reading skills were getting faster as his knowledge of written English came back to him from wherever he had obtained it in the first place.

Moving on their own and not in concert, Wilder's eyes tracked two separate stories. "You think politics is all a struggle for personal power."

"Some people can never get enough."

Wiley smiled to himself as he turned the large page. Mind #3 studiously kept up with notes to be presented in his report to Stoan. "You're not very opinionated, are you?" he asked.

"Hell no, I'm just right all the time." Lina paused. "I don't like bullies. I don't like people who misuse their power. I don't like people who lie. I don't like people who abuse others, whether they be other people or animals or the planet. And it's a downright shame that people are conditioned to think that they have to put up with those who do. I certainly am, and that's one of the things I'm trying to change."

She decided to switch subjects and put down her section. "If it's Sunday morning, and it should be since I'm reading the Sunday paper, no matter how old it is, you should have some classical music playing on your stereo system," she hinted.

"I am glad to say I have no music system."

An emergency from the monitor board called Wiley away. He looked up a few minutes later as a strange sound started from the break room, too softly to interfere. A monitor showed Lina adjusting a knob on a black box from which music was coming. Odd that it had no discernible drumbeat to it. She poked her head out the door to give him a questioning look and he nodded okay to her.

"For a little while only," his voice told her. It had come from just next to her ear, though his mouth hadn't said it. He was talking to his screens. She'd known that he had all kinds of electronic input to keep track of his world, but it seemed he could also output to it without using any normal human means. Wow, technology.

She had so much to learn. Lina sighed and returned to the rest of the paper.

It was perhaps another forty-five minutes before Jae reappeared in the lab. Lina was explaining musical themes to Wiley, switching from track to track to make her point. She alternated between *The Moldau, The Blue Danube,* and the theme to *Star Trek: The Motion Picture* to illustrate how music could convey the idea of running water.

Finally she frowned at him and asked, "Have you ever been near an actual running river or ocean?"

"Not to listen," he replied.

"Then that's the problem." She shook her finger at him but before she could continue her lecture, Jae asked, "Wiley, have you become a music aficionado?" He sat down and cocked his head. "That's not one of Londo's," he stated. "I take it we had a breakthrough?" He looked expectantly at Lina.

"It's one of mine." Her face shone with triumph.

"It's good to hear something new," Jae said. "Lon promises to bring in new music, but he keeps forgetting. Ten demerits for porting without–"

"I've already seen to that," Wiley assured him. "She understands not to port without permission and guard."

"Very well. I'd stay and listen, but I'm starving. The mission had a few unreported complications." Jae got up and held the back of his chair. "Wiley, can we get you anything?"

"I'm fine," Wiley said, moving to answer another monitor call. "Make sure she wears the jacket."

3

"Shall we go?" Jae gave a little bow which Lina acknowledged with a smile. "Very nice," he gestured to her new outfit. "One hardly ever sees shoes any more. The tights are borderline; next time make 'em darker so they don't insinuate skin underneath. But Wiley is correct."

He waited for her to pull on her jacket before escorting her out the double doors that guarded Wiley's primary lab. In the hallway outside Jae stopped next to the opening of a clear vertical tube that reached from floor to ceiling... and beyond. "Get in," he said.

"Get in where?" Lina examined the tube. It was as wide as a car was long, open on top and bottom, going who knew how far in either direction. "Down" was the direction she was most concerned with.

"Here." Jae wrapped his arm around her waist and pulled her in beside him. They dropped suddenly, but after the first surprise it was a comfortable descent.

"Ah," Lina observed, trying to be urbane. She held her skirt down with one hand. "An elevator." Kind of like the pneumatic tube the Jetsons used. She was uncomfortably aware of his arm around her, not because it was a touch, but because Jae was a very handsome man, and not her husband.

Get hold of yourself, she told herself firmly. *Ordinary people touch all the time.* But it just seemed so intimate. Where should she put her own hands? She should ease away from him but for all she knew, Jae was holding her up. Could he really fly?

"How do you tell it which floor you want?"

"We've got a way to go yet." Jae smiled mysteriously.

Lina looked into the bright abyss below them and guessed that they'd already passed more than ten stories. Still they fell. Something seemed to solidify transparently under her feet and finally Jae put out his hand to almost touch the tube's sides. "Ground floor," he said, and they gradually slowed to a stop.

The elevator opened to a series of lounges with greenery and comfortable seating arrangements radiating from a lobby. A few people milled about, uninterested in the two of them. Perhaps that was an information kiosk near the exit doors. It held many screens with lots of large, decorative writing on them.

Jae led her through a dark corridor with small flashing lights embedded in the walls. "Security," he explained as they passed an unsmiling, uniformed man. Then they emerged onto a paved plaza.

Turning around to face the building they'd emerged from, Lina looked up. And up. And up. "Good lord!" she cried. She knew it was big, but this–! Mega-Legion Headquarters was immense: not only tremendously tall, but it stretched wide to take up a few city blocks along this side at least. This was a veritable mountain, solid, unreflecting black against the bright city sky awash with sunset.

Over the main door sat an oval emblem that must have been five stories high at least. Overlapping the oval was a symbol or perhaps the first letter in whatever was Panlingua for "Mega-Force Legion," or maybe "Affiliated Systems," for it was the same letter that was on Londo's Legion ring – and Jae's and Wiley's, for that matter. A child's indication of a bird in flight: a "V" with wingtips.

"Should I be impressed, or are all Sarastor buildings this big?" Lina asked. She didn't want to look at it any more. Its sheer immensity made her dizzy.

Jae chuckled and pressed the top of a short post next to the doorway. A panel lit, words scrolling across it. "Legion Headquarters is one of the largest structures in the AffSys," he said as he slid a finger along the writing. "You can be impressed if you want. I think that its size is the reason why they came up with these." He held up his right hand, but received only a quizzical look in return. "My Legion ring." He wore it on his middle finger, same as the others.

"I've noticed them. So?"

Jae crinkled his finger and the air around him crisscrossed with the slightest of linear distortions that she wouldn't have noticed if Jae hadn't made such a production of it. The distortions focused on eight, or maybe twelve equidistant spots about a foot and a half out from his body and were anchored not only by his ring, but by his wrist and ankle bands. With a subtle lift of his chin Jae rose a few feet in the air and then touched back down.

"Wow! Look at you! Is that an anti-gravity field? It really lets you fly? But why does Londo wear one? He can fly by himself."

"It's also a communications device as well as a locator. It does a few other things as well. And it serves as identification."

"You must sell millions of cheap copies to your fans."

Jae shook his head as a small, brightly-reflecting saucer with flashing lights descended from the sky to land in front of them. "It's illegal to duplicate the design of a Legion ring, a minimum of ten years imprisonment. Here's our cab."

They ducked into the plush, circular interior, but the vehicle had no driver. A window a good yard high ran completely around the craft, and passenger seats were arranged to take in the panorama. Lina was about to ask who or what controlled the saucer, but how would it sound? The primitive Terran, here on the wonder world of Sarastor. May as well call her Granny Clampett, gawking at her ce-ment pond.

She decided to put her suspension of disbelief on overdrive. She should enjoy her situation and not be frightened by her lack of information. The challenge was not to lose herself before she started to find her way in this world. Her stomach gave a little lurch as they took off because things didn't match up from what she saw going by the window to what she felt. She just had to ask.

"Artificial gravity?"

"I guess so. I never thought about it before." Jae put his hand on a red panel and said, "Pares Restaurant in Thessander." The cab changed direction suddenly, but the motion didn't register inside. They might as well be in a theater with the scenes of the city projected on a screen.

Lina stared out at the city as they flashed across the sky. It seemed to stretch out forever. She'd been to New York, had seen the cityscape there, but this was much, much, *much* bigger.

"How big is this place?" she asked.

"As in…?"

"I don't understand. What didn't you understand about the question?" she asked.

Jae nodded. "That's right, Terran cities only go so far into the wilderness. Here on Sarastor, parks are placed within the city sectors. The surface of the planet is one city with different sectors. Legion Headquarters is in Lirravon, which is about, oh, a hundred fifty square miles. It's only a sector, the site of an ancient city, I think. The modern city itself goes on and on."

"How awful."

According to Jae there was still wildlife left, although most of it could only be found in the larger connected parks and waterways, plus two and a half wide belts of rain forests that were off-limits to any kind of development. Smaller city parks that were spaced every few miles or so couldn't be expected to have much diversity in them.

Lina had problems with the lack of wilderness back home, much less here. "Are all the planets in the AffSys like this?"

"They'd like to be. Sarastor sets an example to the entire sector. You'd find other worlds much less built up."

"Feith wasn't like this." For some reason she was sure of that.

He was silent for a moment. "No, it wasn't. We had a small population that kept to central cities. We shepherded the land but did not control it."

"So what's your take on all this?" The lights from down below sped past them in a steady stream, unlike the frantic lights of higher air traffic around them. She craned her neck to see light patterns on the ground, as if there were regular streets down there. But there weren't many. Why would they need streets on a world with flying cars? The city spread out low and vast, with a few centers here and there requiring clusters of towering skyscrapers.

Jae shrugged. "I got used to it."

"That's not what I asked. Whoa! Look at that!" It wasn't for another half-minute that Lina realized that she was kneeling backward on her seat, staring out the rear of the vehicle at the trail of a rainbow-colored something that had just swooshed past them like a traveling fireworks display. "What was that? Was that a spaceship? Are they all right? How close were they flying? Aren't there any traffic laws here?"

"Relax. That was just an official communications drone coming out of hyperspace. Some planets like a little fanfare when they send an important message to Sarastor."

"A drone? Like the one you made?" She settled back in her seat. "There was a miniature thing like that, that came through Wiley's lab."

"Just light by now. The solid part converts to light frequencies when it exits hyperspace. Look, we're almost there." He pointed out the window as they went into a long swoop. From here, high above the unending city, she could see a narrow grid of lights. Yes, there were streets in this area. Over there was a square patch of absolute dark. Maybe that was one of the parks. She hoped so. She suddenly felt very sorry for Sarastor and her inhabitants never to know the wild areas.

"Put us down here; I feel like a walk," Jae said to the air, and two beeps replied.

The drop down to street level should have been stomach-wrenching, but it wasn't. And it wasn't so much a street as a pedestrian mall following the canyon between buildings. They strolled past large-screen displays of garments, sparkly electronics and room-sized lava lamps. Movies also played showing 3-D people who walked alongside them, then ran off into the walls of the buildings through strange landscapes. A few of the actors talked to them, but Jae waved them off with an affected gesture like people here used to talk with computers. Sometimes the actors on the side screens would jump high or twist at impossible angles, like they were characters in a videogame. Once an explosion went off next to the street, safely encased in the screens.

Jae let her stop and stare, but he didn't offer much explanation. It must be too ordinary to explain. Maybe he was just in a mood.

Real people were sparse down here on the street. Jae told her that most Sarastorans never went outside; there was no reason to. The pedestrians they saw were non-natives. Those hurried through the cold past them with a definite goal, not bothering to enjoy the evening or the shows to either side. Their footsteps echoed metallically through the empty plazas, except for the alien-alien with cloth-covered tentacles who slithered down the pavement at a quick pace.

Lina's breath frosted in the cool air of evening, but otherwise the amazing Climalon jacket made her forget how cold it was. Her simple floral print stood out like a weed in a parking lot among the op-art geometrics of bulky Affiliated Systems dress. She hoped again that she wasn't giving away her provincialness.

Jae's outfit branded him as well. He'd wrapped his cloak around himself like a coat, perhaps for anonymity more than warmth. Even so, every now and then Lina would turn her head to see someone stopped behind them, staring back at Jae. Or rather, staring back at the Legionnaire Neutrino, the Last Feithi.

Then she looked up at the night sky but couldn't see stars for all the city lights. If the city stretched all around this world, the skies would be like this everywhere.

You don't like me? she heard Sarastor ask, and she shook her head.

No, it's not you. It's what they've done to you.

Ah, yesssss...

Lina murmured in sympathy.

"What was that all about?" Jae demanded. "You were talking to someone."

"Just Sarastor," she replied with an apologetic smile. Jae and most of the Legionnaires were used to being around telepaths who got the special spacey look when they silently communicated. There was a telepath on the Legion rolls. Two, she corrected herself, now that Londo was telepathic. "She thought for a moment that I didn't like her. I corrected her impression."

"Talking to a planet." Jae gave her a beat on that one as he digested it. Then he shook his head. "Well, you'll like this place," he said.

They entered an open archway into a mall. Suddenly everything was warm as summer, without any noticeable air curtain effect. Inside was bright. People strolled around in indoor dress.

"I like this part of Thessander." Jae said. "It's busy. There's not that much politicking going on."

Lina asked, "Are these Sarastorans?"

"Off-worlders again, for the most part." A small group of people gaped at him. Three in the group dropped into deep bows. He nodded to them all and went on. "Sarastorans don't like to leave their quarters. Here." He led the way to a wide, glittering doorway and pressed his fingers to a plate on the door frame. The plate glowed for the merest instant before the entire door pneumo-popped into the wall.

"What's that all about?" Lina asked with a gasp as they stepped through.

"The one who's paying opens the door. They have my ID now and can bill my account. Londo says that on Earth you actually have to wait for a check after you eat. What if you're in a hurry to leave? What if you sneak out? This way the restaurant gets its revenue."

"Oh." Exotic writing scrolled within a floating screen that greeted them. What did it say? "I'll have to learn Panlingua, spoken and written. Ugh."

"So you can read on Earth?" Jae asked.

"Of course I read!"

A thin smoke layered the air of the darkened restaurant. It didn't smell of cigarettes, thank goodness, but rather of meats grilling. Lina's stomach rumbled despite her new aversion to animal flesh.

The restaurant consisted of a long corridor with black doors every ten feet or so. Closer to an open floor area, the walls turned into three-sided cubicles that formed the backdrop to interior tables. The cubicles set a grid pattern, all facing the open floor.

Jae gave Lina a push, and she realized that a bald waiter with deep orange skin had appeared to lead them. He bowed to a darkened door and Lina touched it. Her hand passed right through.

Inside was almost as dark.

"Very funny," Jae muttered and waved his hand. The waiter seemed surprised when the interior lights came up to decent levels, but he bowed and waited.

"I need a drink," Jae said. "Lina?"

"Nothing alcoholic, please."

Jae gestured with two fingers and thumb to the waiter and got another bow before the waiter turned and left.

Two lounging couches flanked their low table at right angles to each other. Jae kicked one. It scooted to the opposing side of the table. "Sit," Jae told her, and he slid lengthwise onto his couch, rising to brace himself on an elbow.

Lina sat uncomfortably on hers. She had to swing her knees to the side so they would squeeze between couch and table.

"No, no," Jae waved a circle at her and then at himself lying there. "Like this."

"Roman style," Lina said, and tried to keep her skirt decent as she wiggled around to a good position. "Do they expect us to eat like this?"

"Sure. It's all the rage: Argoji-style. People are fascinated and repulsed by it, so the Pares carries it. The Pares specializes in the controversial." With long, slender tongs, he sorted through a bowl of brown, bite-sized whatevers on the table and then popped one into his mouth.

At his nod, Lina fumbled for the tongs set at her place – and a picture of a steaming plate of live worms appeared in front of her. The tongs clattered as she dropped them.

Jae waved and the picture disappeared.

"What was that?"

"Just the menu." He ate another thing.

"I didn't order it, did I? Worms!"

He gave her the barest of bored nods. "Controversial and repulsive. I hear they're delightfully chewy with a robust aftertaste." A slight tilt of his chin, and he met her shocked eyes. "No, you didn't order them."

He explained that for now the tabletop contained a menu. He raised up to point out the two places that needed to coordinate to confirm an actual order, and Lina heaved a breath of relief. She got the tongs to work and fastened upon one of the brown things. "This isn't a fried bug, is it?"

"I'm a vegetarian," Jae told her as he ate another one. The air beeped quietly and he said, "Come."

Through the dark air curtain of the door, the waiter appeared with a tray of drinks. He set a tall glass of brown liquid in front of Jae and a squat one of frothy green for Lina.

"Keep 'em coming." Jae waved the waiter off. He lifted his drink to Lina. "Here's to Aiko," he said.

Lina tinked her glass on his. "Aiko," she said, and tasted the stuff. It was light, not sugary as its appearance suggested, and tart as a good Granny Smith. It was also darned difficult to drink it in this position.

Jae had no problem with his. He downed the majority of his glass in two long pulls.

"Technically, I'm not on duty," he said for her benefit. "If I get a call, I'll just neutralize the alcohol in my system."

"Oh. Your power…" Lina wondered. "You can change things. Chemical reactions and compounds. Materials at an atomic and molecular level. You command devas of form and structure."

He gave a slight snort. "Don't let them hear you say that. The concept of devas is altogether too unscientific for civilized people to discuss."

"But you do. I guess all your people did?"

"And you hear me do it." He gazed at her through the rim of his glass as he tipped it to his lips.

"Wiley said the Feithi kept the technique of their powers a secret. I won't tell anyone if I'm not supposed to."

That made him nod. "What do you want to eat?"

"I have no idea what foods there are on this world."

"Then do you mind if I order for you again?"

She shrugged. "Sure. I trust you."

"Ah, never trust me, Lina."

"You're my confinement officer so you don't want to poison me," she retorted. "If you did, they'd make you fill out a lot of pesky forms."

He chuckled at that and agreed. Jae's fingers skipped across the tabletop. Dozens of pictures of food popped up momentarily, then were gone. "Done," he announced after a few seconds. He reached out to touch her wrist, then slid his hand around it. "Just an experiment," he said as she immediately jerked away out of habit.

But it was a healed habit. He'd noticed. So she let him grip her wrist. She bit her lip.

"Fear?" he asked.

She shook her head, staring at his flesh on hers. People did this kind of thing all the time. "It's just going to take me a while to get used to it."

He released her. "I thought something was different. Part of our little miracle this morning?"

"I think Londo did it last night. It was an accidental side-effect."

Jae threw back his head and laughed. "So that's what he was up to. An entire phobia – gone, *fsst.* He'll have to teach the method."

"No, that's not what he was up to. It just happened."

"So. You can touch others now."

"It's so strange." How could he laugh at something as serious as this? "You don't understand. I've never been able to touch others before. It's weird. Everything's weird." She glanced around at this strange cubicle, this strange world. "I mean, it's not bad weird. I'd love to explore this place, but–"

"You're under arrest. No exploring."

"Right. Arrest." Lina supposed that she shouldn't even be here. She should be a cell.

A sudden crash from outside their cubicle made her jump off her couch. It was followed by a shrill whistle and series of thumps. "Fire alarm?" Lina stood next to the door and looked back at Jae uncertainly. He hadn't gotten up.

Instead he lay back on his couch and howled a huge laugh: "HAH HAH HAH HAH HAH," like a machine-gun, holding his stomach and then pounding on the table with his fist.

"What? What?" Lina demanded. Outside, the sound continued. Lina peeked through the brief darkness that was their doorway, only to note the absence of any mass exodus. A few people were now up and about. They weren't moving to the exits, but rather to the open floor area. The sound raged at hair-raising levels. She ducked back in to find the sound diminished some, and Jae wiping the tears from his eyes.

"Oh, that was good," he wheezed. "Fire alarm. Hah."

Lina plunked herself back down on her couch in proper seated position and stuck out her lower lip. "So what is it? Can we make it stop? It's really annoying."

"No it's not. It's music."

"Oh, ha ha." She crossed her arms and glared at him.

"No, really. You don't like it? I thought Terrans were so into music."

"We are. That is not music. Or is my translator malfunctioning?"

Jae sat up straighter and made a strange gesture. Immediately, all sound from outside stopped. Lina breathed a sigh of relief.

Jae tapped on the bottom of his now-empty glass. "They've been telling me here for years that they had the best music on the planet and I just wasn't able to appreciate it properly."

A momentary blast of "music" assailed them as their waiter appeared with a new glass for Jae and spirited the empty one away. When the door barrier stood intact again, the music silenced.

"Even experimental music has some kind of organizing element to it," Lina said.

Jae nodded. "They stop the band when Londo's here. He threatens to wreck the place every time they play. The barrier doesn't tune it out for him."

"Lon's been here?"

"You'll see," he said mysteriously.

"Lon says you play guitar," Lina said. "Is that allowed?"

"In public I play the jibble and rialla."

Lina glanced at her translator marble hanging in the air beside her. "Didn't translate," she reported.

"Jibble's something like a *zy-ler-fun*," Jae said.

"Xylophone," Lina corrected.

He nodded. "Rialla's percussion section."

"Drums?"

"More than drums. Drums are permitted."

But he didn't elaborate. He regarded his glass, ran his finger around its rim, and then sipped. "Aiko's gone," he said.

"I'm sorry. Maybe your message will–"

His stony glare came up to her eyes and her voice faded.

"No, it won't," she said and he nodded.

"There's nothing you can do," she told him.

"No. And that's the hell of it, isn't it?" He said *hell* in English. "So. So. You don't like being under arrest."

"Am I required to?"

One side of his mouth twitched, though he didn't look at her. "No. You planning an escape?"

Lina pressed her lips together. What should she say? What did he expect her to say?

"Don't even think about it," he growled.

"Oh, so my thoughts are being regulated now. Isn't that mind control?"

"They control everything here."

"Who?"

"Rules for everything." His eyes were overly bright. "Even more rules for Legionnaires. We're in the spotlight. Have to be perfect. And team leaders have to be the most perfect of all."

"You're a team leader, aren't you?" Lina asked. "I read that in your bio. And Lon says he's a team leader. What is that: a major? lieutenant? Of course, I don't know which of those is the higher rank."

Jae made a cross between a chuckle and a grunt. "Londo is Team Leader Alpha-nine-unlimited-NB-PT-247-status-prime-spec563. Although…" Jae rubbed his upper lip, "that may change with his new telepathic powers. Yes, probably be a new responsibility or two in there somewhere in a few days."

"What does all that mean?"

"It means he's an Alpha Team leader. Sometimes he takes orders; most times he gives them. It depends on the situation and specialty of any other team leader in on an operation. In rare circumstance a team member will outrank the leader."

"Oh." Lina thought. "I suppose it's the same gobbledygook with you? And an Alpha Team?"

He nodded and she gave him a small smile.

"Glad I'm a civilian then," she said.

He shook his head. "Not a civilian. You're a Legion spouse. In the system you've already got a string of numbers and letters after your name that shows your rank."

"Rank?" Lina blinked at him.

"Legion Protocol will be getting in touch with you soon. Probably tomorrow. You'll learn." He cocked his head at her. "Just one of the many things Lon should have explained to you beforehand."

"He was going to explain at our lunch," Lina remembered, "but he was called away. So you tell me what he would have told me."

"No. You'll have to wait until he gets back. Then we have our little lunch, all three of us. He might forget to tell you something unless I remind him. Marriage is a complicated thing for a Legionnaire."

"Is that why you're not married? Is it too complicated, or because you don't want to abide by the rules?"

"Maybe the rules don't want to abide by me," he said. He nodded at her empty glass. "You tap twice on the bottom to get a refill. They cook the food here. It can take a while."

But instead she regarded him. Something about him wanted her attention… "You're gay," she realized.

Jae put his hand to his chest, cocking his head this way and that as he checked himself out. "I don't feel particularly happy," he said.

"Damned translator," Lina muttered. "Gay, as in homosexual."

His elbow slipped under him, but he caught himself. "Why would they call it happy?"

"Not happy, gay. Stupid translator, just say 'gay.' Gays and lesbians. I think it started out as joke but it's stuck. Gay pride and all that."

Jae stared at her, dumbfounded. "*Gei* pride?"

"Part of the human rights movement. Equal respect, equal civil liberties, that kind of thing. I'm surprised Lon hasn't told you about it."

"Lon doesn't talk much about Earth. *Gei* pride…" He ran the phrase around his mouth. "Here there's no pride involved. It's kept in dark corners and hidden. If it's not mainstream, it's not proper. If it doesn't conform to the rules, it's bad."

Lina leaned forward sympathetically. "That's terrible. On Earth if someone announces themselves as gay, it's called 'coming out of the closet.'"

"We're all still in the closet here."

"Is there a network, secret signals, ways of wearing clothes?" Lina asked. "Places to meet where a lot of illegal stuff goes on, as if being gay is wrong as well?"

Jae nodded slowly. "That's it exactly. Not the kind of situation a team leader is supposed to get into."

Lina slapped her hand down on the table. "Well, we'll just have to fix that. I've got a friend down in Atlanta who's really into Pride. You'd like him; he's great. Tells the most off-color jokes you'll ever hear, as long as they're funny. I'll see if I can get some sort of 'welcome out of the closet' kit from him for you. Huh, I guess it's true."

"What is?"

Lina shrugged at the amazingly beautiful man. "The saying is, 'All the good men are either married or gay.' I took care of Londo, so that leaves you to be gay. You did say you weren't married, right? Can gays marry Out Here?"

Jae put down his drink. "I can't believe that it's out in the open so much that there's a maxim about it. There are that many *geis* on Earth?"

"Does that mean you want to visit now?" She gave him a mischievous smile. "My friend Mace would love to meet you. Have I said what a great guy he is? Mace was always interested in gay rights, but ever since he got sick – he's got a medical condition that's associated with gays, though anyone can get it – he's practically made himself world commander of the movement. He knows everyone, simply everyone. Are you sure he doesn't know you?" She squinted suspiciously at Jae as he chuckled.

"I would have remembered a *gei* commander from Earth. We don't get too many Terrans Out Here."

Lina settled more comfortably on her couch, though she didn't lie on it. "So this is an improper restaurant serving witchdoctors and gays, and we're naughty just being here?" She gave him a conspiratorial smile.

Jae propped his head on his hand, looking innocently at the heavens. "I'm afraid so."

"Good. Rules be damned!"

"People also come here–" Jae paused as the waiter showed up with their food, gingerly settling covered plates in front of them and turning the table off its menu mode – "for the food."

The waiter removed the lids with a flourish before he left. A large cheeseburger with grilled onions and french fries sat on Lina's plate. It smelled heavenly, but – She flinched and then checked it again. It gave off zero dying cow vibes.

"It's vegetarian," she said slowly. "Or at least non-animal." Then she laughed in delight at Jae as she scooted forward on her chaise. "It smells wonderful."

"Try it."

She took a bite and almost swooned. "Oh god, it tastes just like the real thing. Thank you for ordering it."

Jae didn't comment as she continued eating with her hands and not silverware. Londo did the same thing when he ate this. It must be Terran form. They'd both eaten some things with their hands at the reception, too. "You said you wanted to have your last hamburger. Now you can have it a few more times."

"How in the world–? Lon had something to do with this."

Jae dug into a mound of white and purplish, spicy-smelling stuff as he talked. Silverware was sporks and knives. The waiter brought drink refills for them both.

"Lon came in here a few years ago with all the ingredients, demanding that they learn how to make a real hamburger. He stomped back to the kitchen and grilled it over real fire."

"You're kidding."

"You should have seen the chief cook – they have humans cooking here – making way for Valiant. Of course, there's no way for anyone to get… what is it, *boeuf*?" Lina nodded, and Jae continued. "No way to get *boeuf* here, so the chefs worked to find a fiber substitute."

"My hat's off to the chef. This is not only a good burger, it's one of the best hamburgers I've ever had in my life." She paused. "And Lon made the original? I didn't know he could cook. Why in the world is he stooping to eating McDonalds if he can do this?"

"I've heard him mention McDonalds," Jae said. "A restaurant, right?"

"A chain of fast food restaurants, serving burgers that taste like… Well. Very low-brow."

"Maybe he's slumming?"

Lina shook her head. "I sure will like having some time together so I can get a handle on him," she said.

"But you married him," Jae said softly.

Her eyebrows scrolled up innocently. "That's right, I did. And some day that'll sink in. Look, Jae, I know the essential Londo, I know that he's absolutely the man I want to spend the rest of my life with. It's the details that escape me."

"Sometime the details are what get in the way."

"So I won't allow them to. I am a willow; I can bend." She waved her arms overhead in the non-existent wind. "Did that translate?"

"No, but I get it." Jae had to shake his head at her. "I know I officiated, but I don't believe it. You two not knowing… okay, not knowing the *details* about each other and still getting married."

"So tell me some details. Tell me about Londo, some of the other crazy things he's done around here."

Jae took a long swig of his drink. He squinted his eyes for a moment, looking out onto nothing but memories, and then related a stunt he and Londo had pulled off in the heart of Legion Headquarters when they were both new arrivals, just kids.

Another few swigs brought another tale. Jae's voice got louder, the details more embellished.

A new glass: a civil event from maybe five years ago. Because he and Londo were available, they were told to show up and uphold the dignity of the Legion even though the two of them had their own opinions about the honorees of the evening. By the time he'd finished telling the tale, the woman honoree had fallen into the ceremonial pastry pot with sauce splattered hither and yon, and the accompanying male official had one of her boots on each ear and a panty that remarkably matched the outfit she was wearing, hanging out of his uniform sleeve.

Lina had to put her hand over her mouth so she wouldn't scream with laughter. Jae was pounding the table with his fists, his HAH HAH HAH machine gun laughter spraying the cubicle.

"And they never caught you?"

It took Jae more than a moment to catch his breath. "Wiley himself was called upon to search for clues," he said. "Of course, they didn't know that he'd supplied the alarm-bombs that triggered the fire-suppressant system."

Lina giggled, and noticed that her guides were nudging her, whispering. She laughed some more as she said, "I don't know what, but *they* say something else happened. They couldn't prove anything, but–"

"But Lon and I were still confined to Sarastor missions only for a month after that. Brügz was Commander back then. He said that we looked guilty, and that was good enough proof."

"And Wiley?"

"Got off scot-free. It pains me to talk about it." Jae's face took on a theatrically pitiful mask as he held his hand to his heart, which made Lina laugh even more. "So let's talk about something else."

"Okay. You now, Jae. Hobbies?"

His eyes crinkled. "Mostly sex."

Lina snorted at that. "I really do have to get you and Mace together. He mostly goes after brunets, but he'd make an exception for you."

"You think so?"

"I noticed when we walked here that all the heads were turning, and I don't think it was just because a Legionnaire passed by. Let me guess: you're on the Most Eligible Bachelors or the 10 Most Beautiful People list on whatever society program they have around here."

"You'll turn my head." He was busy with the little crunchies that had been paired with the purple stuff. Apparently this was an old subject. He knew he was beautiful.

"So come up with some other hobbies for us to talk about. You like music. Real music. Feel free to grab some of my CDs when we port home tonight."

"Oh? We're going to Earth?"

"Goal A is not complete yet. I need to feed the cats. I only port sober people, though."

"Perhaps I can arrange that. Good, I like Terran music."

"How about Feithi music? There must be records of–"

"You know how the AffSys feels about music. I've never dug that far to find any. It wouldn't look right."

Slowly Lina nodded her head. Denial was understandable. But with music?

The waiter brought Jae still another ale – how alcoholic were those things? And how much liquid could he hold? – and Jae continued, "Mostly I hang around with everyone in the Legion. It's been a family to me since… A real family. We've got some interesting members."

"Londo said you were like brothers."

"Yeah. I'd been here almost a year when he joined. We were both kids, about the same age, and we palled around together." Jae gave an ironic laugh. "And we both had years of experience with psychiatrists under our belts. People had a tendency to stare at us both back then, for all the wrong reasons. The survivor of Feith, and Maximus' kid with no past."

"It must have been tough. Thank goodness you had each other."

"Yeah. And now Londo has you."

Lina stopped as dark emotions rolled toward her from him. Jealousy? Maybe not, but it was close. Sadness. Loss. "How about this: you haven't lost a brother, you've gained a sister?"

Jae smiled a little at that. "We can try that for a while, if you're game."

"Good." Lina got a warm feeling toward Jae. He couldn't be the kind to harbor jealousy, not if Londo really liked him. Not if all those millions of spirits who gathered around him loved him so. "Now that you have a teleporter in your midst, you can come visit Lon on Earth any time and see him on his home turf. I'm sure you'll find out a lot of new and blackmailable things about him that way. I know I hope to."

"I like the way you think."

They talked some more, and when he discovered that Lina loved to play flute, he asked her what one was. She teleported hers in from Earth, which let him check it for contagion when it arrived. "Very good," he decided after a floating screen confirmed that it was safe. He examined it himself closely, fiddled with its foot joint, then had her play for a few moments before she ported it back to Lon's apartment. "Interesting," he concluded.

Jae looked at her plate and his, both empty for some time. "Are you full? Do you want some dessert?"

"Do they have brownies here?" Lina asked.

Jae looked blank. "Brownies?"

"A sort of… um, chewy chocolate cake with nuts."

"I don't think so. No chocolate here."

"And they call Earth barbaric." Lina set her mouth into a determined line. "I guess I'll have to stomp into the kitchen here some day and whip them up a batch of my famous brownies. I was just curious if they had some. Brownies are the epitome of Terran cuisine, you know."

"No, I didn't. I don't think Lon's ever mentioned them."

It seemed odd not to wait for the check. As they stepped out of their booth, the "music" caught them at full blast.

"Great hairy *grigach*!" Jae shouted. He started to stomp toward the source of the noise, the open section of the restaurant. A band had set up on a stage. People were hopping about on the floor in front of them.

Lina pulled on his arm. "Let's go. I can't believe people really come here to listen to that racket."

"People on the edge do."

The "band" let out a shriek of whistle and cymbal.

"Shards and splinters, what are they doing now?"

Drums pounded and nothing else kept up with them, not even all the drums themselves. The whistle screamed at hair-raising levels.

"That's it!" Jae brushed off Lina's hand and turned to face down the band. "Stop it!" he yelled as he lurched between cubicles.

"No! Jae!" Lina ran to catch up to him. She grabbed him by the elbow. "You're drunk!" she hissed into his ear.

He started to say something to her. His eyes were wild; his nostrils flared.

"You're right," he finally decided. And then he said something, a secret so silently that Lina almost didn't sense it. He spoke with the devas of his body.

A blink. Another blink, this one long and deliberate, and then the gaze that met hers was focused and sharp. He gave her a private grin.

"Let's teach these *frickurns* how it's done, shall we?" With a snap he turned back to the dancers, some of whom had paused at his approach. He strode across the dance floor to the stage and motioned behind him, a come-along signal.

Lina had paused at the edge of the dance floor, but now she scurried to catch up with him.

"Stop!" Jae commanded again, letting his cloak fall naturally so the band would recognize him. Most of them did. The whistle player didn't see him and only stopped when she noticed that no one else was playing. All the dancers murmured. Some bowed in Jae's direction.

From its midst Jae stared the band down, chest out, fists on hips, like he was addressing the troops. "If you can't play well, don't play at all," he ordered. He pointed at the guy in the middle of a complicated but non-electronic drum kit. "You. Move it. Let me show you how it's done." He exchanged positions with the drummer and picked up the drumsticks. "You keep a beat. That's what they're for."

Jae picked out a simple beat on one drum and added to it with a bass drum, punctuating it with cymbals which were triggered in a way Lina couldn't see.

The drummer nodded his head out of time. Jae stopped.

"Listen to it. It has a beat. Even Sarastorans know that much." He started again, nodding his head to the drummer so the drummer would nod along with him.

Lina put her hand to her mouth so she wouldn't laugh out loud. The others watched Neutrino the Legionnaire in awe and didn't pay attention to what he was teaching. One of the band members – were they male or female? Hard to tell – held a tambourine, and Lina took it from them.

"You keep the beat with the drummer," Lina explained as she demonstrated simple straight time. "You accentuate." Using the palm of her left hand, she hit the tambourine with the downbeat. "You accent. You provide a frisson." She gave it a shake roll. "You listen to the drummer."

Jae was still demonstrating for the guy as Lina started to play along with him. Jae glanced at her and varied his beat, so she could show the guy/girl how to change their style. Lina wasn't an expert by any means, but hell, it was just a tambourine. She handed the instrument back to the guy/girl and they tried it, catching on quick enough for someone who had no sense of rhythm.

Jae released the drums to the drummer, who hesitantly tried a steady beat. An avalanche in slow motion had more rhythm than this guy, so Jae resumed his place, concentrating on two basic beats.

Now Lina moved to the bald woman with the plastic whistle. It had holes in it resembling those of a recorder. "This plays more notes than just the one," she pointed out.

"It does?" The woman looked at her instrument curiously as Lina rolled her eyes.

After experimenting for a few minutes, Lina managed a reasonable version of "Mary Had a Little Lamb," keeping up with the drums. The woman's mouth opened and closed as Lina handed the whistle back to her.

"Oh wow, I didn't know."

Jae heard the remark and laughed outright. He was allowing the drummer to operate just on two drums now, refusing to let him expand until he'd gotten those right.

"And you," Lina went up to the fourth member of the group, a lanky male with the same aqua skin tone as Wiley, though his sprigs of hair were platinum. "What do you do?"

"Um, I hang around," he said. Then he straightened and gave her a slow smile. "I encourage them. They say this is art, and I'm their inspiration."

"That explains their playing," Lina said. "Do you sing?"

He looked at her like she was crazy. "Sing?" he said, clearly insulted.

"How about just non-verbal vocalizing?" She waited for the drummer to begin his simple beat, and sang "Little Lamb" with "la la la's." He flatly la-la'd along with her for a while as she nodded her head encouragingly.

"You can throw in a 'hey nonny nonny' if you want," she confided. "It doesn't mean anything. People won't think you're weird."

She stood back to hear if she could discern any difference in the band. It was now in rhythm. A simple, slow rhythm, to be sure, but everyone was on the same beat, and the non-percussion people were nodding their heads in time. The woman with the recorder was playing softly, trying to figure out the different notes available to her while the inspiration guy la-la-la'd, now landing a slight majority of his notes on key. Mr./Ms. Tambourine played their instrument too loudly, but at least on the proper downbeat.

She imagined where she'd left her flute and ported it in. These guys might need more help. Jae alone couldn't guide the entire group. With the trusty instrument assembled and in her hands again, Lina felt more complete. She pointed to the two non-percussive players and drew them aside.

"You," she pointed at the recorder woman, "need to sit down – not in public – and learn how to play the thing. Play real tunes on it. Play it at a volume that shows you're a part of the group and not trying to drown out everyone else or call the cops. And you," she pointed to Mr. Inspiration, "need to learn what a tune is. I'm sure there're some kind of reference materials available. But whatever one of you comes up with, the other one has to know, too. You make the same tune. Or you can do harmony."

"What's that?" Inspiration asked.

What would be simple enough for them? "Sing this," Lina said, and sang "la la la" to "Puff, the Magic Dragon," but adapted to the plodding beat coming out of the drums. It took him a while to get the chorus, but he did. "Good," she told him. "Sing it again." He repeated it, and she played harmony on her flute. It tripped him up. He thought she was correcting him. "No, you keep singing what I told you to. Listen. I'm playing complementary notes."

He sang again as she played harmony. "Ah," he and the recordist said together.

The drummer had graduated to three drums, all in methodical rhythm, with Jae keeping strict watch.

"Got it," the drummer proudly announced. "I can do it now, thanks."

"Up," Jae ordered, again changing positions with the drummer. "You can tell me you've got it when you can do this."

And he began to play.

He started simply, then expanded into a more complicated rhythm, then branched out to incorporate the entire set, which made tonal sounds Lina'd never heard coming from a drum section before.

The drum solo wove to new levels and changed into something else entirely. Man, Jae was good. He radiated concentration as he lost himself in his own world, in tune with his instrument and his muse. He finished with a flourish, a clash of cymbals, and Lina applauded. The entire room applauded.

"Bravo! Bravo! Encore!" she yelled.

He stood up and bowed to her as the band's drummer wilted.

"And now a little dance music." Jae bowed to her again, but this time expectantly. Lina blinked. Oh.

Raising the flute to her lips, she decided on the "Swallowtail Jig" she liked to play in her woods with her stream burbling beside her. Soon Jae joined in, the variations of his drum set adding an other-worldly echo to her flute. The people still standing on the dance floor hesitantly broke out of their congregations and began to hop to the lively tune in patterns of four-part line dances across the room.

When done, they both had to take a bow from the appreciative audience, who talked excitedly among themselves. Lina could well imagine: having a Legionnaire be their avant-garde entertainment must have made their week.

"The important thing," Jae sternly instructed the band as he stepped out from the drum kit, "is to rehearse and get it right before you even think of inflicting yourselves on an unsuspecting public. Do I make myself clear?"

"Yessir, Neutrino sir," the answer came from around the stage as they bowed to him.

"Then my work here is done." He nodded to Lina and they exited the dance floor. Behind them, the band started up again. It was feeble but you could hear a rhythm to it now, and a la-la-sort-of-la instead of the piercing whistle. Jae whirled around, his arms outstretched and fingers grasping as if he could choke them all, but Lina restrained him by the shoulders.

Jae turned back with a laugh. "We'd better go to Earth before I do something I might regret. Might."

She brightened up. Earth! Maybe she could figure a way to stay there when she sent Jae back. "Right now?"

"Let me check in." Jae touched his Legion ring. "Wiley?"

"Jae, I'm here." Wiley's voice replied through the ring. It was very clear, just as if he were with them. Lina wondered what kind of speaker that tiny would give that kind of sound, especially since so many other gadgets were crammed into the ring.

"We're heading off to Earth now, if there are no emergencies on the horizon."

"Noted. There are, but I can handle the load for a while. Estimated length of visit?"

Lina figured quickly. "Would an hour, an hour and a half, be too long?"

"I can live with that," Wilder said. "One and a half hours before I send out a locator signal."

"Yessir," Jae said, and looked at Lina expectantly. "Shall we?"

4

L ina tucked her flute into her belt and then rubbed her hands together. "First
  stop: a cash machine."
   In his time Jae had seen others rub their hands in that way to gather energy. How much energy would teleporting eighty parsecs take?

He should never have sobered himself. What was he doing, volunteering for this?
He should insist that she stay on the planet at the very least, if not in the lab. If the
commander were here, he'd have slapped her in a force field solitary cell from the
first moment.

But this way, by not only taking her out of HQ but into her supposed home territory, he could see how she functioned from a new angle. Would she try to escape?
Signal to others? Would she be familiar with the Terran venue or would some action
give her away as an immigrant, an Imperial? No, he had to do this.

Jae masked his qualms at the prospects – interstellar teleporting by a beginner! –
as Lina's lips parted and her eyes unfocused for a full minute. Without warning,
everything went black. He was somewhere else: no floor below him, no food smells,
no noise from that blasted quartet. He couldn't hear himself breathe, but he was
breathing. He said something but only silence wrapped him. No sound bounced to
tell him he was inside a space.

He hung there, not weightless but not *not* weightless, for how long? Was it supposed to be like this? Had something gone wrong? This must be the stasis she'd
talked about. She had a five-minute limit for holding things outside normal space,
then molecular cohesion of the teleported material fell apart. Had they been here five
minutes? Blindly he reached out and met her arm. He grabbed it before realizing that
he might have distracted her concentration.

All at once he was blinking at spotlights shining in the darkness. His knees felt very weak, and it wasn't a result of the barely discernible difference in gravity from Sarastor.

A cold but fresh wind rushed past, and when he looked up he saw clouds against a dark night sky. Only a small amount of light from below bounced off those clouds. Between them, stars peeked down.

He was on Earth. First things first: he swept a sensor around himself and triggered his personal padd screen: no contamination present. Excellent.

Lina approached a man-sized construction that held a solid computer screen in its middle. A clear roof and two sidewalls gave bare shelter to the tiny structure. Beside it, stark pavement was bordered in the near distance by low buildings with glass fronts, the whole poorly illuminated by occasional orange-colored lights.

Jae inhaled deeply. The air was sweet and wild. Definitely not the slightly stale stuff of Sarastor. Artificially bright signs marked several of the buildings here and places off in the distance. He turned in a circle, saw nearby ground traffic. Not much of it. Perhaps it was because of the night; perhaps there just wasn't much at any time.

The vehicles did not run silent. And what – Those were animal sounds coming from the opposite direction. Jae turned to see forest behind this stretch of buildings. Smaller, individual buildings had been built within the park. Houses? Something barked. A Terran word clicked in Jae's mind: *chien*. Londo said domesticated *chiens* barked and could often be found around Terran residences. He'd barked at Jae to demonstrate the sound.

Lon had also mentioned undomesticated wildlife. Jae's head swiveled as he considered possible dangers of this barbaric world and how they should be faced.

Lina squinted against the lights at the ATM. The time difference had startled her. "Jeez, it must be midnight or more."

This strip mall's bank machine was at the darker end of the parking lot. It was the only one of two in town belonging to her bank. Though the other one was set in the front wall of the main branch downtown, it almost always had an "out of service" or "restocking; will be back online in ten minutes" warning flickering on its faded screen.

She could count only three cars parked elsewhere in the parking lot. Two cars were leaving, or perhaps cruising. The street beside the parking lot was almost empty of traffic.

"I don't like these things after dark. I could get cash at the grocery store, but I need to see my balance. Hang on, let me get my extra card from the desk at home."

She concentrated, apologizing for the time it took. "It's got a magnetic strip on it. I need to get it perfect or this won't work." The plastic card materialized in her hand.

Jae watched as she fed it to the machine and touched screen buttons. "What are you buying?" he asked.

"I'm not buying. I'm getting money out of my account." As she waited for the screen to change, she gave him a quick explanation of cash versus debit and credit cards and threw in some information about checking accounts as well.

He frowned. "Too complicated."

"Compared to Sarastor, it probably is." More buttons to be punched to see her balance. The machine was taking a very long time to get from screen to screen. Had she truly gotten the card transport right? Maybe there was a problem with the network. Maybe this ATM was in the process of dying.

Jae turned as a van that had been leaving made a U-turn. It pulled up to the ATM, bass vibrating its windows as music blasted within. The double stack of bright lights on the vehicle blinded them for a moment. Another car, this one marked by a dark, indented polygon venting system of some kind, pulled up beside it.

"Oh god," Lina told him quietly. "I don't think that those are bank customers."

"Thieves? Can you port us?"

"I can, but I've already punched in the security code. With that, they can get my entire account out, practically. There seems to be a holdup with the network. This shouldn't be taking this long. You're the expert. What should I do?"

He gave her an elvish grin as he nodded at her. "This is Earth; I'm a Legionnaire," Jae said. He rolled his shoulders, shaking out his arms. "Hell, I'm the most dangerous Legionnaire there is. Keep on with what you're doing. I can handle whatever comes up. It's good music, too. I can dance to it." He made a motion to her translator marble and it flew over to hover almost invisibly by him.

The headlights stayed on as its doors opened, bringing with it deafening new skool rap with a pounding beat. Lina could see a man in back and two in the front. Those two emerged with swaggers. Jae stepped between them and her. From the car, two men joined the first group.

Jae began to dance.

Lina wanted to yell at him to stop, to get away, but he must know what he was doing. Instead she silently pleaded with the deva of the ATM to hurry, hurry! The screens refused to change. Her hitting the "cancel" button accomplished nothing.

Jae gyrated and shook his shoulders and hips. He whipped around his cape as well, prancing the short length of sidewalk like he was Jagger on ephedrine. He *was* the music. He was Dance personified.

Stopped in their tracks, the thugs boggled at him until the track ended. "Hey, pretty boy," the van driver decided to say. He sneered at Jae in his costume, though the ugly jacket he wore told its own unlikely story. "It's too early for Halloween, even for drama queens. Look, we've got ourselves a Halloweenie! Thinks he's a para or sumpin'!" The men all laughed and moved into a semi-circle around Jae and Lina.

The next track began and Jae strutted down the line of them, unimpressed. He whirled and high-kicked toward the center of the circle, then bounced on the balls of his feet. His steps turned into quick, deep squats in time with the music, interspersed with fancy footwork, armwork, and more kicks.

The blue-haired passenger from the car tore his gaze away from Jae to give Lina a thorough up and down examination. He slapped his buddy on the stomach with the back of his hand and pointed. The other let out a wolf call. "Row, yow ow! Hey, sweet lady," he leered.

"My kind of woman," Blue-hair declared.

Hurry, hurry, Lina begged the deva. At least the screens seemed to be changing now, if slowly. She vibrated with fear. She'd seen what could happen when men drew out guns. These men definitely had guns somewhere. She willed Jae not to make too much of a scene. He just didn't understand these things.

But a scene was just what he had in mind. He paused in front of Ugly Jacket, still stepping with the music to the left and then the right. He bobbed his chin at him.

"Hey, man," Jacket shouted to Jae, above the blare. "We were wondering if your girlfriend wanted to join our little party in the back." He craned his neck to catch Lina's eye. She gave him her best baleful glare, trying not to look like a deer in the literal headlights. "We got some great stuff back there. Anything your heart desires. We can show you a good time, sweet thing."

Lina ignored them and now silently screamed at the machine's deva. She'd never been anything but polite with a deva before, but this was an emergency!

The deva wasn't concerned with time, only numbers. She pounded on the side of the ATM to drive her point home. The picture on the screen wobbled in response and took time to reform.

"I don't think she's interested," Jae told Jacket. He shimmied his shoulders at him.

The four stared at Jae as sound came out that didn't match his mouth movements.

"How'd you do that? Hey, Weenieboy, how'd you do that?" Jacket's scuzzy buddy, much shorter and dirtier than his companion, demanded. He pulled a gun from his pocket. "Come on, we'd really like to know. Hey, girlfriend, why don't you just step back from there now? Let us get a good look at you, why don't you? Show us what you got."

Lina turned to see the gun. Another guy was climbing out of the back of the Lexus with a gun, too. She looked at Jae. "Port?"

"Oh, baby!" Scuzz said. "I get her first. I saw her first."

"Nah, no problem," Jae told her, and she turned back to complete the transaction, trying not to let her fingers stumble on the buttons. Hadn't she had enough of guns for a lifetime! She should port them anyway – but she couldn't concentrate with all this. Form a picture of home! Sense the space Jae took up…

"Hey, stop that! Get away from me!" As Jae stepped closer, Scuzz stuck the barrel of his gun in Jae's face.

Whipping his arm like a whirligig, Jae knocked the gun away and struck him with his elbows in the stomach, then his throat. Scuzz fell like a puppet with its strings cut. Jae kicked Jacket next to him, never losing a beat. The blue-haired passenger from the Lexus stumbled backwards, shocked at the suddenness of it, while the remaining driver, the howler, pulled out a gun of his own. It snagged on his coat. Jae grabbed it before he could even start to aim. Howler let out a wail and cradled his hand against his chest.

A gunshot rang out in the night. Howler looked down at a line of red pooling on the side of his shirt, unbelieving. His neck twisted as he sought out the face of the buddy from the back seat who'd accidentally shot him. Howler sat down hard. In shock, the shooter dropped his gun but scrambled to grab it as it fell.

Two men jumped out of the back of the Lexus to run toward Jae. They pulled out pistols as he pointed to the weapon of the shooter. A whisper: it turned to mist, steaming on the pavement. The shooter scuttled back with a shriek.

Jae trotted to the far side of the van, away from Lina. He threw himself over its hood to pivot on his free hand, propelling himself at the two remaining armed men. His feet slammed into both their faces. Bouncing up from where he fell, he took a ready stance and eyed his dazed opponents, then the others. He tossed the gun he'd taken to the grass, far from Lina. He made sure it landed pointing away from everyone.

Jacket scurried to hide behind his vehicle. Blue Hair still cowered on the ground in fetal position, his arms wrapped around his head – no threat there. Jae reached down to take the two guns of the men he'd just kicked. As he stood up, he could see one last man inside the van pointing a long gun, a rifle of some kind, at him.

"Put 'em down," the thug said.

Jae grinned and let the guns dissolve in his hands, dripping in a shower of thick, wet chaff onto the pavement.

The thug's lips drew back in terror. "Get back! Get back… or… or I'll take out your girlfriend there!" His rifle swung to point at Lina.

"And how will you do that?" Jae growled low as the rifle sizzled in the man's hands. Smoke began to pour from its joins. The barrel drooped in the middle. The punk dropped it as if it had been acid, looking wildly first at it and then at Jae.

Jae leaned forward against the front of the van. Metal began to rust at incredible speed around his fingers, the air eating holes through it. "I'm coming for you now," he hissed, and the thug inside turned white. He twisted his head looking for some-place to escape to, and then jumped out the back door to run across the parking lot.

Almost faster than Lina could make out, Jae leapt into the air and swooped down on him from above. He caught him by the back of his belt and laughed. "Oh no," he said. "You come back with your friends. They wouldn't like it if you deserted them." He dropped him on top of the twin gunmen. The thug landed with a squeal of fear.

Jae rose again to dip over the back of the van. He dragged the hiding Jacket into the open by his ugly collar. The man's mouth hung open in terror.

"You don't have a gun? You expected to come up against me, and you don't even have a weapon?" Jae let Jacket go and even turned his back.

Muttering an oath, Jacket swung at him. As if he saw it coming, Jae ducked and whirled, butting the man sharply in his stomach. He finished him off with a doubled fist to the jaw.

The passenger from the car still stood in shock, staring at him. Jae gave him a "come here" crook of his index finger and then pointed to the line of crouching men. "Don't even think about going anywhere," he warned. The man shuffled to join the prisoners.

How long had it taken? Lina knew all in all, it couldn't have been more than five minutes. She watched Jae take stock of everyone, even the blue-haired guy who still sat on the pavement wrapped in his own arms, and then Jae turned to her. She gave him a helpless look and he flashed a triumphant grin.

Then she saw another lovely sight. Using both hands, she waved at the car ap-proaching with its blue and red lights flashing. *Whup whup,* its siren sounded. Jae turned to take it in, and then stood by the van where these new people would have a clear view of him.

"Do you have your *skurny* money yet?" Jae asked from the side of his mouth as she approached him.

"I do," Lina said. "Are you through – being dangerous?"

He looked around at the bodies strewn on the pavement and curb and gave a grim laugh. With his back to the van, he gave the front tire a kick with his heel, and it fell flat with a hiss. The very tip of his tongue stuck out at the world from between his teeth. He wrinkled his nose, his eyes bright. "For the moment," he decided.

She let out a breath she didn't know she'd been holding. "Good. Thanks, Jae. That was, well, pretty amazing stuff. Absolutely amazing stuff. And you didn't even work up a sweat!"

"It's a living." The police car pulled up to block the backs of the two vehicles. "These are–?"

"Police," Lina said, smiling and waving at the cops. "They tried to hold us up," Lina called to them as she pointed. "They pulled guns. This one's shot. Oh, and I think they were talking about having drugs in the van, too."

"Is that a fact? Stand over there, miss. You with her?" The officer eyed Jae and his parahero getup doubtfully.

"He's with me!" Lina declared quickly.

"Okay. Keep her out of harm's way," one of the cops said to Jae, as he drew his gun on the rest.

A final man had been hiding in the SUV. He now crouched in the driver's seat, desperately trying the ignition.

"Everyone out. Hands up! Hands up!"

Cautiously the man put his hands in the air. His eyes flicked from one officer to another as he eased out of the van. His buddies on the ground in front of the money machine stayed where they were, taking their turns being handcuffed. The air filled with police radio crackling as one of the cops called for an ambulance for the injured man.

Another police car stopped for backup. That officer investigated the van. "Nice little haul we have here," he told them. "Pills, guns, and some interesting stuff in baggies. A couple TV sets and laptops, too."

"I think the ATM camera might have gotten them on it," Lina added helpfully. She bumped Jae to the side so she could give one of the cops a statement about the incident. Mustn't let them see the translator marble at work.

The officer who'd been investigating the van's interior checked out the car and then did a double take when he noticed the hole in the van's hood. "How the hell – Hey, there's no engine in this thing!"

Jae turned to Lina, his face a mask of innocence and astonishment. "Imagine that."

She shook her head and ported them to a nearby grocery store.

"Sorry about that, Jae," she said. "First minute on Earth and you run into a bunch of thugs. What can I say: we were in an area only a stupid person goes to after dark. It was asking for trouble. It's not usually like this, I promise you."

"These things happen," Jae shrugged, then tilted his head. "More music."

Lina noticed the canned soundtrack too, such a change from Sarastor's silence. It was nicely warm in here, and brightly lit. She ported her flute home. Taking a hand basket, she led Jae to the pet food aisle. While she pointed him to the extra-large bag of dry food, she chose 28 cans of regular cat food and seven of the gourmet.

"All this?" Jae asked, lugging the big bag. "I thought cats were small mammals. That's what Wiley said."

"They are. But there are seven of them. Plus I think that the neighbor cat knows how to use the kitty door and comes in just to eat."

They checked out at the lone open register. Jae watched the process curiously. The cashier, who was even shorter than Lina, with tiny pustules on his blotchy face, scrutinized Jae the same way but didn't say anything about the white cape or the thigh-high leather boots.

Lina laughed inwardly. He must get all types at this time of night, even in this podunk place. They got their bags, went outside, and Lina ported them–

"Home!" she shouted with a whoop. She clicked on the lights. Tiny hurried foot-steps skittered everywhere. Jae set the big bag down next to an electronic keyboard as small, furred animals darted about.

"C'mon, kitty-kitties!" Lina called. She opened the front door and let out a loud, complicated whistle.

"Great shards, what was that?!" Jae exclaimed before she shut the door again.

"What, you've never heard anyone whistle? It's quicker to do that than to stand out there and wake up the neighbors by calling for them."

Sure enough, Jae could hear a clicking sound from another room.

"Cat door," Lina explained, and one by one more cats ran in.

"Hey, babies, babies!" she cooed at them. She picked up a fat one whose fur came in thick white, black and brown patches and kissed it on the nose. "Mama's here, honey, see? Aw yoo a sweedie, Kady-wady? Yes yoo aw! Diddoo miss me, Ember? I'm back for a little while. Yes, I have food, nom nom nom. Was you hungwy while I was away?" The cat wriggled out of her grasp. They made their way to the kitchen, past the remains of at least two dead mice and a pile of feathers.

"I see they haven't starved," Lina said ruefully as one small cat tried to climb her leg. "Yes, Bwanny-wanny, Mama's home. Yes, I missed you, too, baby. Now get down, sweetie. I'll feed 'em and clean these poor things up a bit, Jae. Oh – there's the CD player over there, if you want to try out a few. Wait, you don't read English."

"I can handle it."

She showed him how her CDs were arranged and how to operate the unit. Jae triggered a small computer screen that hovered over his wrist and translated the albums' writing to Panlingua. The music started as she fed, rubbed and kissed the cats. Jae would listen to a few selections from each CD and then switch to the next one in the carousel.

Lina knew she had big bands and ballads already loaded: Bonnie Raitt, Adele, Glen Miller, and Barry Manilow. Londo would probably laugh. Maybe he wouldn't. As she gave Fafhrd her thyroid pill and nutrient paste, Lina wished she knew Lon's tastes better. She smiled to herself. They had the rest of their lives to learn about each other. If only he would hurry and get back!

While the cats were too busy eating to demand petting she called her parents. She explained to the voicemail that she had been quarantined, due to get out in maybe a week or less. Not to worry. Having a good time on vacation despite quarantine.

Her mother picked up as she was finishing. Lina realized that Jae was standing next to her listening in and watching the cats as they were finishing up their supper. No, Mom, don't have any disease. It's just a precaution. Yes, she had been in Tiawa; didn't she remember? Lina let slip that the international calling rates were quite high, and her mother hurriedly said goodbye.

"They didn't even notice that I was gone," she said with a sigh. Jae was watching one of the cats.

"What's wrong with it?" he asked her. The larger black one *hooooled* softly and then its stomach began to undulate. The cat stuck its tongue out as it braced itself. "Is it going to–?" The cat threw up on the linoleum floor. Digestion hadn't proceeded too far, to judge from the pile.

"Moosie does that," Lina sighed again. "He eats too fast. He has a nervous tummy. Are you okay now, Moosie-woose? Aw yoo okay, hunny-bunny?" After a few moments of petting, Moose trotted back into the great room, tail in the air, leaving Lina to clean the mess with a paper towel. "Ick. Well, we have to play with the cats, remind them that there are humans in the world. Oh! The car."

"Car." Jae cocked his head at the word. "A ground vehicle. Like that thing those men rode in?"

Lina washed her hands at the kitchen sink. "Same thing; mine's not that fancy. A ground vehicle that is sitting in a rented space at the airport, that's going to cost me a fortune to bail out at this pace. Do you mind if I sneak it out?"

"I have to accompany you."

The airport fascinated Jae, and he flew high in the air to watch planes land. Then he had to peer inside the cars they passed as Lina searched for hers. He asked her question after question, his subjects ranging from how long Earth had had flight to what the parking lot pavement was made of. He turned as cars drove past, their sound systems evident.

"Do all cars play music?" he asked.

She explained about radio, satellite services, and MP3s. "You don't see this," she told him when she ported her car and them to her driveway. "I just cheated the airport out of a hundred dollars, maybe more," she admitted. "I'll get around to paying them. But we are on a deadline, right?"

"Right," he said. Forest almost overgrew Lina's house. Another small house sat across the street with two more not far away. Pinpricks of faraway lights shone through the woods. Everything else was trees. They rustled as their branches swayed.

The waning moon hung just above the treetops, and the cold, clear sky was alive with stars now that the clouds had moved off. "Whew! Large moon," Jae said, breathing in the green-scented air. "No wonder it's mentioned so much in the music. At least the stuff Lon has."

"You should see it when it's full," Lina said as she examined the sky. A shooting star left a streak across Cassiopeia. "Make a wish," she told Jae, and had to explain the tradition.

"I hardly ever get to see the stars on Sarastor," he told her.

With that he grabbed hold of the bulky, angled trellis over the front porch and hurled himself up. Lina knew it would hold him; she'd certainly shooed enough neighbor boys off it. The 2x4's were spaced so it was like climbing a jungle gym.

"Ow!"

"Watch out for the rose bush," she warned. "It has thorns."

He kept climbing, right up onto the roof. With a resigned sigh, Lina climbed up as well, glad no one was behind her to look up her skirt. She ported them a blanket and they sat on the south side of the roof where the angle was flatter. At this height the forest opened up, letting the heavens shine down on them. "That's the Milky Way." Lina pointed. "And that's Mars, I think, and Jupiter. Those are planets. And isn't Orion bright tonight!"

"Which is Orion?" Jae was squinting, trying to see which gleam of light that gesture had been pointing to.

"It's a constellation," Lina told him. "Those three stars are his belt, and there's his shoulder and there's his other shoulder, and those are his knees, or maybe his feet. And that arc there is his shield." She told him of Orion's dog, Sirius, and how Orion was chasing seven sisters, the Pleiades.

"We told stories of the stars, too," Jae mused. "Heroes and direction-finders. Not many orgies, though."

They sat there and watched the heavens as Lina told Jae the story behind Cassiopeia. Ember and Moose wandered over the ridge of the roof to join them. Lina petted them both as Jae listened. She told him of pyramids lined up with the stars, of Stonehenge and making wishes on the first evening star.

"I thought you made wishes on meteors?"

"Falling stars. You can make wishes on lots of things." She lay back on the blanket. "Can Londo see the stars where he is now?" she asked forlornly. Now that things had slowed down, she was aware of the great gap in her heart where Lon belonged.

"You can't see stars in hyperspace."

"So we can't even wish upon the same star."

"He'll come back. Safely."

She nodded and then sat straight up. "Bother – How much time do we left? I need to play with the cats." She brushed herself off. Had she really climbed up on the roof?

"I'll let you have a half hour. That's maximum."

It was easier to port them all inside than climb down. The two cats weren't sure if they liked the sudden relocation or not, but they didn't freak out about it. Lina gathered some clothes quickly while Jae sampled more CDs, choosing a stack to take back.

"I'd give you my iPod, but it got blown up," she called from her room. "Besides, I don't know how you'd recharge it."

The cats rubbed up against her, demanding to be petted. They meowed piteously at having been left alone. Bran kept trying to attach himself to her left leg. She rolled balls for them that tinkled or just rolled, and they scampered and dove to catch them and bat them back and forth.

One golden cat insisted on climbing up on some bookshelves and jumping onto her back. "No, Molly," Lina scolded, and spanked the cat with light taps each time she did it. Still the cat did it again.

Jae scratched his neck as he watched. He saw the way Lina fussed over the cats, and when the short-haired gray one, Ember, came up and rubbed against him, he reached down to perform the same duty to her. She rubbed and purred. "Even the animals sing on this world," he observed.

He let it go on for a few minutes more, and then announced that they needed to go back. Lina turned down the heat, turned off everything else, made sure the doors were securely locked, and ported them back to Wiley's lab. Brushing cat hair off her jacket as they arrived, she said, "That Molly! I've just got to teach her better manners."

"Thanks for the ride," Jae said, only slightly pale from the interstellar port.

He reached into a pocket on one of his belts and withdrew a small marble to toss at Wiley. It was the same size as the translator marble, but seemed to fade into the background. Camouflaged? Lina had to target it to see it. "A record of the experience," Jae told Wiley. "Complete with man-eating, ferocious cats. Let's see, there were Bwanny-wanny and Pookie-wookie and Molly-wally and…"

"Jae! I do not talk like that! That was Bran and Obi and Molly, and you know it." Lina huffed and then settled down. "Thanks for the dinner and the company," she told him. "Maybe tomorrow we can hit during daylight hours and I can take you to someplace you can buy some musical instruments."

"You could just port all the cats here," Jae said. "I'm sure Wiley wouldn't mind them roaming his lab, throwing up on his experiments."

Lina was quick to protest even before Wiley could open his mouth. "But then we couldn't go back tomorrow! And besides, cats are sensitive. They don't like strange places. As it is, they'll have to move when Lon comes back and we all go to Starhaven. Let's let them stay where they are for now."

"I suppose we could," Jae admitted. "And I would like to see more of Earth."

"It was fun, except for those thugs. We won't see anything like that tomorrow," Lina promised him.

"Thugs?" Wilder looked up at that. "Did you have some trouble?"

"Nothing I couldn't handle," Jae said offhandedly. He saw the puzzled smile Lina was giving him, and realized that she was reevaluating him. He'd been showing off a bit, he realized. Well, everything had turned out; there was nothing to worry about there. And maybe he wouldn't dislike her after all. He'd observe like the professional he was, but he'd give it another few days before he decided for sure.

"How's everything on the home front?" Jae strolled over to look at Wiley's board.

Wiley showed him the log notations on calls. Twelve remote teams had been reassigned missions, but there was nothing local going on. "I believe Protocol wants to talk with you," Wiley said.

"*Grigach.*" Jae grimaced, but Wiley was already motioning down a viewscreen. It brightened to show a man in a dark, baggy suit with pinfolds crisscrossing the shoulders.

"Neutrino, sir," the man said with a little bow of his head, "Flim, Mega-Legion Protocol. I believe we have a problem."

"Let me guess," Jae muttered.

"There was an incident at the Pares Restaurant in Thessander tonight," the man prompted.

"Yes, yes, I was upset at the so-called entertainment they had hired," Jae said. "I just gave them a little lesson. It was for everyone's good."

"I'm sure you think of it that way, Neutrino, sir," the man said condescendingly. "Nevertheless, Legion Protocol clearly states that–"

Jae interrupted. "Does Protocol know about Lina O'Kelly?"

"Who?"

"Valiant's wife. They just got married this morning. Poor girl's straight out of Earth of all places, doesn't know a thing about Legion Protocol or Sarastor protocol either, for that matter. I think that's a shame, really I do. Don't you, Flim?"

"Valiant? Married?"

"What, haven't you looked at today's briefings?" Jae asked innocently. "Oh, that's right, Commander Magnos put a lid on the entire affair for about five days, I think. Still, an important division like Legion Protocol should know this, especially since Lina's a prisoner here right now. It's all a need-to-know security exception. I'm releasing the info to you now on that basis."

"A… prisoner? Valiant married? A prisoner?"

"Come over here, Lina, be a dear," Jae clucked at her, and pulled her in front of the screen. "Here she is, innocent as a babe about protocols and civilized things like that, isn't that right, Lina?"

He pushed her at the screen. "I, ah…"

"As long as she's under house arrest, we might as well put the time to good use," Jae said. He pulled himself up straighter, speaking crisply. "One of Legion Protocol's primary duties is to see that our people know how they're supposed to function in society. I want Protocol to start working with Ms. O'Kelly – and that is her name, not 'Rand'; it's a Terran custom – so that she won't have to waste – pardon me, I mean *squander* – more time with you people once Subcommander Nurunori gets back and orders you on the job. Am I understood?"

"Y-yes, sir, Neutrino!"

"Good. When shall we schedule you?"

The man looked to the side of his screen. "Yency reports in in the morning, sir. She usually briefs civilians and spouses on protocol. We don't have procedures for briefing… prisoners."

"Very good. Yency will do. We'll expect to hear from her tomorrow. Ms. O'Kelly is confined in Lab 1-A and her own quarters for the duration; no visitors in quarters. So it will take place by monitor."

"Yes sir, Neutrino." The screen blanked and disappeared up into the ceiling.

Lina and Wiley stared at Jae, who allowed a slow, satisfied smile to creep across his face. He gave his belly a scratch.

"I want to run that back and look at it again," Wiley finally said.

"What he means is, you're despicable," Lina huffed. "You signed me up for something horrible just to save yourself from a lecture."

"Yes I did," Jae crowed. "And to celebrate, I'm going to hit the sack. What, about an hour and a half, Wiley? Can you stand that?"

"I could even take three more hours here, if it remains this quiet," Wiley replied.

"Two hours; then I'll relieve you. Call me as needed," Jae instructed Wilder. He turned back to Lina. "You can stay here or go to your quarters for the rest of the night," he said. "But like I said, no guests in quarters. You never know who you mind controllers might drag in to Legion HQ."

She made a face at him. "I think I'll start off here," Lina said as she ported her stack of clothes to Lon's apartment. "Here, take the player with you." She handed it to Jae to add to his CDs.

"Thanks," he said. "Wiley, she needs to start learning Panlingua. And if you could find her some kind of introduction to Sarastor…"

"Got it," Wiley said. "Lina, if I'm called away, you have to stay here and not port to quarters. You'll confuse the security puter."

"Okay."

"Right. Good night, everyone." Jae left the two of them alone.

Wilder pointed out the secured places of the lab. Though they'd all been stuck there for a few days because of quarantine, she no longer had free range if she was on her own. Now she could only go into the break room, the corner next to it that held two couches and a couple of puter terminals, a lone chair next to those, and a narrow path that led to the bathroom at the rear of the lab. Step out of that area when there were no other Legionnaires present and an alarm would sound. Wiley opened his mouth as if he were about to detail the dire consequences of that, but said instead, "Bad things will happen," and Lina didn't want to know.

So she straightened up the newspaper she'd left on the break table, refolding the sections. She was about to port them to her recycling bin on Earth, when Wiley said, "Please leave it here. I'd like to study it."

"Sure."

"Give me a moment."

She watched as he swiped some more lights on his board. He picked up a business-sized card with touchpoints on the bottom and held it to a terminal on the desk for a moment. When it beeped, he presented it to her.

"A very simple study padd. I've just programmed this with a Panlingua course as well as the Sarastor information." Lina turned the card over and then righted it, marveling at the compactness. When it was on a comfortably-large viewscreen appeared out of nowhere.

"You can utilize the screen, but use this to begin with the language." Wiley held a dot about the size of a large ladybug. "You put it on like this," and he adhered it between her eyebrows like a piece of sticky vinyl, "and you set the screen like this." He showed her. "You run this mode when you sleep, and it integrates into your brain's linguistic center. It's a very efficient way to learn."

"Sleep learning? That's got my vote."

"Of course you'll need to back it up with conscious study, especially for the written word," he told her as he peeled the ladybug off.

"So I'm a student again," Lina said. The ladybug secured onto a corner of the card for safekeeping.

"You look tired," Wiley said as he triggered the nanos he'd injected her with this morning. "You can sleep over there if you want." He motioned to the couch.

"Tired?" Come to think of it, she suddenly was. Plus the room had become very warm. "Maybe porting so far took a lot out of me," she decided. She almost didn't make it to the couch before she fell asleep.

It took Lina a few minutes to wake completely from her nap. *It must be some kind of jet lag*, she thought, and then, *Darn, didn't use the ladybug thing.* She settled down to explore her new study padd. Though everyone else around her controlled their computers via gesture or even the way they moved their eyes, this one ran by touch screen, even if the screen were just a projection of some kind. Sure enough, there was tourism info next to the language course.

Wiley came out of the break room with a drink. "You can also access libraries or school systems through your padd," he told her.

She spotted the link portal on the desktop. "I suppose I'll have to start with kindergarten level," she said. "Or would nursery school be more appropriate?"

Wilder considered. "Start with third level and scan through it, at least through science, sociology and galaxography. Here, might as well run you through something else first," Wilder said. He guided her to the other side of the lab to stand in front of a computer screen as large as a door. "Just some tests. I'm designing culture-inert testing procedures to be used as standardized materials. You can't get more culture-inert than Terran."

Lina considered it doubtfully.

"Try two or three. They won't take too long."

"I can't read the screen."

Wiley waved his hand, wiggling his fingers as if he were sewing air, and suddenly most of the readouts on the screen were in English. "Better?"

"Much," Lina said, looking at the menu. What would a "Confirmation Numerical Lock" do?

"Good. I have to get back to my board. You do this until I return."

"I could have sworn Londo told you not to put me through any tests."

"He did?" Wiley asked innocently.

She snorted. "How do I start?"

"Computer, begin test," Wilder said, and the screen lit up with new written instructions in the air that the computer read out loud to her.

There were symbols to match, hue families to group together, number series to figure out and continue, shapes to work with. The computer read her some interesting stories to which she had to answer follow-up questions. Some stories she had to give an ending for.

When she got stuck on trying to pass one test, the computer explained that the object was to re-sort the suggested solution steps to an order that could be followed for best efficiency. Lina had thrown out two steps, deeming them unnecessary or redundant, which was not allowed.

One game reminded Lina of the violent video games at home. She was never any good at those. The people she'd seen scoring big points had done so by constant, indiscriminate fire as they murdered their way through the field. Brute force and unlimited power always won the day, where her careful aiming never did.

But here she was, and a life-size three-dimensional maze the size of a classroom awaited her, blotting out the lab. The computer slanted the view for a few seconds to let her see over the outer wall to the pattern inside. When the view straightened, a closed door stood in front of her. Further down the outer wall was another door, with an armed man waiting to go inside. She'd have to actually walk the maze rather than tracing a path through a map of it. Wouldn't she bump into real lab equipment along the way?

#There is a great treasure at the center of this maze,# the computer told her. *#The maze has a guard whose gun is set to kill or maim. Your gun can kill, but only if the shot is clean; you cannot ricochet it off a wall or around a corner. You must avoid or kill the guard and run the maze. After one minute, the guard's speed will increase by 5 percent. After two minutes, another 5 percent, and so on. Get the treasure and the system will vaporize the guard. Do you have any questions?#*

Lina considered. "No," she said.

#Begin,# the computer commanded. Lina kept her position outside the door.

Down at the other door, the guard stood frozen in his position. Apparently he wouldn't move inside until she did. *#The clock is running,#* the computer reminded her.

"I know," Lina said. She remained where she was and checked the condition of her fingernails.

The guard came to life and began to taunt her to enter. He made rude noises and what she supposed were rude gestures at her.

#A short running time gives higher point score,# the computer noted. *#Are you afraid?#*

Lina leaned against the outer wall of the maze, which thankfully supported her. "Points, shmoints," she said. "Who cares about points or treasure? That guy's going to try to off me. My life is worth more than points. Or treasure. I think I'll stay where I am."

#You must go into the maze.#

"Says who?"

#This is a game.#

"So there's a rule against staying outside and alive?"

Silence.

#We will try the game again,# the computer said. *#Now there is a rule that you must go in.#*

Lina thought. "All right."

#Begin.#

Lina stayed where she was, outside the doors. "Hey, you! Guard!" she called to the person there. His head turned to her.

"What?" he asked.

"Look, if you catch me, you're going to kill me. And if I get the treasure, they'll kill you. What say we strike a deal here? You get the treasure, I stay alive."

The guard opened his mouth to reply but the game suddenly reset.

#The guard is no longer sentient,# the computer said. *#You must go inside.#*

Lina muttered something.

#Begin.#

She turned and shot the guard while he stood waiting for her to go in. He crumpled, dead. She then entered the maze and took her time to find the treasure, muttering about the violence of children's games these days and how they needed to teach problem-solving and not brute force. After all if this were indeed a test of intelligence, it took more intelligence to try and compromise than it did to blow someone's head off.

The computer didn't try that game again.

"I'm tired of this. Hey, computer, do you know Reversi? It's a game," Lina asked.

She taught the puter how to play and beat it three times before losing consistently to it.

"Tell you what, puter," she told it. "You figure out an intermediate level on this game, and I'll play it with you. Tomorrow."

That got her two beeps of acknowledgement.

"One more set of games," Wiley said from behind her. "Just two mazes."

"No guard to kill."

"Just a maze. All right?"

"Well… okay. Two mazes." She stood up from her chair while Wiley went back to his monitor board.

#Maze number one,# the computer announced. Lina could see the maze set-up for five seconds before it tilted back up. *#Begin,#* the computer said. It took her a while, but she made it through.

The playing field blanked. *#Maze number two requires the input from spiritual beings for guidance.#*

"That's cheating, isn't it?" Lina asked.

#Those are the rules of the game.#

Lina shrugged and lined up her chakras with the universal white light, not bothering to look at the aerial five-second view of the maze. It righted itself, and she let her guides instruct her on where to go. She bumped her nose on a wall twice, certain that she was going in the right direction. That made her pay more attention to her guides, and she then made only two false turns that she almost immediately corrected. By the way they pushed her, she thought her guides might be having a little too much fun.

#Game over,# the computer announced.

"Thank you." Lina disconnected from her guides and stretched, wandering back to the front part of the lab and the central monitor board. Wilder was watching a blueprint with three moving dots in it, displayed on the tabletop. A configuration of five related scenes floated above it. One was an exterior view of a windowless building. The others held detailed charts and diagrams, plus one with still pictures of people's faces and writing beneath.

Wiley's hands moved on his board. Blinking yellow double-lines appeared across what might have been hallways of the blueprint, blocking them. The dots came to one set and stopped, then retreated, only to be stopped by another set.

"They're held now," Wilder reported to the air. A screen with a woman's worried face on it appeared.

"What kind of weapons do they have?" she asked.

Wilder consulted a side-screen. "Sonics," he reported. "One moment; I can alter your security system from here to deal with that." He touched one of his rings and then gestured with two fingers at the new screen that appeared. "There. I believe they should be unconscious from the feedback. Release the force field on circuit 7-F and enter from the southeast door."

"Thank you, Dr. Mem-Bazer," the woman said as her face washed with relief. "You've saved at least one life, maybe two, and the diplomatic secrets of two planets."

"My pleasure," Wilder said. Most of the screens faded out. The blueprints disappeared from the desktop. His left hand remained on the dark plexiglass with a string of writing running across it now, charts unfolding with either numbers or letters on them. Lina couldn't figure it out, but she did get the impression that whatever his right hand was doing had nothing at all to do with what his left hand was up to. He must be working on two entirely different operations at once.

"Finished, are you?" he asked rhetorically. "My assistants in the minor labs can handle the data from the more mundane of your exams. I've just come up with some new ideas I'd like to put to the test. Are you ready to do some more?" His hands didn't pause in their movements.

"I'd really rather just–"

The monitors buzzed for his attention and he snapped the fingers of his left hand, gesturing with his other as his pinky curled back to touch one of his many plain rings. Three new floating screens appeared. Lina waved her study padd at him and he nodded, so she returned to her prisoner's chair.

Lina preferred the slight background noise here in the lab to the silence that would be in Lon's quarters. Lon wasn't there. If she could avoid the silence, she could avoid the loneliness.

In a few days, though, he'd be back. She'd bet money that within minutes of that, Stoan would bring her to trial or have her thrown into a real jail. He'd want to get rid of the Terran witchdoctor as quickly as he could.

Once Lina had filled in for a courtroom artist for a local TV station. The trial had been a neighbors' dispute: loudmouthed, trashy white woman versus a Hispanic man who had done some equally trashy things but at a lower volume. The public had squared off firmly along racial lines in the conflict, creating a furor ripe for the evening news' ratings.

The judge saw Lina sketching him and had puffed up, striking a series of judicial poses throughout the entire afternoon. His office had contacted the station afterward to buy her drawings. Unfortunately it was the station that got the profit, not her.

The defendant hadn't fared well. "Look at that wetback. He's obviously guilty," Lina had heard someone behind her say during a recess. "He doesn't even bother to argue. And his lawyer's court-appointed."

Lina thought the man couldn't speak much English. Innocent or guilty, he seemed lost in a system that he didn't understand, and the babbling reporters and cameras that swarmed him every time he left the courtroom couldn't have helped.

He'd been found guilty.

Would that be the way it would be with her? Wife to Valiant – that alone would spark publicity. But a trial? The Esteemed Affiliated Systems Mega-Force Legion vs some no-name Terran barbarian witchdoctor who can't speak the language or understand the system.

No. Unacceptable.

She had to make a plan to survive. She'd learned to port safely back to Earth: check. Cats fed and medicated, double check. A-level goals had been met for today. So here was her new Goal A: learn the local language. Lina grimaced. She'd struggled through French for years and still didn't have the courage to speak it out loud. Now she was married to a man whose native language was French.

Goal C was to learn French well enough to speak it. Important, but not immediate priority.

Second A-priority Goal was to learn where the hell she was and get a general idea of things. Find her center here so she'd be in a better position to fight. Or run.

Ordinarily she'd write down her goals, but this study padd of hers was likely monitored, she being a prisoner and all. She'd have to keep these unwritten or coded. "Goals," she wrote in a notes section of her padd. "A: Learn language, culture." That was safe enough to say.

Goal B: find a lawyer. Get through to the legal system – which would mean a second Goal B was to find out how to convert her assets on Earth, meager though they might be, to whatever currency was used Out Here, so she could pay for a good lawyer. Maybe they'd let her make payments.

"B," she wrote. "Call Denny Crane. Can he give me a loan?" Let them look that one up. She doubted they'd discover Captain Kirk's *nom de TV lawyer*. Maybe she should use "Samuel T. Cogley" instead. That was Kirk's lawyer in the episode "Court Martial." Obscure, which could be both a good and a bad thing. If she got rattled, she might not make the connection as well. "Denny Crane" it was.

With her primary goals firmly set Lina studied her padd with single-minded fierceness. There was an enormous amount of information to sort through. She started with a general overview of Sarastor, which was very touristy and repeated some of the quick look she'd gotten the other night: museums and galleries and landmark government buildings; some natural wonders encased in those parks Jae had mentioned. Mega-Legion Headquarters was a major tourist attraction, of course, and there was a Legion museum not far from here.

She'd like to see that. Maybe Jae would take her tomorrow if he had time – if he forgot again that she was a prisoner. It had been nice to go out tonight so she could pretend that she had some freedom of action. But she didn't, not really.

Most of her life she'd been helpless. Life had taken delight in running her down, backing up, and running over her again. But she'd come up with a plan. She'd escaped. For the past almost twelve years she'd been free, on her own and running the show as much as she could. She liked the feeling.

Okay, so the past week had been unlike anything she'd ever imagined. The universe had insisted on taking control again. It left her trapped in a whirlpool of confusion, but by now Lina was a strong swimmer. She'd figure a way out of this, just as soon as she figured out what exactly was going on in this Future World. She had to be strong. She had to be smart. She had to learn.

She was a Sagittarian, one who excelled in learning. This was a plan she could utilize.

She scrolled down the screen seeking more information. Sarastor was the capital of the whole blamed AffSys, which took up a galactic sector, however big that was. There were city-sized governmental complexes, three of them for redundancy, scattered across the globe and two more secreted in Sarastor's planetary system.

Government – She made a note to come back and check how it was set up. History could wait a bit.

Geography. Enormous banks of computers used up most of the land space on the planet. Couldn't they have set those up on satellites or buried them underground and left some of the land natural? The southern hemisphere was the more populated one, and Lirravon, the county or whatever where Legion HQ was located, was in that half of the world, a Sarastoran Down Under.

She moved on to a section labeled "personal matters" and found instructions for using bathrooms, showers, and something called a *mittrisin*, which looked like it would only interest truly alien-aliens. Her curiosity overtook her priorities and she found herself scanning sections detailing body salon services. There were places where you could get moving 3-D fashion tattoos. Biological changes of eye color could match your clothing for the day. Creams could form a plastic barrier over your skin in case you had body odor from hell…

Another section: getting around Sarastor. Lina read about the aircab system, the subway system for both local and intercontinental travel, how to get booked onto an interstellar flight.

There were different classifications of interstellar travel. Hyperspace had three levels to it, with three levels of difficulty to attain. The hardest, of course, allowed the quickest trip and was the most expensive. Planetary teleportation was not available to the common person; only high-ranked officials and emergency law-enforcement were allowed to use that…

With a start, she discovered she'd been napping again. What time was it? She turned to the section on telling time and realized that she'd have to learn Panlingua numbers toot sweet. It could be worse. At least they were on base ten.

Lina looked around for what the study padd said was a timepiece and found one. Comparing numerals, she decided that it was the local equivalent of a little past midnight. If she wanted to get on any kind of schedule here, she'd best think about turning in. She had to get over her interstellar jet lag.

Wilder was handling an emergency call as a web of lights crackled over his head and into his board. "I'll have to leave for this," he told her, and started to activate the transporter on his board.

"May I return to quarters?" At his nod, she ported to Lon's room.

It took time to figure out the alarm clock there and set it. In her absence, the bed had made itself. Lina propped herself up on the pillows, looking around the hollow room. Even though the clean sheets no longer smelled of Lon, his presence hung over this place as he permeated her mind. Except for two nights, she'd slept alone all her life, and now sleeping alone just didn't seem right. There should be a warm body next to her. She was missing the better part of herself.

He was alone, too, and in danger.

"God," she thought and became uncomfortable. It had been a long, long time since she'd really prayed. She'd used one of those Last Chance prayers a couple days ago for Londo. God probably didn't appreciate those if they weren't accompanied by praying on a regular basis. But no, God didn't see sin; God was unconditional love.

"God," she said deep inside herself again, "watch over Londo, please. Keep him safe. Let him know that I love him. Oh, the others – watch over them as well, and please send lots of angels to help everyone. And Aiko. If it doesn't have to happen, please save Aiko. If it does – Please make it quick and painless. Please help them all through this."

She visualized angels gathering around wherever the group would be: angels that would heal, angels that would warn and guard, angels that would love. This was all she could do for him, for them. She hoped it would be enough. The rest would be up to the angels… and God.

"Please send him back to me safely. Thank you." "Amen" always seemed so artificial, a fancy way of saying "over and out," but without it the prayer's ending hung like an unresolved chord in her mind. "Amen," she finally said.

Lina stuck the ladybug on her forehead and punched up the linguatape program. Almost immediately she fell asleep.

5

She dreamed of Londo holding her close and whispering to her words she couldn't understand at first, though the sweet tone of his low voice put his message across. They made love as he asked her where the nearest hyperspace station was? How far was it to the embassy? And when Dad walked into the bedroom, pointing his finger at her and shouting, *"Charrant!"* she knew he was calling her a whore.

As usual, he yelled that she'd wind up in a gutter someday, but Lon stood defensively in front of her. Dad's words bounced off Lon's invulnerable chest like bullets, to hit Dad instead. He lay bleeding on the bedroom floor, dying, still cursing her.

Lon climbed over the body, back into bed. "How far to the nearest medical facilities?" he asked her. "And is there a good restaurant nearby?"

A soft buzz woke her. Where – Oh. She looked over at the clock to puzzle it out. It seemed to come easier to her that it was after four o'clock in the morning. Four fifty-one, which translated as maybe 6 AM her time. Sarastor days were twenty-seven-ish Earth hours long, but there were only twenty Sarastoran hours in a day, one hundred minutes in an hour. Noon was 10 o'clock, and they used military time for PM. She eased herself up to a sitting position and took off the ladybug, replacing it on the padd. She'd have to study consciously today. Oh boy – not.

The other half of the bed was cold. He wasn't really there, of course. Gone one day, four days or so to go. *Hurry home, Londo. Be safe. Don't regret that you married me.*

She could see him lying there with the sheet draped over him, his eyelids half-lowered, that naughty smile quirked to one side and radiating mischief to come. He loved her! But now he was off saving people and she had the audacity to want him here instead. Why couldn't he snuggle with her, his legs intertwined with…

Enough! Back to real life. She clambered out of bed to shower and change into some by god comfortable clothes, old jeans and sneakers and a tee shirt that said STARFLEET, with the *Enterprise* insignia on the back.

Turning on Lon's music, she searched the kitchenette and found a food replicator. With the study padd propped next to it, she compared control panels. Although she could figure out how to work it, she couldn't understand what the foods were that it could produce. She'd eaten the only energy bar yesterday. There was that one hunk of cake in the freezer…

"I'm sorry," she told the air, and concentrated on the market from last night. A half-pint of strawberries appeared on the counter in front of her. What was that, three dollars? Four? She'd have to pay the store back, but right now she was hungry. She sliced the berries. A carton of vanilla yogurt, a small ported bottle of orange juice, and she had a breakfast fit for an empress. She giggled and tried not to feel wicked in her decadence.

Oh – It wasn't just decadence. She was stealing. How much was this now? Um… estimate high just in case. And then there was all that food they'd eaten on the island. And that parking spot at the airport.

She wasn't going to become a thief! All this had to be paid for, and she'd pay everyone back just as soon as she got back to Earth to stay. But for now she had to make a solemn pact with herself: no more stealing.

How it would look if Lon had to drag her into court? "Sorry, Your Honor, but my idiot wife's a klepto." No no no!

Still, everything had been prepared and opened. It would be a shame to let this go to waste. Okay, it was the last stolen meal she'd have. She made a to-do list on her padd and noted the repayment. Then she watched the news – incomprehensible even with the translator marble working – and tried an experiment with her powers that took a very long time and left her exhausted though she hadn't fully succeeded. Even so, it was a neat trick and she felt a little giddy for having tried it. She added that to her goals list ex post facto so she could take check it off and see she'd accomplished something.

Now it was time to see what was cooking down at the lab. No, over and above at the lab. Now she could sense the relationship of some of the rooms within Legion Headquarters.

No one was there. No wonder no one had called asking her where she was. The monitor board seemed to be set on automatic. Translucent red walls lined her security space. "Puter," she said to the air in case she should, "prisoner reporting in for the day." She got two beeps for that, so something approved.

Eventually the red walls disappeared. "Good morning," Lina greeted Jae as he arrived in the lab. His blond mane stuck up in places. Dirt and oil smudged his face and the front of his uniform. "Are you okay? Was it a rough one?"

"A little. Stratospheric rescue. Everyone's all right now."

"Oh, good. Would you like something hot to drink?"

"Thanks. A *larex*?"

She used her study padd to program the food replicator. A steaming mug of brown stuff that smelled like a cross between bouillon and compost came out. She brought it to Jae, holding it far away from her nose. "Is that it?"

"It is. Thanks." He took a sip as he checked the monitor station, which had awakened. He didn't seem to mind the larex. "You're getting the hang of things."

"Let's see. I set the alarm. I know what time it is now. And I practiced hard for a new trick for porting."

"What's that?"

She held up an index finger and ducked into the break room. She could feel Jae's sudden suspicion, but within a minute and a half she managed to switch her clothing by porting and emerge dressed in different Starfleet tee and jeans than she'd begun the day in.

Okay, she might have been able to do it faster manually, but it was the concept that was so keen.

"Ta dah," she said as she gave her bra straps a final tug. "I'm hoping to get faster."

"Very neat trick," he laughed.

"I thought so."

"Arms, Lina."

Lina looked down at the bare arms below her sleeves. "These shirts come with short sleeves, not long."

"Arms. You're a Legion spouse and you've got to dress appropriately. I can requisition standard prison garb if you–"

"Oh, hell." Lina ported in a sweater from home and shrugged it on. "It's too warm in here for a sweater. Wiley must be having cold flashes. What have you done this morning?"

He told her about the stratospheric rescue between two airbuses, a medium earthquake on the next world out in this system – just a few seconds away by hyperspace – and an energy bomb scare within the computer core of an interstellar bank.

"Is that a quiet morning?" What kind of workload did Lon have, anyway?

Jae considered. "Moderate. Because we're actually located on Sarastor, the officials feel free to call on us for any emergency that they'd otherwise have to work up a sweat over. Other worlds only call in case of dire need. Usually their job is to contain the emergency long enough for someone to get there." The board beeped. "It's for you," he said mysteriously.

Lina sat at attention in her seat as the screen hung in the air before her. "Ms. Rand," the woman on it said, as she referenced her own screen. She was so real she might as well have been seated right there, though the sides of her shoulders and lower torso were cut off by the screen's framing. "I hope it doesn't surprise you that these… conditions we find you in have shocked Legion Protocol."

"They have shocked me as well. And my name's O'Kelly, not Rand," Lina told the lime-green-haired woman. Her eyes perfectly and artificially matched her crew cut, and there was an outer ring of gold around the irises that matched the trim on her vest, making the back of Lina's neck prickle. *Please, God, let those be contacts and not some kind of corrective surgery just for the day's cosmetic requirements.*

Ms. Yency's mouth pinched condescendingly. "It is 'Rand,'" she told Lina. "Here on Sarastor, the rule is to take the more prestigious partner's name in a contracted marriage of over six years. Sarastoran convention takes precedence over Terran. I'm sure you understand. We have rules for many things which may seem confining at first, but are for the greater good. They make life run much smoother for everyone."

"My name is O'Kelly," Lina repeated. "There will be no compromise about that." They'd made her a prisoner, and now they were trying to take her name!

"But with a husband as famous as–" the woman faltered before she found the courage to say the civilian name – "Londo Rand… and his father being – Huh- Henry Rand…"

"Exactly." Lina smiled tightly back. "Who am I to be a Rand? My name is O'Kelly. Please correct your records."

Ms. Yency's perfect lime-green eyebrows trembled. She was obviously trying not to lose her temper to this Terran barbarian. "This is the Affiliated Systems Mega-Force Legion, Ms. Rand. There is no higher law enforcement group, no higher *social* group of any kind. We must have our rules, and one of those is–"

"I'm sorry," Lina interrupted. "Did you want to talk to Lina Rand? There's no one here by this name. You must have the wrong number. Please check your directory for the correct listing. Puter, terminate call." She spun around in her chair, missing the startled expression on Yency's face as the screen blanked and rolled back up into the ceiling.

"Lina."

She looked over to see Jae leaning his chin on his hand at the main console.

"What?"

"Be good."

Behind her she could hear the screen unfolding again. "Ms… O'Kelly?" Yency's strangled voice came from it. Lina turned with a sweet smile on her face, all innocence. "Ms. Yency," she said. "How nice to see you again."

There followed a long and exhausting introductory lecture about Proper Legion Spouse Deportment. People were elevated to near-Legion social standing when they married into the Legion. They were expected to walk and stand at least one pace and usually three behind their spouse on all but the most formal social occasions, when they were permitted to stand side-by-side. The primary reason for that was for each spouse to privately remind the other of etiquette at those oh-so-proper functions.

A civilian always addressed Legionnaires by their costumed names in public. In that arena, only Legionnaires could call other Legionnaires by their civilian name, and then only if it had been cleared by Legion PR to do so. If Lina were in public with her husband, she would be addressed as (the Panlingua word actually meant "contracted spouse of") Mrs. Valiant and not as Ms. O'Kelly.

"Why is that?" Lina blurted.

Yency pursed her lips yet again, as if blocking her first instinctive retort. "We are the Legion," she chose to say. "The Legion remains by and for itself. It defines itself. It is forever apart and forever above all other society." From then on Lina noticed that Yency never addressed her as "Ms. O'Kelly," but as the more formal "Mrs. Valiant."

Yeesh.

Yency explained the general configurations of Headquarters: that levels ten and below were available to all Legion spouses. Some higher levels were open to those spouses with higher security ratings. Lina's security rating was a total mystery, since she was a potential death-row criminal and should be a zero, but since she was a Legion spouse she couldn't be less than a 2. Security puters would track her presence anywhere she went within Headquarters and make sure that she stayed within bounds. Since she was a prisoner now, she was restricted anyway.

Guests were permitted if blah blah blah, family was permitted on levels blah and blah, tours were given for guests on blahday and blahday. There were in-house cafeterias for families with children and a few for couples who didn't want to be bothered by children, and also some for Legionnaires who didn't want to soiled by the presence of non-Legionnaires.

Lina would be required to speak only Panlingua in all her dealings with the public, which would be monitored by L-PIC, the Legion's Public Information Center. If she kept up her studies, she should be fluent by the time the commander returned to determine her status.

Recreational facilities were such. Regularly-scheduled social occasions were such and such, but since Valiant was only a part-time member, she was not expected to show up for every one of these. (Lina did not volunteer news about the availability of rapid interstellar teleportation.) Regular spousal appointments were scheduled once a quarter with Legion Subcommander Nurunori, whom Lina recognized as just Andri, but Yency never referred to her by her actual name, heaven forbid. Weekly group meetings with Protocol were required of all spouses. The conception of children should be scheduled with Gorgeon, the chief of medicine here, and L-PIC kept consulted for input as to proper birthing schedule.

"What business is that of theirs?" Lina demanded.

"We are the Legion," Yency insisted.

There were sure to be press interviews when the marriage was revealed to the newsnets. It was unfortunate that Lina was a Terran; Protocol and L-PIC would work together to see if they could cover that up. Lina would be carefully briefed in advance of each interview, and her first ones would be taped so they could be edited in case mistakes were made, before sending them to the press.

A Legion spouse never said anything, *anything* negative about the Legion or any of its activities to the press or to guests or even to family. A Legion spouse never did anything in public to embarrass the Legion. Spouses leaving a marriage would be debriefed, and if their security rating warranted, hypnotically or surgically blocked so they could neither libel nor betray the Legion in any fashion. L-PIC would be available for Legion exes to cover up any faux pas they might make later in life.

"And they've got me for mind control," Lina muttered angrily. It was too hot in here; she wriggled out of her sweater as she frowned.

"Now about your hair and the way you dress," Yency began.

"It's Terran standard. Modest Terran standard," Lina blurted. "So I've got arms. Sue me. *What's the matter with the clothes I'm wearing/ 'Can't you tell that your tie's too wide?'"* Lina pointed at the screen for emphasis, bobbing up and down in her chair to the song's beat in her head.

The woman on the screen was positively blanching as she drew back in horror. If Ms. Yency had been a barbaric Terran, she would have made the sign of the cross. "We will continue this discussion tomorrow," Yency said quickly and the screen blanked.

Lina blew a particularly juicy raspberry in the screen's direction as it folded up to the ceiling.

"What was that about?"

She turned to see a puzzled Wiley just entering the lab. Jae had buried his head in his hands at the console. Lina pointed to Wiley and bobbed, *"Everybody's talkin' 'bout the new sound / Funny, but it's still rock and roll to me,"* she sang and played the final air guitar notes, "Dit dit dwaaaang!"

"Orb," Wiley sighed.

A screen unrolled in front of Jae. "That will be Protocol," he told Wiley. "Please tell them that I've taken her to Gorgeon to get her head examined. Gorgeon reminded me earlier that we'd promised to bring her by. C'mon, trouble-maker." He held out his hand for Lina to take as he walked quickly out of the lab. Lina grabbed her sweater, scurrying to catch up to him.

"There's a rumor going around that you're insane," Gorgeon mentioned as she checked her sensors against Lina's skin.

"Just trying to fit in," Lina replied pleasantly, and then intoned, "We are the Legion!"

"She's been talking to Yency in Protocol," Jae explained.

Gorgeon shuddered in sympathy.

"So, Doc," Lina said, "how'm I doing?"

"Just call me Gorgeon," the friendly, round-faced woman replied offhandedly as she studied her results. It wasn't the lights in here that had made her look orange when Lina saw her before by monitor. She truly was, just the slightest tinge, as if she'd eaten too many carrots or dandelions. Lina wondered what color hair the doctor would have, but her head was covered in a tight cap with folded flaps above the ears, and her eyebrows were either shaved or naturally missing.

"That's something I don't understand," Lina said. "Wiley is Doctor Mem-Bazer, but you're just Gorgeon. Don't you have a degree?"

"I have many advanced credentials, I assure you," Gorgeon replied, looking up from her personal mini-screens. "More than His Highness Dr. Mem-Bazer does in the field of human medicine, although he never admits it."

"Then why can't I call you Doctor Gorgeon? Don't you deserve it?" Lina asked. "I mean, if you call one person 'doctor,' you have to call all doctors that. If no one wanted to be called doctor, then I'd say fine, but why Wiley and not you?"

"We are the Legion," Gorgeon chanted and her eyes sparkled at Lina.

Lina thought about it. "So you have to be reminded of your place so you don't outshine all these high-falutin' Legionnaires, is that it? I don't like it. I'll call you Doctor Gorgeon, if you don't mind. Even if you do mind. But I hope you don't."

Gorgeon folded her hands in her lap and gazed evenly at Lina. "My name's Riz."

Lina broke into a grin; Riz grinned back. "Nice meeting you, Riz," she said. "Now how'm I doing? I think I've developed narcolepsy. I'm always falling asleep without warning. And Wiley said he thought the porting was permanent. But he mentioned some kind of brain damage…"

"The same brain damage that makes you sing to Protocol agents?"

They discussed Lina's medical condition, that she seemed entirely healthy despite having come a breath from death just days before with burns all over her body and a hole drilled through her arm.

"I'm feeling much better," Lina declared.

"But how?" Gorgeon wondered. "How did it all heal so quickly? So completely? I'd never guess you'd had a laser rifle hit you if I hadn't seen it myself."

"There were–" Lina began, but Jae cleared his throat.

"Security, Lina," he told her. "It's a double-Level 5 Need to Know Only basis."

"Well, Riz needs to know. She's my doctor. She's Lon's doctor, too, I assume. He died the other day, and I want to make sure he's fully healthy when he comes back."

"That's classified, Lina!" Jae barked. "You've just broken security!"

"Oh, nonsense. The doctor-patient relationship is higher than a double-Level 5 whatever. It's absolute. A doctor has to know certain things in order to do their job to the best of their ability. Right, Riz?"

Riz opened and closed her mouth. "No wonder, no wonder," she murmured. "It explains so many rumors, the damage to Headquarters, the evacuation alarm…" She shook her head. "I'd have to agree with her in principle, Neutrino. The Legion knows that I can be trusted with anything. I've had a lot to handle through the years and I've always come through. And I do need to know extreme medical emergencies when they happen so I can treat them."

"His name is Jae," Lina insisted.

Jae stood there with his arms crossed, a frown on his face as he considered Lina. She gave him a sunny, innocent smile.

"I suppose," he said slowly, "that this would be a Need to Know occasion."

"Doctors always need to know," Lina piped up. "I trust Riz. Her guides are all giving me thumbs up."

"Guides," Riz said. "What are guides?"

"Guardian angels," Lina told her. "Spiritual beings. Look, Jae, even your guides are patting her head. You can see them, can't you?"

"No, I can't."

"Sure you can. You just don't try."

Jae set his mouth and queried Riz on Lina's brain damage. According to cellular evidence, it had happened when Lina had been four, and appeared to have been a series of hard blows to the head.

"I don't remember it," Lina replied blankly. "It wasn't a fall? I fell a lot, they tell me."

"There were three blows," Riz said. "Very distinct, very hard. I don't think they would have put you into a lengthy coma, but you were rendered unconscious for a time. There would have been definite scalp swelling and bruising visible. Of course, under all this hair–"

"No, Mom kept my hair real short," Lina said. "It made me look more like a boy. I just started to grow it when I got out on my own."

Riz nodded. "Then it would have been very noticeable for a period of two weeks, maybe more. There would have been a lot of blood at any rate. Someone had to know."

That made Lina shrug. "In my family, if they had known they wouldn't have cared. So this stopped me from porting?"

"I'd put a bet down on it. The brain healed incorrectly – not enough for a norm to notice the difference, I suppose. But within the past week it seems to have suddenly rehealed. There was another blow to the same area – just one blow this time."

"The brick," Lina said. "We were caught in an explosion."

Riz nodded. "All right, a brick. It affected the same area, but this time it healed properly. I take it you healed it yourself?"

Lina rubbed the back of her head. "Well, nobody hit me again, okay? I like porting. I want to keep it."

The tricorder-like sensor buzzed in Riz's hand as she ran it the length of Lina's body. "This brick happened the same day you lost your virginity," Riz said as she studied readings on a hovering screen. "What did he have to do, hit you to get you to–"

"Excuse me!" Lina exclaimed. Jae started laughing in that loud rat-a-tat way he had. "Some things are private, okay? Does *he* have to be here?" Irritating, that's what this was becoming.

"I'm in charge of the prisoner," Jae chuckled.

Riz scanned Lina's reproductive organs, the results displaying on her screen. "No tearing, no ruptures, no damage at all," she murmured as if that were a surprise. Her gaze flicked to eye Lina. "How is that possible?"

"Ah, I'd rather not say."

"I know how they do it," Jae put in.

"And if you know what's good for yourself, you'll shut up right now," Lina declared.

With a sigh of defeat, Riz switched back to scanning. This time she concentrated on Lina's head. "It will be educational to research such a specific area of the brain and deduce how it's tied into a megapara power," Riz said. "So are you and Valiant planning on having children right away? I can schedule them for you today if you want. We can start your half of the procedure now."

"What?!" Lina blushed a deep red.

"Is there something the matter with that?" Riz asked.

"I don't think Terrans do it the same way," Jae said.

They escorted Lina to another department of the medical section where they could gaze through a window into a room in which mylar wine sacks dangled from a moving track. Gravity in the room was a little lighter than normal, Riz explained, and the temperature was kept at standard body levels.

"Are you trying to tell me that those are… embryos? Fetuses?" Lina gaped at the scene.

"Yes," Riz said. "That's Bove's little girl, and there's eMage's; she chose a girl, too. Of course, they're not much to look at, just the amniotic bag system. The fetuses can be held in stasis when they're ripe, to be born at the convenience of their parents."

Lina stepped back from the window. "That's sick," she declared. It struck her as: "Obscene! That's… an insult to the life that's inside them! What about the mothers? Why aren't they carrying these babies? Hell, if the mothers won't do it, how about the fathers?" Sheer, unnatural fury permeated her.

A part of Lina stood back from herself. *Calm down,* she told herself. *You've just met Riz. Mustn't make a bad impression in front of a good person.* But she couldn't stop herself. It felt so good to let all the frustration of the past few days out as anger.

Riz regarded her. "What, hold a fetus in the womb for full term? That's dangerous to the mother's health, and it's a *skurny* inconvenience."

"Inconvenience! You're having a baby; you're supposed to be inconvenienced!"

"This way the entire process can be monitored," Riz said calmly. "The baby is as healthy as it can get."

"Physically," Lina said. "But what about emotionally? What about the bonding with the mother? With the parents? Babies can hear and feel through the womb. How are they going to get any of that this way?" Lina turned and strode down the hallway, waving her arms and sputtering, "Inconvenient! Might as well squirt 'em out with a Salad Shooter on a cookie sheet and stick 'em in the freezer!"

Looking after her, Riz said, "I guess she doesn't want to schedule after all. I was looking forward to having Valiant's child in the nursery, to see if the equipment could handle it."

A steady stream of unintelligible mutterings followed Lina.

"You should suggest that Dr. Mem-Bazer reduce the dosage he's giving her," Riz told Jae. "It's making her irritable. Or do all Terrans go through such wild mood swings?" Riz turned back to the nursery window and gave it a reassuring pat. "Who in their right mind would prefer the barbarian method of having babies?"

"Lon's never been fond of this nursery either, as I recall," Jae said. "Neither have I."

"I've never heard you mention it, Neutrino," Riz said.

"Jae. My name's Jae, Riz."

They smiled at each other and turned to the babbling. Now Lina was barreling down the hallway towards them. "Where the hell am I anyway? And aren't I supposed to be in your custody, Jae?"

"Coming, Lina," Jae sighed.

Lina woke up fuzzily, but she felt calmer than before. Riz said that her sudden naps might be the result of PTSD, but should wear off soon enough with no further aftereffects. Before she'd blanked out, Wiley had been attending to business while Jae took off for something, but now Wiley was gone and Jae was back.

"You awake?" he asked.

"Um. I didn't realize I was so tired." Lina stretched. "I've never had interstellar jetlag before. Or PTSD. It makes me cranky, I guess. I'm sorry about back there in medilab. How long does jetlag last?"

Jae shrugged noncommittally and glanced at the chronometer. "When did you want to hit Earth today?"

"Sometime during daylight hours." She tried to compare times between the two planets, extrapolating from last night. In the middle of her computations, she remembered she had stashed an extra MasterCard in her desk. Money! She could buy something for Londo. Or Jae, to thank him for his kindness. Then again, maybe a bribe to the guard would be a better idea.

Jae checked his monitor board. "Wiley's asleep, due to be back on duty in two hours – unless Dellen shows up from her mission, in which case I can take off about an hour. Either way, it'll be a while." He motioned to the air. "Neutrino here."

He took an emergency call and left (the translucent red Security walls outlining her prison appeared as soon as he'd teleported out) and Lina returned to studying, trying out words and phrases that seemed kind of natural once she'd said them out loud. Jae appeared in a transporter effect twice more, and twice more departed.

Lina got up to get a glass of water from the break room, but it tasted horrible, as if someone had used it for washing filthy dishes. She dumped the glass down the drain and wondered where Wiley had gotten the water he'd given her the other day. It was still too warm in here; funny how before the lab had always seemed cold. How difficult could it be for these guys to maintain a decent room temperature? She took off the sweater, regarded it disgustedly, and ported it back to quarters. At least she could turn on some music now.

When she turned back to the main lab, a woman blocked her path, silhouetted against the red lights beyond. She was somewhere in her early thirties – short, spiky black hair with medium brown skin – and she held a gun in her hand.

6

"Who are you?" the woman demanded. "Why is security running?"

"I'm Carolina O'Kelly," Lina replied quickly in English. Every Panlingua word she'd learned had fled. Thank goodness her translator marble hadn't.

"Not enough information." The woman's gaze clicked down to Lina's bracelet, then back to her face. "Prisoner. A prisoner in the lab?"

"Uh, uh, Jae's on duty, but he's been called away. Wiley's sleeping. They said it was okay for me to be here as long as I stayed within bounds."

The woman pointed her non-weapon hand at the bracelet. Now Lina noticed the Legion ring she wore. With the ring aimed, the bracelet glowed a dull lilac.

"Neutrino's prisoner." The woman said it with certainty.

"Yes. But Wiley's in charge overall while the others are gone. That's what they said."

"Charges?" She cocked her head at Lina, weapon still aimed.

Lina grimaced and closed her eyes so she didn't have to witness her own death. "Mind control. Suspicion of, suspicion of!" she quickly amended. "Incorrect suspicion. Unfounded. Not guilty!"

"Suspected mind controllers aren't kept in the lab under computer recognizance."

Lina cracked open her eyes. The woman's position hadn't changed. "Jae said I was under house arrest." What else could she offer in her defense? "Protocol tells me I have a security grade of 2." That was better than zero. Mind controllers were zeros, if not negative numbers.

"Two? *Cheerah,* what in sunfire is going on here?"

"You could check the records before you vaporize me," Lina suggested. "Um, maybe you'd want to wake Wiley? Get a second opinion? Or third?"

"You." The newcomer pointed with her weapon at the bench that wrapped around most of the break table. "Sit. Slide to the far side."

Lina did so. From here she was penned in, at least from the woman's point of view.

"Now, sit and don't move. Hands on the table. Spread your fingers."

"Yes'm."

A small screen emerged from the woman's ring and she spared it quick glances from Lina. But one point made her stare at it instead.

"Valiant?" She gaped at Lina. "Married? You?"

"I'm sure it was an oversight that he didn't invite you to the wedding," Lina hastily assured her. "It was yesterday morning. Very, very early."

"Valiant. Married." She glanced at the screen again. "*Grigach,* you're Terran?"

"Guilty on that part. He doesn't know about the arrest. Yet."

Chuckles rocked the woman's chest, though they never made it out of her throat. "I guess not, or he would have brought it to our attention. Violently. Unless you really were controlling him, in which it's best if he stays out of range."

"What's the range of mind control?" Lina asked. "I haven't had time to research it. Should I? I've been thinking. If I research and learn a lot, couldn't that be misinterpreted as evidence against me? Jae said 'Dellen' was due to arrive soon. I take it you're her?"

The woman's mouth twisted slightly, but she lowered her weapon. "And Neutrino declared you under house arrest?" She added in an undertone, "He's going to get so many demerits for this it's not even funny." After a beat she decided, "Yes, it is," and laughed out loud. "I can't wait to watch when the commander finds out."

She now directed full attention and a frown to her info screen. "Man, no one ever tells me anything," she mumbled as she read. Finished, her eyes flicked toward Lina. "Around here we like our wedding nights. Same for Terrans?"

"Haven't had one yet," Lina said forlornly. She remained in that same splayed-hand position she'd been in. That gun could be re-aimed too quickly for her tastes.

"Hunh. This isn't a full report," Dellen told her. "I need details. You and Valiant? I assume you met on Earth?"

"Yes. Protocol says I'm supposed to call you by your cape name. What is it?"

"This says injuries were involved, but some idiot's assigned them to Valiant." Dellen gave an unbelieving sput at that idea. "What, you got hurt? You should know not to fool around with him. He can make one mistake and–"

"He was hurt. I'm not supposed to tell. It's some kind of security thing."

"I'm a Legionnaire."

"Dr. Gorgeon is a Legion doctor, and they didn't want her to know."

"Hm." Dellen folded her arms across her chest, the gun dangling from her left hand, and studied Lina. "The cape name is Multiplex. I'm Level 4.2. Beta team member."

Lina shrugged. "I have no idea what that means. Jae said something about a double-five, or maybe triple-five level of whatever."

"Double-five security block," Dellen mused. "Now, that's interesting. Does it have something to do with the lab being a mess?"

"They're supposed to release part of the story in four days," Lina added. "At least that's what Stoan said."

"'Stoan?' You know the commander well?"

Lina wrinkled her nose. "Oh, right. Cape names. He's what, Magnetman? Mr. Magnet?"

"Magnos."

"Well, he made me mad. He was a jerk with all this mind control stuff. And Lon and Jae and Wiley all call him 'Stoan.'" She sighed. "Lon says he's a good guy. I have yet to see it."

Wiley's voice announced, "While I'm seeing all too much of you. Cover up, Lina." He appeared in the doorway behind Dellen, and she whirled.

"Doctor! I was just–"

The red walls had disappeared as soon as Wiley had come into the lab. Lina ported behind him so he stood between her and Dellen. "She tried to shoot me! Why don't you people hang signs around here? Maybe she has an itchy trigger finger, huh? Did that ever occur to you?"

"Itchy…"

Dellen let out a shriek. "How'd she do that?" She pointed at the table in the break room. "She was there. And now she's–"

"Teleporter," Wiley told her.

"Interstellar teleporter, the report said," Dellen declared hotly. "No word about localized power. She could have sneaked up behind me and–" She threw her hands into the air, including the one with the gun. "Nobody ever tells me anything!"

Wiley peered at a small screen he'd summoned. "Hm. Yes, this should probably mention that right up front. I suppose one could think she was merely long-range. I'll correct it." With that, he nodded at Dellen and moseyed to his monitor station.

"Thank you for not shooting me," Lina told her.

"Hunh," was all the answer that merited.

"Cover up," Wiley told Lina. "Computer says that you've made good progress on your studies, despite terrorizing Protocol."

"Ah, privacy," she said as she ported in and put on her sweater. "Well, you won't be able to keep track of me when Jae and I go out. I may even wear shorts. Anyone else want to come along? No guns allowed." She looked at Dellen.

"They allow you to walk around outside? A mind control suspect?"

Lina huffed a protest at the thought. "I need to go home to feed my pets. I thought I'd treat Jae to lunch since he bought supper last night. Is that all right?" She looked at Wilder for confirmation.

"A short trip."

"Waitaminnit," Dellen said. "Is that translator working, or did she just say they were going to hop off to planet Earth for lunch?"

Lina grinned and said clearly, "<We are going to visit planet Earth this morning,>" in Panlingua.

"Very good, Lina."

"Thanks. I like the linguatape way of learning languages."

Dellen considered. "Does any of this have to do with all the construction? Like that hole over there?" The bottomless crater in the back was still a major landmark in the lab.

"Just a little," Lina confessed. "Stoan didn't like that we messed up his nice headquarters."

The main console buzzed for attention. Wiley perused his screens and then pointed a finger at Dellen.

"Sure thing," she said. "I mean, just because I just got here…" Dellen shrugged her shoulders and split into four people. The extra three just materialized around where her central persona stood – all perfect replicas.

Lina's mouth dropped open, and then she gave the central Dellen a big grin. "That is so cool," she said.

After a moment Dellen grinned back. "Yeah," she said. "I guess it is." With that she pixilated into a teleport.

"I see I'll have to learn my Legionnaires," Lina told Wiley. "What other kinds of neat powers are there?"

"Many," Wilder replied unhelpfully. Now that everything was under control, he plucked on a chunk of pocked gray styrofoam with glowing tweezers as he waited by his monitors for Dellen and Jae to return.

Lina picked up the miniaturized *igglin* on the edge of his desk. "Don't touch," he commanded her, and she quickly set it back down. Wiley waved her back to her study chair.

He had just finished another small project when Dellen walked back into the lab and took his place at the command monitor board. "Here, Lina," Wiley said as he left his post. "Put this on." In his hand he held another bracelet, but this one was made up of golden links.

"Ah, a wedding present." Lina didn't touch it. "What does this one do? Anything like this one?"

"Just put it on," Wiley said patiently.

"Not until you tell me what it's for," Lina said. "Do you want me to take this one off first?"

"You can get it off?" Wiley raised an eyebrow at that.

"Of course. You mean I'm not supposed to be able to?" Lina asked.

"Have you tried it?"

Lina ported the bracelet off into Wiley's hand. Simultaneously a klaxon of alarms went off. He sighed as Dellen reset the monitor board. "Please put this back on, Lina."

"Okay, but only since it goes so well with the outfit." She made a face at the new one. "Now, what's this other thing for?"

"It will help determine how your porting works. Among other things, it will show me what kind of medium you travel through when you do it."

"I don't think I travel through anything. I figure it's either a fourth kind of hyperspace–"

"You know about the levels of hyperspace?" Wiley's eyebrows shot up and both eyes rotated to focus on her. "You are supposedly a Terran. You shouldn't know–"

"It was in the tourism section of the Sarastor information you gave me, sheesh," Lina said, exasperated that everyone saw conspiracies on top of conspiracies. "Since it doesn't take any time to do, it can't be any of the known kinds of hyperspace. So it's either a new level, or else I'm creating some kind of wormhole in normal space. Wormholes explain everything, don't they? I have no idea what one is. Or my process is something else entirely. I'm not putting all my money on the hyperspace theory yet."

"I'll keep that in mind," Wiley said as Dellen snorted. "This instrument will keep me constantly informed as to your coordinates and time passage."

"And it also doesn't clash too badly with the outfit," Lina noted. "Okay, put 'er on." She pushed back her sweater sleeve to let him fasten it in place. "It buzzes," she reported. "Can you make it stop?"

"I don't hear anything." But he took the bracelet off and fiddled with it a moment, then replaced it.

"Much better, thanks," she said.

"Let's try it out," Wiley told her.

"Okay, where to? How far out?"

"Let's just start around the room."

Lina obliged and took about twelve ports around the room, circling it four times, getting her orientation going faster with each port. She reappeared next to the monitor station as Dellen jumped. "How's that?"

Wiley checked his readouts. "Excellent. Now… How far have you been on this planet?"

"Jae took me to Thessander last night."

"Be back in under a minute."

She was back in thirty seconds.

Wilder checked his data. "Let's try one port to Earth, there and back directly. Just to calibrate."

"Okay. Anything you want me to pick up as long as I'm there?"

Wilder thought about it although his left eye never stopped reading the invisible news screen he kept next to himself. "How about a book? A printed book? I'd be interested in learning about Terran culture."

"Sure thing. This'll take a few minutes," she said, and then disappeared after her eyes had gone misty.

"Can she really do this, Doctor?" Dellen asked Wilder. "And what's all this about mind control?"

"The commander is being over-cautious," Wiley reported. "I think that Lina is just what she appears to be, and he's not used to people who don't have hidden agendas. However, the more people we have in HQ, the better. Most mind controllers can handle only one mind at a time. The maximum we've ever discovered is three, but we know the Empire is working on computer enhancement of the process. If they're successful, there's no limit to how many they could control, albeit at low levels.

"She has no control implants. So far we haven't detected outside signals to her brain. Of course some mind controllers have never needed implants. Her personality tests indicate a strong belief in free will – definitely not a mind controller trait, though there are ways around the tests: deep conditioning, possibly RNA programming that could be triggered on signal. Hm. Odds are against it, but I'll check that angle. This marriage may be a little premature, but since they're both telepaths now…"

Dellen blurted, "Are you talking about Valiant? Valiant's a telepath?"

"It would seem so. A fairly strong one, too, although I haven't tested him as much as I'd like. Yet. But as I was saying, telepaths seem to jump into emotional situations quickly, and this seems to be no exce–"

"Got it," Lina said as she appeared again. "Here's your book. I ported it in from the return bins at work. They'll never miss it." She tossed the volume down in front of him: *101 Ways to Pick Up Women.*

"Very funny," he said, knowing that Dellen couldn't read the title.

"I thought so." Lina grinned. She pulled another book from behind her back: *Timetables of History,* and set it down on the board. "How's the calibration?"

Wiley consulted his readings and then cross-indexed to the central Legion computer. "There's a skew at interstellar distances. Let me compensate… There. It should be ready now."

But soon enough he was busy researching an annoying glitch in one of Sarastor's older planetary defense programs. It gave Lina and Dellen a chance to get to know each other – or at least for Lina to know Dellen. She was quite the talker, and was eager to fill in this new person, prisoner or no, on the various and more colorful characters around Legion Headquarters.

In particular, she passed along some gossip concerning their missing confinement officer, Jae, who was indeed "Jae" to her. Juicy rumors always followed him around, Dellen explained. This time the prevailing word was about him and a missing ambassador, who, when finally found (in roaringly inebriated condition), produced an interstellar treaty with one of the Unaffiliated Worlds that the AffSys had been trying for years to procure.

But it wasn't until Dellen had exhausted the current round of gossip that Jae himself returned. "Hey, Dellen, you're back!" were his first words. "How'd it go?"

"Okay. No great shakes," she shrugged her shoulders but couldn't hide the special smile she had for him. "All they needed was for someone to knock their heads together until they saw eye to eye."

"At least they didn't knock you around."

"They tried."

Jae laughed and looked around. "So everyone's up and around. Does anyone mind if I go off to Earth for an hour or two? I could use a break."

"Wiley's going to let us go for three Terran hours," Lina said in Panlingua. "Dellen said she'd pass."

"Listen to you. Okay, three Terran hours. Are you ready?"

"Um." She didn't know how to put this. "Last night was okay for that outfit, Jae," she said. "A lot of weirdoes and crazies run around at night. With the translator and your height you already stand out. Could you find something a little more normal to wear?"

"Like what?"

"Like jeans. That's what these are. Londo's got some jeans and tee shirts here…"

"Let's look."

Lina ported them to Londo's apartment, where Jae fished through Lon's bedroom drawers. He pulled out some jeans from one and a tee shirt that said TERRAN PAR-ANORM NETWORK in stacked, faded type behind the word PARANET with a big lightning bolt cracking through the logotype. Lina laughed and read it to Jae.

"I might even be able to wear these, too," Jae said. "How about shoes?"

They quickly discussed Terran fashion and how Sarastoran could be suitably altered. Jae went to his quarters to search his own closets.

Jae modeled back at the lab. He'd had to replicate the jeans in his size and his dark boots were much shorter now. The tee shirt that might have been snug on Londo hung loose on Jae's more slender frame. Its thin material showed his shoulders and chest slabbed like Londo's. While Lon looked ready for a boxing match, Jae had a lean swimmer's body.

"Arms, Jae," Wiley said as Dellen grinned and ogled the Feithi Legionnaire.

But Lina approved. "Very Terran," she said before they ported to Earth.

First stop, of course, was for the cats. They all trotted out except for the second black cat, this one a small, scrawny one as opposed to the large tom who'd gotten sick the other night. This one lay still on a bookshelf. Very still.

"I think it's dead," Jae hesitantly told Lina.

"She's just old," Lina insisted and waved a tube under the cat's nose. "Fafhrd," she urged. "Faf, wake up. Time for your pill."

One eye opened and then the other, and the ancient cat stuck her butt high into the air and stretched, clawing at the shelf. Then back end went down, front end went up and forward and streeetch again with an enormous yawn. Jae noticed that the cat was missing some teeth asymmetrically even before Lina pried open its jaws.

"Pill gun," she explained to him, and pressed a rubber-tipped syringe into Fafhrd's mouth. The cat wasn't pleased, but when Lina took a tube and squirted out some brown gel on her finger, the cat followed her actions attentively. Lina again opened the cat's jaws, but this time squeegeed the gel onto the roof of Fafhrd's mouth. The cat settled to worry the stuff off, smacking its lips.

"She's got a thyroid problem, plus she needs to gain some weight. That's a food concentrate," Lina said as she set the cat down on the floor.

Jae decided to play with the creatures, too, and he learned all their names, but again noted that Lina had her own versions of them. The grey cat he had petted the night before apparently remembered him because she came up to him and purred, standing on her hind feet to rub her chin against his knee.

"Ember likes you," Lina said as she opened the back door to let some cats out. Thick forest surrounded the house.

Jae gave Ember a good rubbing and she came back for more, a look of utter adoration in her eyes. Jae laughed at her. "Cute little Ember," he cooed at her, and she seemed to understand his Panlingua.

He noticed that Lina kept opening and closing the door for the cats to go out or come in. "I thought they had a door of their own," he said.

"Ah, but they have their human here now. Why use their own door when they can prove their superiority by using me as their servant? It is my pleasure to serve you, sir," she said gravely as one cat exited and another came in, their tails high in the air.

As Jae finished washing up, Lina gave him his choice of what to do. "We could shop for CDs or we look at musical instruments, if you'd like. After that we go to lunch. And… oh."

"What?"

"When Lon and I spoke to the Bolt the other day, we said he'd be home in a couple of days. They might worry when Londo doesn't show."

"Good point. How do you contact the ParaNet from here?"

"I have no idea."

That shocked Jae. "You don't know how to get them in an emergency?"

"I know 911, for the local police emergency number." Lina tried to reason it out. "They've got to have some kind of toll-free number set up. Let's see."

She turned on her computer and then Googled for "ParaNet contact." There were personal appearance listings, hero agent listings, regional offices… and as she worked her way through more specialized links, an emergency number.

"I hope I don't get into trouble using this," Lina murmured.

"I authorize it," Jae said.

That's right, Lina realized, Legionnaires seemed to outrank ParaNetters. But did the Legion have any jurisdiction on Earth?

She called the emergency number on her landline.

"ParaNet emergency," a male voice said.

"This is not an emergency, but it's the only way I could get through," Lina said. "I have a message concerning Valiant."

"All right," the man said. "What's the message?"

"I'm Carolina O'Kelly," Lina began. "Valiant and I called from Sarastor the other day and we spoke to the Bolt. We said that Valiant would be home in a couple of days after he got out of quarantine. Well, he was called away on a mission, and now it looks like there's going to be a state funeral after he gets back to Sarastor. So I just wanted to say that no one should become concerned if he doesn't show up for, what, another five or six days or so. Do you have that?"

"Um hm," the bored voice on the other end of the line said.

****I said, do you have that?**** Lina accompanied her message with a good telepathic shout.

"Yes! Message noted," he said briskly. "Valiant, five days."

"Thank you so much," she purred and hung up.

As long as she had the phone in her hand she punched in another number. "Hi, Sharon? I finally got through. Yes, it's me." ****I'm checking in at work,**** she explained to Jae. Her supervisor was relieved that Lina hadn't caught the disease she'd been "quarantined" for, and that the famous Bolt himself had called to explain things, causing all kinds of excitement at work. Lina assured her that she'd be back in about a week.

Jae considered the landline phone as she set it down. "I can see definite advantages in not having a screen with one of those," he said.

"Absolutely," she assured him. "Have you decided what you want to shop for?"

"I wouldn't mind visiting a store with instruments, just to see what's available," he said, "but I'd like to get some music and my own player. And something to eat; I'm starved."

"Let's go to Chapel Hill then," Lina said.

They strolled down collegiate Franklin Street in the afternoon sunshine, taking in its modern, yet Nineteenth Century brick ambiance. In the shade it was chilly without light jackets, but the sunny side was warm enough. Still, the heat inside the music shop was welcome. There was no one else in the store, and the saleslady let them roam around once they explained that they were just looking. She seemed content to gaze at Jae.

Jae examined the electric guitars lining the walls with lust. He ran his fingers over some of them, took two down from their hangers.

"You're familiar with them," Lina said.

"Londo brought me one years ago. Taught me to play. Mine is acoustic."

Then he tried the drums and Lina held her breath. His performance the other night had been robust, and if he broke anything… But he didn't. After running each part through its paces, he gave a nod of approval and proceeded to explore the rest of the store's varied contents. The dazzled saleslady let him handle – or fondle – the brass instruments. He peered through mouthpieces, fingered the keys on everything.

"Tell her I'll be back," he told Lina in Panlingua, so she could translate "from Swedish" without being unsynchronized.

Out on the tree-lined sidewalk, Jae bounced as he walked, listening to the various melodies leaking from all around him. "This is so great," he said. "I wish Sarastor were like this."

Lina had to bounce to keep up with him. People stopped to stare. Jae was probably the most beautiful person they'd ever see, and his height just added to the effect. Sometimes it was difficult to look at Jae, he was so pretty, but then Lina reminded herself she shouldn't think of him that way. He was Londo's best friend. So he had perfect genes. He was still a nice guy underneath it all.

"Look over there," she pointed. Some people had set up a folding table in front of the post office.

"What's that?"

"Gay rights. And gender identity rights. See the rainbow symbol? Let's go see what they have."

Lina read Jae the pamphlets over a lunch of veggie pizza and a selection of local beers for him, tea for her. She was excited to be home, showing off the place to Jae and talking all the while, so she only had one slice.

Jae easily took care of the rest, even though at first he was uncomfortable eating the food without silverware. But after seeing everyone else in the shop eating with their hands, he tried it, then had to lunge after some dripping mozzarella.

"Hot hot hot!" he cried when he could catch his breath. Only the ice-cold beer could extinguish the heat. By slice number three he was a pizza pro, shaking on red pepper and folding the slices as those people across the aisle were. ("They're New Yorkers," Lina said, as if that explained it.) He let the grease dribble down his fuzzed chin.

He proclaimed the beer good, too, except for the second one, which he tasted and then pushed away. Lina peeled the labels off all three bottles he so that he'd know what he'd already tried when he came back for a visit. The one he didn't like she drew an unhappy face on.

"Efficient." Jae tucked the labels into his hip pocket.

The sound system blared heavy rock, so Jae kept the beat on the table and glass. Someone had put a life-size cutout of Captain Picard in the window with cardboard word balloons next to him telling customers, "You are Number One with us!" and "Any topping combo – We'll make it so!" Lina used it to demonstrate that she wasn't the only *Star Trek* fan around. Jae noted the matching symbols on their shirts and she assured him that, yes, she was indeed wearing a *Star Trek* shirt.

Jae's drumming fingers froze. "What the orb–?" he exclaimed softly. Lina tried to see what had startled him, but it was just a couple walking into the restaurant.

"Is there something wrong with her?" Jae asked, looking from Lina back to that woman. That enormously pregnant woman. Before Lina could say anything, Jae whispered, "Is she pregnant?"

"Very," Lina said. "Don't get in her way if she lets out a yell. She looks like she could drop at any time."

"Pregnant," Jae murmured to himself, his eyes round with wonder. "A baby's inside her."

"That's the general idea. And it's impolite to stare."

With a startled sound, Jae returned his attention to his pizza. He made a production out of handling the next slice with its dripping cheese so he could steal one more peek at the mother-to-be.

"Very covert," Lina approved. "Haven't you ever seen a pregnant woman before?"

"No. I know they did it this way on Feith, but I never witnessed it. I was the last child born on my world," Jae said offhandedly. "My sister was the second to last, and she was much older than I was."

"Oh." They ate in silence for a few minutes. Lina tried to understand what kind of a childhood Jae must have had with no other children around.

He was such a surprising man. Moody, yes, but he had interesting moods. And he was so golden-ly beautiful. Someday, perhaps, he'd be merely handsome, but she couldn't picture it. Jae Rallene seemed the picture of eternal male youth and beauty. That is, if he'd just do something about that blond scraggle of beard he'd allowed to grow since Stoan had left.

Manly stubble should be dark and a little threatening, like Lon's, mmm. But Jae's? First, it had grown in too fast. It was beyond the stubble stage already, the first wisps of a beard. To Lina, beards were a way of hiding a perfectly fine face. Such a shame.

She laughed to herself to imagine Jae trying to get away with a beard in the Legion. She suspected that beards were definitely a Rule Infringement of some kind, probably dictated by His High Holiness, Commander Stoan Kinrol.

And she laughed again, trying not to let Jae see. Now she realized Stoan's ulterior motive for leaving Jae as her arresting officer. What woman in her right mind could resist the charms of Legionnaire Neutrino, the Last Feithi? One smile from Jae and any sane woman would turn to putty.

And then it could be pointed out to that woman's new husband how fickle she was. The marriage could be quite handily annulled and the woman thrown into the farthest gutter that existed from Legion Headquarters.

Yes, for Jaeson Rallene any woman would fall hard. Any woman who wasn't already quite insanely in love with Mister Londo Falcon Rand, the man who shook her personal universe. And any woman who didn't know that Jae was gay.

Got you on this one, Stoan, Lina gloated as Jae set down the third beer bottle, half of it gone. He looked like he was almost finished with lunch, but he had to give his neck a good scratch before he took his final bites.

He did that a lot: grooming motions. He'd be walking like some panther on the prowl and then suddenly reach around and scratch his backside. Or you'd be talking to him and he'd start to pull on an earlobe, gnawing at it with a fingernail. Even during his interview the other day she noticed him scratching his chest, scratching the back of his head, even scratching his armpit while the camera focused on him.

She didn't think it was fleas.

No, Jae knew how unholy gorgeous he was, how set apart from humanity his looks could make him. He knew that sometimes he could just look at you and you could tell that an ancient mind was operating behind those blue eyes, seeing you from an ethereally alien point of view. Scratching was entirely human. It brought him back to a realm where others could relate to him.

She could certainly relate to him while he had a smear of tomato sauce on his fuzzy cheek.

Lina said as casually as she could, "This used to be a Mexican restaurant. I worked here. I lived upstairs – illegally."

Jae stopped in mid-bite. The pregnant woman was forgotten. "And why are you telling me this?"

"I figured you were doing an investigation. Might as well get it all out."

He fished in his other hip pocket and drew out a flattened marble, one of those cameras he'd used before. "We'll see it when we're through," he told Lina.

Upon hearing Lina's "old home" explanation and boggling at Jae, the manager let them walk through the kitchen. Jae watched cooks patting out great circles of fragrant flour-covered dough and using wooden paddles to shove them into the large, flat ovens that gushed out dry heat.

Lina gathered her courage for her new ability to touch in order to pull him up a narrow stairway in the back. The floating camera followed them unobtrusively as she explained trading off her half of her scholarship-paid dorm room for cash from her roommate's boyfriend so she could find a less expensive place to live and yet afford the supplies that weren't covered by the scholarship. She'd found a mattress-sized cubbyhole at the top of the stairs here, opposite the attic space.

"The manager let me stay here real cheap, and even cheaper when we arranged that I would work from 3 to 7 AM. I mean, I was always here; why shouldn't I make myself useful at the restaurant, too? I strung up a curtain, bought some earplugs, and no one ever bothered me. I imagined I was Harry Potter in his little cabinet under the stairs. Oh, you don't know Harry Potter."

Jae wrinkled his nose. "I know Londo Rand; therefore, I know about Harry Potter. Boy wizard, right? Fictional."

"How about that? Well, here Christian – he was the owner – even paid me real wages, gave me free meals, and never asked my age."

"Your age?"

"I was a little young. I told him I was eighteen, but I was only fifteen. That's underage for almost everything. The university's right next door, the bus stop's out front. The location was perfect. And I love Mexican food."

Jae had to steady himself against the low, sloping ceiling over the staircase as they climbed back down. "How long did you live here?"

"Until I graduated. Christian sold the restaurant practically on graduation day. It worked out fine, didn't it?"

Campus greens spread out from the rear employee entrance. The two passed the backs of a group of old red-brick buildings with abstract statuary beside the sidewalk. Music emanated from an open window. Lina paused so Jae could hear the college chorus practicing.

The group would stop and then repeat phrases over and over, sometimes splitting up into single sections to do so. It seemed to puzzle him.

Lina realized that he didn't know. "It's live," she told him. "Come on." She took his arm and pulled him around the side of the building, to enter through an arched door. Inside, they could stand in an alcove and see the practice without interrupting. Jae watched, fascinated at how the chorus put their parts together and what the director came up with as criticism. Enunciation. A note not held long enough. The sopranos coming in too late after the tenors.

They watched for a few more minutes and then wandered through the rest of the building. Jae peered at people in soundproof practice rooms working on many instruments – practicing a legitimate art form at an institution of higher education. The more they saw, the wider Jae's mouth stretched across his face.

"You majored in music?" he asked.

Lina laughed. "I thought about it. A lot. But me? No, I took commercial art instead, with a minor in business administration."

A raised eyebrow.

"I couldn't see me performing in public," she explained. "Even as a backup singer, which is what I had in mind when I was a kid. Too scared. The past couple years I've managed to play piano at parties, but I only began that when I was dead broke and had to find extra income or else. The lack of money makes you do crazy things. There aren't that many parties in this area requiring piano for entertainment, and all too many penniless pianists. So I started doing private psychic readings, too."

Out on the green several small groups had seated themselves around people with guitars, enjoying the cloudless March day. A few students with music players mingled with others on the sidewalks, and the faint sound of car radios drifted through the green from the streets. Jae startled and then looked up as a bird broke into song from its territory in the trees. A loud answer rang out from another tree further down.

Two young men strolled by wearing cutoffs and torn tank tops. Jae swiveled to watch them, his bright blue eyes flashing in the sun. The men kept him in sight even as they walked past.

"It's not that warm," Lina muttered. "Look at those goose bumps. Showoffs."

"Yeah," Jae said. "Goosebumps."

Lina pulled on his arm.

"The Wreck Room," a music & movie warehouse, was just on the other side of the more expensive restaurants across the street. "Will this have competitive pricing?" Jae asked, trying to grasp the concept.

"There's usually a price war going on among the places that aren't chains. We've got three world-class universities within just a few miles of each other here with a zillion students, all trying to get a good collection started. Plus there's the entire Internet to compete with. So prices are rock bottom. And–" she pulled a plastic card out of her pocket. "I have a membership card. An extra ten percent off any purchase."

"A discount," Jae approved, rubbing his hands as they entered. The store was two stories high. Walls were studded with TV screens showing popular shows and games silently, while loud music blasted from speakers. Row upon row of product displays filled the space. His mouth opened in awe. "Shards, where do I begin?"

She showed him the sections of music and how he could preview some of the albums. Plus, the majority of the warehouse stocked used CDs, which meant low prices and the ability to buy more music than if he chose new.

The salespeople began to look up as Lina began a pile of Jae's selections at one checkout counter. "He's an exchange student," she explained. She tried not to cringe at the lie, but in emergencies sometimes you just had to if it was the only way to help someone. "From northern Scandinavia. They don't have many CD stores up there. He's getting them while the… customs taxes are so low." They nodded as if they knew what she was talking about. She certainly didn't.

Jae was flipping through some World Music selections when Wiley's voice came through his ring. "Jae."

"Wiley. I take it we're a little late?"

"You passed 'late' ten minutes ago. No thieves?"

"No thieves. Sorry. We're having too much fun. Let me purchase these items and then we'll be right there."

"Right."

Jae reluctantly tore himself from the sections he hadn't gotten to yet, and Lina added the final CDs to the pile. She flashed her membership card at the checker and then her MasterCard, hoping they wouldn't ask to see any other identification. That was all gone in the fire of… was it less than two weeks ago?

They didn't and the charge went through. Three hundred dollars. It was worth it to see the look on Jae's face as he finally got his own music. She ported them out even as they exited the store.

Jae gave a laugh of relief as they popped into Legion Headquarters, then deposited the CDs on the table. "Ah shards," he said. "I forgot to get a player."

"You don't need one." Lina pointed at hers. "That's yours now. I even got some new batteries for you until Wiley or Lon can hook you up some kind of adapter for the cord."

"Really? Thanks, Lina. Thanks a lot." Jae flopped down in a chair. "Dellen, Wiley, you should see it. A great planet. Trees. People not dressed properly at all. Spicy food. Music everywhere – Most of it's singing." He picked up the bags and started to empty them. "And they have this store that's nothing but music. I didn't have time to go through a tenth of it."

"Sounds as if you were playing while we were working hard," Wiley said, but the side of his mouth crooked. He held up one of the CDs. "These seem mass-produced."

"Of course they are!" Lina was exasperated with preconceived ideas about Earth.

"Singing," Dellen made a face. "How barbaric."

"Ah, but it's not. It's not that way at all," Jae's enthusiasm was undimmed as he struggled with the plastic wrap for a CD. Just as Lina was about to show him how to unpeel it, the plastic evaporated into nothingness. He popped the CD in the player and turned the volume control all the way clockwise.

Lina turned it back to the center. It was the first track from *Goodbye Yellow Brick Road*. "It'll get loud enough toward the end," she warned, and Jae nodded.

"She says that any collection has this album in it."

"It's an old classic," Lina declared. She dug out the liner notes and showed them to Jae. "Words, too. You'll have to sharpen up your English."

"Okay." Jae squinted at it for a moment, but then concentrated on the music as it became louder and the beat took over. He drummed along with it. Dellen and Wiley watched him indulgently.

"I could dance to it," Dellen admitted.

The instrumental became vocal, the beat went faster. Elton John began to sing. Jae shook his head. "The translator's not picking this up," he said. "What are the words?"

Lina spoke along with the record, not bothering to check the lyrics on the liner sheets. She could remember each and every word clearly. *And love lies bleeding in my hand. It kills me to think of you with another man…*

When it was over, Jae stopped the CD. "Just couldn't wait to test it out," he said. "What was the title of that? I liked it."

"It was two songs in one," Lina said and suddenly realized… "Oh. It might not have been the best thing to play."

"Why?"

"The first part was 'Funeral for a Friend.'" She saw Jae deflate. "I'm sorry."

Dellen looked at both of them, saw the frown on Wilder's face. "What? Who died?"

"They say that Orenya is going to, during this mission," Wiley said.

Dellen's eyes narrowed suspiciously. "How do they know that? Jae?"

Jae told her what they'd seen.

"That's superstition."

Lina checked in with her guides. "*They're* confirming it," she reported. "It hasn't happened yet, but it's soon. Real soon, as within the next day soon. I am so sorry."

"And no way to give a warning other than what Jae's already done," Wilder said. "If indeed it is true."

"It's true enough," Jae said bitterly. "C'mon, Lina, help me take this stuff to my room. Out of Wiley's way."

"Sure. Do you have a picture of–"

"Let's go the normal route."

"Okay." She gathered up three bags of CDs, he grabbed the player, and they left the lab.

"I'm sorry I brought it up," Lina told him as they took the long drop in the Jetsons tube down to the levels of living quarters. Definitely on these higher levels at least, it was Jae who was flying both of them down the chute with just his arm around her keeping her from falling to oblivion. In the lower levels, some other function kicked in under their feet so she didn't need a Legion ring. Those must be the levels open to Legion spouses and families.

But the knowledge didn't help the fact that intimacy of the touch still made Lina nervous. *Get over it, get over it,* she chanted to herself. *People do this all the time. It doesn't mean anything.* "You were in such a good mood," she said.

"I still am," Jae said determinedly. "I mean, there's nothing we can do about it, is there? She led a good life. No one accomplished more than she did… unless it's Londo. I just wish I'd known a little sooner."

"Why? Would you have done anything differently?"

"I would have seduced her one night. I'd have had crazy sex with her."

7

L ina blinked. "I thought you were gay."

He cocked his head and shrugged. "Mostly *gei*."

"Bisexual."

"I always wanted to have sex with Aiko, just once. And maybe it would have been something she could look back on and smile for at the end. Now there's no chance of that."

"Definitely Pisces energy mixed in with the Gemini," Lina shook her head at him. "I've been trying to figure it out."

"What's that mean?"

"Astrology. Pisces means you're always a surprise," she replied, and gave a little laugh. "Come to think of it, it helps you to swing both ways." He did laugh at that as the lift stopped.

They sat in his room as the new music played. She explained some of the words and concepts in the songs, gave him background on the artists, put the music in context for him as they sat on pillows on the floor. Draperies billowed in an unseen breeze next to faux windows that looked out onto a green-skyed world and forest. There was a waterfall around somewhere; she could hear it between tracks.

"Bathroom?" she asked, and Jae pointed the direction out to her.

"Don't explore," he warned as she got up.

But she was in a strange house. You'd think that all these Legion apartments, at least for the single Legionnaires, would have the same general floor plan, but Jae's living room was so much smaller than Londo's. Why was that? Of course, Lon's was huge; most people wouldn't want a living room that large. Kitchenette over there, dining area, office area, trophy room, a bedroom door slightly open – she could see the corner of a bed back there in the darkness.

The bathroom was Sarastoran standard. Sarastoran plumbing was way better than Terran, Lina decided. No muss, no fuss. Off the hall on the way back was the final door, the guest room. What would it look like? People were allowed into guest rooms; that's why they were there. Lina wanted to peek. Her fingertips touched the "open" doorplate but nothing happened.

"I said, no exploring." Lina jumped at the suddenness of Jae's voice behind her.

"Sorry. I didn't go into your bedroom. I just wanted to look at the guest room."

"Not here. That's private."

The way he said it was strange. "Not for anyone?"

"No one goes in there except me." There was no compromise in the statement.

If it weren't a guest room then it must be someplace very large indeed to make up for all the missing square footage. "Sorry."

A secret garden, a voice whispered to her. Perhaps it was, a place like in that movie where Jae could store his memories without fear of intrusion. Yes, Jae would need that, a room full of scrapbooks and old movies.

They returned to the living room by way of the kitchenette, snacks, and a waft of subtle perfume from flowers "outside" the fake windows.

"Was this what Feith was like?" she asked as they settled onto the carpet against a sofa made of securely piled pillows. She remembered the holosuite program that had been a Feithi landscape. "Was it this tranquil? This is nice."

"Most people don't talk to me about Feith."

"I'm sorry. If it makes you uncomfortable…"

"It doesn't. It's just that most people don't talk to me about it."

Lina considered. "Do you think about it much?"

Jae set his drink on the floor, picked up another CD and looked at the picture on the cover. "I used to think about it all the time. I used to dream of it constantly."

"That's not what I asked," she said quietly.

He put the CD down. "I suppose I still think about it too much," he said. He picked up another CD as if the conversation weren't bothering him, but it didn't look to Lina like he was really seeing the CD.

"What's too much?" she asked him.

"Too much is anything," Jae said. He glared quickly at her and then returned to his CDs.

Take it easy, Lina. But that vision she'd had days before filled her mind: Jae lying dead in a self-inflicted pool of blood, his future unless he turned things around. "So… So there's really nothing particularly nice or warm or loving that you want to remember? I bet people would love to know the good things about Feith. Unless there wasn't anything–"

"Feith only had good things. There was nothing bad about Feith. Nothing at all." His words came clipped.

"So remember the good things. Celebrate them. Or don't you want to be happy?"

"Drop it."

"Sorry. I just thought you might be one of those people who don't allow themselves to be happy."

He looked like he was about to say something else and then decided against it. "You don't *allow* yourself to be happy. Some people just are and some aren't. It's been scientifically proven. There's a… built-in happiness index. It's biological."

"What a load of bullshit," Lina said. "I mean, in your case. There might be some kind of biochemical basis for others, but… *They* say not for you. Besides, doesn't Sarastor have miracle medicines? Are they helping?" She answered herself, shaking her head, her eyes defocused. "A bit. Not entirely. Not nearly so. Jeez."

Lina took a breath. "So, you think it's biological. Was your gene pool so unhappy? Was Feith such an unhappy place that you got all the sad genes?"

"Lina…"

"All I'm saying is that if you aren't genetically challenged happiness-wise and there's nothing medically wrong, no PTSD or anything – oh, is that what they're treating you for? Good; that's definitely a part of this but only a part – then the thing that's holding you back must be you. You're hanging on to all the horror and grief. You're not moving ahead; you're living in your wound. You must get something out of being unhappy in order to keep yourself so grim. At least, Dellen says you're grim more than half the time."

"I'm not grim, I'm–"

"Dangerous." Lina smiled at him to take the sting off. "Very dangerous and one hell of an impressive Legionnaire. You have the entire universe terrified of you." She kept her smile on. "So why doesn't that make you happy, if that's what you want?"

"Are all Terrans this nosy?"

She *harrumph*ed. "Avoidance."

"And I need to take all this from the girl who couldn't even let herself be touched until a few days ago."

"Ouch."

That brought a look of triumph to his face. "Just calling them as I see them. Why did you *allow* yourself to get into that position? I can't imagine not being able to touch people."

"It was a lot more comfortable for me to keep away," Lina said. She lay back on the bank of sturdy pillows, gazing at the ceiling. It was misty and palest green, and seemed very far away. "It was safer. Until I found someone who desperately needed to be touched more than I needed to be safe. Maybe. I don't know."

"Of course you know. We all know our true problems. We just won't admit them to ourselves."

"Sometimes it's safer not to." The look in her eyes was distant.

Jae swung his boots up on the coffee table and leaned back on the pillows as well. He scratched his chin. "A phobia for touching, and safety as an issue…" he mused. "Fear of being touched indicates to old Dr. Rallene here that someone's hurt you in the past, and you don't want to be hurt again."

Lina was silent at that.

"Okay." Jae tapped his fingers on his thigh as he thought. "Best place to start is always the family. Did someone in your family hurt you?"

"Do I have to pay you for this session?" Lina asked.

"Avoidance. Got it on the first try." Jae looked pleased with himself.

"You just enjoy being the shrink instead of the shrunk."

Jae had to pause as the translator gnawed its way through the sentence. He thought. "I am allowing myself to enjoy being a… shrink," he told her. "Would you deny me that pleasure?"

She had to chuckle at that, so she told him bits of her dysfunctional childhood, concluding with, "I don't think you'd like my parents."

"I'd like anyone's parents," he said, and there was a sudden mournful tone in his voice.

Lina rolled over to touch his hand. "Oh, Jae, I'm so sorry that you don't have a family. And I'm glad for you that they were people whom you'd miss. But me, I just want to get away from them. That was one of the reasons I took this vacation in the first place, to get my head straight. Then I could quit my job, sell my place and move the cats and me to some remote corner of the mountains with no forwarding address. My parents would never miss me. I had it all figured out."

"Except for–?"

She gave him a small smile. "Londo."

"And you don't know if you can go through with it now."

Lina's smile evaporated. "Lon's only got his adoptive family – and they all sound wonderful, if you ask me, but he wants… He wants…" Should she be telling Jae this?

"A real tie to the world."

Lina looked at him. Lon and he must be truly close friends. She nodded. "Exactly. So he's got a real wife now. What happens if I cut myself off from my family? That means that we're afloat as a couple instead of a single, but still afloat."

"Don't do it." Now Jae reached to squeeze her hand. "Leave as minimal contact as you can survive, but don't cut the rope all the way through."

Releasing her, he lay back farther and gazed at the ceiling. Wispy clouds were making their way across its sky-scape. "Everyone needs family, even if it's an artificial one. You can think of family as people or as a concept. Cut yourself off from the people if you must, but not the concept."

Lina considered. Cut off from the horrible feelings. Honor thy father and thy mother. Say, yes, I have them, but not necessarily to love them. The Commandment didn't say you had to love them. Send them Christmas cards and birthday cards, but no more than that. No more dreading holidays because she was expected home. "I'll miss seeing the dog," she decided.

"Dog?" Jae's brows furrowed. "Is that the same as *un chien*?" At Lina's nod, he said, "So you can sneak back now and be nice to the dog and your parents will never know it."

She blinked at him as the realization hit her. "You *are* dangerous."

He smiled to himself and drummed a beat on his chest with the flat of his hands. "Absolutely."

"It's a very good thought." She rolled onto her back and put her feet up on the edge of the table, too. "So when you say everyone needs a family," she said, "old Dr. O'Kelly can't help but notice that you haven't gone out and gotten you one, Jae."

Jae opened and closed his mouth in surprise at the suddenness of it. He had to laugh at her audacity. "The Legion is my family," he began, "aunts and uncles and cousins and…" His mouth suddenly twitched in pain.

"What is it?" Lina twisted around, reaching out to touch his shoulder.

"Aiko. Grigach, she's dead. I know she is."

"Not yet. I don't think so. There's absolutely no way to contact them?"

He shook his head. "They won't take the drone seriously. She won't be coming back. Nothing we can do."

"There are… I know of some cultures on Earth that celebrate death. Death is returning to one's natural state; it's going home. They know that it's only the body that dies."

"Wake up and face reality, Lina!" Jae leapt to his feet and began to pace the room, flailing his arms. "This is a blaze of a universe we're in. It likes to take you in its fat hand and twist you, twist all the trust you ever had out of yourself. Orb, it squeezes you dry!"

He picked up a trophy from his desk and threw it against the wall with such force that Lina was surprised that it didn't shatter. "Life is a farce. Whoever came up with the concept was insane!"

Warily she eased herself upright. "If you're so dry, you should be thankful that you won't feel anything about Aiko." Lina tried not to sound too harsh, but his mood frightened her. She wanted to shock him out of it. "Physical life is about relating to others. About improving ourselves and taking tests. Life is a mystery we'll never be able to understand completely. That's why we're here."

"You just don't understand," he told her bitterly. "No one could."

"I can't understand what you've been through, no. But I do know that whatever you're going through now, whatever direction you're aiming yourself for, is not the direction you want to go."

"Butt out, Lina. Keep the blaze out of my business."

"Tell me about life, Jae. Tell me what your people taught you about it."

"What the *frickurn* blaze does it matter? They're gone. They're all dead. Except me."

"And you're still alive. It's so easy to die, isn't it? There are a million ways you can do it. But you're still here. I can't help noticing that. Something inside of you thinks that you should be alive. What is it? What's keeping you here?"

"I said, butt out–"

"Hold hard to whatever it is, Jae. If there's anything in your life worth hanging on to, it's that."

Jae gave her a terrible look. "Whatever it is–" his voice washed her like ice– "maybe it's gone now."

"I don't think so. I won't pry, but you need to look for it. Cherish it, make it grow within you. Life's got its ups and downs, but there are times when it's very, very wonderful. I don't think you've experienced that for a long time. I don't think you've *allowed* yourself to experience it. It may be there, waiting for you to grasp it, but damned if you aren't going to allow yourself! Damnfool stubbornness. I see that in you. And white-knuckled fear. You drink a lot, don't you? Too much?"

"I thought you said you weren't going to pry?"

"Drinking is the classic cover-up to fear. I know. Damned if I can stand the taste of alcohol, or I'd be in some gutter with a bottle next to me today."

He turned his back to her.

"Don't drink yourself senseless over this, Jae."

"I'm going on duty in a while. I don't drink on duty."

"Good. Take some time and face it. Just face a tiny part of it, if that's all that you can manage. From what I see you have friends – You have *family* all around here at the Legion. If they're any kind of friends at all, they want to help."

"I want them to leave me alone."

"Then tell them that. But come out of it every so often." For a moment Lina hesitated, but then hugged him hard from behind. "They say a broken heart heals up stronger than before. I know that the universe has taken your heart and shattered it so long ago. But maybe it's time to let it heal. It can, Jae. I believe that."

He didn't answer her.

"She'll be free now. You said that no one had accomplished more than she did. She's completed her life, and it was a wonderful one. Inspirational. How many of us can hope for something like that? To be so well-loved, to be as loving as she must have been. And now she's gone home and she can rest.

"Do you know that people have a tendency to reincarnate in groups? You'll probably see her again. She'll only be gone from you for a short time. Just a lifetime. That's not long at all in the eternal view."

He nodded his head, not saying anything.

"Grieve for yourself, but don't grieve for her. She's happy. People who've come back from the other side say it's the most glorious place they've ever been."

"So why don't we all go back there? We could all be happy."

"Because we're here. Because physical life is given for a reason. You still have so many wonderful discoveries to make, Jae. Find your core and cling to it during this time. You'll find your balance sooner or later."

"You didn't let Londo die."

That stopped her. She released her hard grasp of him but put her hands on his shoulders. *Give him the strength to carry the burden he must bear, Lord.* "It wasn't his time. There was still a chance for him to live, and I took it. That may have been selfish. And you helped me. Londo's still alive because of all of us working together. He didn't want to go, either; he told me. I know a little about Lon and Aiko, what they were to each other. He's going to be devastated, even more than you. I need you to help him through this, just as he can help you."

Jae was shaking, trembling under her touch. "Help him, priest," Lina whispered sharply to him. Jae's order had the same vows hers had. "Help yourself. You took an oath; don't back out on it now."

"Shit. Shit, Lina." But he let her stand there and hold him in another hug as long minutes passed, both silent.

He took a shuddering breath. "I think you should get back to the lab now. I'll be there in a while."

"All right," she said so softly and squeezed his shoulder before she ported.

Wiley and Dellen looked up as she came back alone. "Jae had some personal business to attend to," was all she told them.

Later Jae came back in full costume, neatly groomed. He didn't glance at Lina, but the way he moved was more alert. The tension in the back of her neck eased. She returned to what she was doing: filling out reports, for whom she wasn't quite sure, either Legion Security or Legion PIC. Ms. Yency oversaw it all as her image hovered over the padd. Name, address, occupation… Skip that one and go on to the next question.

"You must answer the questions in order," Yency told her brusquely, and the program wouldn't let her progress any farther. "Occupation?"

The prim woman's insistence was annoying in a new way that Lina couldn't put her finger on. Every time she looked at Yency, Lina got a mental picture of Gollum from *Lord of the Rings*.

Wait. Gollum was special effects.

"Don't take this the wrong way," Lina told Yency, "but are you real? Are you a real person, sitting there?"

"I am a computer-generated construct based upon a real person," "Yency" replied. "Basic information gathering does not require true human interaction. State your occupation."

Lina told the CGI Yency a rather generic "graphic designer" because Lon had said people might not be ready to be told that she was in the pornography business. Birthplace, education, mother's name, father's name, mother's mother's name…

Meanwhile, Jae ported off to a mission. Another wave of electrical sparks rushed into the lab. They crackled right past Lina's head – possibly through it, if she hadn't ducked in time – and snipped over to Wiley's station. She pulled the back of her sweater up like a hood and crouched down, scrunching her knees to make herself as small a target as possible.

Father's father's name, father's mother's name… A million dull questions later, she put the CGI Yency and the formpadd down and settled instead to studying her Panlingua, surprised that it was much easier. Maybe as her subconscious worked on last night's lesson, it had time to incorporate it more thoroughly.

She swiveled in her chair to read upside down (it alleviated some of the hours she'd already spent just sitting around on her backside), and Wiley cleared his throat loudly. He'd done that a number of times before when she hadn't sat in a chair in the standard way. She ignored him and kept studying.

Dellen was teleporting in and out as well amid waves of incoming sparkler messages. Wiley tended to ignore the sparklers. Lina deduced that such messages were meant to impress and thus somehow slide up the queue of emergencies. Wiley filed them in proper incoming order under strict triage guidelines.

It was a busy afternoon with new wonders to digest. As problems arose, a Legionnaire would sometimes meet with the people reporting it – by holographing in them as well as the room they occupied. It wasn't the actual people and their actual offices, but it looked real. The holograms around here were tricksy things. She should be wary of them.

But the technique allowed the Legionnaires to walk over to the people's own displays or windows or whatever and check out the situation themselves before beaming over. They could conference with a group as if they were actually in their presence. From this side of the conversation, it seemed as if the callers had come to Mega-Legion HQ in person to confer.

It was a most efficient way to conference call. Still Lina could still see the truth in Lon's remark that local duty was boring. In the few minutes between emergency calls and filing notes afterward, if there were two Legionnaires in the lab they were talking about the others and gossiping, just like people back at work. This gossip never seemed to disintegrate into people-bashing, though.

Once the conversation concerned Andri, the Legion's subcommander. Lina had met her for few minutes. She'd impressed her as efficient, thoughtful, and not possessing the habit of accusing innocent people of being mind controllers.

How interesting that Wiley suddenly started mentally broadcasting when they spoke of her. People gave off images or feelings or sometimes exclamations when they felt something strongly. Now vivid images of the pink-haired woman flashed in Lina's mind, though Wiley's voice remained in a conversational tone.

Wiley and Andri. And Wiley not letting on.

It was so nice that she could assign a name to the image she'd first seen Wiley broadcasting days ago. Even so, Lina shook her head and tried to guard against the images. That was personal stuff, not meant for her to overhear. Instead she concentrated on her studies, but she kept an ear out for word about Londo – of which there was none, probably due to her presence – and now also for anything on Andri. Apparently she was unattached but popular. Maybe Lina's decision to port in that *101 Ways* book had been inspired by one of her guides. She'd noticed that the book was no longer sitting out; Wiley must have tucked it away somewhere.

Lina woke abruptly from yet another unexpected nap. Only Dellen was present, tapping here and there on Wiley's communications console as if she were making mission notes, but when she saw that Lina was awake, she ambled over.

"I thought you were going to sleep all day."

"Sorry."

"I have to do some things in my office. I don't want to leave you here alo–"

Jae transported back to the lab in a haze of glittering dots. Dellen told him her situation, but almost as soon as she'd finished speaking, the board registered an emergency that Jae could handle easier than Dellen, so he left again.

Dellen gazed at his after-image and then signaled to Lina to follow her out of the lab. "I don't trust auto security, even if it's Dr. Mem-Bazer's system. You're coming with me. I'll make it quick." They entered the bottomless lift after Dellen signaled the computer to give Lina a floor surface to stand on, and Dellen blew out a breath. "It takes me by surprise, even now, that a man can be as beautiful as Jae. Or that cold."

Lina stared at the floor. If it could do that, why did Jae – "Jae, cold?" she asked when she realized what Dellen had said.

"Nothing touches him. Or maybe he doesn't allow himself to be touched." They hadn't gone down that far before the floor came to a halt and they exited into a dark corridor. Dellen strode off to the left at a determined pace. "I think he needs a good woman to show him the way. Settle him down, you know?"

"And you're just the woman to do that?" Textured floor, bare walls, ceiling... even the *lights* were dark.

Another sigh. "I wish."

"Can you turn up the lights?"

Dellen looked around. "The lights *are* up. We like it dark here. It gives a break from all the bright offices, reminds you that you're between duty at the moment. Tell you what, how'd you like to switch places? You can handle my missions and I can be Jae's prisoner for a few days."

For an instant Lina forgot the darkness and wondered if she could actually finagle a way out like that. To be out of here, free–!

Dellen caught her eye. "Joking," she said. "You're still–"

"A prisoner. So Jae needs settling?"

Dellen's small smile was a sad one. "A long time ago I was his flavor of the month" – or at least that was how the translator whispered it in Lina's ear – "and I thought, this is it. He really loves me. I was crazy about him and then – whump – it was over. He dumped me."

At their approach, a section of side wall brightened, and Dellen gestured at it. A hidden sliding door swooshed open to reveal a blindingly bright room inside.

"I'm just here for a few minutes," Dellen told the orange-skinned woman who sat at a monitor station.

"Yes, Multiplex. I'll hold your messages."

"My secretary," Dellen told Lina as she entered an inner office. Lina lingered in the doorway as Dellen fiddled with a few things on her desk, then grabbed a couple of coin-sized crystal disks from a shelf. She held them to her Legion ring for a moment.

"I thought so," Dellen murmured, and gathered one more disk. She searched the slight clutter on her desk until she found a tiny metallic packet, then deposited disks and packet on the secretary's desk. "This needs to go out right away to Terrippa Prime. Special messenger. Make it look like I sent it yesterday. Hand-delivery can be so slow."

"Terribly slow," her secretary assured her. "But it's the old-fashioned touch that personalizes it."

"Absolutely." Dellen shared a grin with her before she turned to Lina. "We're finished here," she announced and waved her out into the hall. They retraced their path back to the lab, but as soon as they were out of the secretary's earshot, Lina whispered, "Jae dumped you? He would do something like that?"

"He does that to everyone. Oh, about a year, year and a half later, he comes over to my place and apologizes profusely. Tells me how much he thinks about me. We had a crazy night." Her smile was faraway as Dellen recalled. "And then the next day he tells me, 'Thank you very much, but I've got to be going.'" She frowned as they exited the lift. "At least that time he was polite about it. I think he has improved his dumping skills over the years. You don't feel like such a piece of flotsam once he gets done with you."

"So you're saying he's had a lot of practice at it?"

"Hah! Jae is known for his affairs. Sometimes you don't know who it's with, but it's obvious he's at it again. Then someone gets dumped, and they're crying in the corners. It happens about every two, three weeks as if he schedules it. One thing Jaeson Rallene never has a dearth of is potential lovers, lined up and waiting for their chance. He has plans to give everyone that chance."

Dellen settled back at Wiley's monitor station and checked what they'd missed in the few minutes they'd been gone. "When it's going, he's totally immersed in the other person. And then you notice that he's drawing away, almost flaunting someone else in their face, and then – dump!"

It was the way Dellen spoke that made Lina think that she knew. Something in Lina's face may have betrayed her as well, for Dellen said in a very low voice, "Keep this confidential, treat it like Level 5 information. Jae likes other men... if you know what I mean."

Lina nodded to show Dellen that she already knew. "That's not uncommon on Earth," she said. The tidbit caused Dellen's eyebrow to rise.

"That kind likes short-term affairs," Dellen told Lina.

"I don't think that's necessarily true," Lina said. "I know gays who are in relationships just as long-lived as straights. Maybe Jae's background is the reason why he can't make a real commitment. He lost so much; maybe he's afraid of losing people again. Maybe he wants to be the one who lets them go, to have that kind of control in his life."

Dellen made an I'm-not-convinced sound.

Lina continued, "But I can't believe Jae would dump someone so unkindly. He seems so nice, so… enthusiastic. When he's in a good mood."

"Enthusiastic?" Dellen shrugged. "Maybe in an enthusiastically-going-toward-a-breakdown way. The same way he's always held himself apart from everyone else. After he dumped me the first time I thought that it was just him being Feithi, you know, the ultimate in evolution, looking down on us silly humans as if we were children. But from what I've read, the Feithi weren't that way at all. Sure, there was the Great Silence, but I don't think that was the same thing."

"Great Silence? What's that?"

8

Dellen pursed her lips, considered whom she was telling. She glanced at the board; no calls. "Feith wasn't a part of the Affiliated Systems," she began slowly. "Never was. They said that they couldn't agree with our ways of doing business and dealing with people, so they remained outside of the union, although they kept the alliance close. They always welcomed whoever wanted to visit their world, but it was rare that any of them would venture off Feith. They said they didn't need to leave Feith to see the universe, whatever that meant. Still, there were ambassadors and a few teachers, and every now and then a Feithi tourist would come through and attract attention.

"But then the AffSys developed new technology, the Focus. It… How to explain to a barbarian? It concentrated solar radiation, I guess you'd say. Sunshine. Word was that we were going to use it to warm up outer planets and make them habitable."

Lina could guess: "But the military had other plans?"

Dellen gave her a sharp look and then nodded. "So Earth's been through that as well. Yes, offensive uses were suggested. The Focus was a huge, bulky affair, expensive and incredibly complicated to make. There'd never be more than a handful of these Foci available. The military took the one working model and wanted to run it through some war games to see what it could do, to give the AffSys a reason to hand over any future Foci to them.

"There was a lot of debate in legislative chambers about it. A lot of public debate, too, but mostly governmental, behind closed doors." Dellen stopped. "I'm assuming you're going to be a Level Two when everything shakes out," she told Lina. "Most Legion spouses are. So this is Level Two I'm telling you."

"Not to go outside of Legion HQ or to Level One Legion personnel, or to family members of an age of minority." Lina nodded gravely.

"Yes. One day right in the middle of the Grand Assembly floor pop three Feithis, just there – no transporter, no nothing. Maybe they walked in while they were invisible.

"Mega-Legion HQ; Multiplex here."

Lina stepped back as an emergency call came through. She almost didn't catch the slight chew Dellen gave to her lips before she relayed it to the nearest Legion outpost for response. "Southred can handle this best," she told the Legionnaire there who was on comm duty. "And no, I don't know why Defense Systems didn't spot it sooner. I'll make a note for Dr. Mem-Bazer to check it out." Only after she was sure she'd relayed all pertinent information did she lean back in her chair. "Where were we?" she asked.

Lina dared to speak again. "You said the Feithi popped in. Maybe they weren't invisible; maybe they ported."

That made Dellen pause. "Maybe so," she said and continued. "The Feithi said that they'd been keeping tabs on the Focus situation and strongly suggested that the AffSys not even utilize it for peaceful purposes because of the potential of accident or misuse. The records show them actually begging the members to destroy the Focus and all data pertinent to it."

"But they didn't."

"The Feithi would never come out and make anyone do anything; it wasn't their way. The Assembly members talked their way around the ambassadors and finally said that they'd give the military one chance, just one try, with the Focus. Only to see what it could do. Satisfy everyone's curiosity. The Feithi tried one more time, insisted – *insisted!* There'd never been a record of a Feithi insisting on anything – that the AffSys drop the weapon, and the members politely told them no. They would take their advice into consideration after the war games, but no, there'd be war games. It wasn't right to censor scientific inquiry.

"And the Feithi left. Poof – Gone. Everyone thought that was odd enough, but when people started to look around, every last Feithi was gone from the AffSys, just disappeared. If they'd brought possessions, they'd left them behind. Non-Feithi who'd been on the planet suddenly found themselves back on their home worlds with no explanation.

"The word came in from the Unaffiliated Worlds, too: no Feithi. When the AffSys sent a communiqué to Feith, we got a brief return message that Feith had recalled all her people in order to hold a planet-wide council about the situation and discuss what they'd do. Then came the Great Silence: no communications in or out of Feith."

Listlessly Dellen drew a finger-picture against the writing that scrolled across the monitor's table. "It went on for three months. Three months with no word coming outside that atmosphere. Our best spying methods couldn't pick up the first frequency; our cameras went blank as soon as they pointed at the world. And still – and *still* – the military got their precious Focus to play with.

"Who was the idiot who talked the Grand Assembly into having the war games set up near Feith?" She shook her head. "They said it was so the Feithi could see first-hand how well we managed our own matters, how our weapons were not toys for children, but equipment for adults and handled responsibly. This would make the Feithi respect us. This would bring us closer to being their equals.

"But something went – The fleet gathered outside the Feithi system, the Focus was strung out and tuned, and just before the war games were scheduled to begin, one of the admirals actually landed on Feith – understand, no ships had been able to do that since the Great Silence had begun – and invited them to come back to his ships and oversee how the AffSys handled the operation.

"He was refused. It's on record, his last conversation face-to-face with the Feithi, and the Feithi told him and the recording camera that Feith had to do with life, not death, and would always uphold life. They said that they understood the AffSys's reasons for doing this, but that if people would step away from their own fears, they'd see that this weapon was not necessary.

"It's eerie. Fe-lisha Neallon, the last adult Feithi that anyone ever saw, turned right to the camera and said that whatever happened in the future, Feith forgave the AffSys for what it was about to do. Childhood was a difficult process, she said, and sometimes you have to make mistakes to learn. She hoped that the AffSys would learn from this mistake.

"She dismissed the admiral and he took his ship back to the war games. He wanted to have a good view of the proceedings – they had frozen asteroids set up outside the system, well away from any habitable anything – but something went wrong. Someone boggled the Focus. It hit Feith and vaporized everything on the surface. Everything."

Dellen clapped a hand to cover her mouth and closed her eyes. The memory was over fifteen years old but the wound was still fresh.

"What about the Focus?" Lina asked quietly. "Is it still being used somewhere?"

"Anything from it that was left we destroyed. All records were destroyed. The people who'd developed it had mind-wipes; they took them voluntarily. The mind-wipes were localized ones, so they still were able to function afterwards, but even so, a good three-quarters of them have committed suicide since."

"How was Jae able to survive? If the entire surface was–"

"He wasn't on Feith. He'd stowed away in the admiral's ship before it took off. He was a kid; he was curious. He'd never been off-world. And then they found him in the ship's wreckage–"

"Wreckage?"

"It caught the very edge of the blast. It was amazing that Jae could have survived at all, but Jae was Feithi. They say he reacted with instinct, using powers that he's forgotten now in all the trauma. He managed to stay alive long enough to get to the only intact lifepod, but even it was in bad shape by the time Maximus found it. The Focus itself, too, was lost, as was its control ship. The power was too much for it. Half of it disintegrated."

Silence hung in the room as Lina thought and Dellen remembered.

"So Maximus saved Jae," Lina realized. Londo's adoptive father.

Dellen nodded. "Psyche was commander back then. The entire Legion – every last member, we left headquarters and all outposts deserted – ran to Feith to help, but there was nothing left. No sign of life showed on any sensor, just AffSys personnel who survived the wrecks of some of the fleet. Maximus got there the same time as the first ships of Legionnaires, which was almost a day after it happened. It was a day later that he found Jae's lifepod – sheer chance, a tiny, powerless lifepod drifting in a star system. It could have been missed for centuries, considered another piece of system junk floating around."

"Space is pretty big," Lina said carefully. Dellen didn't respond. "How much of a coincidence was it that a weapon so far away from a world as to be outside its system manages, by sheer accident, to hit that world? If it was a Focus, someone would have had to focus it to make it work, right?"

Dellen's voice was bitter. "Don't think about it and it won't worry you."

"Is that what Jae meant," Lina said.

"How so?"

"When he said that it didn't matter if it were deliberate or an accident. That everyone who could have been responsible had died."

"That's about it," Dellen said. "Feith is dead, and the people who killed it are, too. Only Jae remains. Only Jae." The monitors buzzed and Dellen went back to work.

This jetlag was embarrassing, especially after such a chilling story, which should have kept her wide awake. It seemed to Lina that she was falling asleep all the time. What must these paras think of the lazy Terran? After she woke Lina tried searching her padd for information about cures for interstellar jet lag and wondered if she should bother Riz to see if she could do anything. Riz probably had a lot more important things to do.

You need to exercise, her guides told her.

"I know. But there's not much I can do about it, is there?" **Is it some kind of trick? Something to do with the arrest and mind control?**

Don't let them hear that theory, they quickly insisted.

"Ah."

Wiley cleared his throat again from his station. He didn't like people talking to themselves, although he did the same thing in mumbles.

On a whim, Lina requested information within the tourism section of her padd about the Pares Restaurant and was informed that it featured the best cuisine in obscure interstellar fare as well as an eclectic mixture of entertainment. The site sampled what she now thought of as The No-Talent Quartet. They had a beat now but it plodded and skipped, accented with tambourine. The whistle had three notes instead of just the one. Stupid was la-la-laing like there was no tomorrow, paying no attention to what the whistle was playing or if he had anything even resembling a tune.

At least the joint had good food. Her stomach growled. It had been such a long time since lunch. She was not going to steal any more food! These people hadn't eaten that she'd seen. They'd go on missions and save the world and sometimes they'd go back to quarters to rest, like Wiley was doing now, but they hadn't gotten any food from the break room. They'd been working hard and hadn't complained.

So she meditated to pass the time, reminding herself that she really needed to do so more regularly than she had been. When she finished she felt a lot holier, but she was still hungry. Dellen came out of the break room with a mug of something green and slimy-looking. It did a lot to curb Lina's appetite.

"Is there any place I can go to run or do something active?" Lina asked.

"You can access a full range of gym programs," Dellen said. "Let me–" The monitor board buzzed and Dellen trotted to the comm station. "State your emergency." The main screen lit up to show a woman reporting from a call station with chaos erupting behind her.

Follow her!

Lina jumped out of her chair, dropping her study padd. "I'm coming with you," she told Dellen.

"This is no time–"

"I have to come. *They* say so."

"No." Dellen teleported away.

"Too bad," Lina said, porting to whatever place that was on the screen.

She appeared in the middle of a smoky plaza. Shrieks and excited shouts pierced the haze. People ran in every direction. Glowing lines of silent laser fire rippled through the billows of dark gray that fell slowly out of the sky. Sniper – maybe plural.

Dellen did a double-take at Lina. "Go back!" she hissed.

"There's a command center, watching the reaction and coordinating." Lina pointed to the fog above and ahead of them. "But it's… a diversion. This isn't what they're really here for."

"Get the blaze out of here! That's an order!" Dellen multiplied into three and darted up into the smoke.

Lina looked around. A diversion for what? There was something going on down the street to her right. Her guides gave her a push.

She started to run at an easy pace as she tried to focus. Whoever and whatever it was, they were being very calculating at something, trying to blend in with a crowd. Her guides showed her Joe Cool, James Bond, slick characters with sunglasses and sneaky attitudes.

She passed the first long block, part of the sparse but fervent stampede away from the attack. By the second block, the few bystanders were stopping to watch the runners curiously. The smoke didn't reach this far. A low level of panic gathered as word spread.

In a wide city square, people collected in small groups to exchange information. News screens hovered over the pavement. Two aircars sat on ground level. Lina slowed to a jog. It was so difficult to try to figure out what was out of the ordinary in such an alien environ – There.

Lina zeroed in on them, thanking her guides. A woman and child were walking toward one of those flying-saucer taxis. People looking like they were just part of the various gathering clumps shuffled toward them. More came in from another side, creating a box around the two. The woman never noticed. Gathering the child close, she paused to gawp at the runners.

One man grabbed the woman before she could realize what was going on. Another took hold of the kid.

Lina ported the four involved over to her, unable to differentiate between bodies this quickly. They all seemed stunned as she ported them again, splitting them up. "Don't worry," she told the woman as she clutched at her child. "I've got 'em. You just go where you want to now."

"Th-thank you," the woman said as she caught her breath. The child was wild-eyed, his mouth hanging open. "Are you a Legionnaire?"

"No, ma'am," Lina replied. "Just married to one."

Lina teleported the two would-be kidnappers back to the group she had pulled them out of and sat down to wait for Dellen to track her bracelet. The woman and kid quickly took another taxi and left.

Anytime one of the bad guys tried to escape the area, Lina would port them back into the middle of it. It didn't take them long to figure out that they weren't going anywhere. A couple pulled what looked like guns out of their pockets, but Lina ported those into a pile next to her. She hoped the guys didn't have teleportation capabilities. She didn't feel confident following them. She needed a picture for a landing target.

Her wait lasted for some time. At last Dellen flew down beside her. "Lina! You've got to get back to Headquarters right now. I'll only issue a warning this time, but–"

Lina pointed at the group. "I have no idea what to do with these people. Your advice, please."

Dellen frowned at the people. "What's going on?"

"Attempted kidnapping. And they pulled some guns, too." She pointed at the pile next to her. "They were using the snipers as a diversion."

"Kidnapping? Who?"

"Some woman with a kid. They're gone now."

Dellen stood there with her hands on her hips, surveying the situation. She spoke into her ring. Within a minute an aircar with what Lina recognized as police markings swooped down on the plaza. Dellen flew over to meet it and Lina followed on foot while making sure her sweater sleeve covered her prisoner bracelet.

They had already started gathering up the suspects by the time Lina reached them. She hung back so she wouldn't interfere. An officer approached her. "This is police business," the woman told her. "Stand back from the area. These are dangerous criminals."

"Sure, officer," Lina said and ported back to Headquarters.

Wiley's lab reverberated with alarms.

"Shut up!" Lina shouted. "I'm back!" The alarms quieted.

It didn't take long for Dellen to return. "Shards, Lina," she said as she appeared. "Did you know who those guys were?"

"No idea," Lina said, setting down her study padd. "Did you get them all?"

"Every last one. They were from the Ogier Liberation Front."

"Ogier. I don't know that one."

"Let's just say they're a nasty bunch. They were going after one of the Signet heirs."

"Somebody rich? For a ransom to finance their cause?" Lina guessed.

"One of the richest people in the galaxy. Dari Signet." Dellen said it as if of course Lina knew.

"How's the kid?"

"Scared. He knows what almost happened. Dari's quaking in her boots. Maybe next time she won't go out without a bodyguard, especially with her son in tow. Shards and splinters, the stupidity of some people!"

"Was anyone hurt with the snipers?"

"One critically, about six others less so." The sides of Dellen's mouth quirked. "No one hurt after I arrived. Good thing they managed to get a call through so early in the game."

"That's good. And you?" There was something wrong…

"Oh, I just caught the edge of a shot on one of my dupes' wrists. Lina, I won't make a special notation of this, but don't do anything like that again."

"I'll try not to." Lina looked at Dellen's wrist. A three-inch ribbon of seared flesh scarred it. According to the Legion record, Dellen's solid-holographic duplicates, although controlled by her, could be damaged and thus injure her with feedback. One of her duplicates must have been severely hit to make this much mess.

"I might be able to handle that," Lina offered.

"What?"

"Heal it. Psychically."

"You can do that?"

"I can at least make it feel better."

Dellen considered and then shook her head. "It'll wait until I can get to Medical," she said. She glanced from her wrist to Lina's face. "Does this ability have some-thing to do with how you and Valiant–?"

The monitor beeped and a screen scrolled down in front of them. Lina automati-cally moved to get out of the picture, but she heard someone say, "That's her!" She turned to see the woman she'd rescued, Dari Signet, and her son with some officers.

"Hello again." Lina bobbed her head. "I hope you're all right."

"We are, thanks to you," the woman declared. She ran her hand through the thick blue stubble that was her hair. "How can we thank you enough?"

"Dellen, I mean, Multiplex here says that you should consider using a bodyguard the next time you go out. A pity things have to be that way."

The woman looked abashed. "I thought I didn't need one any more. I was wrong." She peered at Lina. "You said you weren't a Legionnaire."

"Just married to one," Lina said, conversationally. She didn't think she should have told that much. Too late now; downplay it. "There are a lot of Legionnaires."

"Yes, there are. At least tell me who you are."

"I'm Carolina O'Kelly from Earth."

"Earth? That's where Valiant's from, isn't it?"

Lina smiled pleasantly; it never even occurred to this woman that Valiant could be her husband. "Oh, you've heard of the planet. Yes, I believe Valiant's from there, too."

The woman straightened up as she obviously felt more in control of the situation. "Earth. Well. Can we meet somewhere? I'd like to thank you in person."

Lina remained pleasant. "Thank you very much, but I'm under house arrest." She raised her wrist so they could see the locator. "I wasn't supposed to be out helping anyone. I think if I broke out again I would get in serious trouble."

"House arrest?" The woman looked puzzled before her brows came together and her smile turned into a straight line. "Whom do I speak to about this? Where is Commander Magnos?"

"Ah, we have an emergency call coming in," Dellen lied hurriedly. "Legion Headquarters out." The screen blanked.

"Well. At least I got a nice run out of it," Lina said as Dellen frowned at her. Lina picked up her study padd and plopped sideways into her prisoner chair, back and legs supported by its arms.

"This is all very fun for you, isn't it?" Dellen said.

Lina looked up from her padd. "Not really."

"This is a serious job. Life or death a lot of the time. I stretched the rules for you this once only. If you hadn't dealt with the OLF, I wouldn't be so lenient."

"And I appreciate it, really. I'm a prisoner. Noted and logged, ma'am."

"Right. Don't do it again."

Jae got back from a particularly grueling mission and left to get an hour's sleep. He had perked up remarkably from his earlier depression. He was a funny guy when he wasn't suicidal, and like Lon in a lot of ways. Lina could see how he could be Londo's best friend. It was good they had each other especially now with the looming crisis about Aiko… Orenya.

On impulse, she asked her study padd if the word "Orenya" had a meaning. She sorted through different languages until she came to what she thought was the correct one: a flower that withstood extremities of weather on some distant planet. The worse the storms, the more beautiful the bloom.

Lon had said Aiko was strong and nearly invulnerable. Lina remembered that she was very beautiful, too. Lina determined that she was not going to be jealous of the dead or soon-to-be so, especially when Londo had chosen her over Aiko while the woman was still very much alive.

Well, not very much jealous. Lina was so new to love, she wasn't sure what she felt any more.

She could cover up the jealousy with grief, but she could only grieve for Aiko if she knew her better. Londo needed her to know Aiko better, so as Wiley returned, Lina went through the public Legion records and reviewed Orenya's career.

"Monumental" would be an understatement. Aiko was a turning point in her world's history. She had saved entire continents from disaster, had diverted hurtling asteroids from collisions with space stations. It was a record that rivaled Londo's or Maximus', and the public adored her.

She was not only heroic, she was young, beautiful and refined. Lina wondered if she spent all her off-duty hours going to medal ceremonies, for Aiko had earned every one there was, it seemed, maybe twice or three times over. She had buildings and schools named after her by the grateful public. Hundreds of thousands of little girls were now walking around with the first name of Orenya in her honor.

Lina scrolled quickly through recent celebrity news articles. There they were: the galaxy's hottest couple, Valiant and Orenya. They'd kept it at rumor stage, never quite saying that they were an item, but they were seen together enough. "Just friends," they'd tell the press.

But Lina had seen the look in Aiko's eyes. Maybe Londo had just been friends with Aiko, but it had not been a mutual feeling. Aiko burned hot for him.

And now Lina had taken Londo away from her, just days before she was to die. *So God, what is that all about? Are You playing a cosmic practical joke on her? I don't think it's very funny. I think it's damned pathetic. What kind of person would do that to a woman like Aiko?* Certainly she deserved better!

Trust in the ways of the universe, her guides whispered.

"Well, that's damned hard to do at times like this!"

Wiley cleared his throat.

She was famished. And thirsty. She was the Sahara come to withering life. She would have asked Wiley, but he looked very busy over there tabulating results from her porting to Earth earlier and coming up with theories when he wasn't handling break-ins by remote control and rescheduling available Legionnaires at Outposts to trouble spots on the far side of the galactic sector.

Dellen was in and out on minor missions. She grumbled about the stupidity of people that they'd get in such messes. According to Dellen, the entire population of Sarastor's system knew when she was around, so they could do these idiot things and bother her. Lina dozed off yet again over her study padd.

She came awake when a loud-speaking man came on the monitors. Lina blinked. Wiley was here; no one else. She'd slept for maybe fifteen minutes. Maybe if she could get herself to take a long nap, she wouldn't take so many of them. It had to be some kind of drug they'd slipped her, even if they hadn't given her pills or an injection. Sneaky bastards. The situation was irritating, and she was irritated enough as it was. Being tired always made her cranky. Being tired and hungry made her doubly so. She needed water, caffeine and calories.

Jae came in to check in with Wiley. Lina got up to join them. "Is it okay if I go back to quarters for the night?" she asked.

Jae opened his mouth in surprise. "Night? It's not even evening yet. You stay in here when you're up and about," he said, so Lina sat back down and studied some more.

She was so hungry. She was starving, but no one here sat down to eat, not even in the break room. Why had she only had the one slice of pizza for lunch? She'd been excited to be back home. She'd been stupid! She didn't understand the foods available here on the replicators. It was Greek to her, and even the food definitions on her padd were incomprehensible. So what if *ropeji* had a texture reminiscent of *ces-ces* and would interest those who also liked *anto*?

She tried one selection and couldn't dump it into the recycler fast enough.

Everyone on duty had their awful drinks. Watching them caused Lina's throat to contract with thirst. She tried drinking out of her hands from the bathroom sink – the water there was better than the stuff in the break room (next thing you'd know, she'd be drinking out of the toilet like a cat, except that there wasn't a Terran-style toilet here) – and the Legionnaires' medium-busy day went on.

She studied more verb conjugations. Who the hell used past class-sensitive imperfect? Her anger at the damned Sarastoran language raged as she became tireder and hungrier.

If they hadn't eaten so early on Earth she wouldn't be so hungry now! But they had, because Jae had been hungry. He'd eaten all the pizza, not leaving her a second slice. Of course, she hadn't wanted a second slice then. So what? He should have left her a slice. Selfish Jae! She sat and fumed. When Dellen asked her a question, she snapped back an answer and shut up.

Dellen and Jae were talking at the main console while Wiley worked constructing a small gerbil habitrail across the room. A habitrail with flamethrowers built in. When Lina came over to check it out, he tapped the thing and pointed at her hand. So she'd picked off one of the little blinky doodads from the side of it, so what?

"Do. Not. Touch," he insisted, and she replaced it even as it began to vibrate slightly in her fingers. Wiley wasn't any fun, so Lina approached the other two. "What is the acceptable time for prisoners to return to quarters?" she asked carefully. Maybe a little too precisely.

"What, you don't like our company?" Jae asked her. "We still have a long time yet."

"Sarastor days are too damned long!" she grumbled.

"You've been studying too much. Find something recreational on that thing." Jae waved at her study padd, dismissing her.

Sarastor games were stupid. You had a bunch of complicated rules to follow and everything had to be done perfectly, no exceptions. The computer caught her every time she tried to take a shortcut and speed things up. She threw her padd on the floor and it skidded a satisfying distance.

She woke again with Wiley standing over her with his tricorder in his hand. He frowned at it.

"Please tell me I'm dying, Doc," she groaned.

"Don't call me 'Doc.' I don't understand how you healed so fast yesterday. Jae!" Wiley called without looking around with either eye. Over there Jae glanced up from whatever he and Dellen were doing. "When was the last time you fed Lina?"

"Huh?"

"He didn't," Lina said. "I fed him when we went to Earth, about two million hours ago. He took all the pizza. And now it's, what, midnight? Can I please go back to quarters now? I'm starving!"

"No wonder your blood sugar's so low. Dehydrated, too. Jae!"

The blond Legionnaire ambled over. "What, didn't anyone take her to the cafeteria?"

"She's your charge. If you wanted us to do that, you should have assigned someone."

Jae scowled at Lina. "Why didn't you say anything?"

She scowled back. "I don't know what the rules are. You have such a long day, I thought maybe y'all ate at a weird time. Or that there was no eating on duty. And y'all have rotten-tasting water here. It's crap."

"All you had to do was open your mouth and speak."

"I've been trying to get back to quarters for the past—" She checked the chronometer "—two and a half hours, Sarastoran. Lon's got some snacks there."

Jae rolled his eyes. "What, do you think we starve our prisoners?"

"I don't know. For all I know, you guys spend all your money on big buildings and all this fancy stuff in here and can't afford food. How am I supposed to know what you do?"

Wiley was much amused with Jae's situation. He shook his head. "I may have to make a note of this for future discussion," he said solemnly. "Lina, do they starve prisoners on Earth?"

She paused. "In some countries."

"Grigach!" Jae exclaimed softly. Back at the monitor Dellen was watching them, shaking her head and holding her hand over her mouth as she tried not to laugh. How irritating.

"And have you ever been starved? Food withheld for some reason?" Wiley asked as he made notes on his invisible computer.

"What did Londo tell you?" Lina rose up out of the chair. Londo liked to brag about sex; would he tell people everything she told him?

"Okay, okay! My fault!" Jae said loudly. "Put it on the record. *Mea culpa!* One half hour for dinner break. You can go to quarters, Lina."

"Can I buzz back to Earth for a couple seconds?" she asked quickly. "Lon's got a bunch of crap in his cabinets."

"No!" Jae's reply was sharp. "I'm sure that whatever's there is just fine. Or you can get something from the replicator."

"Yes SIR!" Lina considered the white bracelet on her arm. She glanced up to see Wiley watching her. She kept her gaze even with his as she asked, "When does my half-hour start?"

"Now," Jae said, turning away angrily, angry at himself, angry at her for not having said anything. She disappeared behind him.

"So…" Wiley said conversationally, glancing at the Legion Security monitors screen hovering above his wrist. He connected its data to his main board to keep watch on time and distance, and engaged the kickback array to bring in sensors from halfway across the sector as well. "Exactly what does Lon keep in his room?"

"I'm sure it's good, Terran food," Jae growled.

"Um hm. I once saw him eat a container of solidified acid," Wiley remarked as he made his way back to the main board, "and then washed it down with four liters of Ligorian sour beer."

"Ohh… Grigach!! I'll take care of this!" Jae threw his hands in the air and stomped out of the lab.

"This should be interesting," Wiley told Dellen. "Care to place a wager?"

"What?" Dellen blinked and understood. "She went to Earth."

"I gave her five minutes before I report an escape." He bit his lip thoughtfully. "I may need to cut back on her nanomeds."

"It'll just take Jae a few minutes to get down to her quarters…"

"So. Who's going to get there first?" The two of them hung over the readout of the betting boards and considered.

Lina arrived back in Lon's quarters out of breath. She held two bags of cans and boxes she'd reached into the pantry for, just letting them tumble into the bags. She'd sort later. Every time she'd tried to move, there had been Bran-Bran the feline road-block! She couldn't blame him; he never liked when she went away for days, but why did that widdle fuzzy guy have to choose tonight?

"Your porting is taking longer today," Jae's voice said from behind her.

She whirled and gasped. He stood there scowling like Londo could, his arms crossed in front of his chest.

"Whether you like it or not, Lina, you have to obey orders."

"I'm a prisoner."

"You're under house arrest."

"Equals prisoner."

"Right, equals prisoner. So you have to follow orders. Puter!" Two beeps. "Get me Wiley. Wiley, didn't you get any kind of alarm on Lina?"

"Alarm?" Wiley answered mildly. "Let me check. No, no alarm. Is there anything to be alarmed about?"

"Pay up." They could hear Dellen's voice in the background.

"Rallene out!" Jae almost said something that he'd regret, but managed not to. She was dumping the contents of those bags onto the dining table, catching tins and smaller bags and glass jars before they could roll away. "Lina."

"Yes, Jae."

She didn't look at him.

"I know that this doesn't seem very serious to you."

"Whatever gives you that idea? I have had my freedom taken away from me. I'm not allowed to control my own life. Of course I take it seriously." She sorted through things, stacking them on the counters in the kitchen.

"And it is serious. It's a serious charge."

"Um hm. Would you like some hot tea?" Boiling the water might get rid of the taste.

"No. So for a serious charge – like this – you have to toe the line. You have to follow the few, simple orders I give you and it'll count in your favor. It really will."

She glanced up at him. "I will be happy to do that as long as your orders are reasonable. This order was not. I can't live on chips and contaminated water for four or five days. Well, I can, but you wouldn't like me if I did. Have you eaten yet? I can fix you something."

"Lina–!" He scratched the back of his head to keep what he wanted to say from coming out. "I've had my dinner. And two snacks. I'm fine." He added with almost no pause, "Thanks."

She nodded and turned to scrounge through drawers for implements. Lon had a pot. One pot. That was all she needed for now, she supposed. "If it'll make you happy, I don't have too much here, either. I was going on vacation, so I tried to clean out my supplies so nothing would go bad. These are all dried or canned goods. And I hadn't gone vegetarian back then; I can't eat half this stuff." If she made enough for two, she could have more time next time to eat. Or maybe tomorrow morning she could start something first thing and then just reheat it for lunch.

Jae watched as she drew tap water into the pot and then poured the contents of an envelope in. She was going to cook – to cook food.

He went through Lon's refrigerator drawers and found nothing that he would classify as making a solid meal. Ducking around Lina, he investigated the cabinets. Snacks. Not real food. He checked the liquor cabinet – Lina watched him curiously; maybe she hadn't realized it was there – and there were only alcoholic beverages. Sometimes Lon stored drink mixers and fruit in it.

"Oh damn, forgot the can opener," Lina muttered. She looked at the can she held and thought for a moment. The top disappeared, and she poured the contents in with the rice. Beans and rice. She didn't have any onions or herbs to jazz it up, no tomatoes or green peppers, but it would be nourishing. Now how did you use this heating unit again? She tried to read the panel instead of cheating with her padd.

Jae sniffed the pot suspiciously. "You like this?" he asked her.

"No," she replied as she put the rest of her cans and packets away. "It's plain and it's going to taste plain. But it's calories and fiber and vitamins. It'll keep me alive until this prisoner shit is over with."

"Lina."

"Jae. Officer Neutrino." Her eyes flashed at him as she faced him stiffly. "I have worked most of my life to keep a roof over my head and food on my table. Apparently now I have an impervion roof over my head, and by god I'm going to have food on my table one way or another. You don't own me. The Legion does not own me. I provide for myself, do you hear?"

Jae cocked his head at her. There was something under the words… "So are you saying there was a time when you didn't have food?"

She ignored him as she turned to continue her work.

"Why no, Jae," he imitated her in a falsetto voice. "We always had lots to eat. My parents gave me everything I ever wanted."

"Drop it." She slammed a cabinet door and went down the hall to the bathroom to brush her hair in front of the mirror there while the food cooked. Jae peeked around the open door at her, satisfied that she wasn't doing anything private.

"Pushed a few buttons tonight, did we?"

"I don't know why Lon has to blab everything."

"He didn't."

She spared him a glance. "But Wiley said–"

"Wiley was investigating the culture of Earth. Some planets do starve prisoners, Lina. And some parents mistreat their children."

"Some do," she told him too blandly as she washed her hands. She pushed past him in the hallway. "And some children learn to take care of themselves, no matter what others may do to them. It's called growing up."

"So when did you have to grow up, Lie?"

"A little earlier than others. When I finally figured out that my father wanted me dead."

Jae paused at that, watching her get the pot of rice out of the thermo-unit and set it on the counter. "When did you realize that?"

She took her time in answering. "One very long weekend when I was eight. I was a dumb kid. I should have realized it years earlier." She turned to him, looked him straight in the face. "Whatever you do, don't tell Lon. He has a temper – worse than mine."

"What, you can keep things from him?"

"I don't know. We haven't had much time together to find out, have we?"

She hunted through the cabinets for a bowl and spoon. Fifteen Sarastoran minutes left for supper, and the rice still had to sit for five minutes, Terran.

"Get your jacket, Lina. Puter, get me Wiley or Dellen." Two beeps. "I'm taking the prisoner out for a while. Give me a buzz if you have something big."

"Will do, Jae." Dellen's voice.

Lina stayed in her place at the counter. "We're going out?"

"Get your jacket," Jae said slowly in a sing-song voice, as if he were talking to a child. "Pleeeease."

"Well. If you put it that way." The jacket appeared on her hand. The beans and rice – "Will these cold drawers take a hot pot without cracking?"

"Why not?"

Lina ate in the main family cafeteria, down four levels from Lon's quarters. It was late evening on this 20-hour day, but some families were still there.

The place was more like a nice restaurant than a cafeteria. You could either go straight to your assigned booth to be served, or there was a line where you could peruse cooking stations to make your choices. You didn't get a tray. Floating monitors followed you to record calories and food type as you made your choices, dutifully clicked off from daily food allowances.

Jae pointed out the fresh foods available and she chose the ones that he recommended. She ordered two large goblets of water, fresh, cold and wonderful. He explained that drinking water had to be ordered specifically as drinking water; regular water was not anywhere near as pure. Wash water was a little better than that. When they'd finished making their choices, servers in white jumpsuits and swim caps emerged from behind a wall with cloth-covered carts and domed plates to follow them. The service of knives and sporks was golden. Definitely not the K&W Cafeteria back home!

Jae pointed at a booth near the far wall, and they proceeded across the room. In attendance were children and single parents; the other parent would be a Legionnaire and all the Legionnaires were gone.

When they were settled, Jae started to quiz her about her own parents but some of the Legion spouses came up to introduce themselves before returning to their family groups. One woman in particular came over with a curious smile.

"That was such an interesting wedding ceremony," she said. She looked not much older than Lina, despite being bald except for a patterned fuzz of platinum-white hair that came across as almost lace against her dark, orangey head. Of course she was tall, but her limbs were long in proportion to her torso, making her seem coltish and exotic. "Hi, I'm Deranged. Congratulations again."

Lina kept a straight face. Names were just names, weren't they? "Deranged."

"Derainjt. Call me Rainj."

"I'm Lina. I'm so pleased to meet you away from the crowds. Everything was a little crazy yesterday." Had it been just yesterday?

"You're from Earth, so you don't know everyone in the Legion, much less the families. I'm Jikker's wife… He's Kinesis."

Lina nodded and lied, "Oh yes," as if she remembered someone named that and was impressed.

"You must know that rumors are flying," Rainj disclosed. She glanced at Jae quickly and gave a uncertain bob of her head, a half-bow. "Of course everything's being kept from the Outside. But Inside… We've been wondering why you haven't been around. There was a spousal meeting today–"

"I'm under house arrest," Lina said, holding up her arm to show the bracelet. Now she could understand the words "PRISONER LOCATOR" that ran along it in big black block letters. "I'm sorry; I'd love to figure out what's expected of me as well as meeting everyone. But they've been keeping me in chains up there. Whippings every hour on the hour."

Jae sat with his head propped on his hand. "Go on, go on," he urged. "Get to the part about the steel slats under your fingernails."

"Those, too," Lina nodded. "Ouch."

The woman had turned a little pale. "But…" she began.

"It will be cleared up immediately when Commander Magnos gets back," Jae reassured her. "We're only taking some minor precautions. There've been some odd things going on and we thought that we'd just play it safe."

"Hot oil torture twice a day," Lina told Rainj. "Call Amnesty Interstellar. Do they have lawyers Out Here? I mean, seriously?"

"Does… Does this mean that the marriage was false?"

"Not on your life!" Lina declared quickly.

"Absolutely not," Jae reassured Rainj. "We'll have this all cleared up in a few days and I'm sure the Rands will be having a big party – which you owe us, Lina – and everyone will get to know each other."

"O'Kelly," Lina told him. "My name's Lina O'Kelly. Not Rand."

"Uh huh."

"So nice." Rainj smiled hesitantly and backed away.

Jae groaned very softly as he turned back to Lina. "I hate to hear what that's going to turn into by tomorrow morning," he said softly to her. "Chains and whips?"

She examined her fingernails. "And steel slats."

"When we go out…"

"Hm? Out? As in 'out'?"

"You're going to disavow all knowledge of anything having to do with Londo and being a prisoner."

"That's kind of hard, isn't it? I mean with…" She held up her arm with the locator and watched as the print turned from black to a white that precisely matched the material. She could feel him talking to something within it. "Oh."

"It's just a bracelet," Jae told her with a serious smile.

"So… who's this Valiant guy anyway? Have I met him? He's the cute one, right?"

9

This time the drop in the clear lift tube wasn't far. Down here the lift was definitely different from upper levels. Lina could step into the open space and feel something solid underneath her feet. Jae explained that above the fifteenth floor the mechanics on the tubes didn't work unless officially commanded by someone wearing a Legion ring. That ensured that non-secure personnel didn't go where they weren't allowed.

Outside, Lina made a big deal of getting out in the fresh air.

"Would you like some more?" Jae asked mischievously.

"Sure," she said, wondering what it was about. "I trust you. Lead on."

He picked her up in his arms and flew straight up!

"Yow!" Lina clutched his neck.

"Didn't I tell you not to trust me?" Jae bared his teeth in a frightful grin at her reaction.

"Oh god, don't look down!" She tucked her head under his chin to protect herself.

"Relax. You'll get used to it," he assured her. "Just think: you're out of headquarters now. Enjoy."

Jae's arms around her seemed strong and safe enough. He was a parahero just like Londo, right? Londo wouldn't drop her and neither would Jae. These anti-gravity setups had likely been around for years, with all the kinks worked out. Jae's Legion ring was probably equipped with special air bags, just in case. Despite herself, Lina cracked opened her eyes and peeked around.

The city stretched out to the ever-so-slightly curved horizon. Now and then she saw what might be a park, but she couldn't be sure. Streams of air traffic made light-ribbons in the sky below them.

They swept over the city in silent flight. Wind and air pressure changes never bothered them, a function of the wondrous Legion ring. Ahead loomed an area even more brightly lit than others. There lights flashed and bright pictures of people and symbols hung in the air around structures big as arenas. Jae landed them lightly on the pavement outside a wide, garish entryway and set Lina down. He walked quickly toward the entrance.

She hung back. "Um, am I dressed for this? I'm a little informal," she said. Jeans and tee shirt, tropical jacket, while he was in his snazzy Neutrino uniform.

"You're fine," he said. He took her hand and practically dragged her inside.

It was a casino or a mammoth sports bar. The entry opened into a rotunda with several smaller but related sections scattered through lower arches. Server stations sat behind longer tables with stools. Those couldn't be anything but bars. Wall-to-wall people laughed and drank under multi-colored, shimmering lights, shouting to each other to be heard. Some just sat at tables and silently watched 3-D screens. Trash-can-sized tables scuttled food and drink to the customers: robot servers?

Against one wall was a set of whirling, multicolored video screens that stopped soon enough, setting off a round of cheers and groans. Jae pulled Lina past some patrons moving in the opposite direction. Here individual tables held lit centerpieces that involved a spiral game with juggling multicolored balls of light.

Drums beat insistently within one of the smaller casino areas. Lina could see people's heads bobbing over the crowd as if they were jumping in unison… or maybe dancing. Brrr – Very primitive.

An awed murmur of "Neutrino," rippled through the crowd, and a path opened before them even as some of the floating TV screens began to show his image. The area around them quieted in amazement. One by one, the onlookers bowed to Jae. Lina reminded herself that Jae was as famous here as Valiant was on Earth – or here. She hurried after him as he strode past the throng, ignoring them. Beyond their immediate area, the roar and dazzle of the casino continued unabated.

Lina was afraid to speak out loud with these people listening. **Where are we going?**

He didn't hesitate to reply, in the over-enunciated way Legion non-telepaths were taught to speak to telepaths, **You'll find out. **

They reached the back side of the casino and Jae ducked through some double doors. Blessed silence lay behind them. A long, empty white hallway stretched ahead. Jae leaned against the doors a second to catch his breath.

"I hate that," was all he said before he strode off again.

"Why were they doing that?" Lina asked as she caught up to his side. "Because you're a Legionnaire, or because you're the Last Feithi? They wouldn't do that for Londo, would they?"

He scowled at nothing. "It's getting worse."

Okay, so he didn't want to discuss it. Change subjects. "So, is this a casino? It looks like one. I've never been in a casino."

"You might call it more of an entertainment club," Jae said. "There it is." He pointed at a door to the right. A handwritten sign had been taped – tape, here? – to the wall. It said "Terran Zone" in English with more written underneath it in what Lina could only deduce were other languages. Yes, there was French, then Spanish. And there were some Cyrillic letters, Asiatic characters, and what looked like the flowing language of Arabic.

"Terran Zone?"

"You seemed a little down to me." He gave her an innocent look. "Maybe more than a little homesick."

She broke into a radiant smile. "That I am. Well, let's see what this hive of villainy has to offer. 'We must be cautious.'" She pushed open the door.

What first caught her attention was the music. Familiar songs played softly on boom boxes scattered about the area. C&W came from down and to the left; Broadway, from the right. She got the distinct impression that the restricted volume was to save batteries and not to avoid clashing styles.

The entry lay a flight above the main level of the room, an octagonal affair with Earth-type ferns and brass trim. Through some columns she could almost see a raised dais or stage on the far side from the bar proper, which was tucked below the stairs. Lots of tiny tables held a medium-sized crowd. They were just as noisy as the crowd in the first room, and again, there were those spiral centerpiece games on some of the tables. They *ching*ed as the balls of light went round and round inside them, creating their own internal music.

Jae regarded the room idly. "Too tame for me. No one's even dancing. Does it look like home to you?" he asked.

"At least it has music. And I guess a bar is a bar is a bar. There was a time in my life when I practically lived in bars. Gay bars," she added, to shock him. "It'll do nicely." She had forgotten how much ambience music could provide.

A man looked up from below and rose to greet them. "Neutrino!" he called, climbing the stairs. "You came back again. Good to have you."

"Hello, ah…"

"Ernst."

"Ernst," Jae said, shaking his hand. "What, no fights?"

The big, dark-bearded man spread his arms in a show of innocence. He wore fashionable tarps, but tighter than Lina had yet seen. He was slightly shorter than Lina – what a relief. But he was burly as a dockworker, and had a grin that could rival the spotlights outside. "Not tonight. We're all very well behaved here, as you can witness. But I see you've brought a beautiful companion. Hello, Starfleet," he finished in English.

Lina winkled her nose at the outrageousness of this man. "Nice to meet you, Ernst," she replied.

Jae looked at her. "Why does he call you that?"

"It's what my shirt says, silly. What did you think it said?"

Jae looked at the shirt. "I have no idea, other than the *Star Trek* symbol."

"Well, it says 'Starfleet.' That's the fleet of starships on the show."

Jae rolled his eyes. "If you say so."

"Come on, Starfleet." Ernst held out his hand to her.

She automatically drew back from the touch, but then accepted his arm. She even laid a hand on top of it, feeling a little cocky in her new ability to touch.

"Let me show you around. If you don't mind," Ernst added differentially to Jae. He stopped and took Lina's left hand, holding it up so that her wedding ring caught the light. He looked at Jae. "Should tonight be a celebration?" he asked.

Lina laughed. "I'm waiting for my husband to return. He's gone for a few days. Jae, I mean Neutrino here, was being kind and showing a homesick girl where she could find a piece of Earth."

"So you're friends with Legionnaires. And I'll bet this is your first time in the AffSys."

"That it is."

"How does that happen?"

Lina sighed with a smile. "Through a long series of incredible coincidences. Oh, y'all have a piano here. A baby grand!"

Now that they'd emerged from the columns, she could see it on the dais. It stood alone and proud, as if on an altar.

Ernst showed it off. "A Steinway. We smuggled it in about five years ago. Every now and then someone goes back to the old planet and pays a lot of money to a piano tuner to come out to keep this in good condition. The round trip takes them seven days, you know, and makes them a little crazy. Groundhogs." He wiggled his eyebrows at her meaningfully.

"Seven days?" Lina asked in confusion. "I thought it was one day out, one day back."

"They're only a piano tuner, not the king of Persia!" Ernst exclaimed. "First level hyperspace is all we can afford. How did you get here?"

"Quicker than three and a half days." Lina blinked. "So, who plays? When does the show begin?"

"We all play! No one can play too well, of course, but almost anyone can pick out 'Happy Birthday,' so that's what we do. Every Terran on Sarastor comes through these doors eventually, so that's a lot of birthdays." He gave a considering squint to the way she ran her hand over the keyboard cover. "Say, you don't happen to play, do you?"

She lifted it off the keys. "A bit. Just how many Terrans are there? I've been fiddling with my translator and found a number of Terran languages available."

Ernst drummed his index and middle fingers on his beard as he thought. "Maybe two thousand. I don't think three."

Jae asked, "How did you all get here? It's not as if Earth were part of the AffSys."

Ernst shrugged. "Alien kidnappings."

"You're kidding," Lina laughed. Then she remembered Londo's story and the smile dropped from her face. "Oh. I'm sorry."

Ernst said, "Occasionally they let the prisoners out on AffSys worlds, and some-times we find our way to Sarastor. Sometimes someone goes back permanently, but once you're Out Here, it's hard to go back entirely. Still, we all get homesick. I've been back a couple of times. Seen *Star Trek*, so I get it." He pointed at her shirt.

"I can understand being homesick," Lina said. Framed prominently on the wall was a large, lovely picture of Earth from space. Scattered around the rest of the wall were tourist posters showing cities of the world.

Jae sat down on the piano bench. "How did you wind up on Sarastor, Ernst?"

"Second generation Out Here. My parents were both abductees. Some second-generationers or more have never been," he gestured to the posters, "but we've all heard a lot about it."

Jae doodled at the keys. "I've seen tapes of Londo using a keyboard," he said. "It doesn't look so hard to me."

"Oh, move over," Lina said as he persisted in hitting sour notes. "You may be a fantastic drummer, but on the piano you seem more suited to the Pares Restaurant."

She tried a few chords, testing. "It *is* tuned. Nice sound," she said.

"Lina plays for parties," Jae told Ernst.

"Holiday and wedding parties mostly, so I just do the oldie standards. I've never played a grand in a bar before."

Ernst gaped at her. "A real piano player!"

Lina noticed that many people had turned toward her when she'd played those chords.

"Not classically trained for any length of time. I mean, don't expect Rachmaninoff. I'm not a professional."

"Real enough for here. We'll take what we can get."

Lina thought a minute. What did this piano want to play for these people? "Will I bother anyone?"

"Hell, no, Starfleet. You play as loud as you want, no matter how off-key it is."

That made her laugh, and she waved Jae a little farther down the piano bench so she'd have room. She began the first few chords of the favorite song she had in mind, and the room hushed completely, the boom boxes silenced.

Just play, she told herself. *Make these people happy. They haven't heard this instrument do what it wants.* She swung into the main melody line of "As Time Goes By." It sounded great on the grand piano, and she enjoyed the tone.

"Does it have words?" Jae asked.

"What?"

"Sing for the crowd, Lina."

She gave him a quick frown, but he wrinkled his nose at her.

"I'll get you for this. Wait a minute until it comes around."

She glanced at Ernst. He was second generation, and probably had never heard this before.

"'*You must remember this: a kiss is still a kiss, a sigh is just a sigh…*'" she sang loud enough so Ernst could hear, too.

A handful of people gathered around the piano, but she tried not to think about them. Just sing for Jae and Ernst, but sing a little louder now. Her voice held steady and clear, and she finished the song.

Applause surrounded her; she ducked her head and blushed. Jae's eyes crinkled.

"That was tremendous, Starfleet!" Ernst clapped her on the back. "What else do you know?"

"I don't have my music with me. I know a few others by heart, the party standards, and I can probably fake my way through more if someone gives me a melody line assist," she admitted. "What would you like to hear?"

Lina didn't know whether to laugh or cry at her own embarrassment as people called our requests. They were so needy for music, and she could give it to them. She started on the old song, "Moonlight Serenade," glad that the last wedding she'd played at had requested it, so it was familiar. She even remembered the words without effort, hooray.

"'*I stand at your gate, and the song that I sing is of moonlight…*'"

She sang and played. Her face grew a little sore from wincing at the notes she missed, but no one seemed to mind. It only took a few songs before others wanted to sing as well.

"Waitaminnit, waitaminnit," she pleaded at one point. "That would take a full orchestra – a brass section at the very least. All I've got is this piano and no sheet music. Give me another choice, Hay."

The man thought. "Okay, how about 'It's in His Kiss?'"

Lina nodded. "That's better. Who's going to do the lead? You?"

"I thought you might," Hay said hopefully. "I'm not gay."

"Praise the orb," Jae murmured beside her.

Jae studied the Terrans as more came up to sing along with Lina's playing as solos or in groups they made off the cuff. They seemed starved for the chance to sing without people thinking they were deviant because of it. They lined up around the piano waiting for their turn.

And Lina knew many of the songs. That increased the chances she was a real Terran.

"What time of year is it back on Terra?" a woman asked.

"It's just about spring. In the northern hemisphere, that is. I've got to think on a global level," Lina added as an aside to Jae. Then to the woman, "It's March."

"Damn. I'd hoped it was Christmas time. I wanted to hear some Christmas songs.
"

"So the Holiday Police are here tonight?"

"The Holiday Police?" The woman looked blankly at her.

"You know, those guys with the heavy guns who won't let you play Christmas music except at Christmas?" The woman looked sheepish as Lina said it. "Let's break some rules tonight. I won't tell if you don't. Religious or secular? Or is there something in specific you want to hear?

Lina played "White Christmas" first, and the room grew particularly still, though most sang along softly. "One of my better arrangements," she murmured to Jae, "but then, I know an awful lot of Christmas songs, and they're still reasonably fresh from last year's parties."

The sudden seriousness, no, the homesickness that permeated the place, caught Jae's attention. The song wished everyone a merry Christmas, which he knew through Londo was a family-centered holiday, but people didn't look merry. A few were wiping their eyes by the time Lina was done.

She whispered, "Time to get everyone back up."

This time the music had a lively but soft beat to it, and since Lina wasn't singing, she could concentrate more on her playing, which was more intricate now. The audience nodded their heads along with the beat. There was an easy-going attitude to it that Jae liked enormously. Lina finished amid generous applause.

"I don't know if anyone's familiar with that one," she began, but many people in the audience shouted out, "Charlie Brown! Snoopy!"

"That's right," Lina smiled at them. "What do you know? Y'all aren't as cut off from everything as I thought you were."

They wouldn't let her go until she held up her hands. "Just give me ten, please," she begged, flexing her fingers.

Jae pointed out an enclosed booth in a corner, and the three made their way to it. Ernst volunteered to fetch drinks. "Anything in particular?" he asked first.

"Anything, as long as it doesn't have alcohol in it," Lina said. "Water's fine. Drinking water, I mean."

"A teetotaler?"

"Well, I would claim occupational reasons, but the unpleasant truth is, alcohol puts me to sleep. I don't get drunk; I don't get high. I fall asleep."

"She gets stupid." Jae elbowed her. "I've seen her."

Lina stuck out her tongue at him.

"Then I'll find you something without alcohol, Milady Starfleet. And you, Neutrino?"

Jae asked for some obscure thing that sounded through her translator like a virgin flightline. The crowd around the piano dispersed back to their seats. They respected Lina and Jae's privacy, or perhaps they were too in awe of Jae to approach. Maybe they were just following rules.

"I'm enjoying the show," Jae told her. "You have a nice voice. And you play much better than Londo, or maybe just in a different style. I've heard his recordings. Never heard him play in front of an audience, though."

"Thanks, Jae. He told me he played." She frowned. "There's something about tonight – it's starting to get spooky up there."

"How so?"

Lina shook her head. "At first I thought I must be getting the words and music unconsciously from the people requesting it. But that one woman asked for her mother's favorite song because she had never heard it. So I sang it for her."

"And?" Jae prompted.

"And I've never heard it before either. The words came right to me. The music not as much, but I faked it." Lina raised her eyebrow at him. He did the same for her.

"Racial consciousness?"

"I just say weirder and weirder."

Jae thought. "Are you getting any negative vibes from it?"

"No. In fact, it's nice not having to try to remember the words. These people actually need me to sing to them, and I'm glad to do it."

"So don't worry about it. Enjoy."

She gave a little harrumph at that, but then said, "I'm glad you're Lon's friend."

"Thanks. Here come our drinks. Please note that mine is non-alcoholic."

"Very admirable."

Ernst returned with a tray. "Here we go. Your freeflight, Neutrino. Your fruit juice, Milady Starfleet. And my Coke."

"Coke? My god, they really are everywhere."

"You can have mine, if you'd like," Ernst offered quickly.

"Oh no, I'm fine. It's just that when I do allow myself some caffeine, I like Coke. Fully caffeinated, fully sugared, that is; can't stand the doctored versions. And it's… my husband's soft drink of choice, too. At least, I think it is."

Beside her, Jae snorted.

Ernst bobbed his head. "So you'd like to know where you can find some, eh? Well, we can certainly stock some whenever you want it, as long as you keep coming here and playing for us. So why are you here? Where's your husband, Lord Starfleet? What's your story? And why does the great Legionnaire Neutrino keep company with you?"

Lina's eyes met Jae's. What did he want her to say?

He spoke for her. "Just to keep tabs on her, see that she doesn't get into trouble. Partly because I'm her friend and I know she's never been off Earth before."

Ernst nodded, considering, and turned to Lina. "And Lord Starfleet?"

What to tell him? "I came here as part of a medical emergency that the Mega-Legion became involved with. Now my husband's helping some of them in hyper-space."

Jae nodded approval at her twisting of the truth.

Ernst sat back in his chair. "I'm impressed; I really am. The Legion working with Terra. Who would have thought? I always assumed that Earth was too primitive for the Legion to care about."

"I wouldn't–"

"Now, don't get into an uproar, Neutrino. But just think of all the troubles they have back on the big blue marble, and then think of the times the Legion has come to help out. None. Zero. I've always hoped that Valiant being in the Legion might make them see that they were needed on Earth. Seems like maybe that was right, what? It's taken a few years, but–"

"At least we have the ParaNet, Ernst," Lina said, trying to conciliate.

"But you're new here, Starfleet. The Legion is ten times, no, a hundred, a thousand times bigger and more respected than the Network. True, they have much more than a thousand times more territory to cover than the Network, but…"

Jae and Ernst continued their polite argument, Jae pointing out that Earth was not a member of the AffSys and it had more than enough megas already, including Valiant and Maximus, the two most powerful beings in the known galaxy. Ernst countered with Valiant's Legion membership. He was one of the few members from outside the AffSys. Why wasn't an exception made for his home planet to be regularly watched by the Legion?

Sometimes one or the other became a little too defensive and Lina stepped in to bring the level down a few notches.

She finally huffed in annoyance. This was not her idea of a break. "I think my ten minutes are over. Let's go see what people want to hear, shall we?" She took her drink and coaster with her to the piano, not bothering to see if she was accompanied. Let them argue at the table if they wanted to. She took along an extra napkin to put under the coaster, just in case. Mustn't spoil the prized instrument.

People started to gather as they saw she had returned. She arranged her drink so no one could knock it over and flexed her fingers as Jae sat beside her protectively. She scooted the bench so that he could have some room and still not be in her way.

"Okay," she announced, not nearly as nervous in front of these anxious people, so desperate to hear the music of home. It wasn't quite so scary now that she'd done it once. "Any requests?"

They had a short list, and Lina went through those she knew one by one, including "Happy Birthday" for two people in the audience who were celebrating. The list ran out and the request was just that she play whatever she wanted. The first song that came to her mind was: *What'll I do when you are far away and I am blue; what'll I do?"*

She had to stop for a moment after that, looking down at her hands, trying not to feel so ultimately lonely, longing for Lon.

"Anything the matter?" Ernst asked.

"I'm okay," Lina looked up with a watery smile. "I'm just missing my husband."

"They were married yesterday morning. Very early," Jae explained. "And he was called away right after the ceremony."

"Sweet mother! And you let him go," Ernst exclaimed.

"There was an emergency. People were going to die," Lina explained.

"Ah well. I hope he returns soon. And safely."

"So do I," she said earnestly. "So do I."

She played some more after that, inviting everyone to sing along if they knew the words, and things became boisterous for a time.

Jae laughed beside her as he saw so many people singing, some of them making quite the fools of themselves as he kept the beat on the edge of the prized Steinway. No one begrudged it.

He watched her as she shifted between love ballads and rock and roll songs, how she encouraged the others to participate. How she dealt with the shy people and looked at them for a moment before coming up with just the right song for them.

She didn't deal well with the drunks and the boors. She didn't know how to handle the guys with the come-on lines. Jae ran them all off. The Legionnaire as bouncer: It was a new role for him and he got a kick out of it, particularly since many of these Terrans didn't seem to have any regard for his ranking as Legionnaire.

Lina asked him if he was getting tired. He hated to admit it but he was, so she gave the crowd one more song and they left, amid great weeping and wailing. Lina blushed while Jae chortled anew at the audacity of Terrans.

They ported into the lab and almost ran into a newcomer dressed in electric blue and gray with white flashing sparks all over his jacket.

"Shards, Jae!" the man exclaimed as they appeared. "Next time announce yourself. I almost fried you!"

"And good evening to you, Brügz. Er'k."

Lina hadn't noticed the other man. His costume had yellows and oranges with a clouded starburst on his chest. Both men were quite tall, like so many people Out Here, and their costumes showed off fit physiques. Brügz seemed older, maybe mid-thirties, and the sprigs of hair that showed on his head were navy blue. Er'k's hair was a loose crewcut and spectacularly copper. He looked to be Lina's age, maybe even a trifle younger. Both had medium-brown skin.

Jae said, "May I introduce Carolina R… O'Kelly, Londo's new wife." The men nodded their heads at her. Obviously this was not the first time they'd heard her name. Jae pointed first at the older one, then the younger. "This is Brügz Sikrichat and Er'k Gallad, otherwise known as Ion Emperor and Sunstorm. Er'k is my team's newest member, and Brügz is on temporary assignment with us to help train."

"An emperor," Lina smiled and nodded at the newcomers. "Pleased to meet you, Brügz, Erk." The rule to always use a costumed name for Legionnaires never entered her mind.

"Er'k," Jae corrected her. There was a little clearing of the throat in there.

Lina tried it again and failed, and then said, "Erik, a good Terran name. Sorry; no disrespect. I'll work on it, okay?"

"No problem at all," Erik said as he stepped forward to press his hand against hers. He met her eyes with a piercing gaze. "It's a pleasure."

"And I can guess what your power is," she said as stepped back. She ran her arm through the space between them, breaking the emotional hooks he'd just fired at her, and then shook it at the floor to release the energy.

"Erik's always the ladies' man," Jae said warningly. "Even with married women."

"A ladies' man with more than a hint of telepathy." Lina frowned. "Quite specialized."

Erik looked surprised. "Who, me?"

Jae *humph*ed. "I always suspected he had something up his sleeve. Or somewhere." Then he laughed. "Specialized telepathy, huh?"

"Can't be," Erik said huffily.

"Sacral chakra, solar plexus chakra, throat chakra," Lina explained to Jae and then turned back to Erik. "We can call it telepathy or we can call it psychic manipulation. Whichever, I've seen it before. I also know what to do about it, so please don't try it again with me."

The expression Erik gave her seemed sincerely apologetic. "I don't know what you mean."

"I think she's talking about your line of attack," Brügz broke in. "I've seen you do it with every female you meet. It's so obvious."

Erik gave an "I'm innocent in all this" look, and the other two groaned. "Okay, okay, I'm sorry for whatever I did. I won't do it again."

"Well, it's still nice to meet you," Lina repeated, trying to break the tension. She didn't like psychic bullies either, but maybe he was truly ignorant of what he was doing. Guys tended to encourage asserting power over women in different ways. Someone with this kind of psychic ability could very well think it was all part of the game.

Brügz spoke for the two of them now. "He's not on the rolls as a telepath; he's in charge of weather control. Me, I'm into electricity." He flicked a couple of sparks off his fingers. They popped with a bang, and Lina knew she looked impressed after she jumped an inch or two in surprise.

"Where's everyone else?" Jae asked as he looked around.

"Wiley's on extended break. Dellen's on assignment on Sarastor. Shift command is waiting for your return," Erik said, keeping his distance from Lina. "We were just about to tune into the news to catch up."

The screen flickered to life in midair in front of the monitor station, and whoever had the remote, if indeed there was one, clicked through programs at blinding speed, stopping to play back snippets of public Legion information. The Legionnaires watched coverage of what Jae, Wiley and Dellen had been doing, plus there was footage from Legion teams stationed off-world. When the system settled on a relatively lengthy story about the Legion and a sniper attack with a kidnapping attempt on Dari Signet and son, Lina began to tiptoe backward to her prisoner chair.

"Dellen's been busy," Brügz remarked as the news voiceover gave her hero name. An interview with Dari Signet mentioned the prisoner at Legion Headquarters who had helped her.

Jae's jaw jutted along with his lower lip as he consulted the comm station's records. His head rotated to target Lina. "You ported out without permission." His eyes had narrowed into slits, and as he strode closer he seemed to tower over her.

Lina's first impulse was to cower, but then she decided to stand her ground. "Dellen needed help," she replied as breezily as she could. "She said she wouldn't report it. Do you have to? I really don't think Stoan would approve."

"You didn't inform me."

"I informed Dellen. I didn't think you'd–"

"You broke confinement rules. Blatantly, and apparently without remorse." Jae shook his head. "The crime you've been charged with is a major one, don't you realize that?"

Breezy wasn't going to work on him. "I realize," Lina said. "Do you realize that people were in danger and no one else knew?"

"You could have told someone."

"Dellen didn't believe me. I wasn't sure where they were to tell her where to look."

"I spelled out the rules for you just as carefully as I could, and you still–"

Lina lifted her chin. "Mitigating circumstances," she claimed.

"And how do we know you won't cite that again? You could claim danger and then when we caught you you could say you'd been mistaken."

"I wouldn't lie about that."

Jae stood there, every stony, disapproving inch of him an officer. "I don't want to hear excuses," he said. He made a brisk motion with his right index finger and a screen appeared. "Cell 3FF is ready right now," he said. "That's our force field section. Port your cats into Londo's room and we'll see to them while you're imprisoned."

"No," Lina said.

"There will be no discussion. Port your cats."

"My cats are staying where they are."

"Then they'll starve."

"And I'll sic the Humane Society on the Legion's sorry asses if you let that happen. If you let them starve, it will be your decision. You can prevent it."

Jae's gaze swept Brügz and Eric before settling on something in the distance. The two were still standing in their casual positions by Wiley's podium, but it was a pose behind sharp attention.

"I'm taking the prisoner to her cell," Jae said. "Hold command here for me until I return or Wilder does."

Lina marched with her head held high. "I promised I'd stay in the lab or in Lon's quarters," she told Jae. "I never promised anything about a cell."

Jae didn't respond but kept walking, prodding her every few steps so she'd keep up with him. "PRISONER" was once more emblazoned across her bracelet.

"There were good reasons why I left," she said as they descended in the Jetsons tube. "The first time I plain forgot. I promised not to do it again, and I didn't, until my guides told me that I had to leave. And it was a damned good thing I did, wasn't it? That Dari Signet and her little boy would have been kidnapped and maybe killed if I hadn't gone."

Still Jae said nothing.

At a new floor a long hall stretched before them. Though brightly lit down the center ceiling, it seemed dark because of the unreflecting black walls. Their quick footsteps made no sound.

"I want to see a lawyer."

Silence.

Jae halted before a blue-gray wall. He waved his right hand and with the faintest of *zzt*s the wall disappeared, opening into a white, featureless room.

"You won't let my cats die," Lina said softly. "You'll at least contact the Para-Net, who can contact someone. Tell them I'll pay whatever it costs. And that Fafhrd needs her medicine and nutrient paste once a day."

Lina stepped into the room. She never looked back at Jae.

With another gesture, the gray force field reappeared, the most solid energy barrier technology could devise. Jae stood looking at it for two full minutes before he turned abruptly and strode back in the direction he'd come.

Lina walked beside him, matching him step for step.

"I didn't hear you promise," she said. "I want a promise before I stay in there."

Jae jerked to a stop and whirled on her. "How did you get out?"

"These are lives we're talking about, not stupid rules. I want to hear you promise."

He grabbed her shoulders and shook her. "How – did you – get out of there? Did you just make me think you'd gone in? Are you controlling my mind?"

"For god's sake, Jae, I can port, remember? I just need to make sure my cats are safe before you start up that force field. Are you going to promise me or not?"

"Start up the force field?" Jae glanced back. The field looked perfectly stable to him. No visual moiré, no system lights activated, no sound alarms had gone off. Prisoners couldn't escape a force field cell. It was impossible.

Would a Terran really see a force field as a simple wall, or was it all the act of a mind controller?

"I'll go back just as soon as you promise. Those cats trust you to take care of them if I can't. Pets are a sacred responsibility."

Jae scowled at the field and then at Lina. She just stood there with righteous innocence written across her face.

"Your cats should learn not to trust me," he finally said. "What will you promise if I take you back to the lab? Will you stay there and not port off?"

Lina's eyes shifted to the left as she considered possibilities. As an innocent prisoner in a society where her rights weren't protected, it was her duty to escape if she could do so without harming Londo's reputation. But what would her leaving do to his standing in the Legion? "If someone's in danger," she said, "I can't promise that I won't go to help. If possible I'll try to alert a Legionnaire so they can go instead. I can promise that much."

"Not good enough."

She lifted her chin. "I promise I'll try my best to act in a way that won't bring any shame to Londo."

His tongue rolled that information around inside his cheek. "You promise you'll stay on Sarastor until trial?" Jae said.

"What if I get bail?"

"What's bail?"

Lina's hands balled into fists by her side. "I want a lawyer," she said.

"You're not getting one until the commander comes back. This time I want to hear *you* promise."

Lina stood silent and didn't look at him.

Jae's voice turned low. "You're actually thinking of running, aren't you?"

"It's a trumped-up charge," Lina finally said. "Stoan knows I'm innocent. He's just doing this out of… out of… something. To show everyone he's boss, I don't know. To show he's stronger than Valiant in some ways. It's a power game, and I hate power games. I refuse to play along. I'm taking myself off the field."

Jae flatly said, "You'll play along and you'll stay here on Sarastor. You're not going to mess this up in any way. Londo's waited too long for this."

Londo. Frustration welled inside her. She wasn't used to being part of a couple. She had always taken care of herself and herself alone. Now she had to constantly weigh what she did against how it would look for Londo.

"Damn it," she muttered.

Jae took her defiant chin between his thumb and forefinger and raised it so she had to look into his eyes. "Promise me," he ordered.

Her mouth worked enough to reveal her teeth tightly together, grimacing.

"Promise!"

Lina almost spat the words. "I will stay on Sarastor unless granted leave to go somewhere else."

"Good." He released her.

"But the cats must be taken care of."

"Bring them here. Legion medical will see to them."

"They're set in their territories and habits. Moving them would cause psychological trauma."

Jae scowled at her. "When you break the rules your actions reflect onto your arresting officer."

"If you'd been in my position, you'd have done the same thing."

He seemed to look right through her.

"Honest to god," she said, "I'd never do anything to hurt you in any way. I'm sorry, Jae. I apologize for my actions hurting you, but I won't apologize for what I did. Is there any kind of paper or form I can sign to admit that it was all my fault and you had nothing to do with it? That you couldn't have done anything to stop it?"

Jae gave her a shove turning her back the way they'd come. "Move," he said, and he didn't say anything else for their return trip.

They all ignored her for at least an hour, Sarastoran. She sat in her prisoner chair while the red security lights formed translucent walls that outlined the area she could move around in even though the regular room lights were on and Legionnaires were present.

Lina kept her back to them. It was she who was ignoring them, not the other way around. She was not a prisoner. She could get out if she wanted, right? They had no hold on her.

Except that now she'd given her word. And if she did something wrong, Lon would be the one blamed. Or Jae. Her stomach churned at the thought.

She kicked the headrest of her chair, which was now serving as footrest, and tried to study… whatever. Though the study padd scrolled columns of information at her, all she could think of was Londo and how hurt he'd look when he found out she'd besmirched his reputation.

After a while she merely concentrated on how he looked. When he was pleased with her. When he quietly revealed his heart. A smile stole across her face. All she felt was warm, like when he held her in his arms.

Being in love was wonderful. Something in her now flowed with the universe, steady and calm like a boat sailing in a rising dawn. This was right. Lon had come into her life.

If only he were here.

Unlike her, he was unafraid of anything. He was completely sure of himself. She could still see him chopping a path through the jungle, then swinging his rifle around to ready position when danger neared, or flying down to her like her personal angel, his arms spread to welcome her into them. He was her protector. He was her lover.

He was her husband.

She wrote "Londo" on her padd and then "Londo Rand" and then drew the words into a bouquet of flowers made up of hearts. Flourishes became ribbons, just like the ones at their wedding.

A cacophony of sparks cascading into the lab jarred her back to full consciousness. Good heavens, hearts and flowers. What was she, a school girl? She checked quickly to see if she'd written "Mrs. Londo Rand" or "I heart Londo" anywhere and then breathed a silent sigh of relief when there was none. When she tried to erase it, the image blinked three times before it vanished. Didn't a triple blink mean it was saved somewhere? Rats!

Erik and Jae answered the sparkly call but from their expressions they regarded it as an inconvenience. They referred action to local planetary police and then adjourned to the break room, stepping through the red wall that was in their path, since it was only light.

Jae stopped at her chair. "How long are you going to stay like this?"

"Is my arresting officer deigning to speak to his prisoner?" Lina glanced around as if Jae were invisible and she was trying to see the source of the voice.

"*Cheerah*, and they say I'm moody," Jae said. "You stay like this and we might not go to Earth tomorrow after all. I'll have to call someone at the ParaNet to take care of–"

"Earth!?" Lina scrambled out of her chair and followed him into the break room. Brügz was already inside, crunching his way through a heavy tray of snacks. Lina said, "We need to go to Earth tomorrow."

Jae programmed a replicator for something as Erik retrieved a drink from the same window. "We don't *need* to do anything. I don't think I trust you. When Wiley gets back, I'll turn the matter over to him for final decision."

"What was that? Earth?" Brügz' eyebrows went up. They went through a round of explaining the interstellar teleportation process.

The older Legionnaire chewed thoughtfully on a long vegetable-looking stick that he had skewered with his spork. "So you just popped off to Earth, just like that, for a spot of lunch?"

"That's a fair way of saying it," Jae replied. "I don't think we'll be able to do that after today's little escapade."

"Oh, but Jae!" Lina exclaimed. "I saw a poster in the store for Art 'Round the Park. That'll be tomorrow. I double-checked the date when I was there, just to be sure. I wanted to surprise you." Well, that and use it as an excuse to ditch him without him being too mad at her. Could she still find a way around her promise somehow? Maybe… If other Legionnaires were involved she could trick one of them to order her to stay on Earth.

"And what is an Art 'Round the Park?" Erik asked.

"It's a street fair. They close off all the streets around the ballpark in downtown Durham and let in craftspeople, and there are live bands everywhere…" she glanced to see Jae's reaction to that, "and food and all kinds of things. It'll be fun. C'mon, Jae. Two hours back home. We can take some others, too. Extra security for the prisoner, don't you know."

Lina ported in the poster she'd seen and smoothed it out with a flourish on the table in front of Brügz and Erik. It had a map and schedules listed.

"See… The Rabbit Pellets will be there." One by one, she described the different kinds of music the listed bands played. "Oh, look! Circadia!"

"Circadia?" Jae asked, peering at the poster. "The band on Lon's juke box?"

"Yes. How'd they manage that? Only fifteen dollars admission at the ballpark – Holy hannah, the joint will be packed." She pointed out listings for dance companies. "And here's the Society for Creative Anachronism. They go around in ancient costumes and have tournaments." Lina looked up to take the two newcomers in as well. "C'mon, it'll be fun."

"I'm supposed to be guarding you," Jae said though his voice didn't seem quite so hard. "But I do like Circadia…"

"I can port anyone back anytime they need to."

Brügz grinned at Jae. "I'm willing to go. What, we'll call it a recognizance team. Never been to Earth."

"Great," Lina said. She looked hopefully at Erik. "Half the population of Durham is female," she said.

"Guess I have to go, then," he replied with a half-hearted smile.

"Okay, Jae. We'll just go without you. You'll miss hearing Rusty Estevez or the Pellets. Such great songs."

Jae made a show of pulling his hair out with his fists. "Oh, all right, all right! Someone add bribery to her charges. What time do we leave?"

Through some kind of computer magic Jae managed to coordinate Sarastor time with Terran. Finally they decided on a schedule that left Dellen and Wiley watching HQ.

"Let's hope it doesn't rain," Lina declared.

Erik cocked his head. "What, don't they have weather control there?"

Lina started to protest the unnaturalness of weather control when Jae interrupted. "Don't get her started. Okay, let's see how things look about six or seven hours from now, and we'll consider going."

"The cats have to be fed at any rate. Fafhrd–"

"Yes, yes, we'll feed the cats. Quickly." Jae scratched the back of his neck. "I am never going to be able to explain this to the commander. Maybe I'll just say that we're putting you on a leash. Yeah, a long leash, that's it."

Lina looked from one Legionnaire to another. "So I'm the Legion's pet dog now? I want to see a lawyer."

"We'll just say that this afternoon your leash stretched a little farther than it should have. Short leash after that, Lina."

"One that stretches over eighty parsecs," Brügz muttered to Erik.

10

The timer in his ring vibrated against his finger. Londo Rand woke from his doze and reached into his vest for his hyperspace sensors. Even his para-vision couldn't penetrate the blackness that was hyperspace, so he needed this to navigate.

The faint light from the sensors gave him the time: fifteen minutes to intercept. He hated the absolute precision with which he had to hurl himself into hyperspace, aided by these mechanical measuring devices, and he hated hanging in the blackness, driven by the inertia of his initial propulsion. Most of all he hated missing his target. He couldn't afford to miss and then have to exit from hyperspace and compute a new trajectory that could cost him another few hours travel time. You couldn't make course corrections in hyperspace other than to leave it.

But sensors said he was right on course. They wouldn't pick up anything until Intercept minus two minutes. It was lucky that modern science had ever found anything to sense objects in hyperspace, but it had and he carried state of the art equipment with him. It was his job. It was his joy to help people.

But still it wore on him. He was always impatient for the time to pass, always going over old battles in his mind, asking himself: *how could I have done it better?* Injuries, deaths – How could he have avoided that? Adam had told him years ago that he might be better off to use the time to polish those stories of his, but he'd never started to do that until this last year. It did seem to help. Adam was a smart man, best shrink he'd ever had.

Adam would be good for Lina, too, Lon thought as he chewed on a roll of com-pressed rations. Should married couples see the same psychiatrist? Hm. Adam would know. Londo touched the gold chain he'd blindly put on, Lina's necklace. There in the blackness of hyperspace he smiled at memories, at plans for the future, and then the sensor vibrated in his hand: Ship ahead.

You had to speed up to enormous accelerations to achieve hyperspace, but once here there was no speed, so there were no speeds to match. How was it that one approached something else in hyperspace? Londo didn't understand it. He'd tried to for a long time, and then had just gone with the practical aspects of it all. Maybe someday a bolt of enlightenment would strike him, but until then he just needed to know how to get from point A to point B.

He reached out and in moments felt something solid underneath his fingers. He sank them into the outer hull as if it were stiff clay, creating a handhold for himself as he got his bearings. Hyperspace realities now matched, he could see with his special vision the ship spreading out in front of him, filling up the blackness. He maintained contact with the ship so that he wouldn't lose sight of it, and quickly found an airlock.

"Valiant!" "By starlight, Valiant!" The haggard command crew greeted him like a messiah as he entered the door to the makeshift bridge.

"There are eighty-odd Legionnaires three hours behind me," he told them, noting once again how people reacted to his presence. They had been worn down by worry and fatigue before, but now hope sprung in their eyes. *Valiant will set things right.* So far that had usually been the case, but there was always that black kernel of knowing that things couldn't always turn out well that lived in Londo's guts, pressed up against his spine. He'd learned to ignore it.

For the most part.

It was all the crew could do to get a ship schematic up for him. The captain pointed out major structural damage – the result of three bombs rigged to explode simultaneously, overtaxing the ship's repair systems. Wounded and trapped people were scattered all over the ship. There weren't enough crew even to begin to see to them all.

Hyperspace nav was out completely; they couldn't rematerialize in normal space. The aft third of the ship was barely held to the rest of the ship by one lockway. If it separated, it would be lost to the void forever.

Some food systems were working, some weren't. Gravity was on in most sections, but not all. Temperature and pressure controls were erratic. They'd managed to halt further loss of air, but it meant that some sections of the ship were unreachable because damaged corridors had been blocked or jettisoned.

And of course no one could use lifepods. Lifepods were for normal space. Propulsion systems needed for hyperspace couldn't be put on anything but a large ship.

The engines were too massive, too sheerly expensive to do that except on a luxury yacht.

Londo nodded at the information. The crew gave their recommendations and he pondered them, taking into consideration the group that couldn't arrive soon enough for these people.

A lone bead of sweat dribbled down his brow as he reshaped the walls of the shipboard gymnasium into long girders for bracing. If only Jae were here! He could make these into something stronger than this. A pro-titani-polyalloy, how Lon wished he had some of that!

Lon's ears picked up the groans of the wounded that echoed in the ship floors away from him, but this was the more efficient way to approach the situation. Give the Legionnaires good materials to work with once they got here. That way they could get a handle on this, snap, snap, snap, instead of running around searching for supplies. Fifty girders to begin with, more to be fashioned later by others.

Meanwhile, the crew was collecting all the rope and tubing they could find so that he could literally slip-stitch what he could of the ship together. He'd done a quick job with the aft section that would stabilize it for a while more. They wouldn't be able to repair the ship, but they might be able to keep it in one piece, one hyperspace reality long enough to evacuate everyone.

The injured people who were too wounded to groan held most of his attention now. The small sickbay was at bursting point already, but volunteers were skittering around down there, making ready for the brunt of the disaster to hit them. Scores more than it was ever designed to handle needed it as a triage station. Legion ships were well-stocked with medical supplies, equipment and beds. The last ones in the train would be stocked specifically for a structural and hyperspace emergency.

If only Lina were here. That porting of hers would literally be a lifesaver, even if it would place everyone in quarantine for a few days. Could she port from hyperspace?

Lina! He tried again, shouting as loud as he could through the hyperspace blanket around the ship. **Lina!!**

Nothing.

So they weren't going to have Lina here. Aiko and Stoan could help knit the ship together firmly after they'd finished a more complete structural survey. After evacuation, they could strip what they could from the aft section and then jettison it.

Kuttr would lead the Legion medical effort. His ad hoc team were specialists in battle injuries and quick fix-em-ups. They wouldn't be pretty, but they'd hold together until they could get everyone back. If victims were still alive when they got to the advanced doctors of Sarastor, chances were that they'd still be alive years from now.

Deegel could sense people who could be trapped; that would keep her busy. He'd assign someone with parastrength to free the trapped people she'd find. No, three people. Two to free, the other to run the victim to medical relief and come back for more. Give them some ship's crew to help.

He would send Nesh down to the various hydroponics modules to beef up the oxygen levels. Nesh hated hydroponics duty, but here in space that was the only logical place for her. Nesh's power just wasn't that useful anywhere else if she weren't on planetary duty.

Londo went down a mental list of the other Legionnaires who had been at the wedding and thus were on their way here. His padd had shown him the rescue teams as he slid through hyperspace.

Stoan had left Jae behind for some reason, probably just to relieve Wiley from solo duty. He hoped Stoan was regretting that now. One of the more minor-powered Legionnaires – like Nesh – could have done that job just as well. Jae was needed here. If Londo were Legion commander, he wouldn't have made that mistake.

Londo grunted. He was not Legion commander and as a part-time member he was not going to be, ever. But that was the job he coveted. His father, Hal, wasn't a Legionnaire; he could never be commander. That would be an honor that Lon could best him with, an honor that could be Lon's alone, with no help from Hal or Maximus's legend. Hal's shadow worried at Londo wherever he went, but as Legion commander the shadow wouldn't be able to touch him.

Ah, but Stoan did a great job. Maybe he had other reasons to leave Jae behind. Maybe Jae had had his own reasons. Jae…

Lon continued to shape the last of the girders as he finalized their battle plans.

According to his padd, the Legionnaires would arrive in twenty minutes. "Right down here." Londo motioned to a nervous medtech, who hefted his portable kit higher on his shoulders to pad silently behind the hero. They rounded a corner, and Lon ducked under a robo-service door.

"Don't even try it," Londo ordered into the dark chamber beyond. The medtech ducked, too, and peered ahead.

A cry of sudden pain came from a corner. It lingered into a low howl.

"Lights," Lon instructed, and the room obeyed.

There between small servo-bots crouched an achingly-thin man, his arms thrown around his stomach. He groaned in agony, and his coverall showed an expanding red stain.

Lon pointed and the medtech moved in, as they'd planned. As the tech administered to the injured man, Londo said, "I've disabled the bomb inside you. You didn't trigger it when the others went off. Why? Who was working with you? Who do you work for?"

"You c-couldn't… I don't…" The man convulsed with a cry.

"It's there, inside a coil of your intestines. I burned off the main detonator." Lon's parabreath had seared right through the man's skin and into his gut. Lon didn't feel too badly about it. "Who do you work for? Who hired you?"

The man arched in pain even as the tech injected healing nanos into the cauterized incision. The tech checked his own medipadd. "He's not an AffSys native, Valiant. Cross-checking Unaffiliated Worlds."

"R-Rear Admiral… Nordan," the would-be bomber gasped. He spoke with a thick accent Londo couldn't place.

"Rear Admiral Nordan. What world?" But before the man could answer, Londo made a slightly open fist and blew through it, as he would have a blowpipe, aimed at the would-be bomber's face.

The man shrieked as a hole appeared in his cheek.

"Old-fashioned suicide pill hidden in a tooth," Londo mused. "I took care of it. There's just a bit of the poison left, charred or vapor. You might find yourself feeling… ill. Sorry about your tongue."

The man screamed.

"But you can still hear me. I'll want answers when the tech's through with you." Through his newfound telepathy, Londo could feel the man's terror through his pain. Guilt at his own cowardice. Hunger, thirst, and a burning sensation. And Lon felt like this man was far, far from his home. Could he be an imperial? The accent didn't match, but the Empire held any number of worlds whose populations were new to the imperial lingua-franca. Were there any more saboteurs on the ship? More bombs hidden? "You'll talk. You'll spill your guts. Count on it."

Now that there were more personnel in HQ, Jae got more time off-duty.

"Sure," he told Lina, "there's a blaze lot more we'd be doing if we were up to full speed. But we're not, so the system automatically shunts incoming calls down to a dribble. It's good for the local forces, keeps them on their toes when they have to handle their own crises now and then."

He sat on the couch in Lon's living room with a drink in his hand and recalibrated the coffee table to Lina's new skill levels. He talked about work as he programmed with his free hand waving and twitching through the air, in the way one commanded computers.

Lina surmised that Legionning was not a nine to five job. It was long stretches of empty duty punctuated by moments of concentrated terror. Emergencies were handled by HQ forces within fifty parsecs of Sarastor. Outside of that sphere were scads of Outposts in interstellar AffSys space, and of course each major AffSys world or major space station had a Legion team, even if it were manned by only two people.

As part of normal rotation, Jae had held duty on almost every affiliated world. Londo had served on about a dozen. He'd been full-time only for a few years after he'd first joined. As a part-timer, he and his Alpha team were now assigned to HQ duty.

But there were exceptions. The Legion prided itself on its adaptability. When needed, ranks, rules and duties were flexible. Jae informed Lina that paperwork, diplomacy and PR were also a large part of what she'd previously thought as idle time.

At some point they got off-track and he began to tell her about his home world of Feith. Lina listened raptly, surprised to hear him open up. Jae's moods were mercurial. Just a while ago he'd been furious with her, but now…

Feith had been an almost-magical place, with people living side-by-side with nature. Central cities existed for the small population, but many liked to roam the planet-wide forests and plains, living in nature, oblivious of climatic extremes. They cared for the flora and looked after the fauna, husbanding the environment.

Jae's family had been one of those. They had a territory that they roamed like nomads: his parents, his sister and her husband (she was thirty years older than Jae), grandparents on all sides, some friends and their families.

He remembered that there had been a mild outbreak among some of the trees of a rust that his father had taught him to cure. He recounted how he'd scraped off injured bark so carefully and revitalized the immune systems of the plants, sealing the wounds shut afterward as his father praised him and told him what a great healer he'd be. He'd been disappointed that after that their family had discovered so few problems to heal.

Occasionally larger groups gathered. Sometimes they'd travel to a city and other times just join in circles under the stars by a lake and sing, dance and make music. The devas of the world joined them in their dances as the stars sang harmony above.

Lina knew that her eyes must be big as saucers, but it all sounded so wonderful that it certainly must be untrue, mustn't it? But wouldn't it be nice if things really could be like that? She held her breath as Jae told her about a time long ago when the stones around one lake had been so taken with the people's music that they'd begun to hop around in a jig.

Was he–? He looked very pleased with himself as he told her the tale, and as she made a moue he embellished it: the rocks reached into the ground and gathered up diamonds and rubies and garlanded themselves with them, then grew drunk on starlight and avalanched in a huge orgy. From this there arose a great range, the Jeweled Mountains.

"Uh huh," Lina said devoutly. "And then Paul Bunyan and his giant ox Babe came strolling through…"

"Never heard of them." Jae was leaning back on the couch, his eyes half-closed. "But I remember hearing of one fellow who swam down the Fire Falls in his altogether, and never got singed except for one small spot on his ass that forever marked him for his deed. You should have seen him, he–"

"Are you sure the spot wasn't on his brain?"

He opened one eye. "You doubt, barbarian?"

"You've been spending too much time with Lon and all his stories."

"So you've heard Lon's stories?" Jae asked.

"Um hum. Lots."

"How did he manage to… Well, he claimed that…" Jae ran his tongue across his teeth, trying to think of a polite way to phrase it. "If you two were boinking each other so much on that island, when in the orb did Lon find the time to tell you stories?"

Jae suddenly began to huff and puff in rhythm, deepening his voice to Londo's level: "Oh! Oh! Yes, I'm coming… Did I ever tell you the tale of the two children who – Oh yeah! That was a good one! Anyway, these children ran into the woods one day and–"

Lina punched his shoulder. "You're… you're… a beast!"

Jae grinned at her. "I do try to be."

Lina leaned back with a happy sigh. "Yes, beastly; I'm going to tell Ms. Yency that you need retraining. But Londo does pride himself on being efficient. Just not that efficient, thank goodness."

Jae guffawed.

"He's so wonderful," Lina continued. "Don't you think? And he's got to be the handsomest man there is."

"I thought I was. I'm crushed."

"No, you're beautiful." She glanced at him, glanced back. "There's room in this universe for more than one handsomest man, don't you think?"

"I've spotted many of them." Jae chuckled.

"He's by far the handsomest," Lina declared. She could almost imagine him there with her. "He's so sweet. Thoughtful. And he knows so much about so many things. And deep – I never thought he could have the layers that he has."

"And you've seen them all," Jae said thoughtfully.

"Oh no, hardly any. Sharing minds isn't like that," she assured him. "It will take a lifetime or more before I ever truly understand Londo." She twisted her new ring and smiled at the universe. "He loves me. Isn't that amazing? He says he always will." Another twist to bring it back to rights.

"So you're married now, forever."

"What if he gets tired of me and he can't get out of the marriage?" she asked slowly. "I don't want him miserable."

"A Feithi marriage," Jae reminded her. "There's no divorce."

"I know. Oh, Jae, what do you think he wants from a wife? What does he need?"

Jae rolled his eyes and Lina slapped his arm again.

"Beyond the sex!" she exclaimed. "He's Valiant. Everyone's been reminding me that he's Valiant and I'm nowhere near his level. I'm just Lina Muttbutt… but now I'm Mrs. Valiant." She made a face. "You know him. Tell me what he wants. How should I act? How should I dress?" She sank back against the couch. "Who cleans the bathroom? Oh god, we really rushed into this, didn't we?"

Jae didn't say anything and she popped him again. That made him laugh.

"We did the right thing," Lina told him determinedly. "We just did it a little quick. Lon says it'll be fun finding out about each other. Well, it will. It might be difficult at times, but on the whole, it'll be great." She eyed Jae. "You've had fun all these years with Londo."

He quietly said, "Yes."

"And you'll have more with him. I'll see to that. Every few weeks I'll send you two out into the world with a bag lunch and an order to have fun for the day. Don't worry."

The smile he gave her was weak.

"Jae Rallene, you're going to have to learn to share," she declared. "We'll start having fun with that lunch he promised you. All three of us – the day after he gets back."

"Lunch?"

Why had that impersonal mask slipped onto Jae's face? "You remember," Lina urged. "The lunch where you're going to tell me all about Londo. Tell me now."

"No."

"Oh, come on." Lina nudged him playfully.

"No. That's for another day when Londo is here."

He was going to be immovable on this subject, was he? "You've known him… how long? Wiley said you were both kids here."

"He stayed here for a few years – full-time Legionnaire, almost full-time therapy – and then he was gone. Now he's just part-time. Just visits every four or five weeks or so for a week at a time."

"Earth needs him."

"Yeah."

"Lon wound up here because Sarastor psychologists could help him, right? Help him get over his kidnapping?" She didn't wait for Jae to answer. "So how'd you end up here? In the Legion, I mean? It seems strange that they'd do that when you'd just–"

He closed his eyes. "They brought me here because they were scared shitless what to do with a mega who was rapidly going insane on them. They thought that being around other megas would compensate for me losing everyone. They were…" He was going to say "wrong," but he paused.

"Not necessarily on the right track?" Lina asked. "What you needed was family and friends, not just megas."

"So some of them made friends with me. Chimrin – she was commander back then – went out of her way to try to make me feel at home. Wiley let me hang around while he was studying me. He thought I didn't know. I knew. But he's a nice ol' *grizzich*, he is. I hid myself from him and there wasn't any more for him to study, and he still let me hang around."

"Good for him; I like Wiley."

"And then Londo came to the Legion. I'd been thinking about running away, you know, just run off and steal a ship somewhere and go back home. Live like a hermit there, I suppose, until I died. I didn't have any idea what the conditions would be like. But Londo came here to live and he needed someone, too.

"And Hal! He was the one who found me after the Disaster, did you know that? His was the face I remembered against the shock, but I'd heard of him, before and since. I was fascinated with the legend of Maximus and here he was in person. I got to see him up close. You'll like him, Lie, you really will. He's not like some of the people here. You've seen some of them by now, you've been reading about them. You've seen how people Outside react."

"They bow to you," she said wonderingly, "as if y'all were lords or kings."

"Yes."

"I thought at first that this was a democracy, but it's got feudal overtones, you know? There's some kind of legislature, but everyone bows to the kings of society. Everyone's focus is on the kings."

"It's because no one else has a real life," Jae said. "They have to live through us, so they elevate us into something they think they could never attain, and thus they never even try."

"That's spooky."

He smiled at the ceiling. "It's good to hear someone say that at last. I'm so tired of everyone taking it for granted. Even Londo – well, Lon likes his attention – but every now and then I can see that he's put off by it. But all this is dangerous to the Legion."

"How so?"

He tried to put it into words. "It attracts people who shouldn't be here. The Legion was meant to help, Lina, and not meant to create an entire new class. But it has, and some megas out there apply just to gain the fame, the power that being a Legionnaire imparts.

"There are people here that I wouldn't turn my back on in battle. They're looking after only themselves, only to star in a good story in that night's news reports. In the heat of battle that means that you can't trust them.

"Lon and I decided to bring up the matter to Stoan when he was first elected, and now there are… sub-rosters, I'll call them, who are used for certain jobs and no others. No one knows about the names outside of Stoan, Andri, Lon and me, Wiley, Brügz, Chim… maybe a few others.

"We put them in front of the lights if we think they'll make a good impression, keep their energy centered on what they want. But usually they don't make that good an impression. The rot from within tends to show on-camera. Some of them are true megas, too. It's to their shame that they don't use what they can to help. Take people like Shascrappin or Transit or Neuron. Don't get close to them, Lie. They'll try to get cozy with the wife of Valiant, but don't you let them. They're predators who will turn on you in a second if you don't watch out."

Lina thought about it. "Is that why Legion rules are so stringent?" she asked. "To use that as an excuse if anyone like that starts getting out of line? So they can be kicked out under an official reason instead of 'lack of character'?"

"Could be, Lie. Could be." He sighed. "I've never understood the thirst for fame. Even with Londo, with him trying to get out from Hal's shadow, trying to get the entire universe to love him, I've never understood the need to exult oneself over another."

"And yet you're in the Legion, the biggest, fartingest bunch of celebrities around."

His lips quirked at that and he swirled the almost-empty glass in his hand. "What I want is to live back in the forest for the rest of my days, traveling with my family and tending the world. That's all I ever wanted. No one special, just part of the pattern, just helping."

"You're helping now, Jae."

"That's why I'm here."

Lina got up to program new albums on the juke box. Jae joined her, stretching sleepily, and together they puzzled over Lon's collection. Jae reached into a crook of the CD bookcase and withdrew a long, crystalline tube. "This is pretty good dance music, if you're interested in learning AffSys steps."

She shook her head and continued to scroll through the listings. "I don't dance," she said.

"You don't dance?" Something in his tone made her look up. "You don't dance?"

"Not a single step."

"Let me get this straight," he said, starting to chuckle with little snorts between. "You married Londo 'Don't Hold Me Down Because My Feet Won't Stand Still' Rand, and you? can't? dance?"

"Oh." Her voice was very small. "Dancing involves touching, remember?"

"Touching? Oh. Ah."

She nodded. "And everyone's always told me that I was the clumsiest human ever born. What am I going to do?" She sank to the floor in a heap. "Ugh!"

"What do people do on Earth?" Jae demanded. "I thought they danced there."

"Some do. Not everyone." She shook her head forlornly before she took a deep breath. "Okay. There's a dance studio over in Durham," she said. "I guess I should sign up for lessons. Find someone with very hard feet. Oh lord, dancing!" She moaned with dread. "Ballroom or modern? Or is he into country line dancing? He doesn't have much country music here."

"Lina, Lina, Lina… I have no idea of what any of those is. Let's see…"

Jae reached into a low cabinet, where he fished through more crystals. He mumbled labels to himself and finally produced one with a flourish. "Here." He pulled Lina with him to the couch where he pressed the crystal to the surface of the coffee table. It swallowed it up.

"Play tape," he commanded the air, and a wide 3-D screen appeared. "This was the opening of the new Cozzyvosh over in NiPond a few months ago. It was wild! We went crazy that night."

The screen showed an interior: colored lights flashing upon a crowded dance floor. Some patrons hung in midair on bungee cords; some hung without the cords. All danced furiously to drums with a dash of cymbal and sticks. It seemed to be a line dance with everyone doing the same step at the same time. Roving spotlights picked out individuals who then ad libbed to the basic beat. Many of the spotlit dances were twice as fast as the one everyone else was doing.

Lina felt like sinking in upon herself. "That looks pretty barbaric to me," she mumbled.

Londo looked as if he were having the time of his life there in the spotlight. Even nearby Aiko faded in his presence. The crowd was going wild for him, and why not? His steps were precise, his body graceful and alert, his dance had purpose. He was soul personified.

"Okay, okay." Jae turned the tape off and got up to pick through some trophies hanging on the wall. "Here's one," he said. He touched a spot on it that Lina hadn't noticed before and a scene projected from it: a ballroom, the walls draped in cloth away from tall windows, balls of muted light floating above the dancers, one of whom was Lon. Now the music was soft, steady drumming with lots of tiny bells and tinkling cymbal. It seemed almost medieval. Couples took each other's hands and stepped around each other, coming in to hold each other only for the equivalent of every other verse. This time, Aiko didn't accompany Lon but another woman did.

"Anyone can do that," Jae scoffed. "It's veddy, veddy upper crust, don't you know."

"It is very stylized," Lina agreed. She considered and then concentrated. Two DVD cases popped into her hand. She put one into Lon's DVR and turned on the TV next to it. She clicked through the disc: *The American President,* the state dinner dancing scene. "This is our upper-crust dancing," Lina said, "but a lot of people are into it on a casual basis, too. For wedding receptions and such."

"At least they're holding each other." Jae watched the two-dimensional tape closely. "Nice music. If you're going that slowly, you want to be holding someone."

Lina ejected that and put in *Sunday the Reverend Killed* with the extensive scene inside the salsa disco. "This is more recreational dancing," she explained.

Jae watched as the camera followed the main characters against the background of dancing. People were dancing apart, but they also danced together. And the music! The singing! He shook his head wonderingly. "I want to go somewhere like that. Tomorrow – Can we?"

Lina turned off the TV as the scene ended. "I wouldn't know where to take you. I don't get out to any nightclubs. Besides, tomorrow's Art 'Round the Park."

Jae sighed theatrically. "A teetotaler. A non-dancer. What did Lon have going through his head? Ah, I forgot. A mind-controller!"

Lina set her jaw. "I can learn this. I just don't know if I have the guts to get up there and do it in front of people. I'll take lessons, here and on Earth. I *will* learn. ...Someday."

"You'll learn now." Jae pulled himself up and put on the trophy scene again. "Puter," he called, "loop this for as long as we need it." Two beeps and the music began. He held out his hand and shook it demandingly when Lina didn't respond. "Now, Lina."

"And I suppose you have feet of steel?" she asked as she rose reluctantly.

"I have armored boots in case some criminal wants to do me in. Or if Valiant's wife wants to do the same thing." He placed her in position and took her through the steps, an easy thing to do since it was mostly walking. They'd turn and gesture, turn and gesture, come in together and swing around, then separate and do it all again. After a long while Jae called quits.

"I've always hated that dance," he grumbled.

"They'd do better to learn how to waltz," Lina told him. "Waltzes are lovely to watch."

"What's a waltz?" Jae plopped down on the couch, his arms crossed in front of himself.

Another DVD case popped in. Lina clicked through, clicked through…

There was Anna in her enormous hooped dress, teaching the King how to dance. Another disc and here was a ballroom of Viennese dancers dressed in nineteenth century clothing, swirling around the room as an invisible orchestra played.

"Interesting," Jae said, studying it all. "I can't see the women's feet."

"It's just a mirror of the men's."

He nodded. "Is there any way to loop this music? So it goes on as long as we need it?"

A CD appeared in Lina's hand. "The Strauss Waltzes," she announced, and set it going on the player. She watched as Jae tried out the step, fumbled, and then got it right. He motioned for her to join him and she tried her best. At first all the holding distracted her – *people do this all the time* – but then frustration took over.

He lectured her: "Don't look at your feet! Keep your eyes on mine."

She growled, "If I don't look at my feet, I'm going to fall all over yours!"

"You're doing that already," Jae growled back. He increased his grip on her waist and practically pulled her along with him so she'd stay on track. Finally he turned off the CD and they practiced without music, her humming, humming – ouch! – humming a very slow waltz to keep them going.

"Remind me not to introduce you to any paravillains," Jae finally muttered afterward as he tumbled onto the couch.

"I'm sorry! I offered to take lessons from a professional–"

"And I just gave you some for free."

"Thank you. Thank you very much. But I warned you! Oh god, now I can have nightmares about being the only person in the universe who can kill Valiant just by being on the same dance floor as he is."

Jae glanced over at Lina's miserable expression and had to laugh. "Tell you what," he finally decided. "We'll do this again tomorrow night and the night after that. You may not wind up the best dancer around, but at least you won't be murderously inept. That would be too strange an epitaph for the Legion to bear." He placed his hand solemnly above his heart. "For the honor of the Legion, I will do this. We are the Legion."

Lina tried to scowl at him, but she couldn't. They both laughed and headed to the kitchen for something to drink.

Lon oversaw the rescue of the final survivor from the lower deck of the aft section, carried up on stretcher by ship's crew. "All clear, sir," the Legion medic accompanying the group confirmed to him, obviously relieved to be out of the iffy section.

Londo sealed the lift, then tethered himself to the section airlock and sealed it behind himself. Now firmly attached to the healthier part of the *Travern*, Lon set about severing this, the final connection to the wounded aft section.

He dug the side of his hand into metal, gnawing through it like a chainsaw through cardboard. With his left hand he held on to one wall while making the final cut with his right. Then he grabbed the newly-released area before it could float haphazardly away. He sought clean footing, digging his toes into the floor slightly, just to be sure of contact. Then he heaved the section away.

Five full decks of massive starship pushed off from the main ship in a direction where they wouldn't hit any protruding structure on the healthier part of the *Travern*. It took only a moment for Londo's push to drive the slag far enough – perhaps two feet away – for it to disappear into the endless void of hyperspace.

There was no action and reaction in hyperspace's void; the toss wouldn't have affected the main ship's course. Lon checked his toeholds, then his impervion tether. It still held, so he made his way back in.

Stoan was waiting for him. "Your bomber is trying to talk," he told Londo, "but he's still anesthetized. And he doesn't speak the language well. It'll take time."

"I've scanned every person on board," Londo replied. "No one's got a bomb in their gut. I saw the remains of three who did."

"But no others. Good work," Stoan said.

"There might be bombs hidden in plain sight," Lon reasoned. "Tough to spot those in chaos."

"We'll assume there are no more bombs until we spot evidence of same. So it's just search and rescue from here on out. You and Aiko cover the center portion. Damage there is extensive."

"On it." Londo flew off down the deck corridor.

Wiley looked up as Jae entered the lab, a big grin on the blond Legionnaire's face. "She can't dance," he explained to Wiley. "Can you believe it? Missus Londo Rand. I had to take it upon myself to start teaching her." He flopped down in a chair and propped his legs up on another, feigning pain. "What do you have for mangled toes?"

"You're teaching her to dance?"

"Absolutely. We can't have a marriage I presided over ending up badly."

"She's a prisoner, just remember that," Wiley said absently. He wasn't even using a full mind for the conversation.

"She's not a real prisoner; she's Londo's wife."

That caught two of Wiley's minds' attentions. He turned to Jae, seeing that he'd started detailing notes on the day's activities both with and without the prisoner. "Since when does that make a difference?"

"Since the fact that it's obvious she's not controlling anyone's mind." Jae looked at his comrade in mild surprise and sat up in his chair, setting down his note padd. "Don't tell me you think she is?"

"It doesn't matter what I think. Rules are rules, Jae."

"To blaze with rules if they don't make sense."

"Now this is an attitude from you I haven't seen in some time. You have been in her presence a lot."

Jae swung his chair around to face Wiley straight on. "And so have you. So if she *is* controlling us, we're both sunk. But she isn't, and she's married to Londo, which means she's going to be around here for a long, long time. This prisoner shit is a *kick* of a way to start a relationship with her. I say, loosen the chains. Let's make a friend, not an enemy. And stop the experiments on her. She's bound to figure out what you're doing."

"She thinks it's something called interstellar jet lag."

"It's making her very moody. I don't like drugging a friend."

"It's standard procedure for suspected mind controllers, Jae. And Gorgeon alerted me to the stress levels. I've adjusted the dosage. There are just a few more readings I need to take tomorrow and then they're complete."

Jae fumed in his chair.

Wiley placed the tinker toy on his console so it matched ports with his dimensional infra-cloud systems. "So you're teaching her how to dance. And taking her to

Earth every day. Why not bring those animals here and have them stay in quarters? They're small, aren't they?"

"She says that would cause them emotional trauma."

"And this way you get to see more of Earth."

"People have the wrong idea about the place. So far it's a nice world."

Wiley checked a minor security alert within the building and reset the system. He ran through the results of experiments his assistants were running in his tertiary laboratory on the lower floors, and coordinated one set with those from his offsite lab. "Lina is a very personable young lady," he said as if an afterthought.

"She's a lot sillier than I'd think Lon would have ended up with," Jae said over his notes. "Or maybe she's a lot more serious. You know, I always thought he'd either wind up with a no-mind bimbo or some ultra-noble mega-mega with society coming out her ass. I never pictured him with a nice girl."

"Yes, very nice. And she also might be considered quite pretty. In a naturalistic way."

That made Jae look up. "Are you getting at anything in particular, or just rambling in your dotage?"

"I am only 119, Jaeson," Wiley replied stiffly. "That's barely middle-aged."

Jae shrugged. "So one of your minds is going early."

"All I wish to remind you is that you should be aware of Prisoner Watch Syndrome."

The set of Jae's jaw hardened. "Dr. Mem-Bazer, I know what I'm doing. She's the wife of my best friend. Is there any law against being friendly with her?"

"If I were you I might think about maintaining more distance, at least until Londo comes back. Lina doesn't know about PWS either. She's just been married to someone who's not available right now. She's undergoing a primary emotional shift in her life. It could be confusing for her."

"So why not make it easier by having some friends around, Wiley? If I were in her boots, that's what I'd want." Jae considered the end of his stylus. "I'm a professional. And she's got a lot of common sense. I don't think there'll be any problems."

11

A four-story hole rent the floor in this flickering section of the hyperspace ship, as if the structure had been paper and some giant had punched his arm through it. The damage hadn't been enough to disable the artificial gravity. Lon and Aiko found three kids who'd been trapped on the shreds.

"Valiant! Orenya!" the kids squealed in relief and awe as the famous Legionnaires appeared to their rescue.

The two of them touched down lightly on what was left of the floor. "Are you three all there is in here?" Aiko asked them with an everything's-all-right-now smile. It was bad enough that they'd been trapped here for two days. Behind the *oohs* of awe, they were filthy, terrified, dehydrated, and hungry.

"My mom tried climbing down yesterday," the one girl told Aiko. "But she hasn't come back. Does that mean she's dead?"

"All that means is that she hasn't come back yet, honey," Lon assured her. He handed out water bottles, from which the kids drank greedily. "It's pretty rough going out there in parts of the ship. She might even have gotten lost. Sorry we took so long to get here."

"So she's okay?'

"I hope so. I know that wherever she is, she's trying to get back to you. Let's get out of here. Come on, you ride up here." Lon lifted the girl with his right hand and reached down with his left for the boy. "And you ride here. Orenya?" He used her hero name so the kids would get a thrill.

"I hope that means you're coming with me." She smiled down at the shy boy and hoisted him into her arms. "Let's go," she said, and they all lifted off into the air.

The kids loved it! The heroes drew out the ride a little longer than they normally would. These kids had been through hell.

Damn, the door that had caused such trouble, almost fused with the wall, had slid back into place after they had worked to get it functioning again. "Orenya?" Lon asked. "I have my arms full, but maybe I could take one more."

"If you say so, Valiant." Aiko hoisted the squirming cargo in her arms and turned him around. "You put your arms around Valiant's neck and hold on for a couple minutes. Can you do that?"

"Y-yes, ma'am, Orenya."

"Good. Hold tight. Are you holding tight?" She paused in mid-air and checked that he wasn't going to let loose. Then she glided to the door and heaved, trying to make the small crack there big enough for Lon and the kids to get through. It eked open with a screeching protest. The kids cried out at the noise.

"What a racket! But we're almost there," Aiko told them with a laugh. "I don't want to break what's already broken."

Londo heard a sound.

A sound like a small popgun, a sound that shouldn't be here. **Aiko, hurry up. All of a sudden I don't like this.**

She looked sharply at him then and now she could hear it, too. A series of pops.

With a grunt the door folded in her hands; she pushed the bulk of it out of the way, into the corridor. To blaze with whether it was unusable now or not.

Lon rushed through the doorway. Gently shaking the kids off himself, he shouted, "C'mon, Aiko! Now!"

Could time stop here in hyperspace? Her gaze met his and then the universe halted, frozen. Now so slowly time began again, tick. Tick. Tick. Aiko's mouth opened to say something, her shoulders tensed to make the final movement that would float her through the doorway.

A noise.

A tremendous, ripping roar. Lon threw himself between it and the children, gathering them in a wad of fragile human flesh his body could protect. Then he looked around.

Debris shot from the door into the corridor. It battered the walls in the other room. Skewers of hypersteel cracked through the air. Everything in that ripped area had turned into a projectile as a damaged bomb finally exploded. The interior wall buckled in places, as if meteors slammed against it. They imprinted deep spikes on this, the other side. The children screamed in terror.

Aiko's mouth circled into a surprised "Oh!"

Aiko!

A deep, narrow spike appeared in the remaining part of the door in front of her as she slammed against it, only her face showing through the hatch window, only the surprised expression.

Aiko! Aiko!!

Londo.

The pummeling ceased and Lon rose up, tearing his eyes from hers. The kids were still squalling. He turned them around so they couldn't see Aiko's face. "Go on, kids. I have to see about that explosion. There are Legionnaires down this hallway, not far. Run and meet them."

The kids didn't move but looked up at him, confused and frightened. "Go!" He pushed each of them. "Run! Move!!"

He waited a split-second to see that their feet continued to hurry them to safety before he turned back. He slipped inside the door. "Aiko!"

Londo... He could hear her thoughts with his telepathy.

A spear of metal impaled her into the wall, holding her there like a butterfly on a pin.

"I'll get you to medical–"

Londo. Her eyes sought his. **I'll always love–**

Her eyes were open but he couldn't read her any more. Blood trickled from the corner of her mouth.

"No," he breathed. "Aiko!"

He tried to reach out as Lina had reached out to him when he'd died. What had she done? How had she done it? And that time she'd talked to those dead mercenaries. **Aiko! Aiko!!** his mind howled through the darkness of hyperspace.

Stoan found him there twenty minutes later, her body cradled in his arms, the spear still through her. Londo shook from the effort of weeping.

"Ah, grigach!" Stoan's heart stopped at the sight. Aiko's Legion ring had registered her death and position to his central command. It had taken him this long to work through wreckage. "Aiko!"

Lon looked up at that, through the curtain of tears. He tried to say something and couldn't.

"Here, Londo." Stoan held out his arms. "I'll take her. You're needed."

"*No!*" Lon clasped Aiko closer to him. "You're not taking her away!"

"There's nothing you can do for her, Lon." Stoan tried to keep his voice soothing. Lon's rages were well-known. They couldn't afford for Valiant to go over the edge, not now. "You can mourn her on the way back, but we need you here now."

"She was there one moment..." Londo cried, "a-and the next one she was... I couldn't sense her anywhere."

"You're right. She's gone. I'll take her now, Lon. Let me have her." Stoan kept talking slowly and softly, and finally Lon passed her so carefully to him. Aiko's body was cold.

"Level Three," Stoan told him. "They need you on Level Three, as soon as you can."

Lon covered his eyes with his hands and nodded. He began to curl up in a ball.

"I'm not taking her back until you leave for Level Three," Stoan threatened.

Lon looked at Stoan through his fingers at that.

Aiko's body was so heavy with the spike still through her. Stoan tried not to tremble from the burden. "I'm not. You leave and then I leave, too."

"You… You're a hard man, Stoan."

"There's a time and a place for mourning, Londo. There could be a lot more mourning for a lot more people if you don't get up to Level Three. Now. Move it, Legionnaire!"

Londo uncurled himself and stood up. He wiped his eyes with the palms of his hands and nodded, not looking at Stoan.

"I'm not leaving here, Rand."

Londo snuffled and flew off, out of the room.

It was only then that Stoan allowed himself to cry.

Neither he nor any of his Legionnaires had detected the message from the tiny drone amid the interference along the cracked port comm conduit of the ship some two hours before.

Brügz and Erik both were stand-offish if curious of the cats, but Lina and Jae fed them quickly. They gave them rubs and rolled toys for them as the other two looked around, wondering at the primeval forest around the house and the antique electronics. Lina demonstrated her computer as she checked her bank balance and e-bills, and they had a great laugh.

"I haven't even been upstairs yet," Jae said, looking up at the balcony overhead.

"Tomorrow," Lina promised. "Art 'Round the Park today." She grabbed a wide-brimmed garden hat and sunglasses to go with her pareo and jacket, and made sure that her hair was securely pinned up under the hat. "There will probably be people there from work," she explained. "I'm supposed to be in quarantine on the other side of the world. They'll never recognize me in a dress."

They arrived in downtown Durham in the bright noon. The noise of the event overpowered that of the downtown freeway a few blocks away. Booths and white tents lined the streets. A band blasted echoing hard rock in a blocked-off intersection.

Crowds of people swirled in slow-moving streams and whirlpools of gawking past those tents as well as refurbished red brick tobacco warehouses that now housed apartments and stores. Lina checked the map on the poster, got her bearings, and ported them again to the next block.

The guys all wore replicated jeans and took great glee in wearing versions of their famous costumes as tee shirts, except for Jae's borrowed ParaNet shirt. Here on Earth they were anonymous. They stared as much as anyone, studying people in dance costumes, renaissance costume, their usual costume, and–

"Klingons!" Lina pointed them out to Jae. "*Star Trek.*"

Jae laughed to see some kind of alien-humans. These people had obviously never seen real aliens.

Lina glanced around. "Over there's where Rusty Estevez is playing. And over here are nachos and tacos. Who wants to try some?"

"This place feels weird," Erik complained, looking at the sky. "There's no weather control. It feels wild, like anything could happen." His power was that of forming pockets within weather-controlled conditions.

"Can't do anything?" Brügz nudged him.

That evoked a frown at the challenge. "Let me try," Erik muttered and he started to do… something. It felt to Lina as if he were gathering in the auras of the nature around him to attach them to his own.

"Wait!" Lina cried. She lowered her voice before she could draw attention. "It's a beautiful day. Why bother a beautiful day?"

"All I want to do–"

"I can bring you back someday when we're expecting a bad storm, how about that?" she offered. "Earth says she's blessed this event today and would really appreciate it if you didn't nudge things around."

"Earth says?" Erik glanced quickly at Brügz.

Brügz shrugged, trying to look casual. "It does seem fairly nice already," he observed. "A little cool." Still, the people here were baring parts of their bodies that he didn't normally see bared. His gaze followed a pair of short but shapely ladies who were wearing sleeveless shirts and skirts that left their legs naked from thigh down. Erik noticed where he was looking and gave them a long, considered glance as well.

A group of screeching children ran past them, their faces painted with butterflies, flowers and lightning bolts.

Erik wondered if this were some kind of tribal skin ceremony. "So how far is Earth from having weather control?"

"Earth will never have weather control," Lina declared.

He returned his attention to her. "Never? Not even with the storms Valiant's mentioned?"

"Never. Earth commands: no compromise on this. Sarastor was ignorant to allow it there; now she knows better. Earth knows better." The food vendor handed her trays of nachos, drinks and change. "Thank you," she told him sunnily and licked some errant melted cheese off her finger as she handed two of the trays off to Brügz and Erik. "Now where has Jae gotten to?"

Lina brought Jae some nachos to munch on as he listened to Rusty Estevez. The others joined them.

"I don't get it," Brügz said of the song, and Jae and Erik looked at him. "Where's the spell? I thought songs were supposed to cast spells?"

"It sounded like a love story to me," Erik opined.

"Songs aren't supposed to cast spells," Jae told them. "They can be about whatever you want them to be. They're a class of poetry."

Brügz looked very doubtful at that. "It gives me the creeps," he muttered to Erik.

Erik regarded him for a moment. "You've never had a sense of humor."

"Have so."

"Never for a moment in your life. Now shut up and listen. At least have an open mind like I have."

"You're just here for the girls."

"And just look at them. You can look while you listen, you know."

Jae glared at them. "Shut up! Some of us are trying to hear."

They left Jae to explore the fair. Erik and Brügz, both so tall and with gorgeous builds, attracted stares as they roamed the crowd. They drew attention away from Lina, she noted satisfactorily. Plus, their height made her look short, further disguise. It came in handy when she spotted several co-workers.

They stopped when they got to the Society for Creative Anachronism exhibition. Ladies fair in their long gowns watched warriors of both genders battling with hard cardboard swords and padded armor in a fenced ring.

"Kuttr wouldn't approve," Brügz muttered. "Look at that. Their stance is all wrong." He spotted some swords lying against the barrier and picked one up, tossing another to Erik. "They should be doing more this…" He swung the sword and Erik countered easily. Another swing, another counter, and they were dancing all over the street in their fight of cardboard death.

Occasionally one would connect, and they'd discover with a cry just how hard cardboard could be. Their fight became more serious; neither wanted to gain a painful blow. A crowd of people gathered around them, swirling away as they approached and then following as they retreated.

"My lords! My lords!" One of the ladies fair ran up to them, keeping a wary distance. "Those swords are for tournament use only. They are dangerous out here!" The two Legionnaires paused. "We are allowed to battle only within the barriers, my lords. And Society rules declare that contestants must wear protective clothing at all times."

Erik and Brügz looked at each other. They couldn't respond in English. With their translators tucked behind their ears, their mouths wouldn't match what they said.

Repeat after me, Brügz: I apologize, dear lady.

Brügz bowed and handed the woman his sword, hilt first. "I apologize, dear lady," he told her smoothly, repeating Lina's enunciated but silent sentence.

Erik: I am a pig and undeserving of your attention.

Erik swept an elaborate bow to her as he surrendered his sword. "I am a pig and undeserving of… your attention."

Brügz frowned as the translator in his ear repeated Erik's phrase in Panlingua.

Brügz: Have your warriors spit on me, for I am the lowest of the low.

Brügz gave Lina a suspicious glance and repeated his bow, saying nothing. He went over to her after the lady hastened away. "From now on I think we risk the translators."

"How rude," she said. "You don't trust little ol' me."

"It occurs to me that anyone who would marry a scoundrel like Valiant might not be entirely innocent herself."

"I'll tell him you said that," she replied with a smirk.

"And you'll tell him what you had us saying."

"Well… Maybe we'll call it even this time."

They left the SCA territory to take in the craft displays. Brügz was attracted to a number of black and white photographs, while Erik only saw one sculpture he liked, but he liked it a lot.

Lina steeled herself before drawing Brügz aside. "I might be able to find a credit card to pay for a photo, or maybe get Erik that piece," she told him in a low voice.

"You could," he repeated at her. "But?"

"It's… I… Damn it. I'm doing this wrong. I get the feeling that you're the same rank as Jae, right? Or higher?"

"I might be."

"But Erik isn't."

"No, can't say that he is."

"Could you revoke Jae's order that I can't come to Earth on my own?"

Brügz tipped his head to the left and gave her an amused look, though his eyes were sharp on her. "Ah. So you'll bribe me to do this?"

"It's nice art, isn't it? And really, in the galactic scheme of things, I'm nobody very special."

"And if I don't countermand whatever order Jae gave you, you'll do what? You'll stay here anyway?" He watched her ponder this and then said, "Last time someone offered me a bribe, it was for a twenty-pound block of crystallized *libdunum*."

"*Libdunum.* Is that pretty?"

"Only in one's bank account."

"Ah, but this–" Lina gestured to take in the art. "This you can hang on your wall and enjoy it every day. What price joy?" She turned back to grant him a considering gaze. "It's a good bribe. Cheap, but substantial. If I were you, I'd jump on it."

"While the actual me will take a pass. Did I mention that I used to be Legion commander?"

"Oh jeez, I'm so screwed." Lina wilted.

"So you'll return to Sararstor? With us?"

Lina shook herself and let out a frustrated growl. "Damn it, I promised."

"And besides that, you're under arrest. For a major crime."

"Suspicion of. I don't care about that." Lina shook her index finger at him. "It is the duty of every prisoner of war to try to escape. I want a lawyer."

"You're not a prisoner of war."

Erik moseyed up to them, glancing back at the sculpture tent. "Wish I could get it."

Lina rolled her eyes and stomped off. She got a business card from the artist so that they could return later if Erik really wanted it and could find some Terran money.

"Or she could strike you a better deal," Brügz confided to Erik. "This will be an interesting trial."

"Huh?"

"Forget it," Lina insisted. "Just forget it. I do lousy bribes, okay? It was my first time; I'll get better. Cheez! Here, feed your faces and be quiet."

They sampled cotton candy and funnel cakes and some iced brownies that Lina turned up her nose at, proclaiming them (away from their baker) unfit to eat because an iced brownie wasn't a real brownie.

"Lina! Good god, is that Lina O'Kelly in a dress?"

Lina whirled to see a familiar head popped out of a fortune reading tent. Not a co-worker, hurray. She waved at the "gypsy" woman. "Dinah!"

Dinah motioned them into her tent and closed the flap against the crowd noises. Brügz and Erik boggled at the light-skinned Terran. A bright purple kerchief barely kept a full head of tightly-permed, dark hair under control. Her eyes were heavily lined, her lips a bright red, and a star beauty mark had been painted on her left cheek. She wore dangling coin earrings and a matching group of necklaces over a fringed shawl and long skirt, both in shades of purple to match the kerchief. Even Dinah's long nails were purple. Blossoming from behind the fringe, her neckline left little to the imagination.

A card-reading table had been laid out with tasseled tablecloths crisscrossing it. Interior walls were hung with tapestries, attempting an exotic atmosphere that the metal folding chairs marred though they were anchored by an oriental rug against the asphalt street.

"You'll set the profession back a hundred years," Lina complained as she looked around. "Plus I think real gypsies might object to the stereotype."

Dinah laughed with an exaggerated mysterious gesture. She used a smoky deep voice for the occasion. "But I'll make money doing it, dah-ling. My rent's due in two weeks and my best clients are both out of the country on vacation. C'mon, Lina, how long has it been since you had your cards read?"

"Guys, this is professional psychic Dinah Stewart, who when I first met her declared that I would someday have three husbands and seventeen kazillion kids and be empress over all I surveyed, or something like that. Which goes to show you how good she is."

Dinah stuck her lower lip out in a pretty pout. "One lousy reading and you hold it against me for the rest of my life."

"Okay, okay. She's looking trampy today, but usually she's a very nice person. And quite talented. How much are you charging?"

She eyed Erik with a suggestive grin, which he returned. "Friends get benefits."

"Ho boy. Are you guys game?"

Erik nodded quickly. Brügz shrugged. "When on Earth…" he began. The translator didn't follow his mouth movements.

"Good god, you're married," Dinah interrupted, staring at Lina with an sharp eye.

"Is it that obvious? No, it's not one of them." Lina saw Dinah scrutinizing the other two, who were already impressed.

"But… you're married. You. With your phobia?"

"No phobia anymore." Lina picked up Dinah's hand in hers. "Ta dah. And for my next trick…"

Brügz and Erik glanced at each other, wondering what that was about.

"Whoa, times sure change. One thing..." Dinah paused, looking at Lina's arm uncertainly. "I don't know what it means..."

"What?"

"There's a bracelet that you shouldn't buy. Or wear. Or something."

"This one?" Lina pointed at the tracker bracelet. "Or this one?" The porting measurer.

"No. These are crap bracelets, Lie. Where'd you get them, the Walmart returns table? You need jewelry, you should come borrow some of mine. No, it's something else. It keeps you imprisoned? Are you into bondage now?"

"I don't think so."

"Well then I don't know what it is. Just keep an eye out for strange bracelets."

"*They* can certainly be obtuse at times, can't they?" Lina commiserated with her fellow psychic.

"They certainly can. And they're going out of their way today. They keep saying you've married Maximus or something, isn't that silly?"

Lina laughed. "Oh, he's just my father-in-law," she said as she faced the fellows. "Who's first?"

Quickly Erik took a seat for his reading and Dinah turned to Lina. "Readings are always best done in private," she said pointedly, nodding at the door to the tent with her chin. "I know you; you'll know when we're ready for you to come back."

Lina rolled her eyes at her. "Fine. We'll be around. He doesn't speak much English, but he understands it. He can say 'yes,'" Lina nodded her head with a smile to get the pronunciation across to Erik, "or 'no,'" she shook her head and frowned, "and that's about it."

"Yes," Erik said.

That seemed to interest Dinah all the more. "Not a prob. Go."

As soon as Brügz and Lina emerged into open air again, Brügz pulled her with him to take in the art exhibit next door while Lina reveled in the overlapping sounds of the bands all around. She spotted colorful dancers down at the end of the block. Mambo!

Jae, would you like to see something a little different? Lots of drums, she called.

Sure.

Brügz hardly jumped when he appeared. They watched the dancers in their sinuous dance. The pounding band featured a full three minutes of just drums. Lina could feel Jae's excitement radiating from him as he bobbed in place. When the dancers invited the audience to join them, Jae was first in line, with Brügz three people behind him.

Lina was quite content to be an observer. The two Legionnaires caught the rhythm and steps right away, but clearly Jae was the standout. Though his movements were the same as the dancers', his attitude was beyond them, playfully and unabashedly more erotic. Three of the professional women dancers gathered around him, urging him on, and he delighted in finishing the dance with them. When the drums finally stopped, much of the applause was directed at Jae, who made a show of bowing to the crowd as Brügz dragged him off.

"I should know better than to dance near you," Brügz chuckled. "At least we know now that there's a spot of civilization on this world."

Then Jae and Brügz spent the next ten minutes in a leather goods booth, admiring themselves in the mirror under the awning. Jae in particular liked one black leather jacket. He fiddled with all the zippers on it, peering into the pockets.

"Just like Londo's vest," he told Lina. He studied the lines of it in the mirror and Lina flipped up the collar for him, lifting his hair over it.

"You look very tough," she said and he grinned down at her. The leather fit him well, made him look more the finely-honed Legionnaire he was. Against the black, turned-up collar his face seemed more angular than usual. More dangerous. He was all lean man, hard-muscled and in leather. Lina wasn't the only one admiring him.

"I do look tough." Jae made a tough face at himself and struck a pose, whirling around to strike another pose, getting the feel of it and destroying the dangerous mood completely.

"So you think you're ready for a leather bar now, hm?" Lina teased. Brügz was busy grunting on a pair of boots that didn't want to fit. He was out of earshot.

"What's a leather bar?" Jae asked Lina, still preening. He held a colorful kerchief to his neck to see how it went with the ensemble.

"It's where all the gay boys hang out."

Jae stopped. "Define 'hang out,'" he finally said.

"Like him," Lina whispered and tried to point unobtrusively at another customer. This one was small and dark, but tightly packed as far as she could see.

"Hm," Jae commented. There was a group of five college men at the belt table. "How about that one?"

"Where?"

"That one, that one!" Jae hissed. He pulled her closer and whispered in her ear, "On the left, blue shirt."

"Pretty sure he's straight," Lina told him after a pause. "Sorry."

He made a face at her and she tried not to giggle.

A saleslady came up behind them. "You like that jacket, hon?" she asked Jae. "You look real hot in it, uh huh." You could tell exactly when she actually looked at

Jae's face, the little jump of startlement at the beauty. Her eyes widened, her mouth dropped open. Lina hoped that she hadn't looked that way when she first had seen Jae, but likely she had. He was used to the look by now. She hoped.

"How much?" Jae asked in English. Lina had used the phrase several times already.

The saleslady told him. Jae nodded as if he understood the exchange rate. **She has a lot of silver jewelry over there,** Jae silently told Lina. **Do you think she'd trade for silver ingots? I could make some.**

Lina came up beside Jae quickly, blocking his mouth from the woman's sightline so he could talk if he wanted. "I don't believe my friend here realizes that this is genuine leather," she said politely.

The saleslady nodded, still in a trance from the beautiful man. "It's the best, the highest quality," she urged. "Smooth as butter, ain't it? We sell conditioner, too."

"Leather?" Jae asked. "As in… animal skin? Dead animal?"

"He's a strict vegetarian," Lina confided with the saleslady.

"Oh, I can't buy this." Jae removed the jacket hastily. "I can't even wear it. Sorry."

"I could make you a good deal," the woman called out after them as they left the tent. Jae smiled and waved at her, hoping she'd take it as an apology.

"You could have told me sooner," he hissed at Lina.

"But you looked so hot in it."

"I do not look hot in the hides of dead creatures," Jae muttered. "The idea!" He paused. "Lon's uniform–" he began.

"Is faux leather," Lina finished for him, to his great relief. "Every last stitch. I asked."

"Good. Maybe I can find out what he uses – unless that's secret information."

"I'll get it for you even if it is. I think we can trust you."

"Don't ever trust me."

Brügz limped slightly as he joined up with them. "She told me my feet were too 'damned' big. It's not my fault they don't make boots for normal-sized people," he pouted. He looked toward the fortune telling tent. The front flap was still closed. "Just how long do these readings take?"

"He's not exactly getting a reading," Lina said. "I hope he got all his shots."

"Oh, blazing shards. That Erik–"

"I hope whoever it is has all her shots," Jae said. "Isn't Circadia supposed to be starting soon?" He took note of all the people surging downhill toward the ballpark.

Lina stood just outside the back of Dinah's tent. She heard grunting from within, the scrape of a table on pavement. "My, isn't this weather lovely for this time of year," she said loudly. "Not too cold and not too hot. Of course, being North Carolina, it's liable to turn any minute. But it's a nice day if it doesn't rain."

"Don't come in!" Dinah's voice rang from within. "What a killjoy!" They waited two minutes to the sound of soft giggles and two more scrapes, and Dinah opened the flap of the tent even as she adjusted her gypsy headscarf. She gave Erik a final kiss as he came out of the tent, grinning. "Come back anytime," she said, and then saw who was waiting for them.

"Holy christ," she said, spotting Jae. "Look at that aura. Oo, look at *him!*"

"Isn't it something?" Lina asked innocently, watching Dinah squint to see the aura in bright light. Dinah was the best at reading auras.

"Christ, where did you get these people?" Dinah whispered to Lina. "That translator thing of Erik's – and these weird vibes, like these guys are–"

"It'll become clear in time, Dinah. I'll call you in a few days. I don't think I owe you anything for Erik."

"No," Dinah wrinkled her nose in deviltry. "In fact, I may owe you something." She blew kisses as they left and another client approached her tent.

"Very nice planet," Erik was saying as Lina joined the group. "I like it." He strutted with his hands in his pockets. Brügz and Jae shook their heads at him.

"Even without weather control?" asked Jae.

"We can't take you anywhere," Brügz muttered.

Jae reached out to grab Erik's arm and shake it. "Listen – they're starting!"

Now they could hear the familiar brass arrangements of Circadia above the crowd noise, and Jae led them at a jog down the street. He was like a little boy, Lina realized, one who'd been denied candy all his life and was suddenly let loose in a candy store.

The street became clogged with people, too many to fight through to get to the gates any time soon. They could hear the band at good volume but muffled. "I want to see them, too," Jae complained. He looked up. There was a broad roof over the stands on this side of the stadium.

"That's where I'm going," Jae said, and ducked to the side of the street. He flew up close to the building, looking for a place with a good view. Disappearing over the curve of the roof, he came back and waved them up.

"No!" Lina exclaimed. "There's a whole stadium full of–" She felt arms around her, and Erik was flying her up with Brügz close behind.

The roof was hot and dirty, but it held an excellent view. Lina ported in some blankets from home and they settled on those. A lively but warm breeze blew an occasional balloon their way as well as the smell of food cooking down on the concourse.

The crowd was into it, the sound system good, the band hot. Lina and Brügz ported down for beer and more nachos and brought them back. Jae ate his nachos without even noticing, she thought.

Unfortunately, Brügz found a chunk of jalapeno the hard way, even though Lina had warned him about them. She had to get a Coke for him to wash the heat away. She got him some ice cream, too, to cool his tongue. It didn't help that Erik laughed at him the whole time.

As the concert continued, Lina sat in their aerie watching the crowd, feeling the good vibrations coming from them, hearing the music of Circadia but also the music from other bands throughout the area. She felt the celebration, the peace, the brotherhood here.

Why couldn't the entire world be like this? All the time? Or at least a good amount of it? What was there here that was the basis for all the good will? What could she find and bring the world that it could be like this always?

Music is a start, the earth told her.

But it was just music. Then she thought of Sarastor and the emptiness there, a silent world encased in cement and steel and rules. Did it have no music because it was encased, or was it encased because it had no music? Sarastor needed music.

Earth needed more music from the heart. Music for the sake of music, not for the sake of big money or selling platinum records.

How in the world would you accomplish that? Where would you begin?

Sing something, the earth answered her.

"Lina?"

She blinked, coming back. Jae was looking at her curiously. "You looked a million miles away. Didn't you hear the call?" He waved his hand with his ring at her.

"No I didn't. Sorry. Everyone going back?"

He nodded and reached out to catch the small camera that he'd had recording the event. "Here we go."

They returned to Wiley's lab, but it had changed drastically in their absence. Great three-dimensional grids hung from ceiling to floor around the monitor station, displaying many levels of floor plans and elevations of some huge, thousand-roomed compound. Hundreds of lighted dots moved within the grids. A planetary atlas floated in one corner of the area with one spot – a city? – lit up. Jae slid into place at one of the auxiliary communications screens as the others grouped around Wiley at his console. Dellen already stood by Wiley's side.

A large bordered rectangle, maybe fifteen feet square, appeared between the grids, a gigantic television screen. In 3-D it looked like a massive doorway to another room. Uniformed people there looked up from their own banks of workscreens, some nodding with an awed gape at the Legionnaires.

Lina kept to the back of the group so she could see but not be noticed. Without thinking, she brought in lines of planetary force around her, making herself difficult to perceive.

Here were the Legionnaires at work as a team. The translator whispered next to her ear even though she could understand almost all of the rapid communications.

"This is Rimhold, main prison complex," Wilder explained quickly to the new arrivals. Lina could see them tense at just that much.

"Legionnaires." One of the uniformed people in the square stepped forward and assessed them, her face grim. "I'm afraid it's part of our para wing as well. They managed to smuggle disassembled weapons through the security nets this afternoon. We've cut off material transport to the complex, but the damage has been done. We're at a level four insurrection, with holding energies breaking down across the board. We've slowed the progress, but as I said–"

"There are megas involved," Wilder nodded. "We only have five Legionnaires available now."

"It's said that one is enough to stave off Armageddon." The woman held a strained but hopeful expression. "We're three hours out; we might be able to hold them for that long. Auxiliary generators are online, and we have six more in transit. Once they get here we can establish temporary force fields."

Jae looked up from his screens. "I have the data," he reported. "Only four megas and fifty paras, but there are forty-five hundred normals already out. They're still within the prison complex. Armed."

"As I recall, Rimhold main complex is almost escape-proof," Brügz said, his arms crossed in front of his chest.

"'Almost' is the key word, Legionnaires," said the woman. She exchanged quick orders with someone and turned back to them. "We'll do what we can to contain them until you can get here, but I'm not guaranteeing anything. We've put out a planetary broadcast ordering immediate curfew to keep every law-abiding citizen out of the way."

Wilder nodded. "Good. We're leaving now. Legion out."

Jae swung around in his chair and stood up. "Lina, you're confined to quarters. Computer, lock door in Rand quarters and report any absence immediately to me." He gave her a hard look. "This is serious. You get there and stay put. No arguments."

"All right," he addressed the others, "Erik, you and Dellen get to the armory and check us out some extra insurance. We'll meet you in hyperspace bay…" He glanced at Lina. "I said, get to your quarters."

"Um, I was just wondering if y'all needed any transportation."

"We're taking hyper…" Jae paused. "You mean you?"

"Well, yeah. She said it would take you three hours, and apparently there isn't that kind of time to waste."

Jae glanced at Wilder, then at his teammates. "All right. Yes. As soon as we've gone, you go to your quarters. Everyone get into combat gear. Meet back here in fifteen minutes – no longer."

That left Lina and Wilder in his lab. Apparently what Wiley wore every day was his uniform. Quickly he attached some packed, small pouches to his belt and rifled through drawers to add to them.

"So who handles things while *everyone's* away?" Lina asked.

"The computer's set on automatic answering," he replied absently. "Outpost number one will function as emergency Command Central. The sector will just have to wait until someone gets back here." He placed his fingertip on a small circular area of one table, and his short hair began to stand on end. After about twenty seconds he removed his finger from the area and his hair relaxed.

"This should take – hard to say. A minimum of three hours, maximum of a couple days. Probably six to eight hours with this quick strike. There'll be more Legionnaires returning in about a day. They're already in hyperspace on their return trip. I'll leave them a message explaining about you." His fingers drummed in a pattern on the surface of the table, and something beeped in response.

"Thanks. This is a really dangerous mission, isn't it?" Lina asked. She gazed at shadows.

"It's not run of the mill."

"There's some guy who can… He's one of the megas, and he's looking for something. Something they took from him before they put him in prison. It's there, and… it's looking for him, too. It's a thing, not a person. But they have a telepathic link."

Wiley looked up at that. "The Black Blade. He has a computerized sword."

"A sword?" Lina shook her head. "It doesn't look like an ordinary sword to me."

"It can slice through almost anything. It can even cut through impervion, if he's determined enough. And it can disrupt force fields."

Lina nodded, her eyes still focused far away. "He's more interested in finding the sword than anything else. He's not following the others in trying to get out of the prison. He wants to find it and then escape. If you can use the sword as a trap, you'll be able to catch him."

"I'd figured as much."

"Oh. Sorry."

Wiley fit a nut onto a ballpoint pen that didn't have a writing point. The nut glowed red and he stuffed the pen into a pouch. "Don't be. You might have come up with something that we didn't know. Do you see anything else?"

She grimaced. "Your technology is so strange to me. It's difficult to figure that out, to know what's normal or abnormal. There's something wrong with one of the megas' head. It's got a… steel plate or something, a little circle – *they're* showing me a TV screen and a telephone. Maybe he uses it for communication?"

"Ombrillo," Wiley nodded. "Go on."

"*They* say… scramble the messages; he'll be confused. It'll distract him or off-balance him or something. His mind won't be able to concentrate if you blast some jamming at him. Low what? Oh, low frequencies. Use really low frequencies on him. *They* show me his teeth rattling."

Wilder considered. "It's worth a try. Let's see what I have." He sorted through some more drawers and came up with three small boxes and a coil of blinking wire that he stuffed into a new bag and clipped to his belt. "That will get me started," he said, and returned to his console.

He hit two spots there and the doorway came back on. This time people with rifles were running past the camera. The woman from before bawled orders to a group of uniformed people, her back to Lina and Wiley.

"Warden Baxum!" Wilder called. She turned.

"Yes? You have some questions?"

"Please clear a small space for us. We're going to teleport directly to you within the next five minutes."

Her eyebrows shot up. "Five minutes? Direct transport?"

"It's new technology," Wilder said without smiling. "We're trying it out for this mission."

She nodded. "Let's hope it works," she said anxiously. "Any way we can save three hours will definitely count in our favor."

"They shouldn't be expecting Legionnaires this soon."

Her lips spread into a death's head grin at the screen. "It should scare the living shit out of them." She turned and yelled to people to clear a space. "Is that good enough?" she asked. "Do you need the coordinates?"

Wilder looked at Lina and she shook her head. "I've got it," she said softly.

"That's sufficient," Wilder told the warden as Jae and Dellen skidded into the lab. Dellen carried a sling filled with small guns. Their uniforms looked like armor now. They wore vests and thick bands over their knees, elbows and wrists, helmets that completely covered their heads, even their eyes, and spread down past their shoulders. Jae had left his cape behind. Erik caught the door right behind them, and

Brügz was only a few seconds behind that, both similarly dressed, in colors and design that matched their regular uniforms. Erik had a weapon-filled sling similar to Dellen's. When Lina turned around, she found Wiley with his clothes also changed, the lab coat now a thick, ribbed vest, and his collar expanded to a face-covering helmet. Brügz and Dellen passed out the guns and canisters to everyone, and they clipped them onto their belts.

"You're still to go to quarters," Jae told Lina behind the crowd. She nodded.

"You be careful," she said. He gave a little nod at that and stepped to the front of the group.

"I'm team leader," he announced to the warden.

"Neutrino, my people await your orders," the warden replied.

Jae nodded at Lina. Her eyes unfocused for a few seconds in preparation for the journey. Then the Legionnaires hung between worlds for some time before appearing on Rimhold.

Jae didn't have to glance around at the Rimhold monitor to know that Lina had gone straight to her room.

Two long hours later Lina heard the intercom. "Lina O'Kelly to Lab 1-A. Lina O'Kelly to Lab 1-A." It was Jae's voice. She looked up from the Legion Spousal Protocol rulebook she'd been studying with Computerized Ms. Yency.

"Music off," she ordered the computer and ported before the two responding beeps could sound.

The screen from before was on at the main console, and Jae and Wiley stood in it, with three guards behind them. They were all disheveled, filthy. One of the guards was sucking in air hard and deep, as if he'd had the breath knocked out of him. Jae's helmet was retracted so she could see his face and bangs.

"Lina!" he said, running his hand through his hair, trying to get it out from his eyes. "Good, you're there. Listen, we need you to gather more weapons for us. You'll have to get them from the armory."

"Where's that?" Lina looked around for anything that she could write directions on.

Jae looked helpless for a moment. "It's a long way from the lab," he said. "Listen, can you get a picture from me? From my mind?"

"Sure, I guess so."

"Here's the armory. Can you see that?"

She frowned, feeling him trying to reach out to her, to give her the image as if he were handing over a photograph. "Okay," she finally said as the picture built up within her mind. "Got it."

"Good. Computer, allow Carolina O'Kelly access to the armory," he ordered, and there were the two beeps. "Go."

Lina ported. "Computer, lights." The warehouse suddenly appeared out of the echoing darkness around her. Towering rows of industrial cabinetry with big, bulky locks divided the room into aisles.

The locks closest to her said "Level 3," and the ones across from them were labeled, "Level 4." Security levels needed for unlocking? Power levels?

"Are you there?" Jae's voice asked over the intercom.

"Yes," she said. "Everything's locked up in here."

"*Skurn*, I forgot," he said. Pause. "Port me there."

"Hang on."

She concentrated. It was so much easier doing just one person. He appeared next to her and reached for the nearest cabinet that opened to him without hesitation. "It's touch-locked," he explained, hauling out rifles. "Here. Take these and get me… six more."

"Are they safe to handle?"

"Yes."

She rummaged in the wide cabinet and found six more that looked like these, laid out neatly in horizontal stacks. When she turned around Jae was piling more guns, these shiny and silver instead of the flat black ones she had, into a stack at her feet.

"A few more," he said, and went to unlock one of the larger cabinets by putting his palm against the lock.

They had maybe twenty-five guns and a number of smaller things which reminded Lina of grenades gathered in six bags. Jae handled them in cavalier fashion.

"Back to the lab," Jae ordered, and they went. He trotted to one of the far supply tables there, opening drawers. "Here's some," he said triumphantly, and produced seven flat padds as big as legal pads. He added them to the stash. "Okay, Lina, port me, and then back to your room."

She obeyed, but when her eyes refocused from completing the interstellar port, Wilder held up his hand to her. "Wait," he said, turning to Jae. "You forgot the seifer coms."

"I did." Jae turned to the camera, turned to the image of Lina he saw standing there. "Lina, we need five seifer coms."

"What's that?"

"They're… ah…"

Wilder took over. "They're metal and crystal tubing, about eight inches long. I keep a few next to the communications wall, in the storage chamber halfway between the first two monitors."

Lina ran to that area, surprised that there was a hidden storage chamber. It merely looked like wall with electronic trim. "Hang on," she told them as she figured out how to get in.

But there were three different kinds of tubing, all with crystals, some just a little longer than the others. The main difference was in their diameters. Oh hell.

She appeared next to Wilder and Jae with her arms loaded, five of each kind. "Take your pick," she told them.

The far wall of the room exploded inward.

"Grigach!" Jae exclaimed, pushing her down behind a console. "Get out of here!"

"You needed–"

"These," Wilder said, gathering the thickest ones. "And these won't hurt," he said as he took the narrowest ones.

"There's someone where they're not supposed to be," Lina said. "Don't miss them because they're hidden in the dark."

Jae put his hand on the back of Lina's head and pushed her down farther. "Lina, port back. That's an order."

"Wait a moment," Wilder said. Guards were firing at whoever had done the damage. From the howls of pain, the guards had the upper hand here. "Who's hidden? Where are they?"

"It's the man with the metal circle in his head."

"Ombrillo."

Jae and Wilder looked at each other before they returned their gaze to Lina.

"There are mazes under here, deep within the bowels of the planet." Her voice was as distant as her gaze. "He travels within them, not quite knowing where he's going, but his general direction is correct. He makes little sound. He… He can see in the dark? Special lenses, implanted in his eyes… ew… He's got all kinds of machinery where his flesh should – Oh, he's a cyborg. God. There's a little water flowing through the tunnels, but it's not a sewage system. Tunnels carved through the centuries by those who made it out of the Rimhold Rock." She blinked, her eyes refocusing.

"Don't stop now!" Wilder demanded. "Where is he? Exactly?"

"Can you locate it on a map?" Jae asked in a calm voice.

"A map," Wilder said. He touched a ring on his left hand and now in the air appeared diagrams of this place.

"Lower," Lina said, echoing the instructions she heard.

Another map showed in the air. Lina shook her head. "Lower. About a hundred, no, two hundred feet lower."

"Two hundred feet?" Wilder looked frustrated. "There are no maps of anything existing below this level."

"It's there." Lina was positive of it. "What? Wait, Wiley, bring up that view again."

He did, and she ran her finger around it until it pointed at a small circle. "An entrance point to the lower levels," she told him.

"No maps of any lower levels," Wilder mused. He held Jae's gaze for a moment, not looking at her. "I had Lina running holo mazes the other day. With her guides."

"A civilian–" Jae began.

"She ran through them almost as if they'd been marked. Lina, could you do that here? In reality?"

"I could give it a good try." She licked her lips nervously.

"Yes or no?" Jae demanded.

Determinedly she met his eyes. "Yes."

Jae grimaced and wiped his mouth with the back of his hand. "Ombrillo." He finally nodded. "Wiley and I'll go with you. Let's get these guns handed out first. Make it quick." He grabbed two of the seifer coms from Wiley as he turned away, and stuck them into his wrist bands.

They ported down to a starting point some working cameras showed her. Too many were out of commission now. It was black enough down here, but Lina knew it would be darker below. Wiley and Jae both had lenses in their helmets that let them see through some of this, but she didn't have that advantage.

To make it worse, a haze of burning plastic filled the corridor. Lina choked before Wiley reached into the pouch clipped at his belt and produced a length of cord. As he strung it around Lina's neck it constricted, solidifying to rest snugly but not suffocatingly against her skin. Suddenly the air was breathable.

"Thanks," she said.

Wiley nodded absently while Jae ran out into the center of the dim corridor to peer into the haze. "Which way?" Jae asked.

"Over there," Lina said, and Jae turned his head that way. "Over there" was the direction that shouting was coming from, echoing eerily as a distinct layer of pinkish fog seethed into their area.

"I really don't like this," Jae muttered under his breath. He glanced at Lina and then to Wiley, who was comparing maps on his padd. "What's the fix?"

"Roughly a quarter mile to the destination," Wiley reported. "We'll definitely be going through that."

"Then you go back upstairs," Jae commanded Lina. "We'll get to the other side of whatever that is and then I'll send for you."

Lina nodded her head nervously. Fine with her. The shouting was getting closer.

"Go!" Jae told her and he and Wiley flew off toward the melee.

Lina arrived back in the control room, huddling where she'd huddled before. There were people in uniforms pouring in through the break in the wall, and she decided to make herself small until Jae called. Where was the warden? A big man seemed to be in charge now, shouting and waving his gun, while the others scurried to his orders.

"I don't care!" he shouted at one of his aides. "This has gone on long enough. We're badly outnumbered. From here on in, we shoot to kill. I'll take responsibility. You do it on my orders!"

"Yessir!" Four soldiers hurried out of the room.

A new explosion – The wall next to Lina cracked, smoke pouring through it as a fine powder from the ceiling drifted down on her. She let out an exclamation and tried to get away from the electronic crackling, but when she turned, three guns leveled at her.

"Who's this?!" the commander demanded.

One of the men with the guns nodded at Lina's wrist, and in horror she realized that she was wearing that bracelet that said "PRISONER" on it. Telling them that she was an innocent bystander wouldn't get her out of this mess.

12

S he ported.

It was the same spot as before, but now the smoke was pea-soup dense, yet held distinctly-colored layers. Bright blasts made the entire corridor light up. Some layers conducted the light clearly, and others hid it, like cloud-to-cloud lightning.

Which way? she asked her guides, and blindly followed. Almost immediately she stumbled over a body. Whether it was dead or just unconscious she couldn't tell. It wasn't Jae or Wiley. She'd know if she touched them.

She crept almost on all fours so she could see the floor and any obstacles, ducking when her guides told her to. Flat pulses of light sizzled through the air just above her head in high-pitched shrieks that hurt her ears. Her hand landed in a puddle of sticky liquid. She refused to look to check what color it was.

But she couldn't crawl a quarter mile. She tried to crouch and run. Now her guides told her, **Zig!** and she zigged and zagged.

From out of the fog, a hand grabbed her arm. She struggled against it, crying out. A dark, menacing voice laughed in return. She had to do something. She kicked out and connected. The hand let loose for a moment. That was all it took for her to run! Pulses of light hammered behind her, but she ducked, she zagged, she fell back against the wall to catch her breath and heard the groans of the injured behind her.

The walls of the corridor keened weirdly as if they themselves were injured. It was the sound of metal in distress, metal that was stretching or bending.

Somewhere a voice through the fog gasped, "It's Neutrino!" but whatever it was, it was happening far down the corridor that branched out from the intersection she'd just passed. This was only the echoes of something that must be ear-splittingly loud wherever Jae was.

The big battle was down there, but the entrance to the lower levels was over here and down a ways. A thrumming sound came from this direction, like a million fans turning, and it was that way that Lina went. Perhaps it *was* a million fans. The air seemed to clear the farther she went.

She was about to breathe a sigh of relief at her safety when she heard **Hit the dirt!** and hurled herself to the ground. Light pulses split the air where her head had been, a triple-band of them in different blinding colors. They left a new fog behind.

A scream ahead of her – Something thudded to the ground. Lines of light traced through the corridor. Lina quickly crawled to the wall, huddling against a support beam. She brought a blanket of Rimhold planetary energy around herself to hide under.

Such a flurry of light – and then nothing. Then another volley, then nothing. She was caught in a sporadic battle. A small squad of people stumbled past her in the dimness, not seeing her. She could smell their sweat, hear the inarticulate mutterings as they passed by, inches away. She tried to count three minutes before she started forward again.

Lina!

Jae was trying to call to her, his thoughts faint but discernible.

I'm here. I'm near the opening.

What? I told you to port back to the control room. You were supposed to follow my orders. Damn it, Lina–!

I'm sorry; it just seemed safer down here. I–

Flashes of light broke through the fog anew, and this time the shouts were sudden and close. Lina knew that Jae might hear the echo of it through her, and stopped sending to him. Mustn't distract him from whatever action he was in!

"Lina!" Jae bellowed. His seifer coms were empty, leaving him almost defenseless in this guerrilla warfare. His power needed a minute or two to work; it wasn't instantly on call to him.

He stripped two guns off the fallen prisoner in front of him. "Lina's down here," he reported to Wiley. "She said she was close to the connection point, and then she cut off."

Wiley regarded him silently, his mouth tight.

Jae knew Wiley was out of seifer fire as well. These guns didn't have much charge left. "You stay behind me," Jae ordered, and took off back down the corridor, the way they'd come.

Sure enough, there was fighting ahead. He'd thought that they'd secured the area. These must have come in from a new direction. At least Wiley was triggering the riot doors behind them, sealing off the corridor from that direction as they traveled.

Lina? There was movement up ahead but no answer. He fired blindly at the echoed shush of dragging feet, his blasts showing him shadows moving through the fog. Two people cried out. Wiley's shots joined his. Bodies fell and the Legionnaires flew past.

Two more skirmishes in the dark smoke, and still no response from Lina. Jae landed to collect more guns as his had finally run out of power. The supposedly dead bodies raised up in sudden ambush.

He punched a silhouette in the gut, producing a satisfying grunt. Someone threw himself on him and he fell, tried to roll, but the man was too heavy. Jae wrestled with him, struggling to find the correct nerve centers to decommission, and finally connected. The man slumped on top of him and Jae threw him off – only to have a woman hurl herself onto him.

He didn't have time for this! Lina could be dying. Their mission could be thwarted. Jae rolled, coming around to the woman's back. He could command the systems of her body to die. He held her there, straining in his arms. Lina was in danger. If he didn't kill this woman, Lina could die. The woman's cells awaited his command. Instead, Jae jerked her head back savagely, heard the snap.

Shakily he rose to his feet as a struggle continued to his left. Grunt and punch, a scuffing of a foot. The quick blip of a final gun charge, and a familiar voice in a strangled cry.

Jae launched himself in a flat dive, dragging down Wiley's assailant and twisting his neck until struggles ceased.

"I was just about to take care of him." Wiley came out of the fog.

"I didn't have anything else to do," Jae rejoined. He looked around. "You okay? It seems like everyone's running out of power," he said.

"That could be a good si–"

"Quiet!" Jae put his hand on Wiley's chest as they both listened. Someone was talking. It was difficult to tell in this echoing fog, but it didn't seem so far away. A woman's voice. A man answered, his voice very faint.

He'd take the chance. "Lina!" Jae shouted. "Lina!"

I'm here.

Is that you I hear?

"Jae!"

Right. We're coming.

He spotted her with his infrareds. She was sitting propped up on the corridor wall, a man lying across her lap. Or what had once been a man.

He was missing both legs, an arm and part of his face. Jae stood in horror to watch Lina smooth the man's hair and run her hand across his good cheek.

"Is that better, Heshu?" she asked him. "No, no, don't try to speak. I can hear your thoughts. Just tell me what I can do."

Who is he? Jae demanded. *Is he a prisoner or one of the guards?*

Does it matter? He's dying. There's nothing I can do about it. "Yes, I'll tell her. Tidda, I have her name, Tidda. I'll tell her everything. You don't worry about that. I'll do whatever I can for her. You can watch over her from the Other Side, too."

She listened to something and then said, "No, death is not the end. It's a passage. Life is the test. Then we go back and we rest and we see our loved ones and learn some more. You'll have other lives for other tests. You've had some hard tests, haven't you? Now they're over. You'll meet people who'll help you review your life. I'm sure they'll tell you that you did your best. I'm sure they'll tell you that – You do? You see someone? Is it an angel?"

Lina looked up the same direction the man was looking, his mouth moving, and Jae appeared out of the fog.

Jae regarded the man for a moment. He was dressed in the gray-brown of a prisoner.

Lina returned her attention to the dying man. "Don't be afraid; I'm here. No one ever dies alone. No one ever dies unloved."

He was trying to talk though he could barely open his remaining eye. Finally Jae knelt down and touched the man's cheek. "Rest now," he told the man. "Feel the love of the universe like warm light. It bathes you and sets you free from this life. This life has served its purpose. Time to go home. Make yourself ready." He kissed the prisoner on his bloody, muddy forehead, reached out and snapped the line between etheric and physical.

"Oh," the man said, and he was gone.

Jae closed the man's eye as Lina sat there in shock. He eased the body off her. She was blood and guts all over. The man's disconnected arm lay on the other side of her like a lump of litter.

Jae knew the signs. She was blinking hard, her chin trembling, and he took her in his arms.

"Let it out," he told her softly, and she began to sob on his shoulder. "That's it," he soothed as he wondered at himself. How many people had he killed this afternoon? And now, what had happened? He'd been a priest. He'd been Feithi.

"More are coming down the corridor," Wiley's voice said behind him. The doctor had three screens spread out around him now, diagrams and reports from the guards on upper levels. "There are no guards on this level yet," Wiley reported.

Jae nodded and eased Lina off himself. She snuffled, wiping at her eyes with the heels of her hands, swiping her nose across the back of her forearm, looking at him expectantly.

"I thought as much," he said. "Mini rebellions have fomented within the main rebellion. Good for us that these prisoners don't know about teamwork, or we'd really be in trouble. Is any of this blood yours?"

Lina shook her head mutely.

"Good. You go back up to the control room, like I told you before."

She held out her arm with the bracelet. "Th-they think I'm a prisoner. There are orders to k-kill."

"Shards," Wiley muttered.

"Shards up the grigach's ass," Jae agreed and sighed. "So you stay here. Right here. Don't move an inch until we come back, you hear?"

"Can I–" Lina glanced quickly at the body next to her. "Can I move just a little away?"

"All right, but no more than that. Lon will have my head if anything happens to you. You wouldn't want that, would you?" Jae was rewarded with the tiniest of smiles as Lina shook her head. "Good. Stay here, stay out of trouble. Stay quiet. We'll be back."

"Can you get us some more seifer coms?" Wiley asked quickly. "You know where they're stored now."

Lina nodded, and within a minute they were loading their wristbands again.

Jae and Wiley took off down the darkened hall.

Despite Jae's orders, Lina had to move again. The fighting had come too close, and then there had been another connecting corridor, and the fighting had been on both sides of her. There – through the thinning smoke she saw Jae a ways down. The cavalry had arrived!

She eased back the way she came so he could find her again, but looked behind when the tunnel suddenly lit up with fireworks and flame. Lasers traced paths in the air. She tried to hug the wall and to listen to her guides as to the safest place for her to be.

Glancing back again, she saw that fire was coming out of Jae's hands. No, not his hands; from the seifer tubes on his wristbands. It ran in streams around his hands and then focused in front of them to lash out in a straight beam at the inmates, following the aim of his fingers. Whoever got hit screamed quickly and went down.

Zig zag!

She did as her guides told her, narrowly avoiding a column of flame that sizzled in a flash down the tunnel in front of her, only fading out far, far away. **Down!** She dropped, and where she'd been crackled with ozone as something she couldn't see fried the air.

She stayed there for a moment, catching her breath, looking back to see that Wiley had those seifer com things going, too. The two of them were haloed in gold-white fire as they struck again and again at the crowd.

Lina ran and ran some more before she stumbled to a stop, clinging against the cold wall of the corridor. Three small globes swished by her in mid-air, then turned back. "I am not here," she told this place determinedly. "No one's here." The globes paused and then sped off in their original direction.

Was it her imagination, or was there less fire now? A sudden wind swept through the tunnels back to the Legionnaires' direction. But there couldn't be a wind, not down here – unless there were some sort of vacuum back there. Lina shuddered and ran on. At least the air was clear now.

Here. This is the spot.

A round grate was embedded in the floor. Lina tugged on it to no avail – too heavy. What to do? She could port it, but did they want her to just yet? There was still intermittent fire back there. She stayed linked with her guides and drew the lines of force around herself, hiding her from casual view. Wait for team leader's orders.

There – They came around a bend of the corridor. Wiley limped as he retreated on foot ahead of a mob of prisoners, dimmed by distance and smoke. The seifer coms must have lost their power, because they didn't use them anymore. Instead Jae swept his hands through the air, and then knelt quickly, placing them on the floor.

Lina saw their brown-clad pursuers begin to sink as if they were in quicksand. They screamed in terror. Some even dropped their rifles in fright. The rifles sank into the muck, too.

"All of them," Jae ordered the felons. "Drop your weapons, or I'll make this stuff even deeper than it is."

They knew when they were beaten. They dropped their guns. Wiley pointed at two men and they unclipped hidden weapons, dropping them into the mire as well.

"Very good," Jae told them all. They were still slogging around in the muck, trying to find a way out of it. Lina could hear Jae say something silently, but couldn't make it out. People abruptly stopped moving forward, weaving back and forth as they sought their balance. The floor had solidified with them inside it.

"I'm stuck!" "Neutrino, you can't leave us like this!" "Get me out of here!!"

"You people have gotten in our way enough for today," Jae told them very calmly as he hovered over them. They were waist-deep in concrete now. "You're going to stay here for a while. It shouldn't be more than a few hours. Enjoy it. Talk to each other." He leaned down to face one snarling man eye to eye. "Sing songs."

He landed with a laugh and turned to take Wiley's arm. The genius was really limping now. Jae spoke low to him and then glanced down the corridor.

"Lina!" Jae exclaimed. "I saw you back there. I thought I told you to stay put!"

"I'm sorry. I had to move," she said as she walked to them. "Things were getting a little too dangerous." She shivered in the cold of the place.

Jae scowled at her. "I'll let it pass this time. Now you port Wiley up so he can get some medical attention. One day, Wiley, you'll use maximal protective gear per regulations."

"I'm usually not in c-combat situations."

"'Usually' is the operative word, Wile. You see a medic–"

"He can get medical attention here," Lina said. "He's needed below, *they* say."

Jae set his jaw and pointed at her. "You don't argue–"

"With team leader. I know, I know. Wiley, lean against the wall here. This isn't a combat situation anymore, Jae. I don't think this will take too much time." She looked up at Wiley. "Pardon my hand," she said with a forced half-grin, and put her palm on his upper thigh.

Wiley's teeth chattered with pain of the blaster wound. "Wish I had my p-primary padd," he said. "I'd like to monitor this." He dug into one of the bags on his belt.

"Not to make suggestions on improving my technique?"

"No. N-not that. Maybe in a few weeks I'll h-have those."

Lina laughed, and even Wiley managed a chuckle. As she worked, he fitted together a medical injector from the parts he'd found, then attached a tiny chip to it from another pouch. He gave himself a shot and, after a moment, heaved a sigh.

"Continue at your leisure," he allowed her.

Jae made his way through the corridor, finding the emergency gates that brought slabs of ultralloy slamming out from the walls, creating a riot barrier against the other prisoners who had fallen previously. He sauntered back, radioing the prison's communications center as to their position and what to expect down here.

"We almost made it, Legionnaire," one man muttered as Jae threaded himself between the stuck grouping.

"'Almost' doesn't cut it," Jae responded, and noticed his breath coming out as slight vapor. The air was raw. He and Wiley would be fine, but Lina was still in a thin tee shirt. He could see her shivering from here. "Tell you what; I want a souvenir of this place. Hope you don't mind." He pulled the man's prison jacket off without much problem.

"Hey! It's cold! I need that!"

"You're not going to freeze," Jae told him. "At least, not right away." He shook the jacket out. "We'll have you back in a nice warm cell in no time. Lina? You done yet?"

Lina eased back from Wilder. "I want you to go easy on that leg until you can see Dr. Gorgeon," she cautioned him as she helped him to his feet.

"Much better. Thanks," he told her.

She ported in some more seifer things for him.

Jae handed the jacket to her and she nodded thanks as she put it on. There was that strange non-velcro velcro to fasten it shut. "That grating is the start," she told the both of them. "I tried to get it, but it's too heavy for me. I can port it–"

A communication from the surface drew Jae's attention to his radio disk. He conversed with someone as Wiley reached down to grab the grate.

"Hey! What did I just tell you?!" Lina cried at Wiley.

"I'm not using my leg," he said and raised off the ground, hovering above the grate to prove it. He grimaced with his hands firmly locked on the grate, and slowly it came up out of the floor. He let it come fully out and then slid it to the side so they could go through it.

"Oh, great, so now you'll throw your shoulder out."

"I was careful. Mother."

Lina thought Wilder might stick his tongue out at her, but he didn't and she gave him a shake of her head.

"Legionnaires." She said as if it were "children!"

"Jae, are you through getting out of the tough work?" Wiley asked.

"Affirmative," Jae was saying into his communicator. "See if you can track us from up there. Dr. Mem-Bazer's going to keep a record of our trail. Neutrino out." Jae looked up at them, then down into the black hole in the floor as he tucked the communicator into a slot on his battle vest. He fastened the new seifer coms to his wrist bands. "Lina, from here on's considered combat situation. Anything I say, anything Wilder tells you, goes. No questions asked. Instant response."

"Yes, Jae," she said.

Wiley produced some goggles from somewhere and Lina slipped them on. Suddenly everything was ten times brighter than before. She had to squint against even this dim light.

"Let's go." Jae saw that there was a ladder down the side of the hole. He went in first.

They had to drop the last four feet. It would be pitch black without the goggles here. "Straight," Lina said, and again Jae took the lead. Something skittered in the darkness and she tried not to pay attention to it. They were still a long way from Ombrillo.

She gave them instructions as they descended through the tunnels, which began narrow and became narrower still.

"Long drop," she whispered to them as they stopped over a hole. "Maybe forty feet. Down there's the right level."

Jae put his arm around her and together they floated down with Wilder following them. **Can you hear me?** he asked.

Actually, you're yelling a bit, she told him.

Link with Wilder.

I'm here. His mind-voice echoed as Lina relayed the message.

We communicate like this until we find him. Lina, as soon as we do, you port back up to the control center. No, back to Sarastor until you hear from us.

Confined to my room?

Unless you want to stay here. I'm sure we can find you an empty cell. Wiley, get that jammer ready.

Down here the tunnel was barely wide enough for two. They glided horizontally through the tunnels, very slowly and not touching the sides so as not to make any noise. Narrower and narrower, a hole through the earth just big enough for a large person to crawl. Jae squeezed Lina against himself so tightly that she almost couldn't breathe as they tried not to scrape the walls.

Up ahead, she told them. **Maybe five hundred feet; there's a curve to the left and he's just beyond.**

It's not a side tunnel?

Doesn't feel like it. The actual tunnel curves.

Good job. Wiley?

There. He just showed up on my equipment. Ready to begin jamming on your command, Team Leader.

Begin in one minute. Lina, port back now.

Yes, Jae.

She hated to leave them there, but she did. These were the professionals. What was it that the warden had said? That one Legionnaire should be enough to stave off Armageddon? She hoped that it was true.

She could leave now if she dishonored her promise to Jae. She could go home, gather the cats and a few other things and take off for parts so unknown even the ParaNet couldn't find her before Lon came back.

Instead she sat huddled in the living room, waiting for word from Rimhold, afraid to think anything that might jinx them. After a half hour she took a quick shower, sluicing the blood, dirt and gore from the tunnels off herself. When she came out, the chair she'd been sitting in had been cleaned. It was as if none of it had ever happened. She knew it had. She knew she'd have nightmares about it for months. But Jae and Wiley and the rest were still in that nightmare…

"Puter," she told the air, "I have to send a message to a woman named Tidda, who is married to a prisoner named Heshu who was held in Rimhold Prison…" She tried to phrase her words to Tidda as gently as possible. Poor Tidda.

This was what Londo did – all the time. Having to face people's expectations of him, saving the universe twice a week. Running off without a thought for himself.

How she wanted him here with her! She crushed a cushion to herself, imagining it was Londo. She needed him – now! She needed his arms wrapped around her, his low voice whispering in her ear that everything was going to be all right.

And she needed sex. He'd introduced her to an entire world of flesh. How she wanted to touch him, to smell him, to taste him again! Just to hold him for one minute, was that too much to ask?

To hold on to him and keep him from saving how many lives?

Selfish Muttbutt! How petty could she be? Londo lived to help others. He'd been made to help others. What if she were one of the stranded victims on that ship where he was? She'd be praying for Valiant to come to the rescue, just as she herself had prayed for him a few days ago when the hotel had burned down around her. He'd come to her rescue and the universe had changed forever.

He'd be back in a few days. What would he want when he got home? Calmness, at least that's what she wanted now. A stable place where the universe wouldn't run over him. Safety. Love and gentleness. Laughter. Someone he could talk to.

Lord, let me help him, she prayed softly. *Lord, keep him safe. Keep them all safe. If Aiko has to die, at least let it be quick and painless. They say no one ever dies unloved; send her love so she doesn't fear the transition. And keep them safe. Londo. Jae. Wiley. All of them.*

Suddenly she knew that Aiko was dead. Maybe a few hours ago–

"Lina to the Lab 1-A. Lina to L–"

She was there before the call ended, gaping anxiously at the screen. Jae stood there absolutely filthy but healthy, and Wilder was consulting with one of the guards, oblivious to the fact that he looked like he'd just been buried in mud. Lina breathed a monumental sigh of relief. "You're all right!"

"We're fine. Everything's under control here," Jae said, taking a final glance around. "Erik, Brügz and Dellen are going to pick up the pieces, but Wiley and I are coming back. Port when you're ready."

She brought them back and practically smothered Jae in a hug, than gave the same treatment to Wilder.

"You're all right!" she cried again, so happy.

Jae brushed his hair out of his eyes, his helmet completely retracting back into his costume as he did so. Lina hugged him again, and that made him laugh. "Yes, we're all right. But now you have to find some clean clothes."

She'd gotten their dirt all over herself. "They're just clothes. Not important."

"Hum," Wilder said, and they both turned to him. He had a deep, thoughtful frown. "It's an interesting experience, your porting. So different from the system we use."

"Is yours instantaneous?" Lina asked curiously.

He shook his head no. "And it's limited to planetary distances." He took his place at the monitor board and called up the previous results of her bracelet telemetry. "If I can figure out how you do it, we could save a lot of time from here on out. A lot of time."

"Wiley, take a shower. That's an order." Jae smiled at his companion and stage-whispered to Lina, "If someone doesn't tell him, he forgets."

"I never forget anything. I'll get to it in a few minutes."

"We're still on my mission, not on your command in HQ. After your shower, report to medical to finish the work on your leg. Then take a rest break. I'm for a shower and break, too," Jae declared as he fluffed debris out of his hair. "Headquarters will just have to run on automatic a while more."

He grinned at Lina. "You really are a mess now. How about scrubbing my back for me? We could save time doing two at once."

Lina wrinkled her nose at her silly, wonderful friend. "Right. I'm getting changed before Protocol sees me and starts handing out demerits or something." She disappeared.

"Jae…" Wiley said.

The blond Legionnaire held out his open hands innocently. "Can't blame a guy for trying," he said.

Cleaned and rested, Jae strummed his guitar as he sat at monitor duty, picking out familiar Terran songs that Lon had played over the years, as Lina studied her Pan-lingua study padd on a couch. He knew that Lina had been unusually subdued since they'd returned from Rimhold, or maybe just from Earth, but he'd been unusually excited even after the adrenaline of a major mission had worn off.

All tedious reports had been filed, and this was the first time he'd ever brought his guitar out in public. This was a splendid way to while away the hours on monitor duty. He promised himself that it wouldn't be the last.

Jae glanced over at Lina, engrossed in her studies. She was scheduled for her final nanoscan in a while. It would be a lengthy one.

Ombrillo would have never been captured without her help. With one hand he gestured to add enough credits to her Legion account to counter the – great orb, how had she managed to accumulate so many? – demerits she'd garnered so far.

Jae put the computer on search for a Feithi music clip. Londo's Terran music was fine, but now Jae craved songs of home. Something soft, maybe with a stringed instrument like the *damma*, which resembled a guitar. There. He tried to imitate the sound on his guitar and found with pleasure that he could. Then he tried the song again from the beginning, stumbling over a few places, but getting it mostly right. Once more got it exact.

Two so-called emergencies soon had him fuming when they turned out to be minor difficulties that the local authorities could easily handle. How Jae wished that they wouldn't waste his time. He had actually growled at the last lieutenant who tried to tell him how dangerous one situation was.

A secured Legion audio channel signaled for his attention. "Sikrichat here. Who's there? Wiley?"

"It's Jae."

"What, you're actually putting in comm time? Slacker. We've got everything sewn up here. Ready to come home."

"Let me wake up Lina, Brügz. She's under nanos; it may take a minute or two."

"Standing by."

Jae turned and saw that Lina was already waking up. "They're ready to return," he told her as she blinked.

"Ooo. Okay. Give me a second," she said. She sat up and stretched, then walked over the monitor board. "Are they in the same place? Yes, they are," she answered herself. "Oh. A little injury there. Here they come."

After a couple silent minutes, the three familiar Legionnaires appeared. Erik held his shoulder, his upper lip curled in a slight grimace.

"I need to file our preliminary report," Brügz announced. "Then we're going down to medical. Erik took the edge of a blaster beam. He needs to practice ducking."

Erik sank onto a stool but grimaced as he scooted around to find a comfortable position. Brügz and Dellen sat down immediately at comm stations to file their reports as Jae returned to the central station to answer an incoming call.

"Do you want me to try to ease the pain while you wait?" Lina asked.

"What," Erik asked Lina, "you're a doctor, too?"

"It's psychic healing. Not very scientific. Nowhere near what Dr. Gorgeon can do for you, I'm sure."

He watched her hold her hand about two inches out from his shoulder. "Hey, that feels like something cool."

She opened her eyes and wiped the air just above his arm, shaking her hand out away from him. Then she placed both hands on his shoulder. "Stay still."

The translator didn't repeat her words. "Panlingua," Erik said.

Lina waved the marble away from herself. "I've got to wean myself off it sometime. We'll see how it goes."

"I've been meaning to ask you…" He paused and his eyes shifted uncertainly. "When we met, you said that I'd done something. What was it?"

"Yeah, after a while I figured that you really didn't realize it. You seem to be a bit telepathic or psychic, but only out of certain chakras – energy centers."

"Me, telepathic?"

"Uh huh. I think you get a lot more women in your bed than is considered normal, right?"

He had the nerve to look hurt. "I'm told I'm charming."

"I can see that. But when you meet someone, or maybe it's just a woman you think you might have a chance with, you send out little hooks to reel her in."

"Hooks?"

"Well, that's the way I was taught to see them. Really pushy people, people who want to control you, they do that kind of thing, too, but they don't connect to exactly the same chakras that you do. You connect to the interaction chakra, the sex chakra, and the power chakra. You weaken the other person's power in order to have sex with them."

He considered it. "How do I do that? Are you saying it's… mind control?"

"I wouldn't call it mind control with capital letters. It's more a leaning-in kind of thing. Do you feel like you're pouncing on women when you first meet them?"

Erik cocked his red head, getting a faraway look in his eyes. "Isn't that what it's supposed to feel like?"

"I don't think so. Why don't you try, just a couple of times, not to capture them? To just exude all that charm their way and let them fall instead of pushing them? I think you might find they stay around a little longer. If you're interested in that kind of thing." Lina took her hands off him. "Finished. Now get Dr. Gorgeon to look at it."

He seemed startled to be reminded of his injury. "Shards, it does feel better. Thanks."

Lina eyes defocused. "Ah. One thing. You…" She could feel the words but didn't know exactly what they were. "You extend your self, your aura when you use your powers. You reshape it and bend it."

Erik looked at her curiously.

"If you would, leave this area as it is for a day or so. That will help it heal all the way. It's out of balance right now."

"I think I know what you're saying. Thanks, Lina."

"My pleasure."

"Say, do you know how I can get in contact with Dinah again? For if I ever go back to Earth?"

"You liked her that much? Good. I have her phone number and email address. Wiley can probably rig something, no?"

Erik shrugged and then sucked in a breath at the sudden movement. "I'm sure."

Jae came over to them. "So Erik, if you're going to stick around for a awhile, how about you handling the board solo after you get back from Medical? That'll give you a jump on your next command level promotion."

Erik considered it. "For how long?"

"A couple hours. I want to take Lina back to the Terran Zone."

Lina perked to attention. "Again?" Did the thought of singing in public give her a thrill?

Jae looked sharply at her. "You don't want to go?"

She shook her head quickly. "I didn't say that. Those poor people, cut off from music like they are. Besides, Earth told me I needed to sing to make the world a better place." She twisted her mouth in puzzlement. "I've been trying to figure that one out. Maybe she means it just as it sounds. Bring your guitar," she added.

Jae did a double-take at that. "Oh no. Oh no. I'm not ready for a public performance."

"Then we'll get the No-Talent Quartet from the Pares Restaurant. C'mon, Jae, you're really good."

"Yeah?" He looked at his guitar and considered. "Okay, you sweet-talked me into it. Anything's better than the No-Talent Quartet."

The crowd greeted them with enthusiasm when they appeared, and an "oooo" went up when the people saw Jae's guitar case. He'd changed from his uniform into jeans and tee shirt, with a replicated vegan version of that leather jacket he'd been admiring.

Ernst rushed up to greet them. The guitar caught his eye. "I'll see if I can get a microphone for that," he said, and disappeared.

People shouted out requests as they made their way across the floor. Lina had another Starfleet shirt on, so they kept calling her Starfleet and she didn't mind. In fact, if she were going to perform before this many people she would take all the anonymity she could get.

She slung a knapsack off her shoulder and opened it for the audience. "Music," she announced, dumping a pile of piano fake books onto a nearby table. "So I won't have to fardle my way through a song, AND you can read the words." That elicited another "oooo." Patrons flocked up to look through her offerings.

"Just remind me if I don't get to your request," she said as she and Jae sat down at the piano.

Ernst appeared with his right palm extended. He held three large ladybugs, or maybe beetles. Jae picked up one and adjusted it with his fingernail. It flew up in the air and came to a rest about a foot from Lina's face.

"I take it this is a microphone," she said, and heard her voice carry. "Jae, are you singing tonight? Or are you just going to play that?"

"We'll see how it goes." He released the microphone for his guitar and left the other on top of the piano.

Theatrically Lina cleared her throat. "Ladies and gentlemen, making his public debut with absolutely no rehearsal at all only because he just happens to be the bravest musician in the entire universe, Mr. Jae Rallene on lead guitar." Lina grinned as Jae nodded his head at the crowd and their burst of applause. "How do you want to do this?" she asked him.

He nodded at one of the music books unfolded on the table. "I can read chord changes."

"Okay, let's start out with a lively one, a little more current than what I've been playing," Lina said. She flipped through the books and chose one. Jae squinted at it as she secured it in the music rack, then nodded.

"I thought I heard someone request this. Let's see if we can do it." Lina counted them down and they swung into "Cut to the Feeling." The over-amplified microphone on the guitar gave it a slight electronic sound.

Because of the sheet music, the arrangement was much more complicated than the ones of the night before, though a little formal for the subject. They managed to make their way through the song with only minor mistakes. When they finished, it was to thunderous applause.

"I think we'll have to start scheduling rehearsals," Lina told the crowd. "With maybe some drums and a brass section and a synthesizer."

They had to stop a minute because Jae didn't know what was happening when Lina had gone back to repeat some verses, and she showed him how the repeat symbols worked on the music. She complimented him on making his way through without knowing that.

"I'm good at faking," he said, and they proceeded from song to song.

After another that they tried to make loud and fast, Lina turned to Jae. "How do you adjust the volume on this thing?" He showed her, and she turned hers down.

"How about that song you were playing along with the monitor?" Lina asked.

"It's Feithi," Jae said.

"Anybody mind a Feithi song?" Lina asked the crowd. There was a chorus of "NO!" and she smiled encouragingly at Jae. "Does it have words?"

He gave a surprisingly bashful smile as he picked up the other microphone and let it float in front of him. He sang the love song, as it turned out, to solo guitar accompaniment. His voice trembled just a little in front of this crowd, but he bulled on and it steadied, a low tenor. To his surprise, Lina sang a soft harmony on the chorus in Feithi.

The crowd loved it and called for an encore, to which Jae obliged. When a strange sound merged with that of his guitar, he gave a start and looked over at Lina. She was playing music on that flute she'd had before. Its languid tone melded with the song, making it faraway and soulful.

"I forgot that I'd brought my flute along," Lina told him for the crowd's benefit when they'd finished. "Hope you don't mind."

Jae just wondered how he'd deflect the wrath of Protocol after tonight. "Not a bit," he said and turned to the audience. "Now, who wants to hear a flute solo from my friend Starfleet? You know one, don't you?"

By now Ernst had set up a camera and screen system for scanning the music books so that the words could be projected above the audience even as the two musicians used them. Lina played "Edelweiss," and the audience sang along for the last verse.

Ernst was exuberant. "This is turning into a regular orchestra!" he exclaimed.

"Three instruments do not an orchestra make," Lina replied. "Maybe a trio, if we had three people here."

"Don't be such a downer. This was fun." Jae nudged her. "We'll wait for that husband of yours to come back," he said, "and then we'll get him out on stage, too. I hear he plays a couple of instruments."

"You do that, Neutrino." Ernst drummed his chest with pleasure at being able to participate in the event. "You do that, and the Terran Club will make it worth your time. We'll have the first true band that this world has ever seen in centuries. Wouldn't that be something to see?"

"It would certainly be something to see Legion Protocol dragging me from this building." Jae said darkly. "I think the less publicity, the better."

"I didn't know you knew Feithi," Jae said to Lina when they took a break. "Have you been learning that, too?"

"I told you last night: I know the words to lots of songs now. As I recall, my instructions from you were not to question it."

Jae rubbed his mouth, squinting at her. "Very strange. Have you mentioned this to Wiley?"

"I think his brain's about to turn inside out as it is with the trouble I've brought."

Ernst fought his way through the crowd with their drinks. "What an honor to have a Legionnaire playing for the crowd!" he exclaimed as he settled his frame into the booth with them.

Lina took a sip of her iced tea. It was old and bitter with a harsh mask of false peach – obviously that foul stuff canned for Yankees who didn't know any better – but people Out Here were doing their best. Better than tap water, she supposed. But not much.

"I don't think the Mega-Legion would appreciate me being here this way," Jae told Ernst. "I'm just Jae Rallene tonight, not Neutrino."

"Suit yourself," Ernst said. "So tell me, Starfleet, will you two be here tomorrow night?"

"I should think the crowd would have had enough of us by now," Lina said. "Isn't it time for someone else to step up to the mic?"

"Why should they when they have you two?"

"Tell you what. When… When my husband and I get back to Earth, we'll ask around and see if we can't schedule the Terran Zone on some bands' tours. Maybe they could trade off the cost of a hyperspace ticket for a chance to be Out Here for a few days."

"You think you could do that?" Ernst asked, not hiding his excitement.

Lina chewed her lip in thought. "I'd have to check. I know a guy who knows a guy who… Wait, I know a girl who knows someone. They're first cousins." Lina nodded her head. "Yeah, all you'd need is one good band to start. And they're really good. Once the word gets around, you might have a steady stream of artists. I'll check into it."

They went through more requests, including some songs that the crowd could join in. Lina threw in TV themes like *Cheers* to see if anyone would recognize them and sing along. They did, and they did.

"Oh what the heck," she said, and played the theme to Classic *Star Trek* with all the words. The crowd cheered for that one, and Lina could barely play from laughing when a man stepped up to do it in its original operatic-style, without the words and in blazing falsetto. She finished the night by answering people's callouts of cities they were from, playing for each area that had a special song. Jae was astounded that people would write songs for cities, but here they were. Loud arguments began over which city was better. Jae broke it up by proposing a vote as to which city song was best. San Francisco won.

They exited to a standing and slightly argumentative ovation.

"I could get used to that," Jae said as the bar door closed behind him. His ring beeped.

Erik's voice: "Are you finished?"

"Were you watching?" Jae winked at Lina.

"A little. I copied the performance to Protocol; you don't have to thank me. They said that Lina hadn't finished today's sessions with them, too. I think they gave some demerits for that. But Jae, I thought you'd be interested: That ZoBois of yours is at the club."

"ZoBois! Here?" Jae exclaimed. He edged away from the Terran Zone door, as if someone in there could hear. "Where? What's she doing?"

"Watching you. She stayed close by the bar in the Zone for a half-hour. She could have been trying to pass you a message."

Jae made a sound low in his throat. "It didn't have much chance of getting through the crowd. Is she still in the area?"

"Unknown. Patching in to the Romaki Club security monitors. Give me a moment."

Jae looked at Lina with a frown. "It's personal business," he told her just as Erik came back.

"Got her," Erik said. "She's leaving through the front west door."

"I'm following," Jae said. "Rallene out. Come on, Lina."

13

He grabbed her hand and ran down the hallway, away from both the bar and the casino. After two turns, they barged through an exit door, and then Jae flew her up and over the building. They stood on the precipice of the roof as Jae peered over the crowd below them congregating in front of the Romaki Club. Lina eased back from the edge.

"There," Jae said, pointing with one hand and as he reached for Lina with the other.

They dropped heart-stoppingly fast to land behind a woman – a girl, more precisely, younger than Lina, her splotches of short, bristly hair done in rainbow colors, a different one per splotch. It was Lina's gasp on landing that made the girl turn.

"Neutrino!" the girl exclaimed, and then hurriedly lowered her voice. "There's trouble."

"I thought there might be," Jae said. "Why didn't you contact me at HQ?"

"I was going to, but then I heard you were here." She eyed Lina warily now, giving her the up-and-down. "New flavor? You goin' for Terrans now, Neutrino? Hanging out in their places. Hey girl, you got enough hair there for a dozen gangs."

Jae ignored the insults. "Lina, this is ZoBois. You wanted to see a native Sarastoran. She's one."

ZoBois's mouth turned into a little sneer. "Take a good look," she said. "There ain't many of us out these days."

ZoBois's clothes were as defiant as her hair. She wore the layered look, but her dark jacket and trousers were enormously baggy with not an artistic fold in sight. They were tied to her with bright crisscrossing belts that held crystal rods like seifer coms. Maybe they were some kind of ammunition, too, for there was a grip sticking out of the neck of her jacket, one that looked like it belonged to a pistol.

She wore two layers of gloves, one tight, short and fingerless on top of another that looked five sizes too big and that stuck out of the other one. Her skin was a medium tone of blue-tinged flesh. One eye was yellow with a purple ring on the outside of the iris, and the other was purple with a yellow ring.

As the girl stood there being appraised, she ran her tongue around her slightly-open mouth. The tongue had a bright yellow stripe down one side.

"Apparently Sarastorans don't have much fashion sense," Lina said. She got a sniff in response.

"Better than half-naked Terran barbarians."

"What's up?" Jae asked ZoBois.

"They're going to take out the Back Steps tonight," ZoBois said. "It's going down in less than an hour. Boddie's got the Waste Pack to come in with us." She shuffled a bit, wiped her nose with the back of her glove. How old was she? Fifteen? Sixteen? "I got scared."

Jae nodded. "Don't be," he said. "I can stop this, and we don't have to involve the authorities."

"Just tell me what to do, Neutrino."

By the time they arrived at the cul-de-sac ZoBois had directed them to, the Sarastoran rival gangs were already in place, the Back Steps vs ZoBois's gang, the Undergrounds.

"I don't see the Waste Pack," Jae whispered to Lina as they stood in the shadows of a building ledge well above the pavement. "ZoBois said they'd be here. They must be hiding, waiting in reserve."

"Waiting to see how the battle goes so they can side with the winning team?" Lina whispered back. ZoBois had to join her own gang so she wouldn't be suspected of squealing to a Legionnaire.

Jae nodded. "Wait here. Don't do anything; just observe. I want to know when the Waste Pack move. Keep out of sight and listen to your guides." He looked skyward. "Keep her out of trouble!" he commanded.

And with that, he was gone into the night. There weren't that many lights back here, just three dim ones on street level. Lina huddled in a recessed window, praying that she wouldn't fall.

Down below two groups of people, about twenty apiece, circled each other in loose formation. They dressed in baggy dark clothes with bright accents. All had that bluish Sarastoran skin and patchy hair.

"Hebbling, ya fokka!" One guy yelled at another, just three feet away from him, as if he couldn't hear well.

Lina ported in her translator. She didn't think this guy's name was "Hebbling."

"Whattaya tryin' to do to us? You're stretchin' out in territories that don't belong to you. These are our digs! Our turf."

"They took the fact'ry from us!" the other guy yelled back. "The fact'ry! Do you know how big that thing was? I got too many people, man. We need a space! And you guys got too much space. Seems to me, you can ease over and let us be."

"You got too many people, and that's a fact," the first growled. "But we can take care of that."

"I'm sure you can," Jae's voice echoed loudly through the cul-de-sac. "But I don't think that's your best choice."

He strolled out onto the pavement, his movement liquid and boneless. He'd fluffed his hair out to catch what light there was, creating a halo around his head. No one else on this entire world looked remotely like the Last Feithi.

Jae stopped ten feet from the two leaders. "What we have here," he said, "is a problem that needs solving. But you're not making the right decisions. Neither of you are. You only see two choices but there are dozens of others. Better ones. Choose one of them instead."

"Get out of here, Neutrino," the first man said. "We don't want to hurt you."

"No, you just want to hurt yourselves." Jae paced in his own circle around the two leaders. They followed him warily with their eyes, not letting the other out of their sight. "The way I see it," Jae told them, "it's the offworlders who are easing you out of your own territories."

"Yeah, Neutrino."

"You got that right."

"The offworlders have it all, don't they? They get all the jobs, they get all the perks, they get all the nice apartments."

"We just get the reservation!" one of the gang members shouted. "Screw 'em! We should be killing them and not us!"

"Sure, that would solve it." Jae laughed. He settled on a bin at the side of the road. "Kill a few innocent offworlders. Three or four, and then there'd be room for just the Sarastorans on Sarastor, is that it?" He stopped. "Of course, the few who did the actual killing, they'd be in jail. But everyone else would have plenty then, wouldn't they?"

"Course not," someone said.

"Well, how many would it take? How many offworlders would you have to kill to make room for yourselves again? And who would you kill?" Jae pointed to a gang member. "You. What kind of person would you kill to make room for you and yours?"

"Huh. One of them government tax people. Them rich guys, they take all that money. Kill one of them, let me take their place! Haw haw!" The man looked around for support and was rewarded with laughter from the others.

Jae nodded. "Too many taxes, I agree. But you'd take his place? Take his job, take his wages, take his home?"

"Yeah man. Right."

"Uh huh. How much training have you had to take over his job? Can you handle third-range fiscal planning? Do you even know what that is?"

"Man, no! I'm not into that shit."

Jae jumped up. "Why the *skurn* not? The government and its guilty conscience has made it possible for native Sarastorans to do anything they want. You have free minimum housing, free minimum utilities, free Nets, free minimum food, free education – there's no minimum to that, you could go as far as you wanted – and what the blaze do you do with it? You sit around all day, glued to the Net entertainments, living your lives through whatever you can find out there. Or you wander around at night, looking for others like you, so you can complain about your sorry, miserable lives and work yourselves up into trying to find something that will make the boredom go away. Even if it means killing each other!"

He shook his fist at them all and stood there in silence for a minute, then regained his seat.

"Well, I'm the one who's bored tonight. You people just go ahead. Shoot each other. Kill each other. But please make it entertaining. Tomorrow night I'll have to find some more malcontent Sarastorans who don't have balls enough to get off their lazy asses and make something of their lives. Or are all Sarastorans really so stupid that they couldn't do anything important even if they wanted to?"

"You – You take that back, Neutrino!"

"Or what? Or you'll make something of yourself?"

"Or – Or–" The man withdrew a gun and pointed it at Jae. Lina could see his hand shake from where she cowered.

"Puh-lease." Jae dismissed the threat with a wave. "I'm asking for action here, not comedy."

There was a flash of movement along the line of roofs, under the lights of the city behind the block. **We've got people up here,** Lina told him.

Jae stood up slowly so as not to alarm the gunman. "You people have to realize your real problem is you. Not the offworlders. Sarastorans. You've given up trying to beat the offworlders at their own games. You've withdrawn into yourselves; you've become inert. All of you here know this. You're killing each other to get rid of the sickness."

Jae raised his index finger to the sky. A hundred finger-thin flashes of lightning flickered in a net pattern high above the street. Now everyone could see the members of the Waste Pack, frozen in fright, as they crouched on the low rooftops.

"You play Sarastoran against Sarastoran," Jae told the crowd. "And you have to play dirty to do it. You sicken me! You're smart people but you pretend to be stupid so people won't wonder what the real reason is that you're not doing anything. Why you're not running your own lives. Why you're not running your own world!"

The lightning flashed in a sheet, searing a circle ten feet around Jae. As thunder shook the alley, his hair flew around him. He stretched out his arms, shouting to heavens. "Run! Run off to your holes and fight the boredom for one more day! Don't think about the future! Don't think about your world!"

When the lightning ceased and the last roll of thunder eased back to the sky, an unnatural quiet lay upon the ground. A fine mist, a left-over soft crackle sifted past on the midnight breeze. And only seven people remained in the cul-de-sac.

"Tell us what to do," one said.

"Do you think they will?" Lina asked Jae as they popped back into Wiley's lab. The sudden bright light made her squint and shade her eyes.

"Who knows?" Jae shrugged. "Maybe I made a difference. Maybe not."

"But you certainly stopped bloodshed. That lightning thing was awesome!"

That brought a small smile to his lips. "It's my signature move. I save it for special occasions."

"It's very impressive!"

"Glad you approve."

At the control center, Erik signed off from another communiqué. "About time you got back, Jae. Did you forget how shorthanded we are? I had to give you demerits."

"Sorry. You'll have to go for another hour or so. I need to make some arrangements for ZoBois and company for tomorrow. Well," Jae reconsidered, "Maybe I'll take a little nap in here and do it afterwards. I'm beat. Add another three demerits for that."

Lina spoke up. "Me, too. Not the demerits, the nap. Can I go back to quarters for the night? If that's all right." She bowed towards Jae and he nodded condescendingly.

"Need anyone to keep you company?" Erik asked.

"Everyone here is looney tunes," Lina said wryly. "Here, what have you done to your shoulder? You've hurt it again."

Erik grunted as she touched it. "I forgot about the not using it for a day instructions."

She made some air-swipes in the shoulder's general direction and then laid her hands on it. "If Riz had told you, you would have followed her instructions to the letter, right?"

"Not him," Jae said. "Erik always acts before he thinks."

"Do not. Who's Riz?" Erik asked.

"Doctor Riz Gorgeon." Lina stamped her foot. "Okay, I'm going to give your guardian angel instructions to remind you."

Her eyes defocused for a second and then came back. "If you're doing your thing and you feel something go *thwunk* here," she tapped Erik's head sharply, "then you'll remember to keep your shoulder clear. Right?"

"Are you serious?" He could see her determined look. "I'll remember. But I might try it just once to feel the *thwunk*."

"Maybe I can arrange for it to be a little harder than that."

"Okay, okay. I'll mind my ways for a day."

She smiled at him and Jae. "Good enough. See y'all in the morning." She ported out.

Jae settled down on the couch to catch his nap as Erik scanned through some stations on the screen. "Cute girl," Erik commented. "You've been running her a lot today. The commander will be interested in this tight arrest you have her under."

"Yeah."

"Thinking about making her a member? That is, if she's proven innocent of charges?"

Jae adjusted the couch area lights to dim. "I'm beginning to. She really came through at Rimhold, don't you think?"

Erik grinned at him. "Yeah. And she's got great tits. The Legion needs more of those. I wonder how she is in bed?"

"Good enough for Londo, I guess," Jae said, bunching some pillows under his head. "I wouldn't recommend you trying anything with her; Lon might get a little perturbed."

"I am keeping my distance." Erik made a "hands off" surrender gesture, wiggling his fingers. "Valiant. How in the world do they do it? I mean, Valiant and a norm? How far do you think they can go?"

He studied Jae, and something occurred to him. "You know, don't you? You were confined in here with Valiant. You've been with her for days now. Do they? Really?"

Jae punched a pillow, trying to get it in shape. "They do. Really and all the way."

"Shards." Erik clicked a few lighted squares on the monitor board. "Someone who can handle Valiant in bed. I'm trying to imagine it."

"Maybe it's best if you don't."

"Killjoy. As if you don't."

Jae laughed a little and closed his eyes, trying not to imagine it. He didn't succeed.

Lina popped into the laboratory to find Wiley and Brügz at the monitor board, while Erik talked to someone in one of the holo-partitions. "Morning," she said, and they returned her greeting offhandedly

She settled down to study her Panlingua, glad to discover that her padd let her skip several sections because apparently she had them down flat. Not much more to go on the verbal language, thank goodness. Both goals A could be checked off as completed.

As long as she was in the language section of the padd, she made sure that the previous bookmarks for languages she wanted to learn were still in place. Too bad conversational Klingon wasn't available.

Using this Out There stuff was getting easier and easier. It was also obvious that Wiley and maybe Jae must be keeping close tabs on what she accessed on her study padd. Good thing she had disguised her goals.

B goals were…? Lawyer, right. Learn legal system. Figure Terran currency exchange to finance legal battle. She needed to add research on just what this mind control stuff was so she could start to figure how to prove herself innocent.

There had to be a way to get onto the wider Nets to wherever they kept all the legal info. Maybe by lunchtime she'd have contacted–

She dropped the padd as his presence filled her. **Londo!** "Londo!"

Lina! Lina chérie, tell them–

Londo, I can port you–

Suddenly everything went blank again, a terrible emptiness on the face of the universe.

It was a long minute before she realized that Erik had rushed to her side, Brügz right behind him. Wiley remained at his board, alert to her.

"Skurn, what is it?" Erik exclaimed.

"Londo – I felt Lon's mind. But just for an instant."

Erik looked quizzically at her, but Wiley nodded. "They're on their way back, then. They have to come out of hyperspace to change course and reinsert."

With the sudden loss of Londo, it took her a few beats to comprehend. "Oh! Oh, no! If only they'd stayed out a little longer. I could have ported some people back."

Wiley made a note of the time on his board, coordinating it with the transponder blip from the Legion ships themselves. "This must mean that Lon's coming back with the ships. Otherwise, he could have stopped longer in normal space."

That concerned three of Wiley's minds. Wouldn't Lon be eager to return to his bride as quickly as possible?

There could be a number of reasons. Emotional upset. Most Legionnaires knew that when Lon was in one of his black moods the best thing to get him back to normalcy was to keep him around people. If Aiko truly had died, the last thing they would want would be for Lon to brood about it alone in hyperspace.

Mind #3 had been observing all this using a preliminary hypothesis that Lina was indeed guilty as charged and was controlling Londo's mind. Hyperspace blocked mind control as well as telepathy.

The other minds countered that Lina didn't seem to be the mind controlling personality type. Wiley couldn't quantify it yet, not precisely. He did have a number of psychological profiles of her now, though.

Independent, averse to rules or limitations – no wonder she was so fidgety in here. Fairly passive-aggressive but not alarmingly so. Deep-seated moral values, maybe even too much so; she was inelastic in some of her thinking. But she was also creative and innovative, highly intelligent, with an amazingly deep and hidden level of fears. That last would be what Stoan would point to. Wiley could only point to the data and counter with, no, that's what Londo would want to marry.

But there were these telepathy tests, too, elementary ones since it was next to impossible to get even basic-level information from the experts on Tishan. Lina was a solid five on telepathy, at least an eight on clairvoyance, off the scale when she used those so-called guides. The Legion's Chimrin was an eighth-level telepath, Wiley knew, but she was an eight-alpha-six, and he'd never been able to find out what the other figures meant.

If Lina were to use mind control, she would have used it to break out of here, which she considered a prison. He watched her and Brügz talk. All she really had to do was port, but that would counter those ethics of hers. She had made a promise to stay here and she was going to keep it. The fact that the Legion had her under official arrest was not important to her – except for how it would impact Londo's record.

Even so, the lame bribery attempt yesterday might indicate growing desperation.

"Could you tell?" Brügz asked Lina as Erik helped her back up in her seat.

She shook her head. "It was too quick to get a message through. He was upset; he wanted me to tell you all something, and then he got cut off. But she died yesterday, yesterday morning. My guides told me. I'm sorry. I think – I think it was quick, if that's any consolation."

Now Wiley came over, his padd in his hand. "You say you got a message that she was dead yesterday? And you didn't say anything?"

"Everyone was busy on Rimhold when I found out. No one was in the mood for bad news."

"Next time say something."

"Well, it wasn't exact, nothing you could measure, Wiley. I just suddenly knew that she'd been dead for a few hours."

"And this was when we were on Rimhold."

"When you were on Rimhold. Just before I ported you and Jae in."

He nodded and made a note. "I don't know whether to say I'm curious to see if this is true or not," he said slowly. Brügz grunted in sympathy. "Of course the last thing I want is for anything to happen to Aiko."

"I'm sorry," Lina repeated.

"But if she is and if you knew about it, it would be the first instance of communication through hyperspace."

"Do you do *linder* tricks as well?" Brügz asked her.

"No, no sleight-of-hand." Lina gave him a small smile for his efforts to cheer the atmosphere of the room.

"What, you don't believe her?" Erik asked Brügz.

Brügz shook his head without apology. "Chim taught me a long time ago that this kind of thing is sheer superstition. I don't think we're talking real precognition here." He raised a significant eyebrow at Erik, who was well aware of Lina's score results from Wiley's tests, including some low ones for precognition.

"But for Jae to have seen it, too…" Unwillingly, Erik's gaze flicked to Lina and then back to Brügz.

Lina made a sour face. "Don't tell me you're thinking mind control. I am not a mind controller!"

"I've seen controllers," Brügz said.

First-hand information. Lina turned to him eagerly.

Before she could open her mouth, Erik asked, "Where?"

"On Tishan, of course," Brügz told him. "They were being held in hyperspace cells. Every last one of them had the same look, the same hard eyes. Unfathomed anger at the world. It was as if… if things didn't go their way, by the orb, they'd force people to do what they wanted. They were brutes, closet dictators who didn't have the balls to go out and shoot someone honestly. Instead, they snuck behind people's backs, smiled and then knifed them with their minds. Cowards – all of them."

Brügz jerked his chin to Wiley. "So when are you going to break down and get Tishan in on this? They're the experts. You're in command now; you've got enough power to go to the top if they try to sandbag us."

Wiley shrugged and returned to his mission board. "I'm under the commander's orders not to. And you of all people should know about Tishana security."

"The black hole of the known universe." Brügz nodded. "When is Chim due back?"

Wiley didn't even bother to consult his screens. "Eight days minimum," he said. "Realistically, two to three weeks."

"*Skurn.*"

Wiley grunted his agreement before answering another call. Brügz took it and Lina ported him to his assignment, grateful that he seemed to be on her side. Next time she'd try to find something nicer to bribe him with.

Erik settled next to Lina. He didn't seem to be in much mood to talk, so she taught him the game of Reversi.

"I thought this was called 'chess,'" Erik told her as the computer set up a second game.

"Same board, different pieces and rules. Chess is boring."

"Boring? Maximus doesn't think so. He and Valiant play all the time when they're both here."

"His name is Londo. And chess is boring because I always lose."

"Ah." Erik grinned at her. "Then I want to learn that one. Puter, set up a chess board."

This wasn't just a 2-dimensional game; it rose up off the table in front of them in practical real life. You reached to touch a piece and it moved under your hand. But there was no air resistance, no weight; the piece seemed slightly insubstantial. Erik kept a note of pieces and their movements beside him, and then he won the first game and the next.

"Boring," Lina announced. "Why does Brügz know about Tishana security? Tishan's where all the telepaths go to school, right? He's not a telepath."

"He used to be married to Chimrin – Psyche."

"The Legion's telepath."

"Right. She's from Tishan. And when Brügz was Legion commander a few terms ago, we went through a big mind control scare on Dubblest. He had to deal with Tishan a lot. Checkmate; you didn't even put up a fight."

"I don't like this game."

"Aw, come on. Just one more time," he urged. "It's not often that I run into someone here who has zero sense of military tactics." Instead he turned his head to the monitor station.

"I think that's for me," he told her and went over to converse with Wiley and whomever was calling in. He finally nodded at the screen and gathered some protective gear piled next to the table.

Wiley motioned to Lina to come over. She checked out the bright interior scene on the monitor. When Erik was ready, she ported him there.

Now it was just her and Wiley in this big ol' boring lab. It needed a trampoline. "Have you gotten all the information you need with the porting?" she asked him.

He gave her a sour look. "What I got didn't make any sense. I wish you could port to some other planet so I'd have new triangulation data."

"Is the Rimhold prison safe enough?"

"I think the guards would shoot you before you could port back."

"Forget that then."

"Unless we told them you were coming." Wiley was already gesturing at the communications console, calling up the warden. He told her that they were conducting an experiment with their new teleportation equipment, and someone would suddenly appear where they had yesterday for about a minute, then disappear. He didn't want this person to get shot accidentally.

Perhaps it was fatigue that made Warden Baxum look skeptical, but she was talking to the famous Dr. Wilder Mem-Bazer, so she nodded her head and told him to wait five minutes before sending the subject through.

While they were waiting, Lina asked Wiley if he'd looked at the strange symbols that had decorated her dress as well as Londo and Jae's outfits.

"Search turned up at least five thousand meanings each to the three main symbols," he told her. "The trick will be to find something that ties them together. Having the one partially covered up does not make my job any simpler."

"Erik said you were the man to do it," Lina said encouragingly. People seemed to be dealing easier with her status these days, so she ventured in a casual voice, "So, how do I contact a lawyer around h–"

The screen flared to life. "We're ready, Doctor," Warden Baxum reported.

"Stand by," Wiley announced as one section of his board lit up. "Go, Lina."

She ported to Rimhold prison, just long enough to see smoke still rising from some room beyond the great hole in the wall. Guards regarded her curiously. A stench of scorch hung in the air, with burning plastic backing it up. She ported back. "Got it?"

"Yes." Wiley turned to the screen. "We're done, Warden. Thank you for your cooperation." The warden nodded and signed off.

Wiley ran the data through his computer and his minds, shaking his head. "It just doesn't make sense," he finally said.

"Would it help if you had another first-hand experience with it? Did a more relaxed port just to see what it felt like?"

"A subjective reading?" Wiley considered. "Anything might help at this point. I wish some of the members who have been a few hundred parsecs from Sarastor were here to give you someplace really far to port to. If we stretched you to your limit, we'd get some extremely enlightening data."

"If I survived. I'm not sure I like this stretching to your limit stuff."

"We'd work up to a really long port, of course, and see how you were taking it."

"Thank you for your concern. Wiley, how many levels of hyperspace are there, really?"

He looked at her sharply. "What do you mean?"

"Oh hell, don't tell me if it's a state secret or anything. Over at the Terran Zone they were saying how long it takes Level One hyperspace to get to Earth, and I started thinking about it. Y'all seem to travel around by Level Three, which is advertised as the fastest way to go. But Lon said he was faster than your ships. And the Ruby Guards – they're faster than Lon is. I saw an interview with Rico Carapella once and he said he could make it to Aum from Earth in six hours. He had to use a special homing speed or something, different from what he usually used. Six hours to the center of the galaxy – that's damned fast."

Wiley mumbled noncommittally and rechecked the results of her IQ test.

"So why don't you let out that there are at least five levels? Maybe six, with me around? What could it harm?"

"You're making a lot of suppositions," he told her. "How do you know the other levels are hyperspace?"

"You were the one who said that I couldn't sense Lon because he was in hyperspace. And Rico Carapella talked about the lonely journey to Aum. I was thinking that maybe it was so lonely because he couldn't communicate with anyone. Why is there a barrier? Why can't you communicate? Or is it just that they're going so fast that communications are garbled? Is there a time-slowing like there is when you get close to the speed of light?"

"First of all," Wiley carefully explained, "I am not entirely under the impression – yet – that what you do is hyperspace travel. I don't see any acceleration process involved."

"Neither am I. The lack of acceleration is why I'm so fast," Lina replied smugly.

"Uh huh. You're fast because you don't move yourself."

"Exactly. Space and time are constructs of the human mind and ultimately unreal."

"How much AffSys science have you been studying?"

"I haven't had the time to get around to it. Okay, Wiley, on Earth when we start to talk about relativity, someone usually brings in a set of twins and shoves one of them on a close-to-lightspeed spaceship. Let's begin with…" Lina counted on her fingers, "septuplets. One stays on Sarastor as our control, and the others climb into hyperspace ships, all bound for… Aum, at the center of the galaxy. Each goes in a different level, and one, of course, doesn't need any ship because they're just porting."

"Do you think you could port to Aum?" Wiley asked sardonically. "It's about 6500 parsecs away."

"I've never tried. Anyway, the six travelers all reach Aum and return to Sarastor. Is there any difference in their ages by the time they all join up again?"

"How many minutes apart were they born?"

"A miracle took place and they were all born at exactly the same moment."

"A miracle. You're a good one for miracles." He busied himself with two different functions of his station.

"Give me some informaaation, Wiley!"

He considered her with his right eye for a long moment before he spoke. "There may have been some time experiments done. But only for the bottom three levels. I've been meaning to talk Londo into one."

"And?"

"Sorry, no differences. Time seems to flow at the same rate in hyperspace as in normal space. There are fluctuations, probably the same fluctuations as one finds in relativistic space, but when applied to a hyperbolic curvature of space resulting from–"

Almost immediately, Lina lost track of his meaning. She'd taken basic quantum mechanics, but nothing much beyond that except large doses of science fiction. Every now and then she nodded and Wiley blathered on.

Maybe Londo could explain some of it to her; he had to travel hyperspace all the time. If Rico Carapella were lonely, Londo would be, too. If he were moody, that couldn't be good for him, could it? She didn't want Londo lonely. She wanted Londo comfortable, content. His hand in hers. Her arms around him, making a home for him to return to.

She'd make sure that home was his favorite place in the universe. She'd keep the place clean and neat… somehow. She'd cook his favorite meals. She'd make sure his clothes were clean and people didn't bother him or bow to him when he wanted some privacy, and that his bed was warm and soft and had her in it and oh, why wasn't he here now?

Damn it, three days without Lon was too much. He was the best thing that had ever happened to her.

And he did the best things *to* her.

"And you haven't been listening to a word I've said for the past three minutes."

"Um? Oh sorry. I really didn't mean to zone out like that. I'm afraid you got a little beyond me."

"In that case, I'll give you something you can handle." More forms for Legion PIC, interspersed with another session with the real Ms. Yency and questionnaires about Earth. Sometimes Lina didn't think that some people around here really believed she was from the Big Blue Marble…

"I'm back, Dr. Mem-Bazer. Lina."

She turned to see Erik enter the laboratory, so young! Could he really be in his early twenties? From what she'd seen in her studies, people around here didn't age normally at all. Brügz looked maybe early- to mid-thirties, but that estimate was probably off by a decade or three. Erik *felt* young. He hadn't had his shine burnished by life yet.

"Please don't put so many outrageous opinions in your answers," Wiley was telling her about all those forms she had to fill out.

"I can't help being a little opinionated. How's the shoulder?" she asked Erik.

Wiley did not want her to interrupt. "But I'm trying to get an objective view of Earth."

"I'm very subjective when it comes to Earth, Wile. You want an objective opinion, you have to come to Earth yourself and take a look around."

Erik turned to Wiley, shaking his finger at him. "I'll give you subjective. It was the *skurniest* thing. I was revving up, about to call down a good wind, when *thwunk*, I feel someone tapping my head, and I remembered." He turned to Lina. "Is it really a guardian angel?"

"Yes, it is. He's standing there with his hands on his hips and telling you to pay some attention to the health of your body. Apparently you're letting some other things go, too."

Erik looked at Wiley. "Guardian angels." He shook his head. "Ow!" He rubbed his head and looked accusingly at Lina. "Someone hit me."

Wiley looked at Lina's smirk and said, "I didn't see anyone in this room do anything, Sunstorm. Maybe it's just your imagination. A creature from hyperspace."

"Yes, Erik, it must be your vivid imagination."

"Ow! Lina, tell him to stop it."

"Are you going to start taking care of yourself?"

"Ow! Yes! Okay! I give up." Erik looked at the air to his right, trying to see whoever it was. "Just quit hitting me. That's better."

"And he says to watch that mind control, too."

"Mind control?" Wiley perked up at that. "Who's controlling minds?"

"Not me," Lina said innocently.

"She claims I am," Erik growled.

"Just a bit."

"Is that so?" Wiley pondered for a moment. "Maybe we can clear up this suspicion of Lina if you show me what you're doing. I can quantify it and compare."

"I don't think we should be encouraging his habit."

"I've sworn it off," Erik said, raising his hand in oath taking.

"He doesn't need it anyway," Lina said, meeting Erik's eyes in a long gaze. She sighed happily at him. "He knows he's a studpuppy. Mmm-hm. God's answer to every woman's prayer."

"You really think so?" he said, leaning closer. His mouth widened into a dazzling smile.

"There. Did you get that?" Lina asked Wiley, swiping the air clear in front of her chakras.

"I did, in full spectrum. Thanks for the warning."

"I think you need a little more work on not doing it," Lina told Erik. His lower lip stuck out in a great pout. "Maybe you need to visualize as you practice."

Dellen wore a towel around her modestly-covered shoulders and dabbed at her sweaty brow as Wiley called her on the monitor.

"I've got something for you," he told her. "A fire at the Unaffiliated Worlds Interstellar Trade Center. Emergency units are already engaged, but people are still trapped. I'm calling Jae in, too."

"Give me three minutes," she said, and the monitor cut off.

Lina sat there, the image still in her eyes: a pool, Olympic-sized or bigger, had been in the background, and there was something that could definitely be used as a jogging track. There had also been what looked like strength training equipment, but she wasn't interested in that. "Was that in Headquarters?" she asked Wiley.

"Um."

She assumed that was an affirmative; he had his mind on other matters. Or minds. Good lord, he could do a lot of things at once!

He was tapping on a keypad with one hand and scrolling through a screen with his other, circling information with his index finger, highlighting it as he touched it. Two screens hovered that he controlled like an orchestra conductor, with an occasional touch for one of the many rings he wore. And always, always, that television screen with the news droned on, three tiers of printed information scrolling across the bottom of the screen, and smaller screens popping in and out of the air around him.

One he sometimes polarized so only he could see and hear it, but often he brought it out to bother onlookers. At least, that's what Lina thought. It would appear after she'd been singing to herself, or when she'd fooled around with her flute for a while, too loudly for his tastes.

Wiley kept track of it all.

She stopped working on the endless tests and Terran informational reports that kept her from researching legal matters and watched as Jae and Dellen reported in so Wiley could transport them out.

Only then did she repeat her question: "Was that in Headquarters? That gym that Dellen was in?"

"Mm? Yes, the training complex."

"With a pool."

He turned to her. "Yes. I take it you feel you need some exercise?"

"I've been sitting here for four days, plus. I can feel my butt getting bigger even as we speak. How much would it take to bribe you to let me get in there for an hour? Just in the pool? The track, if I can, too. Nothing else."

He appeared to consider. "How much do you have?"

"I've got about twenty dollars, American, that I can get hold of."

"Lina, that wouldn't even get you into the front door of the Legion Museum." He returned his attentions to his board.

"I don't want to go there, not right now. C'mon, Wile. Just an hour. I can't mentally control anyone there; there's no one to control down there, or up there, or over there, wherever it is."

"What do you want to do in the pool?"

"What? Swim, of course. Goof around. Stretch a bit. What else does one do in a pool?"

"And you know how to swim?"

"Of course I do. Pleeease, Wiley. I'm getting to the point where I won't be able to get up in a day, I'll be so out of shape."

"I don't know if I can confine all the flesh-eating fish we keep the pool stocked with," Brainy said, shaking his head at his console.

"Flesh-eating…"

"It is part of the survival course."

"Give me a break. You don't keep fish in there. Not in a gym."

He sighed. "I'll have to turn off all the security systems…"

"You're a sweetie, Wiley. Ohmigosh. My swimsuit got blown up at the hotel. I'll have to order one off the nets."

"You won't find one," Wiley favored her with a glance from one eye.

"Why not? Are they in a special section?"

"People don't swim, not for recreational purposes."

Lina sat back in her chair. "Don't swim?"

"That's why we use the pool in survival training," Wiley told her, turning down the volume on the news set with a crook of his finger. "Most rookies come here not knowing how to swim and we have to teach them, in case they get in a situation when they have to. Does everyone on Earth know how to swim?"

"In America at least – I couldn't say about other countries – a good percentage of everyone goes to the pool or lake or the shore during the summer, to cool off if nothing else. I was a lifeguard one summer when I was a kid. That means that I had to have advanced swimming and some basic lifesaving skills. It wasn't at the ocean – I was afraid of the ocean – but at a pool. It didn't pay much, but I had a great tan that year. Hardly any splotches."

"And this was a public pool?"

"Yeah, part of the city recreation program."

Wiley let out a long-suffering sigh. "We have some waterproof bodysuits in inventory."

"As long as no one's around, I'll come up with something for myself." Lina grinned. "Don't worry; I wouldn't dream of going skinny dipping in this high-and-mighty Legion Headquarters, at least not without wearing my pearls." Legion Protocol had sent her some more clothing regulations to read through this morning. "One hour?" An hour here was at about ninety minutes.

Wiley considered. "All right," he finally said. "One hour."

Lina wanted to laugh in delight at the prospect. "Do you think Jae would mind if I borrowed his boom box?"

"Music to swim by?" Wiley closed both eyes in pain. "Does everything have to be accompanied by music?"

"Only if you want to have a good time," Lina said. "I'm making a quick stop back at quarters for proper attire. Bye." She popped out.

She showed up on his monitors five minutes later dressed in cut-off jeans and a tank top that said "Keep Calm and Boldly Go." It wasn't per Legion regs, but chances were that no one capable of issuing demerits was in the gym. Though Wiley was likely watching.

Looking around to get her bearings, Lina set down the boom box and CDs and started the music. The gym was large enough to hold an actual jogging track as well as a climbing wall and what might be a giant-sized jungle gym. Individual strength-type machines ranged along the side of one part of the track.

She stuck her toe into the water as her *Beach Party!* CD began. She didn't spot any flesh-eating fish. It looked pretty deep and dark down there. There were no diving boards.

The water was warm. How many Legionnaires would be shocked at the temperature of the water they'd actually encounter on missions? But something else was odd.

She dipped her hand into the water and sniffed. Salt water. Ocean water – not chemicaled pool water. Well, that would be what they'd be running into, for the most part.

She put her towel down next to the boom box and suddenly took off for the pool, long-jumping, rolling herself up into a ball. *Splat!* A very satisfactory plume went up from her cannonball and she surfaced, shaking the hair out of her face. The water had sprayed a good eight feet or more from the edge of the pool.

Lina swam a few laps as "Carolina Girls" played, followed by songs by the Drifters, and then tried to see how far down she could dive during James Taylor's "Up On the Roof" and the Embers' "Under the Boardwalk."

How deep was it? If she went down using all her breath, could she touch bottom? She could always port back up. She took a huge breath and tried. When her lungs began to scream at her, she ported up. She hadn't even been near the bottom.

But she'd ported too high. She fell about five feet into the water and had to catch her breath. Waitaminnit. She treaded water as she considered. No diving boards. But if she ported up there…

She ported ten feet up and twisted into a dive, steep and straight. Her arm strained in vain reaching for the bottom of the pool. She tried again, this time about fifteen feet up.

Afterward she treaded water determinedly. She could see the bottom on that one. She was going to touch it! She tried to pack as much oxygen as she could into her cells by breathing deeply and slowly.

Twenty, maybe thirty feet up, she went into her dive. Lina blasted into the water amid a storm of air bubbles as she let the force of gravity propel her. Then she stroked as strongly as she could, absolutely determined. There. She could see the slight construction design of the bottom. Stroke. Stroke. Straight down. No air. Straight down. Need air. Almost there. *Need air!* Touch! She ported.

She took a huge breath while she laughed, and wound up coughing instead as she swallowed some water, but then she laughed at her own coughing.

"What in sunfire were you doing?!" Wiley's voice boomed in the gym from some speaker. "Stop that! Stop that right now!"

"I just wanted to see if I could touch bottom," Lina said. "Go back to your monitors. You're an ol' party-pooper." She swam to the side of the pool and pulled herself out, then loped to the boom box and put in another CD: Beach Boys singing about old-fashioned summers.

She ran a couple of easy laps around the gym in her bare feet. It must be a half-mile in here at least. What was all this strange equipment for? Did Lon train here? Could some of this equipment handle him, or did he have to have a special area? Or was he considered trained enough so that he didn't have to do this? Did he train others?

She squinted up at the ceiling, so very far above. Five stories at least. There seemed to be some gym equipment up there, too. She stopped and ported to what she could see clearly.

She hung onto a kind of monkey-bar ring arrangement. Up here! Rings hung down from the ceiling, wide and big enough for… oh. Big enough for someone to fly through. A flying training course, perhaps? What else would you do up here?

Movement down on the ground caught her attention.

Jae had come in. He was looking around, turning in a circle, his hands on his hips. His white cape billowed behind him. "Lina?" His voice came through clearly up here. "Lina, where are you? Wiley?"

Don't tell, Wiley! Watch this!

"She was in there a few minutes ago. Sensors say she's still there," Wiley's voice came from the air. "Just a minute," he lied. "I've got a call coming in."

Lina held her laugh inside her. This was too perfect to resist. Jae was standing right beside the pool, looking away from it as well as the boom box. She ported the box farther away from the pool, the instantaneous port not interrupting the music at all.

Then she spotted twelve feet above and about five feet in from the side, almost next to where Jae was standing. Porting, she immediately rolled into a ball, letting out a rebel yell as she crashed into the drink.

Water fountained in an immense column and exploded outward. Lina tried to surface in time for the hit, but missed it. She came up for air to see Jae turn around, his entire body drenched in salt water, his hair and cape dripping as he stood in a puddle.

"That's called a cannonball," Lina hooted. She dissolved into hee-haws at his condition as she treaded water. "Bedraggled" barely began to describe it! What did a better job? "Angry," maybe. Yes, "angry" was a start.

She thought that might be two plumes of smoke coming from his elf ears as he detached his cape and dropped it, advancing to the pool.

"Lina…" he warned.

14

U h oh. She turned and stroked father out into the pool, then faster. He leapt off the pavement and quickly glided toward her. That damned flying ring! Cheater! Lina took a breath and dove. Damned if he was going to catch her without getting wetter.

She came up for air, dove and came up again. He was right behind her in the water now. She gulped air and dove deeper than before, turning to see him trying to reach her feet.

There was something funny about the water around his head, like… A bubble of air. He could change elements; maybe he could carry breathing air with him. Cheater!

She dove as far as she could and felt his fingers brush her toes. Gasping for oxygen after she ported back up to the surface, she saw him deep down there, turning around to return to the surface. He wasn't swimming; he was flying underwater. Miserable cheater.

She ported ten feet up and dove right on top of Jae, tagging him on her speeding way, spinning him around. He followed her, his speed slower than hers. Apparently water dragged at the flight apparatus. Stroking away from him, she swam in loops around him until she had to port back.

Where'd he go? He was floating in mid-pool, about ten feet down. Just hanging there. His arms dangled to his sides. She couldn't detect that bubble around his head any more. Was he faking? He had to be faking. Shit.

Lina dove and grabbed him from the back, dragging him to the surface. He seemed unconscious as he didn't respond to her touch enough to fight back. Very odd.

They reached the surface and she pulled his head above water. Suddenly Jae turned around and grabbed her by the waist: "Gotcha!" he cried triumphantly.

He carried her out of the water, hovered above it, and then tossed her, letting her drop but caught her by her feet. He dunked her head underwater once before she could get her balance together enough to port to the ground. She sat down and pouted.

"What the *skurn* did you think you were doing, getting me all wet?" he demanded as he glided down to join her.

"You cheat," she said.

"And then you didn't port me immediately when I was drowning. That's sloppy, Lina."

"So I forgot I could. Sue me. I was in lifeguard mode. You didn't fight back, by the way. Drowning people almost always fight back, even if you grab them from behind. I figured you didn't know how to drown properly. You were probably following the drowning rules around here." She stuck out her lower lip at him. "You tricked me."

"I told you, never trust me." Jae sat down next to her, lying back on his hands. "I should sic Protocol on you for what you're wearing. Or what you're not wearing. What the *frickurn* were you doing in here, anyway? Swimming for pleasure?"

"And why else would anyone want to swim? I kinda like this salt pool you have here, Jae. I could get used to it. Salt's so much easier to take than chlorinated water."

"So they swim for pleasure on Earth." Jae wiped his hair out of his eyes and shook his head. "I don't like swimming."

"You never had a chance to play games in the water, then," Lina said. "Or maybe you were never out on a hot enough day that you'd want to duck into the pool to cool off. Let's see. You can also race while you swim. Or play team sports. You could bet on those; Legionnaires would like that. Don't they do anything, as long as they can wager?"

Jae smiled at that. "Maybe. Legionnaires also like to watch semi-naked people." He gave her a mocking once-over from head to toes and back again.

Lina resisted the impulse to cover herself with her hands. Instead she lifted her chin defiantly. "I am not semi-naked."

"Are too."

"Maybe if you had a decent pool, it wouldn't scare everyone off and they'd stay around to play."

That he took as an affront to Legion honor. "What's the matter with our pool?"

"It's too damn deep. It should have at least one side that's shallow enough for people to stand in while they learn how to swim. People have strong fears about drowning."

"A sloping bottom?"

"It doesn't have to be that wide for the learning area. You can rope it off from the deeper part, if you need that deep of water to train in."

"I don't get it."

"One hour," Wiley's voice echoed in the room.

"Thank you," Lina said as if she meant it. She didn't. She didn't want to go back to that cramped old warehouse of a prison. "Look; I can show you real quick if you want to take, I don't know, maybe a third of an hour?"

Jae considered. "Wiley?" he asked. "You still there?"

"Here."

"Give us a half hour or so. I think we're going to Earth, and not to feed the cats. It's actually borderline Legion business."

"Make it quick. There's trouble brewing in Celastar."

"Check." Jae stood up and stretched, and suddenly he wasn't the least bit wet any more. He ran a hand through his hair, and it fell naturally back into place.

"Cheater," Lina mumbled.

He smiled at her as he held out his hand to help pull her up. "I am dry," he said. "Unlike some soaked, semi-naked people I know."

"We'll see," Lina smiled, and she ported them. During the final phase, the matching up with Earth part, she tried to imagine herself as being dry. Not too dry; she didn't want to dehydrate. They appeared, and water still dripped from her. "Damn," she said. "It didn't work."

Then abruptly she was dry. "Thanks," she told Jae as he looked around.

They had materialized inside a humid, echoing natatorium lined with bleachers and a small but vocal crowd. Jae followed Lina behind the bleachers to a more deserted part so they could peek out and not be noticed.

People played a game involving net goals and teams of men in the water. At first Jae thought they were naked, but then on closer, more interested look, he saw the tiny suits. Everyone swam in hard strokes as they went after a ball. The crowd let out a scream when the ball was stolen.

"It's hard to see the setup in here," Lina said. "Let's see if one of the other pools isn't busy."

They ported, but the building seemed the same. Was it some kind of pool complex? Here was a pool about three-quarters the surface area of the Legion's, with sparkling blue water. The effect must come from the paint on the sides and bottom. Stripes made lanes on the bottom of the pool, and floating ties sectioned it off.

When Jae turned, Lina was wearing a sleeveless light blue, skin-tight leotard that left no doubt whatsoever as to what the anatomy of a female Terran comprised. Jae choked back a gulp with what sounded to him like a sputter.

"See? I'm getting faster. They still keep the suits in the same place," she said to him. "Sorry I don't know where they keep the guys' stuff, or I'd get you one, too."

"Quite all right," Jae told her in a tight voice. He didn't know if he had the nerve to wear those strips men wore here. Not in public. Not a Legionnaire. And not now. He tugged at his earring in consternation.

As it was, he turned away from the nearly-naked woman but stared out the corner of his eyes. The suit showed off more than a little of her generous cleavage in front and left parts of her buttocks bare, as were her arms and legs and thighs and feet. Was it really proper for people to dress this way on Earth?

She dove into the empty pool. Jae had never seen anyone dive. He'd seen them ease themselves in and fall in and jump in, but not dive. It didn't make that big of a splash at all.

Lina came out midway to bob on the surface. "According to the measurements–" she pointed to marks on the side of the pool – "this part is about three meters deep. It's that way all the way from here to that side over there." She ducked under the floating rope and swam to another mark. "But over here, it should be just about as deep as I am tall. Let's see."

She sank down to the bottom. Jae could see her feet on the floor. The water barely covered her. She rose up and then stroked closer to the side to stand. The water came up to her shoulders – her mostly-bare shoulders that were playing peek-a-boo under the wet curtain of her hair.

"See?" she said brightly. "You can teach people easier how to swim if they don't have to concentrate on not drowning."

"It's still tough on children, though."

"This is a college pool. Regular public pools are geared for kids, and then there are wading pools that are shallow all over. Those are for young kids."

"And you use chlorine to keep the water clean," Jae said from the obvious smell.

"There are other ways. Ultraviolet filters and such."

Lina pulled herself from the pool – long, cool flesh as legs drew themselves from the primordial waters, the inviting wiggle of a firm, half-exposed derriere – and stood up just in time to get out of the way of a shouting, running group of college kids.

Three women wore much, much less than Lina, but the men didn't wear the strips. Instead they wore baggy shorts that seemed almost sedate after what the sports team had been in. They ran around to the deeper edge and jumped or dove in. One kid waited until everyone was in, and then cannonballed them. The girls of the group screamed, and everyone laughed.

Lina gave a sharp whistle. They turned to her, then looked curiously at the tall, costumed man beside her. "This is college property, not a private pool," she chastised them. "No running, no horseplay! Or did you sign waivers before you came in?"

"Spoilsport!" someone yelled.

"School of law's right next door," Lina retorted. "There are a couple hundred lawyers in training who'd love to help the school in their suit against you. They get extra credit for it, you know."

"Aw, she's not going to report us."

"C'mon; join us. We're just having a little fun."

Jae's ring beeped and Wiley's voice came out. "Get back, Jae. I'm tired of sending fools out to track down this planetary defense cascade snafu we seem to be having. I need you in Celastar to check it out in person."

"Cascade?" Jae's voice registered his alarm. "Since when is it a cascade?"

"Since the Harp Line network reset of its own accord."

Jae stood silent a moment in the echoing chamber. "These things don't happen in clusters."

"My thoughts exactly. I want you to find some answers."

"We're leaving now," Jae informed Lina as well as Wiley.

"There's the real spoilsport," Lina told the swimmers. "You people be a little more careful." She ported the two of them back to Sarastor.

"Shouldn't you take your own advice?" Jae asked as ironically as he could as they appeared in the lab.

"I try never to do that," Lina replied.

"What the *skurning kick* of sunfire are you wearing?!"

A crash of glass told Lina that Wiley had dropped something even as he went full-tilt into a fashion police rant. Oh dear, she was standing in the lab in her swimsuit. She'd left her outfit at home on Earth; now all she had to wear was this borrowed thing. Let's see… first port the outfit to Sarastor, then switch, then port… No, a towel first…

"My cape, Lina?" Jae held out a hand and she ported his cape back from the gym. It hung swollen with water, and he made a move to flip it out towards her. Lina stepped back hastily, but by the time it whipped to its full extent, it was perfectly dry. Jae put it on with a grin as he gave her another sly head-to-toe appraisal. In an instant, though, he went into full professional mode and conferred with Wiley.

The morning wore on. Lina studied her Panlingua first, humming to herself to keep awake, but then Wiley would make a small warning noise and she'd glance up to find him looking at her expectantly with his extra screen chattering away. With a sigh, she'd shut up until she forgot again.

He didn't like her humming, he didn't like her sitting any way but straight up, as if she could stay in that position for more than a few minutes at a time… Apparently that fun-loving mind that Jae swore he had was off on vacation today, leaving the other four wet-blanket minds behind. Eventually she finished the final section and turned off the screen with a flourish and a "Ta dah!" fanfare. Wiley wasn't around to hear. No one was.

She wanted to celebrate.

All alone, she was forbidden to go into the lab proper. Instead she schemed. She'd seen Legionnaires use the one computer wall console reachable from her red-walled cell. It must have more access to the galactic Interwebs than did her little study padd. She asked it for a listing of lawyers who would handle cases like hers against the Legion.

#Legal charges against Carolina O'Kelly are classified Level Four security,# the computer informed her.

"So give me a listing of lawyers who can handle Level Four stuff."

#A legal representative from Legion Legal Services will be appointed by the Mega-Legion commander, if needed.#

"I don't want His Royal Highness to choose my lawyer from his brown-nosed flunkies. I'd rather not spend the rest of my life in jail, thank you very much. Get me a list of civilian lawyers. Where're your Yellow Pages?"

But she couldn't find a way around the puter's insistence that the only legal representation possible for a Legion Spouse would come from Legion Legal Services. Lina gave the puter a frustrated bop on the corner of its immaterial screen.

Maybe she could approach this from a different angle. "Puter, show me some educational listings," she told the air casually as she settled in her prisoner chair. "Might as well sign up for some courses."

Two beeps, and the screen came closer, blooming to larger life than before in order to display a list of a variety of classes. She narrowed it down, wondering out loud between art and sociology. She made sure to speak in everyday, easy tones, just like you did before you grabbed a cat to take them to the vet. A few questions about what were the best schools and the list narrowed some more. Upper-level courses… Sociology… Hm, why golly gee, maybe a law course…

"Oh, that looks interesting," Lina mused out loud over a course description. "Can I talk to the professor to see if I have the prerequisites for it?"

Two beeps and a message to wait for a few moments, and then there was a real, human woman on the screen. A law professor.

The woman bowed her head to Lina. "I'm honored that a Legion adjunct is interested in my class, Ms. O'Kelly. In what way are you connected to the organization?"

The puter flashed an off-camera warning that security silence concerning her marriage was still in effect for another two days. "I'm not at liberty to say," Lina replied smoothly. Quickly she added, "Just let me state that I am living here at Headquarters and I'm under arrest and desperately need legal aid that they–"

The screen blanked.

"Damn!" She gave her solid chair arm a good slug. The screen registered twenty demerits for attempting to circumvent Legion legal matters, and then suggested that she continue her studies about Sarastor instead, this time on her study padd.

So she let the padd scroll through the Introduction to Sarastor's entertainment listings, as she played dark, roiling passages of Wagner on her flute. There were no concerts, no music notations of any sort except for the No-Talent Quartet. And – She set down the flute and pointed at the screen to make it stop. The Romaki Club was advertising Terran music. Not singing, just music. When the puter played her a sample, it was her. She wondered if they were going to send her a check.

"Sarastor," she said, "I mean it. You've got some funny people here."

Thank you for making music, Speaker. They appreciate it and I do as well.

"Anytime, Sarastor. It's my pleasure."

Teach my people about themselves.

"What? Sarastor, what–?"

Apparently Sarastor had had her say and wasn't going to talk any more.

Wiley and Erik returned and she quickly put away the offending flute. Wiley made some disparaging remarks not quite under his breath about barbarians as Erik disappeared into the break room for a few minutes.

When he returned with a mug of *tarn*, Erik grinned at Lina. "Has Wiley seen it?"

She'd made a rude drawing of Wiley on the electronic bulletin board in there, shaking his finger and shouting, "Mustn't touch! You touch and Daddy spank!" The lines were too mechanical for her tastes, but all in all it was a satisfactory caricature, especially when she found she could animate the eyes to roll around in different directions. Plus she could show off that she'd begun to learn written Panlingua.

"I'm sure I'll hear it when he does," she told Erik.

Dellen came back and Lina was interested to see that she took a press interview in one of the media cubicles, like Lon and Jae had done while they were in quarantine. Lina could watch on a monitor as the off-site interviewer and Dellen spoke about current Legion affairs. Lina could touch various popups on her screen to find out more about Dellen, sign up for her fan club, or check out in-depth coverage of the subjects the interview handled. Cool.

After a while Jae and Brügz checked in, and Dellen took some time off. With both Brügz and Erik manning the comm board, Jae felt free enough to make good on a major news interview postponed from two days ago. He also used the lab instead of the regular press room elsewhere in the building that Lina had read about, and Lina moved in closer to observe. She sat cross-legged on the lab floor, which kept her out of the way.

As they had during quarantine and Dellen's interview, they programmed the backdrop to show the Legion symbol. Now Jae was really in his costume instead of a hologrammed version, and he looked quite the dashing cape celebrity.

He faced a number of reporters instead of being one-on-one. It was a regular press conference, Lina thought. She could see the monitor at the comm station streaming the broadcast with Jae front and center, with insets that kept changing as different reporters asked questions. All bowed respectfully before they spoke.

Jae answered a variety of queries ranging from his current duties during the Legion's unusual absence, to whom he was taking to the Housers in a couple months (he didn't know who he'd be going out with by then) (and yes, he was between relationships at the present), to the current political situation on some Unaffiliated World, one outside the AffSys but still within the sector. There was even a question about Valiant's mysterious girlfriend, but Jae told the reporters that they should wait to get that information from Valiant himself.

Through it all he was so calm, friendly and dignified, except for the occasional arm pit scratch. He was a Legionnaire, the ultimate star, and Jae carried it with confidence, authority and deftness. It was as if he were a world leader – but then, he was.

As the interview wore on and became more politically detailed, Lina listened with half an ear as she played with a jigsaw puzzley something she'd found on one of the experiment stations. Most of Jae's political references were over her head. But she perked up halfway through a new subject.

She'd missed the start of it. Apparently someone had stolen a hyperspace vehicle in the next system over or so and had been arrested as soon as they'd landed on one of the Unaffiliated Worlds. They'd been deported back to the AffSys and put into slavery.

Slavery?!

"The AffSys Abolitionist Movement is calling for an investigation," the orange-skinned reporter was informing Jae. "How does the Legion feel about this?"

Jae shifted in his chair. It was the first time Lina had seen him pause for some length after a question.

"As I understand the situation," he said slowly – Jae, speaking slowly? – "this involved a slave marriage. The woman was the legal slave in the union and was trying to escape. If she'd thought more clearly about it, she'd have escaped to a world with no extradition policy to the AffSys, and one where slavery was illegal. She missed on both counts here."

Lina dropped the jigsaw pieces in shock as she jumped up. Slavery! And Jae was sticking up for it!

A hand grabbed her arm and pulled her to the comm desk, where a privacy screen was hastily called, standing between them and Jae like a wall of water.

"You've got to be quiet during these things!" Erik hissed at her.

"But he's condoning slavery! Slavery!" Lina pointed wildly at Jae so he could see even through the distortion that she was upset. On the monitor, he glanced her way for a millisecond and then his attention went back to the reporter.

"There's nothing he can do about it," Erik told her as Brügz handled a call. "This isn't even a case of true slavery. It was a slave marriage."

"What the hell's that?"

Erik frowned as he put his thoughts together. "It's one of those three-ways. You get a married couple and they want a third, so they buy a slave. Sometimes the slave's just there for the sex, and sometimes they're a general-purpose servant as well. In a three-way prostitution marriage the third is always just there for the sex, but it's not a slavery marriage. The prostitute gets paid for their services for the length of the marriage contract."

Lina jaw dropped. Speechless.

"A slave marriage is totally different from real slavery. There are worlds out there where slaves don't have the protection that marriage provides them."

"How can there be any slavery Out Here? I thought you people were civilized?" She gesticulated at Jac. "I thought the Feithi were so advanced. But you can stand here and tell me that–" She sputtered incoherently, knowing that her face had gone dark red with anger. "How can any thinking person take another person and claim that they're superior enough to own them? It's insane! Don't tell me that the Legion, the high and mighty Affiliated Systems Mega-Force Legion, actually *condones* slavery?"

"Keep it down," Brügz barked. "I've got a call here!"

Erik dragged Lina away from the comm desk. The privacy curtain split and followed them. "Be quiet and listen!" he told her. All traces of humor had disappeared. "You're a Legion spouse now. There are rules about what opinions you can have and what you can't. The Legion operates under AffSys authority, and the AffSys holds many worlds where slavery and slave marriages are perfectly legal. The Legion has to stand by the law. We can't support anarchy. The entire system would start to come apart if we did."

"You can support basic human rights! The honor and dignity of the individual!"

He pointed a finger at her chin menacingly. "You can't talk like that, Lina. Not anymore. I'll have Legion Protocol sequester you until you understand."

"What the hell is this, some kind of cult? Conditioning the prisoner? A little shock therapy to hammer it through?" Lina pointed right back at him. "I am not a citizen of the Affiliated Systems, buddy; I am a citizen of the United States of America, where it is *illegal* to own slaves, *immoral* to even think of doing such, and I am completely within my rights under the First Amendment to state my opinions any time I want to."

"Not anymore, and not here," Erik told her, but his tone gentled as perhaps he realized that she truly did come from another culture.

Instead he locked her into her chair with a privacy screen around her for the duration of Jae's interview.

And immediately she ported out to stand just outside the camera range in front of Jae. She crossed her arms across her chest, her chin defiantly jutting. Then she turned her back on him and sank to sit on the floor in silent fury.

The questions about the case had nearly run dry. Jae defended the Abolitionist Movement's right to speak their mind, but reiterated that all forms of slavery were quite legal within the AffSys, as long as they conformed to certain conditions.

Lina shook her head angrily but silently as she sat on the cold floor. She bared her teeth at Erik when he tried to come near her. He backed off.

Jae ended the segment. "In order to have this woman released from her slave contract," he said, "it would take more than proving that it had been signed under duress. We may assume that all contracts for slavery are signed under some kind of duress. This would take changing basic Affiliated Systems law, an amendment to our constitution itself, before they could begin proper proceedings." Jae shrugged. "By that time, in all probability, the woman's contract will have run out."

Lina shook her head again, disgusted at Jae for ruining her opinion of him.

"But if the Abolitionist Movement needs help to begin the legal process," Jae continued, "I hope someone in it will give me a call. I'd be happy to be a part of it as I can."

Lina's mouth opened and she whirled around. Jae wrinkled his nose at her for an instant and triggered a new reporter's question.

Brügz called an emergency session with Ms. Yency after that. "We are the Legion," the real Yency told Lina firmly via monitor. "We support the organization with every breath we take."

"So if the Legion's mission is to help people, how can we take that next breath and support slavery?!"

"Slavery is something we have no control over. It simply *is*."

What a wretched view Yency had! Lina folded her arms over each other and clamped her mouth shut before she could say anything that would get Londo in trouble. *Londo! How could you sit still for any of this?* Lina had some questions for her husband that she wanted answered toot sweet!

Jae finished his interview and went out on a mission almost immediately. Lina motioned Erik over. "I'm sorry I caused you trouble," she told him.

"You're new to this world."

"Yes, but you can't help it if you have to live by a bunch of stupid rules and immoral laws."

"I worked hard to get here. I'll abide by those rules."

"Well, it's those rules I'm mad at, not you. I'm sorry."

"Apology accepted." Erik flashed her his dashing grin, and she had to smile back. There were no hooks in it. "Jae left 'feed the prisoner now and then' instructions. Are you hungry? I was about to take a meal break. I could take you to one of the cafeterias."

Lina begged off to stay with Wiley, who had decided to put her miraculous wedding ring under his more high-powered sensors while he waited for some report from his assistants in a downstairs lab. The ring was a sign of her vows to Lon, and she wasn't going to let it out of her sight.

So it was Wiley who eventually escorted her down to the main cafeteria, but this time there were younger children present, different families. Wiley watched the rambunctious kids sourly. Their parents weren't paying them much mind. "Let's try another," he suggested, and they went down to the ground level, to the cafeteria that specialized in non-family outside guests.

"I like this," Lina told him as they were seated. "It's a lot brighter down here. Whoever designed those dark halls upstairs – Well, it's depressing."

"We had the best decorators when the building was constructed," Wiley told her.

"So it's time to redecorate. What's it been, a hundred years?"

He shrugged. "A little over that."

"Dark is depressing. At least put in some more of those phony windows." She nodded at the wall which displayed a view of the plaza outside, and knew that it was a television picture of the place and not a window. "They make all the difference. Where's this Mega-Legion Museum that everyone's always talking about?"

"I wasn't aware that everyone did."

"I've been watching a lot of tourism tapes."

Wiley pointed with his spork to the far end of the plaza. "Down there and to the right about a half-mile."

"Can someone take me there? Can I go on my own? Do they have a souvenir shop?"

"A souvenir shop?" The corners of Wiley's mouth twitched downward at the thought. "No, you cannot go alone; you're still very much under arrest, remember that. Why would we want a souvenir shop?"

"You're kidding; you don't offer souvenirs?"

"The Museum is a dignified place for reflection and honor for our accomplishments. We're proud of what we do."

"And so you should be. People who come here to visit, honor y'all." She'd managed to squeeze the Panlingua to make a "y'all" just for the hell of it. Wiley winced whenever she did, which was another reason why she did it.

"Tourists come here; they want to take a piece away with them so they can remember. If they got the same thing at their local Walmart, it wouldn't have the memories or the impression. You're doing the people a disservice by not offering official souvenirs."

"We are." His voice could sound so dry sometimes. He knew just how to twist each word for ultimate sarcasm.

"And just think. When you up the price of the souvenirs – after all, they did get them from here, and not Walmart or wherever – you can take a little off the top and finance some redecorating projects."

He rolled both eyes but in opposite directions, just like in his caricature. "And this redecorating is the most important project we require."

"Now, don't twist what I said, Wile. It's just that I shudder to think what those kids upstairs with all that depressing and efficient decor are going to grow up into: depressed but efficient adults. Poor things."

Wiley quirked his finger and instead of a screen popping down in response, a waiter in crisp overalls and swim cap hurried to their table for instructions. Within moments he returned with a golden tray from which he served them wobbly pinkish stuff with a crisp top.

"Try this. I think you'll like it." Wiley said as the waiter bowed away from them.

"Thanks. You should be going after an atmosphere that inspires creative thinking and self-determination. Instead you want them to be Stepfords," Lina accused. "You and Ms. Yency and Protocol and that horrible, horrible computer of yours that runs all the quizzes. Stepfords, all of you!"

"I take it being a 'Stepford' is bad."

She considered as she tried the pink stuff. "It's a literary reference. This is nice. You need to surprise yourself now and then."

"I never like surprises."

"You don't learn the interesting stuff without a few popping up now and then. Or a whole blamed planetload."

"Which you have been complaining about."

"Only because I'm bored stiff. Give me something interesting to do and I'll shut up."

"Okay. Reorganize the Legion."

She stopped herself before she could register a spit take. Then she wrinkled her nose at him, lifted an eyebrow.

"Uh oh." Wiley took a deep drink from his glass of sour-smelling brew. "What kind of problem did I just create?" he asked, though it seemed he was asking himself.

"It's a good challenge," she told him. "I'd need to research a lot more. Consult some experts."

"But you'd do it? How?"

"If I tell you, will you tell me where I can find a non-Legion-affiliated lawyer, level four security?" Lina asked.

"No. A lawyer will be furnished to you if–"

"Yadda yadda yadda." Lina leaned back in defeat. "First goal is to avoid going to jail for a crime I didn't commit. After that… Goal A is a nice tourist kiosk. Out on the mall." She gestured at the plaza. "With tee shirts and flags and whirligigs and soft ice cream cones."

Wiley touched a ring and then held a forefinger away from the thumb on the ring hand. Between the two, a miniature 3-D image of a group of Legionnaires – you could tell by their colorful costumes – flew across a cityscape while fireworks went off all around.

"Ooh, yes! Lots of those movies. Can we pack one into a fake Legion ring?"

Wiley and she went round and round with suggestions on how to make it the most flamboyant, most gaudy, most tasteless souvenir spot in town. "Officially-endorsed whoopie cushions." "Glow-in-the-dark Legion bobbleheads." "Talking Legionnaire baseball hats." "No, *singing* Legionnaire baseball hats." "Damn straight!"

Jae checked on her status when he returned and must have seen the new demerits. "Stop trying to bribe or trick people into helping you," he told her. "Follow the rules. You have serious charges against you."

"I'm just supposed to sit here and do nothing."

"Yes."

"We are the Legion." Lina crossed her arms tightly across the top of her chest.

"We are."

"Your commander is off his rocker."

Jae didn't say anything.

"Ha," Lina said. "You agree with me."

"I never said that."

"You never didn't say that. We're taped in here, right? I want it witnessed: Neutrino agreed with me."

"Neutrino did not agree with you. I'll run a playback for you if needed."

Lina gave him a juicy raspberry, which made him chuckle.

"Very mature."

A mission called him away before she could clarify herself.

"I'm going to Earth," Wiley announced when Jae returned. "There are things I need to investigate on site."

"You can't wait?"

"Mind number 3 is stuck on psychic theory," Wiley told him. "It's very uncomfortable and distracting. This could be cleared up in a matter of hours by me taking off."

"We'll need to feed the cats," Lina reminded him, and he nodded absently.

Their conversation paused as Dellen fuzzily teleported in from a mission, and was greeted back. She nodded to them all and moved to a terminal to file her report.

"You should report to the spa for Terran makeup," Jae told Wiley.

"I can supply the necessary illusion myself," he replied. He rummaged through a cabinet to emerge with a small box. Using his stylus to program it, all of a sudden his skin turned a golden Malibu tan, exactly matching Jae's. His short brush of hair darkened from violet to black. Everyone in the room turned to assess the effect.

"That's perfect," Jae said. "I didn't know you had something that could do that. It might be useful every now and then."

"I plan on demonstrating it to Stoan when I have it down to a more reasonable size," Wiley said as he displayed the tiny mechanism on his palm. "I want to see the New Age store Lina has told me about. I'll start from there, but Lina will need a guard."

"What?"

"I told you, one of my minds is stuck," Wiley said to her as he attached the box to his belt. "Under those circumstances, I cannot oversee you and research at the same time. Jae is the arresting officer and should come along. Multiplex, you and Sunstorm will cover for us here."

"Dellen and Erik," Lina insisted.

Before Dellen could protest, Brügz beamed in. She huffed surrender. "Bad timing," she told Brügz, and then to Wiley, "Looks like we can handle that."

Lina told Wiley, "You're going to need Terran clothes, too."

"I'll go get mine." Jae bolted to the door.

Wilder took the box off his belt and fiddled with the programming again. His baggy lab coat turned into jeans and dark boots with a hot pink tee shirt.

"Whoa, radioactive!" Dellen exclaimed as she hid her eyes from the imaginary dazzle.

Wiley looked down at himself and blew a bubble behind his upper lip. Then he changed the program. The tee shirt became a pale yellow one.

"Much better," Lina declared.

"Do they always have to say something?" Wiley looked doubtful.

"Usually they do. But some are just the plain variety, worn by very serious people." She shook her head seriously at him to illustrate her point. "This will do nicely."

Jae returned dressed in his ParaNet tee. Wilder pointed at him. "What if some member of the ParaNet spots that and arrests him for it? Does Earth have penalties for that?"

"Let's just say this, Wiley," Lina said as she straightened her own clothing. "If the Legion were located on Earth, you'd be getting at least half your income from the sale of cheap imitation Legion rings for the tourists, and the other half from tee shirt sales with the saying 'I'm a Legionnaire in good standing,' or something like that. And plus, there'd be all the tee shirts with the Legionnaires' likenesses, and the fan clubs for all of 'em… Come to think of it, whatever y'all take in here you could probably triple your income by relocating to Earth." She pointed a finger at him. "Think about it."

"Capitalism," Jae cocked his head at her.

"Blatant, no-holds-barred Free Market Capitalism in all its naked fury." Lina grinned back. "Ready for the barbarian experience?" she asked Wiley, waiting for him to set his instruments and nod before she ported them to Earth.

They both looked expectantly at Wiley when they arrived inside Lina's house and were rewarded by his faraway, contemplative gaze. "I could feel the final wait quite clearly this time," he said. "It was as if we were here… but we were overhanging the reality from without. On the edge of time-space, perhaps."

Jae said, "It's too dark there to say where you are."

"Here but not here," Lina said.

"I believe you did mention that," Wiley nodded at her. "And I was plugged in to a few more sensory input channels than you were, Jae. All right, I've experienced it with all five minds, and I have one more try on the way back. What do we do here?"

"We feed the cats and play with them," Jae announced. It was dim daytime, and through the large, south-facing windows he could see some cats in the backyard sleeping around a birdfeeder. Bright red and gray-and-white birds studied the cats before proceeding on. A woodpecker flittered up and hung almost upside down on the feeder to reach the seeds.

Wiley settled to observe the fauna of the planet, and looked closer when he noticed the bare forest around the house with tiny red baby leaf buds.

He announced suddenly, "These are deciduous. It's the end of winter."

He turned around when Jae started some music for their stay. Lina switched on the heat; the house was quite chilly. The sky loomed gray and low, so the passive solar hadn't kicked in well. As Lina gathered the cat food, Wilder nosed around some bookshelves.

"Do that thing," Jae said as Lina poured out the dry chow.

"What thing?"

"The whistle. I want to see how you do it."

"If you watch me, I won't be able to." She went to the front door, tried to whistle and failed. "See?" She licked her lips and tried again. An undulating whistle, very long, followed by three short ones, filled the air. Cats came running up on the porch and through the cat door, knowing that their food had arrived. Jae tried to whistle, and couldn't.

"It took me a while to learn," Lina commiserated. "Just keep trying and you'll get it. Wet your lips."

Jae tried and nothing came out.

"Definitely, these animals do not belong in my lab." Wiley joined them at the door to see the other side of outdoors. A cold, wet wind blew through the opening without a temperature barrier. It was beginning to drizzle. A small cat ran up on the porch, saw the strangers and paused, then raced inside between their legs toward food and dry warmth.

Wiley regarded the driveway. "That's an automobile," he said, stating a fact.

"A car. Yes." Lina closed the door with a shiver.

Jae added, "It has a music system in it, too. All cars do."

Wiley peered through the door's peephole at the little Honda. "I wouldn't mind a ride in it," he said.

Lina opened her mouth in surprise. "Well, the stores we're going to are about fifteen minutes away by car. I can port us back if we run out of time; I can handle a car."

"Very good." He showed her some books. "May I borrow these?"

"Sure, go ahead." Lina looked to see what they were. "You found my New Age bookcase," she said. "Did you pass up the others on purpose, or didn't you see them?"

Lina pointed him to a bookcase around the corner from where he'd been, with her history books in it. "All the other stuff's upstairs," she said.

"Upstairs," Jae repeated. "I haven't been there yet."

"It's a mess," Lina said, "but okay." She led them upstairs where they had to go through her studio to get to the library. Jae stopped to look at her paintings. "I didn't know you did this," he said. "What kind of focal system do you use?" The pictures were out of focus, even blobby in places.

"Focal system? As in photography?"

That stopped him. "This is a form of photography, right?"

"Painting. I'm an artist. Focal system is the eyeball and the brain."

"Like in… dabbing paint on a surface?" He sidled up to one canvas so that one eye was almost on the surface of the painting. Gingerly he touched the uneven surface with his finger. "You do that?"

"I don't; that's the problem. If I do two paintings a year, it's a real accomplishment. I know this is all crap, but I keep thinking if I work at it, I might turn out better crap."

Jae noted the easels, tables, and a general multitude of small equipment crowding the small room. "Not too bad here," he said of one picture of narsaws, or maybe flowers. Though too primitive to his tastes, there was a real sense of light shining through the shells.

Lina picked up a brush to show him how paint would be applied. Jae squinted at unfinished paintings doubtfully. "It seems like it takes a long time. I haven't noticed your attention span being too long."

"Which of these are science fiction?" Wiley's voice came from the library.

Lina hurried to join him in the house's one bedroom, which she had converted to a library two years ago, just as she'd converted the family room into a studio. She showed him the science fiction, the sci fi/fantasy, the pure fantasy. Here was her *Star Trek* book collection; she only kept the good ones, which were a significantly small proportion of the published material. Ecology, sociology, biography, travel…

"All my art books are in the studio," she told Wiley, and he nodded absently, flipping through the books here.

"So, what," Jae said, looking around, "You sleep in that big chair downstairs? It looked comfortable enough for sitting, but–"

Lina slid open a full-length double mirror to reveal a storage closet behind it. Jae peered through. A skylight illuminated a small bed tucked into the space.

"My bedroom," Lina announced.

Jae chuckled to himself. He could certainly see that a virgin had lived here. There was no room for more than one, and that one couldn't even move around much. The ceiling sloped alarmingly over the bed.

It gave me room enough to turn this into a library.

He crossed his arms and leaned against the wall. **Reading my mind?**

You're broadcasting.

And you made it difficult for people to get into your bedroom. They had to go through a maze, pass a secret door, and when they got here, they had to contort themselves to fit. Interesting. Didn't you trust yourself otherwise?

Did not. No one ever wanted to come here, and it would have been impossible for them to do whatever they wanted to do if they had.

Says the woman who married that great, lusty oaf, Valiant.

What's that supposed to mean?

But he just smiled elfishly at her, pulling at his earring.

He sat on the edge of the bed and bounced a little, checking out the closeness of the ceiling. **I take it back,** he told her. **I think you could do a little here. Come here; let me try something.**

I'm going to start calling you "Erik."

It's not like that, Lie. It's to make a tactical point.

So sex is just tactics for you, Jae?

A sound as Wiley picked up another book made her turn around, remembering him. "We'd better play with the cats, or we won't have any time to go shopping and exploring," Lina said, and she and Jae trotted downstairs.

15

Lina popped the hood of the car. She wouldn't be able to give the guys a ride into town. And it was Wiley's only time on Earth! How embarrassing.

"It's the battery." She pointed at the black box. "You're supposed to run the car every few days, but the good ship *Galileo* hasn't been turned over for over two weeks now. She's a little on the ancient side. Plus it's been cold."

She looked back at the two men. She'd given them both umbrellas against the drizzle. "I should port you in some jackets for this weather," she said, feeling guilty for wearing her all-weather coat. "Can you picture in your minds where they'd be?"

She tried picturing them both at once. "Oh. Can't do two from separate destinations at once," she said. Instead she ported them one by one.

"Multi-tasking is difficult for the single-minded," Wilder said.

"Guess we'll just port over to Durham," she said as they donned their coats. "I can get someone to jump-start this when we come back permanently."

"For a battery, it feels weak to me." Jae bent over the car. Silently he talked to it and then straightened up. "Wiley, I need some calibration here."

"Right." Wiley didn't even have to take time to think before he reached in the detachable pockets of his belt that he still had under his jean illusion and took some wire out of them. He hooked one end up to one section of his belt and placed it on one of the poles of the battery. Jae continued his silent conversation. "There. That should do it," Wiley announced a few seconds later.

"Just like that?" Lina asked, then realized whom she was asking. "Okay. Everybody in, then." She closed the hood and Jae clambered into the back seat without waiting for Lina to push the front seat up to give him access. Wiley sat in the passenger side, and Lina showed them how to put on seat belts.

"This might indicate the chance of an accident," Wiley said.

"Never had one – yet," Lina tried not to be too reassuring. Might as well make this a thrill-ride. She switched the radio off before she turned the key. For a second the *Galileo* didn't sound good, but eventually the engine *voomed* to life. "Mr. Sulu, take us out," she intoned in her own ritual, and backed out of the drive.

"Mirrors?" Wiley croaked. "You navigate with mirrors?'

How long could she go without cranking up the windshield wipers and turning on her lights? They might not have gotten the battery charged enough. She didn't know how much that would tax things before the battery could reach a full enough charge. There shouldn't be any cops or real traffic until they got to the highway. "Mirrors," she affirmed. "And turning my head and looking."

After a half-mile on the empty country road she switched on the wipers, then the lights. The car didn't protest.

"Gears," Wiley said as she shifted again. When he reached to his side, his tricorder appeared as it emerged from the holoillusion. He turned it in all directions. "Do you mean to tell me that this entire vehicle operates on human power amplified through internal combustion mechanisms? That you physically have to control everything?"

"That's the general idea. There's a computer in there somewhere that's also got a say in things."

"And that, considering the velocities this vehicle is capable of, there are no safety systems whatsoever?"

"You're wearing your seatbelt. That's solid cloth, mister. Newer models have airbags."

Wiley regarded her with his left eye. "The structural components leave a lot to be desired for dissipating the energy of a collision."

"No accidents yet, Wiley. Ease up. Have a little faith. I thought Legionnaires were supposed to be so dangerous?" She glanced in the mirror at Jae and gave him a sunny smile. He looked a little pale back there.

"What's that?" Wiley demanded at the sudden tick-tick, tick-tick as they came to a stop at highway 70.

"Turn signal." She pointed out the signals on other cars now that the road had more traffic and there was a short line at the stop sign. "Damn," she muttered. "They really need a light for this intersection. There've been more accidents here… Come on, come on! You have to put your foot on the gas to make it go, ya stupid–!"

At last the car in front of her lurched across the intersection, and it was her turn to wait. The traffic finally cleared enough for her to step on the gas and swing out. "Finally!"

Wiley clutched the dashboard as the car took off. "Grab that safety device," Lina instructed him, pointing with her chin. "It's probably the most potent thing in the car."

"What, this?" Wiley took hold of the grab bar on the side and pointed his tricorder at it. "It's not a safety device," he frowned.

"Sure it is. It's a 'Jesus bar.' You grab it, shout 'Jesus!' and invoke heavenly protection." Lina grinned at him sideways and he grunted. "There must be some big pileup on I-85 to have all this traffic at this time of day."

"A pileup?" Jae asked. He braced his elbows on either front seat and leaned.

Lina steadied the wheel with her knees as she slammed her fist into the palm of her other hand as illustration. "A pileup," she said, quickly taking back the wheel. "Seatbelt on, Jae. It's a rule that I observe."

"I'm sorry I asked. Is this a park? It's big."

"No, this is just how things are between towns. Up ahead there's a piece of Duke Forest – that's preserved woodland, owned by the moneybags university. They have public hiking trails and such all through it, but otherwise it's left natural. Things have really built up out here in these past few years." She shook her head.

"You call this built up?"

"Mm hm. I used to be the only one on my end of the road," she said. "Cow pastures, horse pastures, and forest all around. I'd come home from work and there'd be a cow in the back yard eating my garden. Now they've got three big housing developments in the neighborhood. Three! There were two robberies at my neighbors this past Christmas. Too many cats around here have wound up as roadkill. It's past time to move."

"What's that?" Wiley demanded as they passed a semi heading in the opposite direction. Wiley pointed at everything. Lina spent the next five minutes explaining the variations of utility trucks to pickups to minivans to trailers to, of all things, an antique jalopy cruising sedately through the rain. Merging onto I-85, Lina thought them safe enough to turn on the radio.

"See?" Jae said to Wiley. "I told you they had music systems. Turn the knob, right?" He pointed, and Wiley ran through the FM stations. Lina identified the different kinds of music and what made them different from each other. Wiley turned the sound down so it was barely audible.

"Why all these signs?" he asked. "Is there long-distance tracking of this traffic? Why is that railing bent back like that? Why is that sign broadcasting current information, when these signs are permanent? What are those orange things in the road? Why are these dashed lines? Is that a dead animal? What was it? Are there many of those around here? Are there animals in the metropolitan areas? What is that? Are all your aircraft like that?" and so on and so on until Lina thought she'd either slap him silent or go hoarse from answering him.

"Hey, look at that," Jae laughed as they went by a sign. Lina wondered what the joke was, but Wiley laughed as well.

"There it is again," Jae pointed. It was an exit sign. "Somebody's got a problem," he added.

He was talking about the curved arrow. The arrow! "Oh," Lina realized. Arrows were phallic, weren't they? "You know how men can only follow one thing reliably," she said.

Wiley made a doubting sound and continued his questions. "All this forest," Wilder motioned. "Earth is mainly covered with it, right?"

"It's got a lot of forest, yes. But they're destroying a lot of it, too. Too much. Up here we've got urban sprawl. Down in the tropics in the rain forests, which produce most of the planet's oxygen, they're chopping down the trees to make room for cattle ranches, to feed people who want lots of beef in their diet."

"Is that the same thing as *boeuf*?" Jae asked.

"Different language. They say that it's to improve the standard of living for the people who live down there in the third world, but I bet you anything that it's the same old rich first-world corporations who are raking in the profit."

"'Save the rain forests,'" Wilder read from a bumper sticker on a car in front of them.

"Uh huh. Use your car to show your political philosophy." Lina pointed out other bumper stickers: "Think globally, act locally." "Mean people suck." "Love your mother."

"What's the symbol on that one?" Wiley asked.

"It's one of those five thousand you told me about," Lina said. "They're talking about Mother Earth, the spirit of the planet. Right, Earth?" **Hey, Earth! I'm married now,** she told the entity. **I married Londo, did I tell you?**

Yes, Little One, came the reply. **I know. I'm happy for you both. You two have been too lonely.**

Lina smiled to be on her home planet again. Earth was such a nice person.

"Whoa," she said, "look at that." In her rearview mirror a car came roaring up in the left lane.

Jae turned to see where Lina was looking, saw the approaching car. "That looks dangerous," he said.

"It looks illegal, too," she countered. "I'm doing the speed limit. They must be doing – look at 'em! – ninety at least. In the rain. They're going to hurt someone."

The car rocketed past them. "Shit! More like a hundred! And coming up on a populated area. Where's a cop when you – Jae!"

He'd rolled over the back seat into the cargo area. Somehow he popped the hatch. He jumped out into midair as Lina gave a strangled sound.

"Keep on going," Jae shouted as the wind and rain raged around him. He hung behind the car as he slammed the hatchback closed, and then streaked through the rain, following the speeding car.

"…Shit!" was all Lina could think to say. Beside her, Wiley laughed.

"I thought you said you liked surprises?"

"And what's he going to do? Does the Legion have jurisdiction on Earth now? He'll scare those people to death!"

"No he won't. Contrary to popular belief, Jae Rallene does have a little common sense. Just keep driving."

They missed the freeway turnoff, but Lina was following Jae. It was all she could do not to speed to catch up with him. Pictures ran through her mind of the shocked driver running off the road, no, running into other cars. Of Jae trying to stop the car carefully, not knowing what he was doing, and the car screeching to a stop, tumbling end over end. Of the driver pulling a gun on the para chasing him down…

They found Jae next to the Guess Road turnoff, calmly leaning against the hood of the car as it sat steaming on the road shoulder. The driver and his passenger pounded at their doors from the inside. Apparently they were stuck inside. And all four tires were flat. Lina pulled off to let Jae get in.

"They finally saw reason," he said with a smile as he saw the expression on Lina's face. He gave her a bow as space would allow.

Wiley snorted. "Showoff."

"I'd like to have seen you do better." Jae brushed at his hair with his hands and suddenly he was all dry.

Lina was so upset she couldn't speak.

"I'm okay," Jae told her.

"But… But you might not have been. People are dangerous, Jae. I know it's just Earth, but they have guns here and a lot of idiots carry them. And use them. If people are crazy enough to speed through a heavily populated area, they're crazy enough to–"

"Hey," he said, spreading his hands across his chest. "I'm a Legionnaire."

Lina set her mouth and stared at him in the rearview mirror as she reached for the glove compartment and the cell phone there to call the highway patrol.

The car started up easily enough. She chose this exit ramp to turn onto Guess Road. Wiley asked about the stores, the parking lots and hotels and churches. She pointed out the capitalistic competition going on in store windows.

Once she had to slam on her brakes as someone cut in front of her. "Sonnuva–!" She gritted her teeth as the moron gave her a one-finger salute as thanks for her not hitting him.

"I see what the seat belts are for now," Wilder said calmly.

"No accident yet," she repeated.

They pulled up to Ninth Street where she worked up her nerve to parallel park, showing off for them even though they wouldn't be able to appreciate the fine skills involved.

Wilder noted that she locked the car as they got out even as he studied the workings of his umbrella. She pointed down the road for his benefit. "One of the best astrologers you'll ever run into lives about six blocks that way. He'd be able to tell you in a flash where that Libran energy you have is coming from."

"Then one day I want to meet him," Wilder said. "Is this the place? 'Signs and Omens?'"

"Best New Age store in the Triangle," Lina declared as they entered the dry warmth. "Both eyes working together, please, Wiley." She waved to acquaintances behind the counter on her way to the back of the store and the bulletin boards there.

Most of the flyers on the boards were for local psychics. There was one advertising someone as a teacher of Reiki, and another one giving a Level I Kolaimni course. Another promoted a course on the history of the universe and the angelic dimensions thereof.

"I've taken that one," Lina said. "The astrologer I told you about teaches it. It's very far-out stuff – well, a lot goofy if you ask me. But it's really interesting. And I've run into some things since then that makes me think that at least bits of it could be true. Soulmates, for one." She caught Jae's eye. "I never believed in them until I directly experienced it."

"Soulmates are true," he said, as if he were telling her that the sun would rise in the east tomorrow. "You're using the word to mean 'pod mates,' souls who were created at the same time and remain a kind of family group throughout eternity. I don't think you're talking about grafted soulmates."

"Grafted–?" Lina asked, but he turned his back and wandered down another aisle.

The bulletin board also gave notices of non-locals coming through the area with their programs. She pointed at one. "Circles of Life. That was interesting. I could never feel it working, but people around me said they could. Maybe I'm just not in tune with it."

"And maybe they merely imagined it by suggestion," Wiley said as he ran an invisible something across the air in front of the board. Lina wondered if he'd actually call the numbers on these notices to enroll. "What's all this other paraphernalia here?"

Lina took him through the aisles. Homeopathics; she had to explain that to him, and picked up a small introductory book and some samples. The gongs and singing bowls, which Jae was playing so beautifully, adding to the New Age music on the sound system. Crystals. The *Course in Miracles* section. Tarot cards, angel cards, bear cards…

"How are we doing on time?" Jae asked.

Wilder admitted that it might be time to move along. Lina took the books he'd chosen and checked out. Because their card reader was on the fritz, Lina wrote the store a check as Wiley and Jae watched, interested in the new form of currency.

The book store was the next stop, just a few doors down. It was one of those cozy Ninth Street bookstores, but after seeing Wiley with her meager book collection, Lina didn't think that her credit card would last beyond this point. She'd prefer not to have to declare bankruptcy next month.

"Look, why don't we just go to a library?" she asked. "It's a lot less expensive, and it'll start you out just as well. The bookstores have the latest stuff, but the libraries sometimes do as well, plus they have all the old standards. You can read while we shop, and you can get a few books to check out. It's too bad you can't access our Internet. Or can you?"

"You have libraries on Earth?" Wilder was clearly astonished. "I didn't think the cultural level was that advanced."

Lina gave him a sour look. "I'll have to get you an ancient history book so you can look up the Library of Alexandria," she said, though she doubted the general populace back then could have checked out the library's scrolls. It sounded good, though. She ported them directly across counties to the main Chapel Hill library, for which she had a card.

"Yes, I think I can read a few books now." Wiley ogled the stacks. "I'll be quite content here for a while. And I'll rig an Internet patch when we get back." He was already moving to the labeled shelves, rubbing his hands.

Lina showed him the computerized card catalogs and listings for the Dewey decimal system. Jae reminded him to coordinate his eye movements in public.

"Okay, Lina, let's go somewhere interesting." Jae grabbed her arm and she ported them back to Durham. "Alone at last," he joked.

Taking her hand, he pulled her along to the store he'd seen before, the one with all the music posters in the window. She hurried to keep up. He grabbed her by the waist and pushed her through the door of the store.

"How much farther will that money card of yours go?" he asked, eying all the shelves with the same avarice Wiley had shown books.

"Maybe a good-sized stack at least, but I don't think it'll last much more than that."

"Do they have good prices here?"

"These are all used, not new. Plus we're a block away from the second of the world-class universities. Well, if you can really call Duke that. Quick English lesson, Jae?"

He turned to her expectantly.

She raised her index finger to center his attention. "Dook sucks," she enunciated.

"Dook sucks," he repeated, and she nodded at him before turning her chin to take in the store. "I think I've got a discount card for this place."

"Okay. Point me to the soundtracks. Musicals. Opera. Something with a story like the ones Lon makes up." They hurried to that section of the store, and Lina tried to guess what his preferences would be. She'd tell him the basic plot of the play or movie, and then he'd think about it. He said yes much more often than no.

Lina made sure he had *Mame*, *The Music Man*, *Funny Girl*, *An American in Paris*, *Rent*, *Hamilton*, *Beauty and the Beast*… They went through the Heavy Metal section where she was lost. She didn't a clear idea of what to tell him to get but apparently Londo had – often – and he dug in. Before she knew it, they had a stack. A tall stack.

She did some mental accounting. "Just a few more, and then I'm cleaned out," she apologized to Jae.

He wrapped his hands around her upper arms. "Don't think I'm not aware of what you're doing for me," he said as they stood chin to forehead. "I know that it takes a long time for you to work to pay for this. I will pay you back, don't worry, just as soon as I figure out how to get some Terran money."

"This is a gift from me to you, Jae," she said. "You don't pay back gifts. I'm enjoying seeing you so happy."

He gave her a crooked smile. "I've been needing music in my life. Thank you for bringing it to me, Lina. I can never repay that."

How warm his blue eyes could get when he was being sincere. She glanced quickly away. "I'm just glad to see you've found it again. C'mon, let's check out before you find another section you haven't hit yet. Ooo, like the clearance table over there."

"Where?" He darted for it and Lina watched his blond head over the displays, saw the women in the store swivel their heads in his direction. Every bit as attractive as Londo, but in an effervescent and yet etheric way, as opposed to Lon's dark and deep good looks. Jae was very restful to the eye. A handsome friend and a gorgeous husband; how lucky could she get? She made her way through the store to join him before he could take her over her limit.

"Excuse me."

She turned at the strange male voice behind her: a brown-haired man a little older than she, wearing a dark blue Duke jacket. "Hi. I couldn't help but notice all those CDs you've selected," he said.

"Oh, but these aren't–"

"Some interesting choices there. It's not often you find a woman with a wide range of musical interests."

"But you would a man?" Her eyes glinted at him.

"I wouldn't say that, either." He smiled easily. "I know this seems forward, but would you mind if I bought you a cup of coffee somewhere? I'd like to hear your ideas about–"

"C'mon luv, 'tis time we was off." Jae was suddenly by her side. He put his arm around her, turning her toward the checkout counter. "Ya left the wee bairns in the car and they'll be chilled ta the bone." He turned to the man. "All t'ray o' them."

Lina tried not to laugh as Jae held her protectively, glaring at the stranger.

"Dook sucks," Jae added.

The man in Duke blue quickly turned and walked, or maybe ran, back down the aisle.

"Oh, you didn't have to do that," Lina giggled against Jae's chest. "He was harmless."

Jae considered, but he wasn't smiling. "Perhaps in some ways, not in others. Trust me, you've got to learn how to drive off wolves."

They walked to the checkout with his arm still circling her. "If it ever comes up again, I will." She realized something. "You spoke English back there."

"Dook sucks."

"Not that. The other."

"I did? How interesting."

"How long have you known how to speak English?"

Jae considered. "Not very well, about fifteen years. Fairly well, about a day. Or do I spick as weill as I think I du?"

"I think you speak very well. You have a thick Irish accent. Was that intentional?"

"I do? Is an Irish accent bad?"

"Oh, very melodious. Everyone likes an Irish accent. And a French accent, like Londo has. One's charming, the other's romantic. Did you get everything you absolutely couldn't live without here?"

"I think so." He handed her a small stack to add to the one she already held. She held her breath as the charge request went through. And made it.

"Whew!"

Jae took the bag with his own glowing pride of ownership. He fumbled with his ring now that the stock clerk's attention was elsewhere.

"Wiley? Ready to go?"

"Not at all. Give me another half-hour or so. Yes, an hour, Terran. I really have neglected my Terran studies."

Jae raised his eyebrow at Lina. "Weill than," he said in his Irish English. "Is theyr a poob around here? A poob with a dance floor? We've neglected yuir dancin' lessons."

She shook her head at him. "It really fits. An Irish leprechaun, that's what you are. A pub." She searched the street's storefronts, then pointed. "Let's try there."

Lina shook their umbrella thoroughly in the bar's doorway as Jae checked the precious bag of CD's to make sure they were dry. A few drops had found the plastic jewel cases, so he told the water to evaporate on them.

The bar was very dark, even though the place had electric lights. A few of the tiny tables and booths had candles on them, but a brightly-illuminated cabinet in the back of the room caught his attention. Music blared from it. Two couples danced in a cleared space on the floor as the rest of the bar patrons ignored them.

The waiter placed a bowl of peanuts in the shell on their table and took their orders. He came back shortly with a Jack and Coke for Jae and a real, non-Yankee, half-and-half iced tea for Lina, or so she described it. Now Lina was the one who tapped her glass and said, "Keep 'em coming."

Jae turned his attention to the patrons watching a sports game on a large TV hanging over the bar. Others didn't watch. One couple, looking as if they'd come from swimming in a river, sat in a back booth and necked. A solitary man read from a tablet over his drink while other patrons just talked and laughed occasionally, stacks of books and laptops beside them.

Duke banners decorated the walls between neon beer brand signs.

Lina showed Jae how to break open the peanut shell to get at the edible part, and he took great delight in throwing the used shells down on the floor.

"You just don't see anything like this in the AffSys," he told her. "Not worrying about what others think. Not playing by the rules. There are too many rules on Sarastor."

"I noticed that the puter doesn't like people who want to bend the rules even a little."

Jae shook his index finger at her. "No, no, no. Have to play by the rules in order and check them off as you accomplish them." He took a sip of his whiskey and ran it around his tongue before he swallowed it. Very nice.

"I would think that Legionnaires would be able to get around the rules, or at least take a few shortcuts."

"You would, wouldn't you?" He grimaced to himself. "It would speed things up. It would allow us to cut to the heart of the matter and get on with things. But on Sarastor especially, the very heart of the AffSys – Uh uh. Do it by the numbers. If you miss one, you have to go back to the beginning. I think that's why so many Sarastorans are the way they are."

"Like those people last night?"

"No. They're… What the orb did Lon call them? Some kind of vegetables on furniture."

"Couch pota–"

"*Couch potatoes*. He told me what it is, and I have to agree. There's too much to do on Sarastor, so everyone just sits around and does nothing. They don't focus on anything real. Their bodies do nothing and their minds decay and stop.

"Their bodies don't know it, though. Their hearts beat and their synapses send out the occasional pulse, but that's it. Sometimes I wonder why the entire native population doesn't commit mass suicide. Maybe they're planning it. No one knows what the average Sarastoran thinks, probably because none of them can think anymore."

Lina crunched a shell between her fingers. "But Sarastor is the capital of–"

"The planet is. The world's run by immigrants, by ringers. The business of Sarastor takes place between the hands of people who have sometimes never seen the face of Sarastor. Remote control, a lot of it. Telecommerce and telegovernment. Netlife and Cyberlove. You think you cut yourself off from the world, Lina. These people have cut themselves from life, and they have no idea they've done it."

Lina swirled her straw. "So what can be done?" she finally asked. "Is anyone working on the problem? Surely someone in the population recognizes that–"

"No one. I've rarely heard anyone mention it." Jae took another sip. "It's status quo, the way things are supposed to be. People have noticed how AffSys vids lately are becoming more and more laid back. I call them comatose. There's been some backlash, some violent thrillers, but more and more, the vids are real sleepers. I think it's a sign of Sarastor influencing the AffSys, and this time it's not for the better."

"I thought…" Lina tried to remember. "I saw a news show about all the violent street crime on Sarastor."

"There's not that much," Jae told her. "Not much of anything on the planet, so when something does happen, it gets blown all out of proportion. But that kind of crime is increasing. That's what we were in yesterday. I've been researching. It's gathering momentum, maybe a kind of anti-lassitude movement among the lower classes. They're the ones being wholly supported by the government system. The people can't get jobs because they aren't training for them, and the government supports them sitting around all day."

"Ultimate welfare?"

"A remarkably similar concept, except that Lon says your welfare systems do help people to find work, don't they?"

"Yes. So you're doing research? Does that mean you want to do something about it?"

Jae sighed. "I don't know where I'd start. I'm just one man."

"A Legionnaire. Neutrino, even."

He gave her a little smile at that. "Even so, I'm just one man against a mountain. This time it's the attitudes that need changing, not states of material existence. That's not one of my powers."

"Everyone has that power, Jae. Maybe you just need to team up with other people. Strength in numbers."

He grunted with a twitch of his shoulders that may have shown agreement. "That's why I'm doing the research. To open others' eyes to this, maybe get a commission or something started. The way I see it, if Sarastor goes over the edge – and it sure looks as if it is to me – then the entire AffSys will follow.

"The world's the foundation of too much that the AffSys stands for. If it crumbles, it'll bring the entire Affiliation down with it. Let's dance." He stood in a rush, and held out his hand to her.

"Dance? In public?"

He pulled her up out of her own chair and dragged her to the back of the bar. "In public. I take it this programs the music?" He hovered over the large bar jukebox with its outline of bubbling lights.

They went through the available songs. "Pick a slow one," he finally instructed her. People had been dancing to slow music before, a dance that looked simple enough for Lina. They took their places on the dance floor as the song began with just the damp couple there now, engrossed in each other.

Jae watched the others and placed Lina's arms around his neck, then put his hands on her rear end. She immediately pulled his hands up to her waist. "They seem to be in a relationship," she told Jae. "They're allowed to be a little familiar."

"This seems familiar enough to me." He gave her a quick smile. They were pressed up to each other, swaying back and forth, Jae moving the two of them slowly around the open area. "This is a common dance?"

"I think so. Is this something Londo would like?"

"He'd probably put his hand on your butt."

A distant light came into her eyes. "Probably," she admitted. It would be so good to have Lon's hand on her butt again.

"And you'd lean your head against him."

"He's coming back soon, isn't he? There won't be another long mission after this, will there? Is this considered a long mission for the Legion?"

"Maybe average. There are longer ones, the two- and three-weekers, but those don't come that often. And Lon's a part-time member, so he doesn't get something like this very much at all. Most of it's travel time, Lina. And now, look – We've got you. As soon as more Legionnaires find out, they're going to start clamoring for you to be chained in the main communications room at our disposal."

"The Legion does like their chains, I noticed." She nodded at her tracking bracelet.

"They'll ask nicely this time; I'll give you odds. No one likes to sit around in hyperspace for days doing nothing."

"Wiley doesn't leave."

"If you noticed, he left the other day. But he's more valuable to us staying put, working on those interminable experiments of his. That's why monitor functions transfer to the lab. He's always there."

"He's lonely. He needs to get out."

"He's perfectly happy there."

She shook her head at him. "I'm sorry if it would interfere in Legion business, but he needs to get out and be around people acting normally. Not necessarily normal people."

"Erm." Jae had never considered that. Wiley was just Wiley, part of the Legion landscape. A good friend, always there. "You say he's lonely."

"Like some other Legionnaires." The jukebox switched to another slow song. Jae was going to stop dancing, but Lina didn't let go.

"'Lonely, hidden soul of sighs,'" she sang so only he could hear, *"'wanderin'
through this world...'"*

Jae was silent as the song went on. He'd heard it among Lon's CDs; it was a
familiar tune.

"'A heart is crying over there,
'Hiding tight and furled.
'Take a step forward; drop your disguise.
'Open your heart and look in her eyes,
'Then watch the new day's sun rise.'"

Lina let the music end as they stood there, not moving. "You, too, Jae. You're
lonely. You have to get out and look. There's someone out there waiting for you.
Your reading said you could find a new love, but you have to get off your butt to do
that. You have to stop faking and put some real energy out into the world."

"So suddenly you know everything?" New, faster and louder music began behind
them but they stood there.

"No. All I know is that you're too fine a man to be alone in this universe," she
told him. "All this parahero business aside, you're too fine a man."

He cracked the ghost of a smile at that that faded. "I know a lot of people who
would disagree with that."

"So you don't even consider them. We'll find a gay dating service for starters,
how about that? Think you'd be interested in a Terran?"

"Tell you what, Lie," Jae said and he tried to bring up his smile again. "You come
with me and screen everyone so I don't make a mistake."

"I'll do my absolute best."

He came back from the restroom – he hadn't imagined that Terran bathrooms would
be quite that primitive and filthy – to find two men checking out Lina. Before they
could make their move, he pointed out the problem to her and had her gather their
things. They ported back to the library with Jae on the lookout for more wolves of
the human variety.

"I really don't think there'll be trouble here," she said and removed his hand from
her waist.

"You can never tell. You need to scan an area before you port in. Get in the
habit."

"Why? Those guys were harmless. Mostly. I could have ported them away if
they–"

"Lina, come here." Jae guided her to a carrel in the back of the empty research section and set her on a chair. He settled on the edge of the table, facing her. "You're Valiant's wife now. He has a lot of enemies who'd love to find his vulnerable spot."

"But I don't see any reason why we should advertise the marriage so his enemies would know. I can't think of very many paraheroes – on Earth, at least – who have announced that they're married. It seems to me that that only happens if they marry another parahero." She tried to think of an example. "Look at Maximus and his wife. I mean, everybody knows he's married, but you never hear about her."

Jae said, "Her name is Else."

"I know, you just never hear about her. I just assumed I'd be the same way."

Jae smiled at her. "Else is a very nice person. Sharp. She even makes Wiley work when he plays a mystery game against her. She won once against him, an Ultimate Skill level, too."

He saw Lina's uncomprehending face. "That's unheard of," he explained. "She likes her privacy; she has her own reasons for not going public. But in case you haven't noticed, Lina, you've pulled off some stunts in the past few days that most of your Terran heroes could only dream about. You're a megapara. How long do you think it'll be before you're in a costume and porting around stopping crime?"

Lina almost laughed out loud before she recalled where she was. "Why in the world would I want to do that? I want to help the world, not beat up criminals."

"Okay, so you won't beat up criminals. But how long do you think it'll be before you become well-known? You're already getting a lot of attention on Sarastor."

"But–"

Jae held up a finger to silence her. "Don't compare your life before to your life now. You married the biggest megapara there is. You have some powerful abilities, which you don't seem to be shy about using. People are going to notice you."

Lina was silent as Jae kept going.

"You have to be more careful, more suspicious of people. Just a little. Get in the habit of checking out the room that you're entering, the people who come in. If you're in doubt, port out. Always keep an escape route open."

"Yes, Father."

"I'm serious."

"I know you are. I'll think about it." She sighed. "It would help if Lon were around so I could talk with him."

"So you talk with me until then. It won't be long now."

"That's what you say. These days seem so long. But I forget that Sarastor's day is longer than Earth's. No wonder I've had jet lag."

A new voice spoke up. "Then you should get some sleep when we get back." Wiley appeared from behind her and she flinched. "You should take Jae's talk to heart, Lina. He made a lot of sense."

"Do you do that? I've seen Jae do it, but you?"

"Of course I do." With a sour twist to his lips, Wiley looked down his nose at Jae. "I just do it subtly."

Jae made a choking sound.

"We're all trained to do that. And we have to go through self-defense courses. Jae and I have both been Legionnaires for a long time, but we still have to refresh our training. Plus, we teach the newcomers."

"Do y'all have a course for Legion spouses?"

"We don't, but we should. Legion spouses are supposed to utilize Legion Security guards." Jae looked at Wiley. "Maybe we could start one?"

Glumly Lina laid her head in her arms on the table. She was sure going through a lot because she'd married Londo, and the marriage hadn't even been consummated yet. It didn't seem a fair trade. Oh well, ask her in another day or two, and she'd probably have other ideas about the tradeoff. Londo. She smiled to herself. Londo.

"I'd say we were ready to go," Wilder said. "I only got to scan through some seventy books. How do I check out more?" He pointed to a loaded cart.

Lina caught her breath. "No way my library card's going to handle that," she said. "You really want that many?"

"For now. I shouldn't take too long with them."

"We'll just bend the rules. You can do that on Earth." She shoved the cart of books into a darkened aisle between stacks and then ported the three of them, cart and all, back to her living room.

"Wait," Wiley started.

"Too late to object," Lina said, and he shrugged at Jae.

"A little larceny," Jae observed as he flipped through some of the books.

"You Legionnaires are leading me down the rocky road to crime," Lina countered. "I'll return these when you're done, Wiley. Make it fast so nobody misses them."

"They'll be done tomorrow," he assured her. "Let me add these…" He reached for the pile of Lina's books that he'd already collected and dumped them on the top of the pile in the cart, along with the bag of books from the New Age store. "It's time we thought about getting back."

"Forgot the car." Lina concentrated, but it was nigh impossible to port things when she couldn't see one of the ends of the port. She opened the door and looked in the driveway. The car appeared in no time.

"One more stop," she told them. "It'll be quick." She led the way outside around the house, down the paths through the forest. The bare tree limbs dripped even though the rain had stopped. They came to a small, rushing stream. It gurgled and gushed around a flat, man-sized rock in its middle.

"Moving water," she told Wiley. He listened for a minute.

"On a small scale," he said. "Those symphonies depicted rivers and oceans."

She ported them again, to the Eno River and an old country bridge not far from her house. Here the sound was not so burbly, but rather a flowing shushing, interspersed with bird song and the chatter of squirrels emerging from the wet trees.

She let Wilder listen, and then she ported them to the Outer Banks and the shore of the Atlantic Ocean. She turned up the collar of her coat against the brisk, wet wind as they listened to the surf boom against the otherwise empty beach. Wiley listened, but Jae watched the birds who darted into the sea and back up. The setting sun was trying to peek through the low clouds, and the birds' plumage flashed white.

He turned to look at Lina, her face and blowing hair backlit with a shining halo against shafts of golden sunlight.

"Oh, I forgot. One more as long as you're here, Wiley," Lina told them.

16

It had once been a smooth white beach. Now a wide, black gash of fused sand ran down from the palm forest almost to the line of surf. It was half-filled with water, a jungle stream trickling through it and not its old banks.

"By the orb!" Jae gasped in spite of himself.

Bodies, not many of them whole or recognizable, lay sprawled in the dawn light. To judge from the stench, they'd been lying out here for days.

"Next time, Lina, give us some warning," Wiley said sternly but brought out the sensor padd which he'd had clipped to his belt. He released a recorder cam. "I take it this is–"

"Where they killed Lon," Lina said.

Jae's eyes narrowed at the bodies, the carnage and wreckage. Trees had fallen everywhere in great piles of charred trunks and browning vegetation. There was evidence of a small forest fire. This rent in the earth – did something boil the sand to fuse it this way? Deep glassy cracks led from here down to the ocean. There were other odd tracks around, lines from wheels, lots of boot prints, people dragging something.

Jae touched his ring. "Dellen?" he said into it.

"Coming back sometime today?" came the answering voice.

"Give us a while. We're investigating a crime scene."

"On Earth?"

"Yes. We'll fill you in when we get back. It shouldn't take us too long."

Wiley crouched over the guns next to a body. "These wouldn't have done it," he said.

"No, those were the low-level ones, the ones I got hit with. I don't see any of–" Lina stopped.

"What?"

"Dr. Menlo," she said and pointed. "He's the guy who lasered me, who took Lon's blood." She stood over the body, trying to breathe shallowly. Thank heavens for the brisk ocean breeze! The dead man had two patches of red-brown on his shirt and a shocked expression on his familiar face. His laser rifle lay next to him, but there was no sign of the bags of blood.

"Dr. Menlo," Jae said softly. "Lon's mentioned him a lot."

Lina nodded. "He's… He *was* a pretty big-time criminal. I'd never heard of Terry Rhodes, but I've certainly heard of Dr. Menlo. I've seen him lots of times on the news."

"Well, no one will have to worry about him anymore," Jae told her grimly. He looked around, tried to count the bodies. "How many did you say there were?"

"We were told 200 in all, but the final confrontation – maybe fifty, sixty men," she told him.

And here were perhaps twenty-five bodies, if you put everything back together. Twenty-five bodies caught in the edges of the blast aimed at Valiant.

"And you never sensed them."

"Not until the last instant. I don't understand that. Even before everything happened, when I was only half-aware of things, I should have been able to sense a small pack of men wanting to do us harm. An army of them – I should have felt them coming miles away!"

"Perhaps your mind was preoccupied," Wiley told her. "What were you and Lon doing at the time?"

She blushed. "Talking. No, not talking. Watching the moonrise."

"Caught up in each other's thoughts and not on anything outside yourselves," Jae offered gently. "I don't think anyone can blame you for that. It happens sometimes."

Rodents didn't even pause from their meals as the three walked around. "Him, I think," Lina pointed shakily at a headless body. "He's the one who was on top of me."

Wiley scanned the crisped, dismembered body and nodded. "The DNA matches," he told her. He moved from body to body, occasionally reaching down to pick up a gun and scan it.

Lina ported one of the large guns in, dripping with sea water and ocean scum from where she'd ported it days before into the ocean. "I can't find the others," she told him. "They must have drifted."

"This wasn't the final one?" Wiley asked as he swung his instruments around to scan it.

"No, this was just one of the ones to keep Lon in line. It could do a job on him, though. It staggered him. They only had to hit him three times before he went down long enough to use the big one."

Wiley nodded. "We'll take this back with us," he said. "Good job."

Jae came back to them carrying some clothes and a blanket. "I found these," he said, and handed them to her.

"Thanks." Lina looked away from the carnage and back to the pool that had once been the heart of their idyll. From the blackened edges of the forest, birds began to sing in the morning sun. "It really was a paradise," she whispered.

"All it needs is a little cleaning up and repair," Wiley pronounced. "Jae, why don't you put these bodies into stasis? We can contact the Network when we get back. I'm sure they'll want to investigate here as well."

Jae nodded. Lina watched as he gathered himself and raised his arms to take in the clearing.

"Stand back," Wiley whispered to Lina, and pulled her away.

Jae spoke to something silently and authoritatively. A blanket of stillness spread out through the clearing from him, the rodents scattering wildly before it, back into the woods.

Finally Jae exhaled, took another breath and exhaled again, shaking out his hands. Clearing himself and not realizing it, Lina thought.

"That should hold them for about three days," he announced. "There won't be any deterioration of the bodies," he explained to Lina.

"Can I still walk around there?" she asked him. "There's something I need to do."

"Sure, it's safe enough. I just stopped the microbial action." Jae looked at her curiously. A round box appeared in her hand. She opened a small spout on it to pour a mound of salt into her hand. Now she walked around the clearing, sowing the salt on the bodies, on the sand, even a little in the woods.

"Ah," Jae said softly.

Wiley chewed on his lip, puzzling even as he recorded the scene. "What? What's she doing?"

"Hush."

She spread the salt until there was no more to be used. Then she used her arm movements and her breath in great banishing gestures and exhalations, all around the area. Standing still at the center of the place, she brought her arms very slowly up until they were over her head.

"Give me a second," Lina told them as she leaned over the glassy chasm at the edge of the ocean to wash her arms in the salt water there.

"And what, pray tell, was all that?"

"These men had finished their lives," she told Wiley. "Whatever they were here to learn had been learned. It was time for them to move on. Some of them were still here. There were vibrations from the crime: terror, fear, hatred. That needed to be cleansed. The souls needed to be urged to move along."

Amused by the shamanism, Wiley glanced at Jae. "And you figured that out."

"I could see that there were still presences here, yes," Jae told him as Lina finished her personal cleansing. "And I know that salt is used for purification."

"So you believe in all this?"

Jae watched Lina come up from the beach, gathering her clothes and the blanket again. "I know that I saw something on this beach and that whatever it was isn't here anymore," he told Wiley. "As for my personal beliefs, we can have a conversation anytime you have an open mind."

"I always have an open mind. Five of them." Wiley stuck his lips out petulantly.

"Uh huh." Jae's gaze roamed the area. "I remember a similar ceremony a long time ago. It was on the top of a bare mountain, and it was winter. I remember the wind. We didn't use salt, but the attitude was the same." He wouldn't say anything more.

"Ready?" Lina asked them.

"Ready," Wilder confirmed, and she ported them back to his lab on Sarastor.

He stood there for a moment. "It's that same feeling of being on the edge of reality," he finally said. "I can't seem to define it." He touched the box on his belt and went back to his yellow-garbed, blue self. He took off his jacket as the cartload of books arrived. It took only a few moments to assign a blast-proof room for Lina to port the large gun to.

Dellen had been alone in the lab. She looked at the books curiously, unable to read the titles, but a few of the fiction books on top had lurid covers of women with swords, men with lightsabers, fanciful starships that could never work.

"I am investigating the culture of Earth," Wilder explained. "Lina, I want to check out a few more books when I'm done with these."

Lina managed a smile. "See if you can manufacture some phony ID, and we can get you a legal library card. That would make me feel better about this." She yawned as she took her usual place in the corner.

Lina looked up when she heard Wiley speaking English but not to her. A monitor hovered in front of him, but it wasn't in 3-D. She couldn't see profiles sticking out of it.

Casually she stood up and eased around so she could see the monitor. The White Puma – good golly, it was the White Puma! – was on the screen, looking more than a little confused.

"You're calling from Sarastor about a Terran matter," the Puma said doubtfully.

"Yes. We encountered a crime scene located–"

"What's the Mega-Legion doing on Earth?"

"We happened to be in the neighborhood," Wiley said with a hint of irritation in his voice. "There is a crime scene located at–"

"Why were you in the neighborhood?" The Puma was clearly suspicious. The long platinum faux fur trim around her brown, well-worn face stirred as if in a breeze.

"I don't see why that would have any bearing–"

Wiley was causing his own trouble, Lina thought. **Don't be so patronizing. She's a parahero, not a child. A colleague of sorts, isn't she?**

Wiley paused ever so slightly. **And you are just here visiting,** he told her. **You are no relation to Londo, understand?** "Perhaps another Terran would be able to explain the situation," Wiley addressed the Puma and gestured for Lina to come over.

"Another Terran? Is Londo there?"

Lina came into the picture now. "No, sorry, ma'am," she said, awed at the legendary heroine. She was her grandparents' age but still running around the planet kicking butt for the Network. "I'm Lina O'Kelly from North Carolina. Wi – Doctor Mem-Bazer doesn't mean to be rude, but it comes out that way sometimes."

"North Carolina? What the hell are you doing at Legion Headquarters?"

Lina quickly held up her bracelet so the Puma could see, and waited for the communication to cut off. It didn't. Be a little subtler this time. "I'm a prisoner, but they've been giving me a break every now and then, keeping me on a loose leash. We were just on Earth a little while ago and there was a place where, um, Valiant had been attacked. It's on Tiawa, French Polynesia."

"Valiant was attacked…" The Puma peered suspiciously at her, but not as much as she had Wiley. The vertical slit pupils of her yellow eyes were farther open than they had been.

"He called in a… an Armageddon Alert the other day," Lina said. "He canceled it a couple of days ago with the Bolt, once he had recovered."

"Recovered?" The Puma's eyebrow went up.

"Yes, he was hurt in the attack. But he's fully recovered now and he's on another mission so he's not here."

"All right. Yes, we got the Alert and the cancellation." The Puma eased back in her chair. "You say you're a prisoner? Are you being held because you're Terran?"

It was nice of her to ask. "I'm not a political prisoner, but I wouldn't mind a little help in getting out of this mess–"

"Valiant will be back in a day or so," Wiley put in from behind Lina. "He will handle coordinating a legal defense."

"I want to get out sooner than that. But what Wiley was calling you about is to report that Doctor Menlo is dead."

The Puma sprang to full alert. "Dr. Menlo! Dead!?"

"Yes, we saw his body. Apparently Terry… oh, what is her last name?… Rhodes, Terry Rhodes or one of her men killed him after the attack on Valiant."

"Terry Rhodes? Terry Rhodes and Dr. Menlo are working together?"

"Well, they won't be any more," Lina reminded her.

The Puma huffed out her cheeks. "No, I suppose not. You're sure it was him?"

"I was introduced to him a few days ago by that name, and he sure looked like he did on TV."

The Puma nodded. "Simple enough to do an absolute ID. Location?"

"It's on Tiawa, the northeast coast." Lina turned to Wiley. "Do you have the coordinates?"

Wiley gave them to the Puma haughtily, upset that apparently this human thought he was lording it over her from his lofty Legion position.

Puma noted the figures into her computer. "So what was the Legion doing on Earth?"

"They've been humoring me," Lina replied. "We went for a little shopping."

"You what?"

"Just for a while. I decided to take them by to see the place where it happened as long as Wiley was there, too. He's been asking about it."

"So… you were there with Valiant when he was attacked?"

"Yes, ma'am. It was pretty rough – well, you'll see. I read in the Sunday paper how the entire population of the island had been forced off. It was so Terry and her mercenaries could have the run of the place. Is everyone there okay now? Back safely?"

The Puma's eyes moved left and right as she sought the memory. "Oh. Ah, you mean this is tied into that atomic test scam. Tiawa, you say?" She checked her computer monitor.

"Apparently Terry wanted to have a clear field for when she and Dr. Menlo went after Lon… Valiant."

"Well. Well, this is beginning to make a little sense now."

"Some of it still doesn't make any sense to me."

The Puma's eyes were crafty, measuring ones. "So you just came to Earth to do a little shopping? And you brought Legionnaires with you?"

"And to feed the cats. Wiley wanted to take some measurements of distances and things."

Wiley stepped forward. "The Network has all the information it needs now."

"Waitaminnit!" Puma exclaimed. "I need more details."

"You have the information you need to investigate a crime site," Wiley said briskly. "There were three of us there today. We did nothing to seriously impede your investigation. As a matter of fact, the bodies were put in temporary stasis to help you."

"Jae, I mean Neutrino, stopped the decay for a few days," Lina piped up, "but you should still take some masks along. There's about twenty dead bodies there and they've been there for a few days. Lots of rats."

The Puma's lip curled. "Look," she addressed Wiley. "You are apparently holding a citizen of Earth… of the United States of America against her will."

"It's a long story and it's not his fault," Lina said but the Puma ignored her.

"And you're handing me a line about being here this afternoon."

"I assure you," Wiley said, "we are telling you the truth. We have a top-security new form of propulsion that…" and he went on about some fictitious process as the Puma eyed him doubtfully.

Lina made sure she was behind Wiley, out of his line of sight but within the Puma's as she lifted the short sleeves of her tee shirt, one side at a time. Nothing up my sleeve… She held out her hand, index finger poised above her thumb, and the Puma's wedding ring soon appeared there. Lina gestured at it, showing it off as a magician's assistant might.

Wiley turned suddenly and discovered her. "Lina!" She jumped. "I am putting you right now into solitary confinement. Puter, give me a view of top security cellblock alpha–"

"Oh, good grief, Wiley, it's not like it's a secret or anything…"

"You heard me giving an alternate explanation–"

"Lying through your teeth. All she has to do is ask the Bolt. They work for the same organization. You do remember that we were teleporting all over the place here with the Bolt watching."

Wiley muttered something dark and threatening as Lina returned the ring.

"A teleporter," the Puma breathed, her ring back on her finger. "You're an interstellar teleporter."

"Pleased to meet you." Lina smiled, trying not to look smug.

"Is this why she's under arrest?" Puma demanded. "Is the Legion trying to snatch another megapara who belongs to Earth?"

Wiley tried to make his face into a neutral expression but didn't succeed at all. "The purpose of this call was a courtesy between law organizations. We have informed you about a crime scene that exists within your jurisdiction. I feel that you've received adequate information. I am terminating this conversation now."

"Hold it! Hold it just one minute!" the Puma snarled. "This conversation has opened up another topic, that being the possibly illegal restraint of a Terran within Affiliated Systems territory. Just because we have no diplomatic relations with Sarastor doesn't mean that we're without recourse here. Honey, have you done anything illegal Out There?"

Lina glanced at the damage across the room. An accident. "Not to my knowledge," she said. "They won't let me call a lawyer. Apparently they don't have bail Out Here."

"What are the charges against you?"

"I'm not sure anyone's ever read me any complete official charges, just general stuff. I certainly wasn't miranda'd. They tell me that the guy who's leveling the charges is going to be in charge of appointing my defense lawyer."

Wiley put one hand on her shoulder and pushed. "You are out of this conversation now," he ordered her in Panlingua.

She threw up her hands and left the viewing area.

"Hold it! Hold it one damn minute!" the Puma roared. "Bring her back here! I want to talk to her for three minutes. Three lousy minutes. Surely the great Mega-Legion can grant a mere Networker that much."

Wiley considered and grumbled almost below audible level. He finally pointed at Lina. "Remember what I told you," he said in Panlingua. "I'll cut the conversation off if you go too far. You don't know… you know who. Don't tell her anything she shouldn't know."

"She's a highly respected member of the Network," Lina retorted. "Don't treat her like a nobody. If she asks something you don't want me to tell her about, you give me a little signal."

"Like maybe an electric shock through your spine?" He let some teeth show through his smile. "Be a good little witchdoctor or daddy spank."

Lina rolled her eyes and entered the picture again with her hands on her head, prisoner of war-style. "Yessir, massa Mem-Bazer," she said smartly in English.

"I am going to search for our Panlingua translators later and rerun the tape of this," the Puma said. "You are under official Mega-Legion arrest?"

"I don't know how they work things here," Lina said as she brought her hands down to her sides. "My guard tells me I'm under arrest, and I have to stay here in the lab all the time when I'm not in quarters. They have a locator on me." She showed the bracelet again. "I tried to get through to a lawyer and they busted me for that, too."

"But Valiant will clear it up?"

"I don't know if he's allowed to. It's the head honcho here who's bringing the charges, Valiant's boss. Besides, Valiant won't be back for a couple days. Sarastor days are damned long."

"But… You say they've been humoring you?"

"I have cats that have to be fed every day. They'll starve if I don't go home!"

"Cats. Every day? You're coming to Earth every day?"

"Yes, ma'am. One of my cats needs meds for thyroid."

"How quickly? How quickly can you teleport humans?"

"Very, very quickly," Lina grinned at the Puma. Wiley cleared his throat.

"What, I can't tell her that much? C'mon, Wiley, I'll be back there in a few days. Out of your jurisdiction. Lon… Valiant said that he was going to take me to the Network, and I'm sure the question will come up sooner or later."

"Then it will wait until then," he told her evenly.

"What are the charges against this Terran, Dr. Mem-Bazer?"

"The charges…" Wiley considered and paused. "The charges are an internal Legion matter, not one for the civilian authorities."

"We don't consider ourselves civilians, Dr. Mem-Bazer. The internal Legion charges are…?"

"Mental control of a Legionnaire."

That made the Puma stop. Finally she asked, "So do you always teleport around the galaxy with a mind controller?"

"Madam, I never do."

Her mouth crooked at that. "They're treating you well?" the Puma asked Lina.

"I could use some *Star Trek* episodes to relieve the boredom. And they have a tendency to forget to feed me. But there hasn't been a strip search or a de-lousing, no *Midnight Express* stuff. I mean, I wouldn't give it four stars… but it's okay. It's fairly interesting here, real-life *Trek*."

"And Valiant is going to clear things up."

"I don't know anything about the legal system Out Here, much less how it operates with the great and powerful Legion commander. They're not big on the Bill of Rights."

"But you think Valiant can help."

"Well, if he can't, I'll just hightail it out of here. It's interesting, but not that interesting."

"You… You can escape the Legion?"

"I haven't seen anything yet that could stop me. Wiley's smart; he'll probably come up with something in a few days. So I guess we'd better have everything cleared up by then, shouldn't we?"

"All right, honey, what about your husband?"

"Husband?" Wiley asked immediately.

Lina wiggled her ring finger at him. "Wedding ring," she told him and then turned back to the screen. "My husband's just fine. At least, I don't think he's in any trouble, is he, Wiley?"

"No. At least, nothing that can't be cleared up quickly within the next few days." Wiley nodded a millimeter at the Puma. "If it sets your mind easier, I'm on Ms. O'Kelly's side in the matter."

"See?" Lina beamed at the Puma. "He's a nice guy."

"Of course, I'm also under your mental control…"

She slapped him lightly on the arm and he made an excruciatingly pained face.

"He's a horrible person who thinks he's very funny!" Lina exclaimed. "Don't you pay him any mind, Puma. He's just an ol' Legionnaire, full of himself and then some. Everyone struts around here saying, 'I'm a Legionnaire; I'm hot stuff!' Wiley, the Puma could beat you up ten ways from next Friday and not even be breathing hard. AND she'd only have to use one mind to do it."

"All right, all right…" The Puma tried to be the peacemaker, but it was clear she was pleased. "You say your husband's safe, Ms. O'Kelly?"

"He's working very closely with Valiant," Lina said sincerely.

"And Valiant says that he'll get you out of trouble when he gets back."

"That's funny; I thought he was the one who got you in trouble in the first place." The two of them turned as Jae came into the lab.

"That's my guard," Lina told Puma. "The one who doesn't feed me. He just takes me to Earth every day and nightclubs every night."

"Seems pretty cushy to me," Puma said, trying to see farther on her screen. "That sounded like Neutrino."

Jae stepped up to the monitor. A translator unit sprang to his side. "Howdy, Miz Puma."

"It *is* you." The Puma eyed Jae thoroughly. "Always nice to see you, Neutrino. Someday you'll come for a visit so we can all enjoy your company."

Why, that horny old lady! Sure, the White Puma didn't look it, but she was old enough to be Jae's grandmother – maybe his great-grandmother – and she was looking at him like he was a five-course dinner and she'd been shipwrecked for a month.

"I was just on Earth a little while ago, as a matter of fact." Jae nodded at her. "Sorry I missed you."

"I've got a granddaughter who's sorry you missed us," the Puma said, pointing an accusing long-clawed index finger at Jae. "Here I've been telling her for years about Londo's friend, and you never show your face on Earth. You come by tomorrow, meet my little Dolores, and we can have the church booked for next week."

Jae just grinned. Behind him, Lina covered her mouth with her hand. Maybe the Puma had a nice grandson instead?

The Puma made a show of dejection, hurling her sigh to the heavens. "Ah well, I tried. You're Ms. O'Kelly's arrest officer? You treat her good, Neutrino. She's Terran. All the best people are."

"Of course I treat her well, Miz Puma. She's got me under mind control. I follow all her commands to the letter."

Lina aimed a blow at his shoulder but he just grabbed her wrist and otherwise ignored her.

"Well, if she gets too powerful for you and you need the Network's help, contact us. And see about getting her some Sarastoran legal help, won't you?"

Jae scratched his chin, which was turning scraggly again, with his free hand. "I'll check the bylaws and see what I can do, but I don't guarantee anything. The Legion has its rules."

"Then have Valiant contact us as soon as he gets back. If we don't receive word about your condition within three days, Ms. O'Kelly, I'll start proceedings on our end. We do have some legal recourses. Don't worry; Valiant can be very resourceful."

Wiley stepped on Lina's toes.

"I'm sure he is," she replied evenly. "Thank you so much." With a sigh, Lina could feel the tension flowing out of her shoulders. Someone knew where she was; someone was going to help. Now there was a definite light at the end of the tunnel.

Goal B had been met. At last, at last.

"Dr. Mem-Bazer, is there anything else?"

He tried to look sourly at the Puma. "I believe we'd given all the pertinent information some fifteen minutes ago." He glanced at Lina. "Time for the prisoner to get back to her holding area. I have some more tests for you."

Lina grimaced but then nodded politely to the Puma. She retreated to her chair. "Nooobody knows the troubles I've seen..." she sang mournfully.

"And no singing in my laboratory!!" It irritated Wiley that the Puma was grinning at him instead of being scandalized at singing in a modern scientific laboratory. The very idea!

"Glory hallelujah," the Puma said, loud enough for Lina to hear.

"Lina?" Jae opened the door to Londo's darkened apartment. "Lina, wake up!" He walked down the back hallway to the master bedroom. "C'mon, wake up!"

She lay on her side in bed with a study padd next to her. Her bare shoulders and an arm were all that weren't otherwise chastely covered by her sheet. Jae smiled; good thing someone from Protocol hadn't come to wake her. But this other thing…

One of Lon's trophies was in bed with her. It had been left switched on. A holopicture of him beginning to smile, then looping back to seriousness, hovered above the trophy. Pillows had been packed under the sheet to mimic another body there. Jae turned the trophy off and set it on Lon's bedside table.

"Lina," he said loudly. He sat on the bed and pushed her over onto her back; she didn't stir. Sure enough, she had the transceiver fastened onto her forehead. She was learning something on advanced speed, and that always put you out cold. He peeled it off. "Lina." This time he calmed his voice so as not to shock her. "Wake up. Lina. There's an emergency."

Her eyelids fluttered and then opened. She automatically pulled up the sheet, although it didn't have much farther up to go. "Jae?"

"There's an emergency," he repeated. "Get dressed. You've got to port some people out."

"*D'accord.* Okay." She took a second to get her bearings, and then suddenly she was fully dressed under the covers. Then they were in Wiley's lab and she smoothed her sleep-rumpled hair.

"What's up?" She was still blinking sleep away. The main 3-D screen was unfurled to full size and a slight woman who resembled Brügz strongly, even down to wearing a version of his costume, looked out from it. She seemed familiar – had she been at the wedding? That's right, Brügz had two sisters, one of whom was a Legionnaire. This was the woman who had to rush from the reception to meet an Outpost shuttle. Oh, was that what "Outpost shuttle" meant? The concept made sense to Lina now.

Wiley stood at the monitor board while Brügz and Dellen stood next to him. Erik burst into the lab, adjusting the cuffs on his costume. Lina guessed he'd been asleep, too.

"Okay, Eila, everyone's here now. Lina, are you ready to port?"

"Who knows where they're going?" she asked, giving her eyes a final rub. "Oh, of course." She addressed the woman on the screen. "Can you open up the picture a bit so I can see your location?" With the slightest of gestures, this Eila's picture widened to show a sparsely-furnished room. "Okay, got it. Just you three?"

"Just them," Wiley confirmed.

"Okay, here you go."

The three vanished from the room, and Eila looked around. "I thought you said this thing was instantaneous," she accused Wilder.

"Quiet," Wiley admonished. "The landing takes a few minutes."

Eila kept looking around and suddenly jumped as the three appeared. "They're here," she confirmed. She looked at Lina curiously. "Nice trick. We'll report back at completion." The screen blanked out.

"That's it?"

"You can return to quarters," Wiley told her.

Lina rubbed her cheeks. "I'm awake now. What time is it?"

"It's just past 0100. Wiley just came in for duty," Jae told her. "I'm due for a rest break. Want to go somewhere? The Terran Zone?"

"Without your guitar?"

"I'll be the audience this time," he said. "Without the others, I'll have solo monitor duty later on. I don't want to get too tired."

"Wiley's almost always here." Lina addressed the doctor. "Why don't you take as many breaks as everyone else?"

"I can rest one of my minds at a time," he told her. "Plus, during the rare instances when we do have such a skeleton staff, I use stimulants to keep my body alert."

"Drugs?"

"They're safe enough for short-term use," he assured her.

"Oh. Okay."

"Glad I have your permission."

Lina turned to Jae. "Are you sure you want to come along?" Lina asked him as she ported in the knapsack with her piano music in it. "I mean, this will make three nights in a row. You must be bored to tears by now."

Jae watched her sort through books and port in some more. "I'd forgotten how much I missed music," Jae said. He followed her to the rear bathroom with its mirror so she could attend to her hair after she brushed her teeth. "I remember hearing it all the time when I was a child. It was like breathing back then, to go through the day singing. I remember how silent everything was when… when I arrived on Sarastor. Besides, I'm your official bodyguard. I'm keeping you out of trouble. Rules say you need an official escort as a prisoner and as a Legion spouse."

"Yessir," she said crisply, putting a hairpin to that pesky lock that always wanted to get in her eyes when she wore her hair in a braid. "Ready to port?"

"Why don't we fly over?"

"It would be nice to get out in the fresh air. I suppose I can trust you not to drop me."

He gave an evil, "don't trust me" laugh, which made her play-scowl at him. Then they both chuckled.

They used that goofy jetsons tube and this time he explained how to operate it. The lobby and security passageway were familiar by now, two uniformed guards coming to attention as they passed, and together they headed out into the night.

They were talking about which instrument Jae preferred, drums or guitar. He picked her up, and Lina realized how strong he was, how beautiful and confident. How wonderful it was to have a man touch her again, even if it wasn't Londo! There was just something thrilling about manly arms and hands and a low voice. Jae leapt off the ground, soaring over the city with her in his arms, but they kept going up and up.

How far were the lights below them? The curving rim of the world came into view but she was unafraid. Jae had her. His ring kept her ears from popping as they rose so swiftly. A deck of thin clouds wisped by, and then…

"Stars," Lina breathed. Here they were at last in all their glory, shining above the competition of man. The Milky Way was brighter than she remembered seeing it on all but the darkest of nights.

"People should be able to see the stars," Jae told her as they hung there in the icy night sky. "People should be able to wish on stars if they want, or to tell stories about them. Or sing to them."

"'Behold, the only thing greater than yourself,'" Lina recited softly. "Sometimes we need to be reminded of scale. And that we fit into the pattern."

Jae watched the stars.

They landed outside the club. The crowd pointed and bowed to the Last Feithi Legionnaire. But things had changed inside in the main lounge. Now large monitor screens had been deployed in some sectors of the room, and Lina goggled to see that they showed her and Jae singing last night. The people who didn't notice Neutrino walking in their midst were watching the screens and talking agitatedly. Some few were laughing in derisive tones; most were not.

The doors closed behind them as they left the main area, and Lina stood there looking back. "What the hell were they doing?" she demanded from Jae.

"Added entertainment for the casino crowd," Jae replied. "Come on." He pulled at her, and she followed him reluctantly.

"If I had known someone was recording you…"

"What? What would you have done?"

"I don't know. It just seems like they're taking advantage."

Jae paused before opening the door to the Terran Zone. "The club owns this bar, too. They do this for each of their private rooms. If something interesting happens, they show everyone. If a celebrity comes through, they showcase it. People want to live through celebrities on Sarastor. It's the only life most of them have."

Lina sighed surrender and stepped into the bar. Immediately she heard murmurs of "Neutrino," but also "Starfleet." She wondered if they'd start to call her "You Are Here," since that's what her tee shirt tonight said, the one with the big arrow pointing to a star in a spiral galaxy.

Though packed in even at this early hour, the crowd parted to let the two of them through to the piano. Ernst wasn't there, and Lina missed seeing his burly, friendly self. Ah well, he couldn't spend all his time here, could he?

She sat down at the piano and asked for requests. The people who were first in line were unfamiliar faces, new people who maybe had heard about a music-maker and had come for a chance to hear the songs of home.

She took the requests as best she could, in the order that she remembered them. And every word was there for her, ready to spring to mind even when she didn't have the music. She had stopped thinking of it as odd, and had even begun wishing that the same thing could be said of piano arrangements. It was difficult keeping up with all these. She was used to playing simple chords and faking a melody line as hired help at parties. It wasn't enough here. These people needed real music!

But how she enjoyed this, singing to the crowd, putting a little style into her voice and singing the song according to its meaning and not just its notes now that she didn't have to remember words.

Even Jae seemed pleased. He'd set his formal cape and gloves onto the side of the piano. He snagged a drink and sipped as she played, keeping a wary eye on the crowd in such a way that only she knew. He was protecting her. How sweet – just like Londo would do. It made her feel special.

Jae was the one who called for a break. Unfortunately, the club was out of Cokes, so Lina settled for that green-apple brew Jae had ordered for her the other night, *laffez*. They slid beside each other into a closed, circular booth and Jae touched the wall. The crowd noises receded.

For the first time in days the silence was welcome. Lina leaned against the walls of the booth and closed her eyes.

"That last song was so beautiful," Jae said thoughtfully. "The words were like a song my mother used to sing. I remember now."

"I'm glad, Jae," Lina said. He seemed so strong before, but the stillness had brought out what lurked beneath the public mask of infallibility he so often wore. The wounded boy in a man's body – lost in the stars. She put her hand on his and squeezed. "Your hands are cold," she laughed softly. "The saying is, 'Cold hands, warm heart.'"

Their gaze locked over those hands. His blue eyes warmed. Intensified. She started to pull her hand away, but he reached out to keep it where it was. His other hand he cupped behind the nape of her neck, pulling her toward him. He leaned forward…

She could not tear her eyes away from his. "Jae," she breathed. "I think that break's over. I need to get back–"

He blinked and released her as if she were a hot coal. "I… Sorry, Lina. Don't know what got into me. It won't happen again. Relax and take your break." He paused, looking away from her. "I'm sorry," he repeated.

"That's all right. We all get lonely sometimes." She patted his hand in a motherly way, trying to take the embarrassment out of the moment for him. My god! She was married now! What could she be thinking? Then she realized that by now she'd known Jae longer than she'd known Lon. Jae was her friend; Lon was her love, her husband. Remember that!

His hand under hers was a man's hand. Strong and yet sensitive. She looked up again into his eyes, and they were not the eyes of just a friend. Londo looked at her that way. A blaze burned there. Deliberately she slid out of the booth and returned to the piano. The crowd eased back for her as she made her way alone.

She refused to think about it. It was a mistake; Jae had been drinking. People who were used to touch must do this kind of thing all the time; they had calluses on their nerve endings. It didn't have the meaning she was putting to it. She was tired and must have mistaken it…

But she knew she hadn't. She shoved the thoughts to the side every time they came around and renewed her efforts to make music for the Terran Zoners.

There were only a couple of requests now (the birthday song needed to be sung for a dozen people who were having very convenient birthdays tonight), and the crowd let her pick and choose what she wanted.

She sang a song so familiar to the crowd that many sang along without looking at the music: "'*When you wish upon a star, your dreams come true.*'"

She finished the last note, letting the applause echo distantly around her and wondering when Fate would send her own wish back to her. Londo. How much longer would he be out between the stars? She was getting things confused here. She needed him, not Jae.

Trying to sense his presence, she sent her mind out calling for her love.

Instead she found… something.

Something tremendously out of balance. What was it?

Sarastor whispered to her: **Notice… Speaker, notice!**

Lina shunted down any shock that might show in her face or voice. "Thanks, folks," she told the crowd around the piano. "But I'm afraid that's it for tonight." Despite the howls of protest, she politely insisted.

Jae! she called urgently. She could feel him give a start.

What is it?

We have to get out of here – now. Something's wrong.

17

Immediately Jae appeared by her side, smiling, gathering up his things and taking her arm as if it were indeed just a whim that she had decided to end her set early. It was an effort to appear natural as they made their way through the crowd. The door closed behind them.

"What?" Jae demanded.

She ported the two of them to Wiley's lab, not surprised to see the aqua-skinned genius at work at two different mechanical projects even as he conversed with a screen. He signed off as they appeared.

Before he could say anything, Lina blurted, "I'm new at all this interplanetary stuff. Is it normal for a bunch of large ships to come out of hyperspace around Sarastor all at the same time?"

"What?"

"What are you talking about?" Wiley put a stylus down and turned his full attention on her.

How could Lina say this so they'd believe her? "As of about ten minutes ago, this planet's been approached by a group, a *fleet* of ships. And I don't think they have anyone's best interests at heart. Sarastor's worried."

Wiley switched on a wide 3-D screen that displayed the planetary neighborhood. There was a thick scattering of light blips in a flat, oval ring around the world. He gestured. Colorful graphics of orbits overlaid on the picture.

"Everything looks normal to me," Wiley said. Tags appeared next to the blips, identifying them as ordinary traffic.

"They're cloaked. Like Romulans on *Star Trek*," Lina said slowly. The two looked at her as if she were crazy, and indeed she felt so. "Bent light rays around the ships, I don't know. Look for distortions. Try–" she went up to the display and put her fingertip at one spot far off in space, matching where a ghostly finger only she could see hovered. The fingertip traced a slow path toward Sarastor. "Try looking here to start. This is the command ship."

Jae moved to the lab computers to tie them into Wiley's other monitors. Wilder rechecked readouts, hit some optical displays to show a close-up of black space with stars in the background.

Double-imaged stars.

"Something's there," Jae said.

"Here; I've found others," Wiley said. The planetary screen lit up with more and more blips. Over thirty of them, scattered but starting to form into a wide but organized wedge as they neared Sarastor space.

"Grigach," Jae breathed.

"Two Legionnaires left on Sarastor," Wiley said. "How many centuries since someone tried to invade the planet? I'll alert planetary defenses, but Sarastor has depended on the Legion for her defense so long… I doubt if they have the firepower to stave this off. Thirty-four, no, thirty-five ships–"

"The Broomline Batteries–" Jae began.

"Off-line until next month, remember?" Wiley corrected him. "What else? What else?" They traded possibilities in brief bursts.

"Off-planet backup couldn't arrive for at least–"

"Nineteen hours. The Coronasphere Shell… I might be able to reconfigure that. We've been working on that."

"How much time?' Jae demanded.

Wiley shook his head in frustration. "Even with all my assistants… Eight hours."

"Coincidence that so many planetary defense units are down with snafus," Jae murmured.

"Blood's *skurny* ice!" Wiley cursed, and almost spat, "Coincidence my eye!"

"Don't you have any other options?" Lina asked. "I mean, to stop a fight before it begins."

"As in…?" Wiley's fingers were flying about his monitor board. Screens showing diagrams and maps were popping up in every direction.

"As in a quick demonstration of superior power," Jae suggested.

"Scare them off, yeah," Lina said.

Another head shake from Wiley, "I don't think we have anything that–"

"We can make them think we do," Jae said suddenly. "What are our options?"

"A bluff?" Wilder considered even as he gestured for the computer to notify his Legion labs staff to report for emergency duty. "What can we work with? Ideas."

"We can blast through some of the ships if we need to," Jae said. "If we could find which ones are the lead ships, we could concentrate on just them. Planetary defenses should be able to handle that much."

"Me," Lina said suddenly. "I think I can get enough of a lock on those ships to port inside one." She concentrated as the others spoke, fishing for some hook to begin. She needed someone who'd been there, or needed to see a picture of it. What would the command area of a battleship look like? She immediately thought of the *Enterprise.* Was there anything out there that had the same feel of the *Enterprise* in battle mode?

A flash of image came to her mind, and she brought it back. A chair. Captain Kirk, yeah. She concentrated on it and the concept, tried to enlarge the view. A chair with a man, a powerful man sitting in it. The view enlarged slowly; she tuned out Wiley and Jae's brittle discussion. Other people were scattered around the bridge, overlooking weapons displays…

It was really more like a submarine than the *Enterprise,* cramped and crowded with stale air. No strobing red lights like in the movies. Was there another similar scene? She knew what the one bridge layout was in general. She looked for something similar but slightly different. "I can do it," she declared, interrupting them. "I've got a couple of 'em."

"There are over thirty ships, Lina. You can't hit them all."

"So you'll give me some drugs, some stimulants along the way."

"Thirty-five ships," Jae warned her.

"Forty-one," Wiley corrected. "Forty-two."

"Maybe I just hit the important ships." She thought desperately, searching for options. "Once I start, I don't come back to Sarastor except for stimulant shots until I'm finished; that way I don't have to waste much energy or time on biofiltering anything. What do I do once I'm there?"

Wiley gave her an odd look before he announced, "As Base Officer, I hereby assign Lina O'Kelly to this mission. If the arresting officer confirms."

He and Jae exchanged concerned expressions. "The arresting officer confirms. Lina O'Kelly is released from arrest for the duration."

Wiley nodded. "Okay, Lina can get us in," he said as they huddled around the comm board. "Now what are our options?"

"We're going to end this peaceably, are we?" Craftily, Jae smiled. "How about this…?"

And he explained to a doubtful Wilder.

The fleet admiral, Bracken by name, watchfully lounged in his command chair as the crescent world grew in his forward screens. Like all his people, his skin fell in the orange range, his in particular being the color of worn terracotta. His hair was dark olive, and his eyes were greenish-gray and sharp.

Muscular despite a proud stoutness, he presented a stark contrast to his slender, sometimes emaciated, crew. He was relaxed but alert, serving as an example to the officers on his bridge. Confident in his imminent success.

Not so long ago he'd been field marshal of the Majority Army of Aldierra, but now he'd organized the planet's new warships into an interstellar navy, and had been made its commander as well. After he completed this assignment and Sarastor was firmly under Aldierran control, he could return to his preferred land-based command.

The Mega-Legion was gone from the tantalizingly rich, powerful and unsuspecting world of Sarastor; his people had arranged that much. Intelligence reported that their saboteurs had been successful, and planetary defenses could not stop his fleet. For the past two hundred years the Legion had been the primary focus of power on the world that held the primary focus of power in this sector. Now the Legion was gone – gone for two more days at least. Just a few stragglers left. His fleet could handle a few stragglers, especially while there was no sign of Valiant being among those.

Sarastor was far from Admiral Bracken's world, and as such it was known only in almost-legendary bits and pieces, but they did know that its technology was on a par with that of Aldierra. Sarastor's main fame was its political power and riches… and of course, the Mega-Legion. He who could conquer Sarastor might also take the Affiliated Systems and its nearest neighboring Unaffiliated Worlds with relative ease, especially in a surprise war.

No major force had even attempted to attack the heart of the Affiliated Systems for hundreds of years. It was well-insulated, lying in the heart of AffSys territory. All the weak people of the AffSys had been at peace for so long. They had no worries about anything except the Yanist-Glory Empire, whose tactics were insidious instead of outright. They would be totally unprepared for this. This action would be quick, deadly and decisive.

His first target, of course, would be to infiltrate Mega-Legion Headquarters and utilize its defense systems to keep the Legion off Sarastor, maybe even strand the large group they had lured into hyperspace. They would secure the planet before help could arrive. Yes, Admiral Bracken was confident of winning the day.

But he jumped when the two strangers appeared on his bridge. They were just there – there was no slow fade-in as happened in ordinary transporting. They were striking young adults, barefoot, with flowers in their long hair. They couldn't possibly be armed. Their silky white clothing clung to them indecently when they moved. Moreover, there wasn't much to it, just two long, narrow panels, front and back, that were tied together with colorful ribbons only at shoulders and hips. More ribbons fluttered at their wrists and in their hair. The bosomy young woman held a basket filled with blossoms that she scattered into the air. She smiled angelically at his officers as they gaped at her.

"Welcome to Sarastor," she said in a voice that was mother's music. She spoke Panlingua, the language they'd studied before this mission. Thus they understood her words, though they also took her meaning from her movements. Her *larn*-colored body swayed like a flower in a soft breeze as she strolled around the bridge. First the fabric clung and then it blew away, allowing tantalizing peeks at what lay beneath. The Admiral blinked and tore his eyes from her, for there was the other stranger as well.

"Welcome! Welcome to our new visitors!" the blond man said heartily as he stepped forward. Sensors confirmed he had no weapons on him, just a note padd. Bracken had never seen a more beautiful being, male or female. His very face seemed alight with nobility, grace and friendship.

Every officer in the room except Bracken pulled their weapons, but none worked.

"My name is Jae, and I have the great pleasure to be in charge of Sarastor tourism. This is Lina, my partner. Please feel free to visit our wonderful world, Field Marshal. Or I should say – Admiral Bracken. Congratulations on your promotion."

Who in coldest hells were these people? For a moment Bracken considered that they might be gods; surely ordinary humans were not this beautiful! But that thought he shoved away with a dose of cold reality. There were no gods, only Hell.

"What is this?" Admiral Bracken demanded.

The man named Jae gave him a deep bow, came out of it with a flourish and then turned to the officers standing in a circle around their commander. "I am your humble servant, your guide to the beautiful and mysterious delights of Sarastor," Jae crowed like a bawdies ringmaster.

He used sweeping arm motions to draw their attention. "All our planetary facilities are anxiously awaiting your visit. We have been preparing for you for some time now. I can tell you, everyone's positively trembling with anticipation. It's not every day we get such exotic visitors!"

Jae turned to his companion. "Lina, why don't you issue an invitation to the other captains to come as well? Perhaps you can persuade some to begin their tours tonight. How we do love having guests! And such tantalizing guests at that, all the way from mysterious Aldierra!"

Intimately Jae leaned on the arm of the admiral's chair. "To tell you the truth, sir, I'd never heard of the world before you came to see us. You must tell me all about it. Oh, but I am skipping ahead. I suppose I'm too excited about all these wonderful visitors. Admiral, which of your captains should be the first for us to invite to the surface?"

Lina popped a flower into the collar of an officer's uniform and turned to her cohort. "I'd be delighted to invite Captains Liji and Duc first – if that's all right with you, Admiral Bracken. So nice to meet you." She curtsied to the admiral and popped out, leaving a sprinkling of flower petals to fall in her absence.

Patting the him familiarly on the shoulder, Jae announced, "Admiral, let me introduce you to some of the natural and cultural wonders of Sarastor. You were interested in the best shore leave your crew has ever had, weren't you? Well by the blazing primordial orb itself, you've come to the right world! We have been readying everything for you."

Jae didn't let Bracken answer as he produced a program on his padd that projected a tourism holotape to circle the small bridge so everyone could see. He orated about vacations and recreational facilities the entire time…

…While Lina ported from ship to ship, strewing flowers and issuing formal electronic notes of invitation to the captains of the invasion fleet. Along with the petals she left a floating camera eye to simulcast the tourism tapes Jae was showing in the command ship – and also to signal Sarastoran forces as to each ship's position. She ported out before anyone could think to fire a gun, pleasantly instructing the captains to communicate with their admiral for further shore leave instructions.

Every two ships she'd return to the lab for refills on flower petals, invitations and cameras, and to puzzle out new ships to visit. On every sixth return Wiley gave her a stim shot. Porting so blindly so often was excruciating work.

"How's it going?" he asked her when they were well into it. A dozen screens filled the area around his monitor station, directly hooked up to Planetary Defense Command. He'd set his equipment to its limits and discovered another thirty-five ships since Jae and she had first left.

"It's damned difficult to find them all. I'm sure they're communicating ship to ship now," Lina replied wearily. "They don't look so shocked when I appear. Of course, I'm not porting to the ships where the guns have already been drawn. I hope Jae can keep up his patter until I return. I don't like the idea of him alone up there."

"Jae's been in far worse situations. He can handle it." Still, Wiley looked grim as he administered her shot. "And we have planetary and AffSys defenses on full alert now, just in case things go wrong."

"I'll keep my fingers crossed."

Wiley spared his hypo a frown. "I'm not sure how many more of these I can give you," he said. "You've almost reached maximum recommended dosage. Try to wind things up if you can."

"Sure." Like she was in control of the situation! Still, with the stim blasting through her system, she felt like she could move mountains if she tried.

"Ms. O'Kelly!"

She turned to one of the screens. A man in military uniform stood there with others behind him.

"Yes? Commander…" What was his name? "Shreitter?"

"Military information. We need to know what kind of weapons they're carrying, what propulsion systems they have, whether they're capable of atmospheric maneuvering."

She opened and closed her mouth helplessly. "I'm from an Unaffiliated World, Commander," she finally said. "I am unfamiliar with this level of technology. If you tell me what to look for, maybe–"

"No," Wiley ordered. "You'll be stretched enough as it is doing what you're doing. I'm not going to take a chance on this phase of the operation going wrong. You have your duty, Lina, and you just see to that. We'll use planetary sensors to assess them from here."

Legion superseded the military; those were the rules. She nodded and straightened the beribboned strap of her dress, turning away from the screen. "I swear, Wiley," she whispered, "I'm going to spend the rest of my days in turtleneck sweaters and jeans. I'll be Ms. Yency's poster girl for proper fashion."

"Has anyone actually pointed a gun at you yet?"

"No, but–"

"That outfit is probably why."

Grumbling, she picked up a refilled basket of flower petals. Then she put on her smile of welcome and ported out.

Ninety minutes and almost thirty ships later, she'd reached the end of her energy supply, even with the stimulants. Wiley had shaken his head at her last time she'd reported back for petals. He'd refused to administer any more stims. She was well past the recommended limit.

Porting didn't look like hard work, but it was, especially when she was under pressure and had to fight so for a landing picture. It sapped her energy bit by bit, leaving just enough for a couple more ports. At least she'd hit what had felt like the most important ships. Now it was time to port back to Jae and see if he needed any help. She was his escape route.

She appeared on the bridge of the command ship and saw there was no fire damage, no missing walls, no blood, no bodies. No bodies was always good.

Jae was smiling, laughing with the admiral and two men in very ornate uniforms. He had charmed them despite themselves. Occasionally he'd stop as another captain checked in, saying that he had been invited by Lina to visit the planet. Lina strolled around the bridge, handing flowers to all the disarmed officers. She opened herself completely to channeling, letting guides chatter at her.

"And how are your two children?" she'd say. "What charming little ones they are, too, a boy and a girl. How proud you must be." "Congratulations on your recent marriage. I was just married, too." "I'm so sorry to hear about your father's illness. If you could just try to get him to breathe deeply and relax a few times a day in addition to his doctors' recommendations, I think he'll improve very nicely. Their idea that he should move to a drier climate is a very wise one."

They'd reel as she would reveal some fact that they regarded as absolutely secret, or at least unknown, certainly to the enemy. But this woman with her warm, brilliant smile and flowers laid each one bare and vulnerable. She knew the secrets of their loved ones; she knew the secrets of their hearts.

Jae kept jabbering his way through the tourism tape. Even without telepathy he could almost feel the admiral's mind racing, trying to come up with a counterstrike for this friendly fire.

Jae had disabled all weapons on the bridge as they'd been produced, and when Bracken's security force showed up their weapons ran out of power. Anyone who approached Jae menacingly found themselves stumbling and weak. The admiral rubbed his chin every time an officer looked down at his weapon in puzzlement, but waved down questions as he measured his talkative opponent. Jae wondered what was he planning?

It was difficult for him to keep his mind on talking out loud as he also spoke to the materials of the air and weaponry that needed to be changed, but he set his mouth on automatic and blathered on.

"Ah, Lina dear, why don't you join us?" Jae finally asked. Grigach, she looked like some sort of flower goddess in that outfit, blossoms in her hair that had been pulled up with tendrils drifting down around her face. The ribbons floated around her even in this breezeless chamber. You could see almost everything she had to offer as the material clung when she moved – definitely the choice to make a non-threatening impression.

She came over in a walk that was more a side-to-side glide. Every man on the bridge was hypnotized by her. "Thank you. I've been meaning to ask if you've invited the admiral's grandchildren to tour the educational facilities on Sarastor. I know they aren't with him now, but hopefully someday in the near future they'll come visit. The life and science museum in Liamar in particular is entertaining at the same time it teaches, and children of five and nine are at just the right age to get the most benefit from them. Your grandson, Mino – he's so interested in biology already. He'd love it, Admiral."

The admiral's mouth opened and then closed again. How could he fight this?

Jae was nodding. "I'd quite forgotten the possibilities, Lina," he said. "How very shortsighted of me! Thinking only of the immediate shore leaves instead of taking the longer view. Thank you for pointing it out." He leaned down to the admiral's level.

"Education is the backbone of civilization. And it's so important to help children find their way through life. Why, I remember the great playwright Im Floutas saying the same thing in his play, 'Permissions Through Life' – have you heard of it, Admiral? Well, you must go to see a show while you're here, it's always playing somewhere. It's one of my favorites…" And he launched into an analysis of the philosophy of the play as it related to the time it was written versus today's more jaded era.

Suddenly he stopped. "Ah me, I seem to have gotten off-track," Jae said. "We were talking about your vacation here, not old plays which you may not even be interested in. Admiral Bracken, perhaps you would like to come down with us as our honored guest right now? Maybe with some of your officers?

He added, "We are strangers, I understand. But I assure you, Admiral, no harm will come to you or your officers. We would be so pleased to discuss shore leave options with you. There are tours to be set up, great feasts to be planned!"

Bracken had no time to consult with his men. These people had seen through their cloaking devices immediately, had boarded their ships with impunity well before their own transporters would even begin to come into range. They claimed to have known about their journey – though not invasion plans – for some time. They knew everything about them, and here they kept talking words of peace and healing. He might not believe them, but he was willing to pretend he did.

The admiral made a show of benevolence. Play their game until he understood their situation better. "I would be honored to come with you. May I bring… six of my officers?"

Lina patted his hand and smiled at Jae, then back to the admiral. She had a smile that made Bracken feel warm all over, maybe a little too warm in spots. "That would be lovely."

Bracken called for his officers and then sent a coded message to the fleet: stand by.

Lina clasped her hand in Jae's, reached for the admiral's hand, and all nine ported down to Wiley's agreed-upon location. It was a plush hotel suite. Wilder, four ambassadors and a Sarastoran general were already there, all in relaxed civilian clothes that tended toward the simple ancient drapery and pose that Jae and Lina wore, though theirs contained much more material. Lina was glad to see that not all the Sarastoran group were male. The testosterone level of the ships had been unnerving in its intensity. These Sarastorans were friendly, they were helpful, they only wished the visitors well. Wiley had coached them ahead of time.

During introductions, Lina telepathed Wiley and Jae the particulars on these officers: family and career information. Data about their world, Aldierra. She channeled health info, recent past events, anything that might give the invaders the idea that they knew everything there was to know about them.

Her head ached from all the channeling. That, plus the last of those stims were wearing off. She knew the symptoms from having had stims before. She shook her head slightly, trying to wake up but not so hard that she'd distract these people. Not now.

Jae, I need to find a bed real soon. Can I go back to quarters?

His eyes slid to hers. **You're falling asleep,** he accused her.

Sorry.

"Gentlemen," Jae rose and smiled all around. "I'm afraid that our Lina has over-taxed herself in welcoming you."

"I apologize for my weakness," Lina said as Jae helped her to her feet.

Before any of his associates could say anything, the admiral said, "Quite understandable; women are not as strong as men. She may share my bed tonight. Which room here is mine?"

Lina's fingernails cut into Jae's palm.

"That's all right, Admiral," Jae said smoothly. "I'll put her to bed. Thank you for your kind offer."

"Are you her husband? Her intended?" Admiral Bracken sounded as if these were the only two options that would allow this action.

"Jae's my fiancé." Lina smiled, and slipped her right arm around Jae's waist. "See?" She displayed her wedding ring as if it were for an engagement.

"If you'll excuse us." Jae bowed and they exited the room.

As soon as the suite door closed behind them, Jae laughed and clutched his hand to his heart, rolling his eyes heavenward. "Why, Lina, this is so sudden."

"Oh be quiet. That old goat! I may share his bed, indeed! Talk about a fate worse than death."

Jae glanced around. A wide corridor extended to left and right down the length of the hotel. They were probably on the establishment's top story. "Tell you what. Let's celebrate a little. We'll need to go in shifts for a while, and I'm tired as blaze of Headquarters. What say we grab a place here?"

"Here?" Lina had noted the decor inside the suite. It was lush even to her off-world eyes: draperies, thick carpets and holographic accents, all tastefully done with elegant flair. "Won't it be expensive?"

"Hell, yes! We just stopped the invasion of Sarastor. Don't you think we deserve a little indulgence?" He picked her up in his arms. "Pick a suite. Pick any suite, as long as it's vacant for the night."

"Are you sure?"

"It's not every night a guy gets engaged." Jae grinned. He flew down the hallway with her, and then shut his eyes tight. "Pick one, go ahead."

"Oh! Jae, stop! Stop!" She clutched him, terrified that they were going to fly into a wall.

"Here? Okay." He set her down and moved his hand to the door's identi-plate.

"Are you sure about this?"

He pressed three fingers to the plate.

"This room is not signed out."

"This is Mega-Legion business," Jae told it. "Neutrino. Coordinate with Mega-Legion Operations. We want one full day, with an option for two."

A tiny blue light appeared somewhere deep within the plate. "Identity confirmed. We hope you have a pleasant stay, sir."

The room door slid open and Jae picked Lina up again before she could protest. "Darling!" he crooned. "Just like I've always dreamed!" He stopped once they were inside and then turned in a circle as the door closed behind him. "Shit, just look at this place! This must be–"

"The presidential suite?" Lina asked. Everything was so ornate, like something out of Louis XVI, not a simple piece in sight. Mirrors on the wall, gorgeous photo-paintings and holostatuary. Lavish furniture in a huge room, four wide double doors and an open archway leading into other rooms.

"Looks more like the imperial suite," Jae said, his voice hushed. Then he perked up and bounced her in his arms. "This way we'll all have our own room," he said. "Maybe we won't have to take shifts at that."

"Just find me a corner to lie down in and I'll be happy. I'm beat."

"Jet lag, eh?"

"I have been doing a little work tonight, not just running my mouth like a carnival barker. Oh, you had them going, Jae, you really did. That was wonderful!"

She blinked and giggled as Jae bounced her some more. The motion didn't seem to match up with gravity, as if time were wondrously out of synch with itself.

"I did have them tonight, didn't I?"

"They were hanging on your every word. Now you just put me down. I'm dizzy." Her body was very noticeably winding down now, sensing a comfortable bed somewhere in the area.

"Not until you choose. Which bedroom? Pick one. C'mon, pick one!" He swirled her in a circle, around and around, laughing at her as she screeched. "Pick one!"

"That one! That one!"

They both laughed as he stopped, swaying and catching himself, her still in his arms.

She clutched hard to him, afraid that he'd drop her or she'd unbalance and fall to the floor. "Oo... my brains feel like they're not connected anymore," Lina giggled. "Are you sure the prisoner is allowed to sleep outside of HQ?"

"Do you want to go back?"

"I don't think I could port, I'm so tired."

"And why should you want to when you could sleep here instead?" Jae asked. He strode over to the doors she'd chosen. They slid open at his approach. He stopped. "By all that's holy," he breathed.

"Oh my."

Inside was a room of carpeting and marble, of curtains around a large bed that sat high above the floor under an even higher ceiling. A tiered chandelier sparkling like a star cluster lit at their entrance. Beyond, a small room showed itself partially, enough to identify it as a bathroom before its door closed automatically. Over there were closets, over there drawers that folded back into the wall after displaying themselves.

"I don't care how much it costs!" Jae suddenly cried out. "We just stopped the biggest *kicking* invasion attempt that Sarastor has seen in an orb of a long time! Just the three of us!" He gave Lina a quick kiss of triumph and threw her at the bed. She managed to roll while clapping what little she wore to herself, but the sheer width of the bed would have stopped her eventually. "Not a shot fired." Jae hopped a Rocky dance in a circle, his fists in the air. "Nobody hurt! Hoo-hah!"

In the movie Rocky wore underwear so that his dance didn't let part of his body do its own, separate dance of triumph. Jae didn't seem to notice that those two flimsy panels of material didn't hide much.

He hopped into a cartwheel up to the mattress, and collapsed onto it as its softness stopped his momentum. Rolling over, he got up on his feet and began jumping on it like a trampoline, circling Lina. She screeched at the close calls and protected her head with her hands.

"Jae, you're crazy!"

"That's what they tell me," he chortled.

She rose up on her hands and knees, and still he hopped all around. "You're not going to let me get any sleep, are you?"

"I don't feel like sleeping!"

Lina rose unsteadily to her feet and lunged for him. "Find your own bed," she ordered.

He slipped by her.

"Let me get some sleep!"

Jae bounced around her. He grabbed at some of the petals that had stuck in her hair and sprinkled them like snow all over the bedspread. "I'm going to order some bubblywine," he declared.

"Jae–!"

"And you'll drink it. You can't be worried that it'll make you fall asleep if you already are."

"Incor… Incorrig…"

"Incorrigible," Jae said. "That's me."

She tackled him and they both fell to the mattress. Her hair came down in curling torrents as she wrestled with him. "Get off of my bed!" she demanded.

Jae rolled her over so he'd be on top. "You don't seem so sleepy to me, my little fiancée of a flower fairy."

He was leaning on locks of her hair. She tugged at them to free herself, but that loosened the ribbon that held the material closed at her shoulder. It was undone before she realized it, and they were still rolling on the bed. The material fell like a sheet of water down her shoulder. She grabbed for it.

"Oh, hell! Now see what you made me do?"

Jae laughed as she tied it up again, awkwardly reaching for the matching tie in the back. Lina scrunched away from him, backing up to the headboard. As soon as she'd tied it securely, Jae reached over and flicked the other ribbon undone.

"Oops."

"Jaaae!" Lina caught his hand and tried to tie at the same time, but now Jae tugged at the ribbon on her hip. She slapped him away. "Silly. Silly-billy-billy. Stop!"

He tried again, and she reached out and grabbed his hand, but she had to hold onto the loose shoulder with her other hand. "I said stop," she told him firmly, trying to focus her eyes.

He just grinned at her. "Think you've got me, huh?"

"Yes, I think I've got you. Now get out and let me sleep."

"No, no, no," he declared, and with her holding both his hands, he reached for her remaining shoulder ribbon with his teeth, catching it and pulling. It untied and the material quickly began to fall away.

Now he was the one holding her hands back from catching the material as it cascaded so gently down the slope of her, falling in a drape that left much of the top and side of her breast exposed.

He put firmer pressure on the hand at her hip and shook the one at her shoulder, until the ribbons there came loose. The gown rippled down her body to pool on her lap.

"Oh," she said, glancing down at herself. She looked up at him in time to see him pull the last ribbon from his own shoulders. His garment fell away.

"Oh," she said.

They knelt there examining what had happened, and then Lina reached out to brush a flower petal from the base of his neck. But her fingertips fastened to his skin as if of their own volition.

Weren't men's shoulders nice, so angular in a soft yet muscly way, calling out to be explored. She slid her hand from his neck to deltoid, and then traced his collarbone back to its center notch. Wonderingly she spread her hand against his warm, beautiful flesh.

His pulse pounded against her touch. She ran her palm over the firm muscle that covered his heart. Could she hear it from where she was? Could he hear hers?

It was only then that she met his eyes. They were dark and endless blue, like the sky over infinity.

"Oh," she said.

In one motion Jae pulled Lina to him, bringing her up to his level. Crushing his mouth to hers, he felt her arms wrap around his shoulders. He pulled her even closer so that their bodies meshed, her back bare under his hands, her belly and thighs crushed against his. Her breasts pressed to his chest, her heart drumming beside his.

Lina tangled her fingers in his hair with one hand, slithering across the layered muscles of his back with the other. Breathlessly they broke from it. He kissed along her jawline before returning to her mouth. Dizzy with passion, dizzy with lust, her breath came fast and hot as Jae moved from there down her body. It was so wonderful to touch skin and muscle, to feel someone holding her again, loving her again, just like she did with–

"Londo," she gasped. "Ohmigod, Jae, what are we doing?! Jae!"

A cloud of stim deprivation hung over her. She shook her head fiercely. *Wake up!*

They were lying on the bed now. Jae raised up to kiss her mouth even as his hands explored the length of her. His knee parted her legs. There was no mistaking what butted against her hip. "Lon will understand this," his hot breath whispered. "Believe me, Lina, Lon will understand."

"Lon will not! And neither will I!" What would get through to him? Ohmigod, he was kissing her again, and she was kissing him back! Their tongues were – She didn't have any control. It was as if she stood in the back of her head, watching her body act of its own accord. "Stop – Umph. The… the ad-admiral… He'll be wanting to–"

"No no, sweet. He knows that an engaged couple might want to take a little time to get to bed."

Wake up! Her fingers were numb, she couldn't seem to work them. The words that came out of her mouth weren't clear even to her. "J-Jae, I don't want to hurt you. Let me go. N-now!"

She managed to break out of his hold as he shifted on her. She turned to crawl away from him and the room spun around her. He reached for her. His grip on her was a little harder than Lon's: not fierce, but it was strong. The chandelier made rainbows on the back of her eyes.

"C'mon, baby," he purred to her. "Lon will understand. We're best friends. He wants us to do this. Relax, sweet." He pulled her back to himself, his mouth behind her ear. "Relax, baby." His hands squeezed her breasts, traveled over the front of her, down to the bottom of her belly and beyond. "You've never been with someone who really knew what he was doing, have you?" His voice was a familiar song.

"C'mon, baby," Lon's voice said. "Relax."

Lon's arms, Lon's strong, wonderful hands on her. Lon rolled her onto her back and his mouth met hers. Londo! Finally he was back! Her dearest, her love, her passion. His mouth moved down on her and she arched under his kisses on her breasts, his hands that were doing all kinds of wonderful things to her…

"Oh, Londo," she breathed, rifling his hair, encouraging him as he suckled so thoroughly.

"Londo will understand," someone murmured as Lon licked and kissed his way down her stomach. She keened and rose as his fingers found their way between her legs, searching until they pressed inside her.

"Lo-Lon…"

Something about the way Lina said the word penetrated Jae's consciousness. He looked up. Her eyes were closed, her lips parted, and he raised up to admire her before he took her.

She was beautiful, angelic and perfectly ripe. Soft and smooth under his hands, an other-worldly perfume in her marvelous hair. Her mouth was warm, moist and inviting, like another part of her was.

"Love you… Lon-do," she whispered.

He stopped at that. She hadn't opened her eyes again. Her breathing… It wasn't nearly as rapid as it should be. Great grigach, she was asleep! Falling asleep during this–!

He suddenly pulled up over her. Stims. She had been on stims, he didn't know how many. She was unconscious too quickly for it to have been anything other than that. He'd been on them enough to know how the sudden let-down was, how you could hallucinate if you'd taken too many – Almost like being extremely drunk.

Great orb. And he'd been about to take her. His friend. Oh shit, Londo's woman. Londo's wife. Suddenly he knew that Londo wouldn't understand, wouldn't tolerate any of this, not at all. Never tell Lon about this, never ever!

What had he been thinking!? He hadn't. His brain had turned off at the sight of Lina's bare shoulder – hell, it had just been a bare shoulder; what was he, some kind of schoolboy? – and another part of his body had taken over his thinking from there.

He had zero excuse for his actions.

Shit, *kick* and utter damnation. They hadn't done much here tonight, had they? They'd stopped in time, right? What had he done? How had he messed it all up?

Everything.

Gone to *skurny tak.*

Lina murmured in her sleep.

"I'm here, sweet," Jae whispered. "Let's just get you to bed, shall we? You can sleep now. I'm here."

"Lon…" she said, and her fingers clenched as if she were trying to reach for him.

Jae folded up her gown and put it on one of the pillows. Carefully, so carefully, he pulled the covers aside and laid her out on the sheets. He paused to gaze at her, to smooth her hair as it fell over the curve of a breast, one lock curling toward a pink nipple. He reached for the cover and tucked her in, put his clothes back on, then locked the suite behind him.

Lina woke when streams of sunlight cascaded against her closed eyes. Mm, such a wonderful evening with Londo. She pulled the covers over her head, blotting out the sun, and sensuously snuggled under the covers.

"None of that now!" a man told her.

"Lon?" she asked, peeking out from the covers to squint against the light. A figure was silhouetted there. "Oh. Wiley. Where's…" No, Lon couldn't be here. He wasn't expected back yet. Why had she thought he was here?

"Good morning," Wilder said cheerily, moving onto another bank of windows. "Time for everyone to be up and about." He touched something along the wall and abruptly a section of what looked like patterned wallpaper became another window overlooking the city, awash in morning sun.

"Is that real? I didn't know they had real windows on Sarastor," Lina said to stall for time. She was on Sarastor, she was in that hotel room they'd found. Lon wasn't here. She searched with her mind to make sure; no, he must still be in hyperspace. But last night… She started to pull the blanket off her and realized that she was naked.

Quickly she pulled the bedclothes up around her neck and shoulders. There on the pillow beside her was that gown thing they'd made her wear, folded very neatly. She couldn't remember doing that. She couldn't remember…

She put her fingers over her mouth, trying to sort through the images of last night. What…? It couldn't have been Lon. She'd left the admiral's suite with Jae. They'd gotten a Legion suite; she could remember that much. Just Jae and her, here. Wiley wasn't with them, was he? No.

Oh, jesus! She and Jae–! What had she done? How could she! But her gown had been folded up so neatly. People just didn't do that after they'd finished… finished having sex. Maybe it was all in her fevered imagination. Maybe. But parts of it seemed too real to be imagination. She could feel lips on hers, hands pressing into her skin, a male body lying on hers…

And if it were her imagination and she was imagining that she'd been with Jae instead of Lon, that was almost as bad as actually doing it. Wasn't it? Oh god!

"You've only been in Headquarters and at the Romaki Club." Wiley was replying to her comment about windows. "Many buildings on the planet have windows. How are you feeling today?"

She was furious at herself. Scared. "I've got the world's biggest headache," she replied irritably. "I've never channeled so much in my life. Remind me never to do that again."

"I can take care of it easily enough." Wiley reached into his belt and removed a small hypodermic, checked its contents and moved a dial. "Try this," he said as he aimed it at the vein in her throat.

"Ooh, yeah, thanks," she replied as it took immediate effect. It seemed a little easier to think now. Last night – maybe it was just her imagination, a dream of her Londo and not Jae.

"A stim now, minimal dose." Wiley gave her another shot. "And please note that next time you find yourself in a strange hotel room, you should order nightwear. Even here you have to remember your status. I thought you were going to be a proper fashion poster child. Do you need more stim? I'd rather not give you more if we can avoid it."

Sourly she rubbed the spot where the shot had gone in and then gathered the blanket up around her. "I think you're getting the wrong impression of me, Wiley. I never, ever took drugs before this. An occasional sinus pill, some cold medicine if I had the flu, but nothing else. Since I've been here I've been given more drugs than I have in my entire life." Maybe that was it, all the drugs in her system.

Wiley nodded and leaned down to examine an ornately-carved table. "That's something we'll have to watch out for, then. But we're in a situation here. We have to have you up and about."

"Yes, I know. How's it going?"

He straightened up. "They're taking a meal break right now. We figured we'd leave them alone so they could digest everything as well as their food and let them talk among themselves. Maybe some of them will sleep. They've been up all night."

"And how's their digestion so far?"

The door to the suite opened. Through the bedroom door Lina saw Jae walk in with an attendant who wheeled a food cart. Jae was no longer in his clinging robe, but rather a heavier version of it, linen instead of tissue paper. It reached to mid-thigh with soled, opaque tights under it so he wasn't showing nearly as much skin, although the taut, bare muscles of his arms were available to view as well as peeks through the sides. It was a daytime version of the outfit, as it were.

He looked like some kind of Greek god, young and golden and vigorous. Vigorous – as in someone who could jump on a bed as if it were a trampoline.

Lina's eyes followed him as he directed the attendant where to park the cart. Had they…? She thought she could taste his lips and tongue; she thought she could feel his fingers on her body. She thought… She thought she knew what that Greek god looked like underneath the tunic and tights. Aroused.

Whatever had happened, it had been far too much. Yet still she watched him as he showed the attendant to the door. He moved as confidently as Lon, but in a different way. Lon's walk was powerful and solid. Jae's was a slow dance like that of a hunting animal. Dangerous. Even to his so-called friends.

"They're definitely not panicky," Wilder said about the Aldierrans. "We've been careful to make no threatening moves. I think we can conclude that their invasion plans have been thrown for a loop, but that they're trying to roll with the blow and come up with another approach. We need you in there to channel some more, toss them off-balance again until our defense systems all come on line."

"Great," she said unenthusiastically.

Jae stood next to the door to her room, barely inside. "Are you going to get up sometime and get dressed?" he asked her, and his eyes settled on the bare shoulder above the blanket. Lina shifted the blanket quickly back into place. Jae's gaze came up, met hers and then looked quickly away. Guiltily away.

Ohmigod. Oh. My. God.

She could feel his thoughts now, thoughts that he imagined he had hidden but that he was broadcasting at primal power. Passionate thoughts of her in his arms, their lips and fingers on each other, of her naked as she swooned with lust, of him–

Stop it, Jae! Not even in your thoughts. You're broadcasting!

Lina deliberately turned her head away from him and faced Wiley. "I hope that you have another outfit lined up for me. This–" she lifted the corner of last night's outfit " – is just a little more revealing than I'm used to, despite what you've seen me in. Things have been unusual lately."

"I brought something along." Wiley motioned to a pile in another chair. "It's a Feithi style like the one you wore last night."

Jae's voice whispered in her mind, **So I can't even think now.**

No. Go away! Get out of here!

Wiley scratched his head as he finished thoughtfully fluffing some draperies that ran along the far wall. He seemed fascinated by all the frou-frouery in the room. "I'm going to eat and then I'm going to go to bed. This suite may be questioned on our accounts, but it was a good idea. It's within shouting distance of the Aldierrans. And by the orb, I think we deserve a little something after all we've been through. What did you get us for breakfast, Jae?"

"Something to go with the place," Jae replied easily. He didn't look at Lina. "Crepes and tuddlies, leaf lichens and bubblywine."

Wiley laughed at that. "I can just feel Andri's grip on my arm now as she drags me into her office."

"Tough," Jae grinned. He glanced at Lina and the grin faded away.

"You two go have your breakfast," Lina said. "I want to take a shower." She sneered the word at Jae and Wiley didn't notice.

"Make if fast; we have things to discuss," Wiley said. The outer door buzzed. "I'll get that," he said.

"I'll make sure that Lina knows how the bindings on these clothes go," Jae called after him. Wiley grunted assent as the room door slid shut behind him.

"You'll do no such thing," Lina hissed. "Get out!"

18

"Lina, Lina," Jae pulled his hand through his hair and grimaced. "About last night."

"Yes, last night!"

"I'm sorry. I am so sorry. I didn't realize you'd been on so many stims."

"And you thought I'd do something like that if I weren't? My god, Jae, I don't even know–"

"Listen. We've only got a few minutes here. I know it sounds really stupid, but I've been thinking–"

"Your thinking is pretty stupid these days," Lina flashed.

"I've been thinking," he glared at her, "and I don't think that Londo will be that upset at this."

"He… He won't be…?!"

"I really don't think so. I'll explain it so he won't be. You let me tell him. I'm going to hold you to this. Mine is the blame–"

"You bet your ass it is."

"That's right. I'll tell him."

"I am his wife. It's my duty to inform him of any… any indiscre – Oh, god, oh, god!" The tears welled up in her eyes and she turned to bury her face in the pillow.

He caressed her bare shoulder. "Lina, Lina, it's going to be okay."

"Get your *hand* off me," she growled into the pillow, and he snatched it away. "Now get the hell out of here before I start screaming!"

"Wiley's wondering what I'm doing," he murmured. "We will continue this discussion later. Get your shower. Everything's going to be all right; I personally guarantee it. Hurry now. Before Wiley begins to suspect."

Wiley! Mustn't drag him in on this. "The bindings," she had the presence of mind to mention.

"Oh yeah. They're just like mine." Jae made sure she was looking at him as he turned around for her to see. She nodded, sniffling. "Make it quick," he repeated and exited.

"Try the tuddlies, Lina. They're the best I've ever had," Wiley said as she joined them. Her bindings were not done well. They were coarse and didn't look like the fine webwork Jae wore. Lina didn't really care.

She didn't feel like eating, but her stomach betrayed her; it was ravenous. She'd thrown up in the bathroom sink – the only place she could find among the Sarastoran plumbing to throw up in – and had tried over and over to brush Jae's foul kisses out of her mouth.

They were still there, polluting her.

"Bubblywine?" Wiley held the bottle towards her empty glass.

"It'll put me to sleep," she said, her voice barely audible.

He glanced at her face. "Aren't you feeling well today?"

"It must be all that channeling." She tried to give him a little smile. "I'm not used to it. I feel very… raw today. This on top of everything else…" She studiously kept her eyes from Jae.

Wiley nodded and paid attention to his plate. The news was on behind Jae so Wiley could look up and see it. "No mention about us; that's good. We spotted two leaks last night and stanched them. I think we got them all."

"Any other Legion teams due to hit return hyperspace today?" Jae asked.

Wiley shook his head. "Late tonight or early tomorrow. It's hard to be sure who's due back when that we have an interstellar teleporter we can use," he smiled at Lina, "but full teams are still at least fifteen hours off. I don't think that's an accident. I think the Aldierrans had a very thorough plan to keep the Legion busy while they proceeded with this. Among other things, it will be interesting to see who triggered the Rimhold riot."

He spooned a hearty sample from a puffed-up dish. "But frankly, Jae, I don't think we're going to need any other help here. I think we've got this thing taken care of." He offered the dish to Jae, who sniffed it and then helped himself generously.

Jae said, "We'll make sure of that today. Get everything glued up in a tight weld."

Wiley chuckled. "The best part is, they never knew what hit them. Stop fiddling with that, Lina."

"Isn't there any way we can get by with some real clothes?" she asked. "I mean with real material, not plastic wrap? Maybe something that has sides to it?"

This time her tunic was downright Victorian next to the outfit of last night. It was shorter, but she could wear the skin-colored soled tights with this since there was a belt of sorts to hide the top of them. Soled tights, she had to admit, were nice. Comfortable, not like pantyhose at all. She could live in these better than jeans. The tunic reached just above her knees, and the gaps in the sides weren't nearly as wide as the earlier version. Instead of ribbons that were so easy to untie, this had wide, sturdy bands that wrapped around and buckled with tiny braids of yarn hanging down as decoration. On Jae the bands were expanded as dark spiderwebs that thoroughly defined his body.

"I still feel exposed in this outfit," Lina said. She couldn't wear a bra with this. Although it didn't cling anywhere near as much as the outfit of the night before, the bumps of her nipples were still clearly evident. She wasn't used to bouncing around in public.

"It'll work in our favor," Wiley said, absently waving his spork. "We're working with a group of males. They can't help but be distracted by a little female flesh. I'll take every diversion I can get."

"Easy for you to say," Lina grumbled as she took some more of the flaky things from the covered dish.

They spoke of tactics and possible tactics from there. It was Greek to Lina. She listened carefully, trying to see the logic behind certain points so she wouldn't mess up anything. It helped her in trying to think of anything except what had happened last night.

"Whatever you can come up with to keep them off-balance but still not threatened – Do it," Wiley said in summary. "We're not only stalling to figure a way out this, but if we can stall until the Coronasphere Shell can be reconfigured by my people, or the rest of the Legion comes back, we'll have some real firepower on our side in case we need it."

"Let's hope we don't," Jae said. He poured himself another glass of bubblywine.

"I don't think we will. At least, if you keep your consumption of the wine down."

"I can handle it," Jae muttered, but Lina noticed that he only took a couple of sips from this glass.

"Unless something extraordinary happens today," Wiley dabbed his napkin at the sides of his mouth, "we have just averted a major war. Oh, it wouldn't have lasted long, but how long does it take to kill a few billion people?"

"So this is your way of telling me not to screw things up for you?" Lina asked miserably.

"Not in the least." Wiley looked a little surprised that she'd say that. "You've done very well. Excellently well so far. I have all confidence that you'll continue to do good work. You seem to have very well-developed verbal people skills. Perhaps that's to be expected of someone who had an aversion to touch for so long. Maybe that's something I can research, an interesting avenue…"

"And he's off." Jae grinned at his friend, lost in his own world of concepts.

Wiley's attention returned to them. "That's a good idea," he said. "I'm off to bed. Give me twenty-five minutes before you need me to call me."

"Right," Jae told him and returned to finishing his breakfast as Wiley wandered over to a room whose door was open.

"I must record some decorating notes here," Wiley commented absently. "These rooms are really quite extraordinary." The door closed behind him.

Jae stopped in mid-bite. "Lina."

"I'm not speaking to you. I don't even know if I should press charges or not. Whatever, I want you to stay away from me. I don't talk to you, you don't talk to me. I don't come near you and you don't come near me. Do you have that?" She threw her napkin on the table and jumped up to pace, wringing her hands. "God! What have I done?"

The television disappeared with a gesture from Jae as she glared at him and his bland mask of a face. How dare he not look remorseful! "And what have you done?! How could you do that! The one thing I remember clearly is saying 'no.' Sarastor is run by rules. How is that there's no rule against… Against…"

Tears spilled from her eyes. She had betrayed Londo! She'd broken her promise to him! Lina wept bitterly at her own shallow nature. Dad had been right, damn him to hell! She was a whore at heart.

She whirled in a maelstrom in the center of a lightless universe made of her own betrayal. "God!" she screamed. She couldn't stop crying. She didn't want to stop. She fell in upon herself until she felt Jae pull her into the bedroom.

"Get your hands OFF!" She began to call him every evil name she knew, but still he dragged her as she struggled. Through the bedroom, into the bathroom. Doors closed as they passed.

"Be quiet!" he ordered. "Let me explain!"

And she told him exactly what she thought of him, stripping every last barrier of politeness from her speech, livid with the very idea of–

He shook her. It felt as if he'd splashed ice-cold water on her face.

"Lina!" he shouted. She cursed him between sobs as he shook her some more.

The ice water splashed through her veins. Shock ran up her spine and she gasped. Another splash; she was freezing with sobriety. The tears had stopped. She saw Jae through crystal-clear vision now.

"What the hell did you do to me?" she demanded.

"You were hysterical. I just calmed you down. I changed your blood chemistry. By the grigach's hairy balls, Lina, Wiley could have come out and seen you like that!"

"So?" Lina shook herself into some semblance of order. "Wouldn't he like to know what a–"

"You've already told me what I am," Jae spat. "I don't need to know any more." His hands still dug into Lina's upper arms and he shook her again. "Now you listen to me and you listen good. You have a role to play today. Four billion people are counting on you putting on a good performance. Four billion, Lie!"

She started to say something but stopped. Four billion. Sarastor was in the midst of an invasion.

"That's right." Jae pressed his face into hers. "Four billion human beings, each with a right to live, and they might all be killed if we slip up. They need you to be charming and sweet and pretty in front of Admiral Bracken and his men. They don't need you slobbering in some corner, crying, 'Boo hoo, I made a mistake and my husband's going to be upset!' They're going to be more than upset if you fuck this up, sweet. They're going to be *dead*. And who knows which world will fall after Sarastor falls? How many more billions will die because you can't suck it in and hold it for one or two more days?"

Lina's lower lip trembled violently, but that was all the outer emotion she allowed.

He shook her again. "Can you do it? You'd better damned well–"

"Stop shaking me!" she demanded. "And get your stinking hands off me! I can do it. I can be your little puppet in front of them."

Warily Jae dropped his hands, searching her face. "You can't let them even suspect–"

She stared him down. "I can wear as many masks as you, Jaeson Rallene. I can pretend and step back and put off things for another time. But believe me, that time will come. You're going to get yours when this is all over."

"Yes, yes," Jae said. "I'll get mine. Now let's–"

Lina spun him around from where he'd turned away. "You aren't listening." Her voice rasped low and dangerous. "I'm very serious. I'm going to do some research into just how bad your crime was, and I'm going to make you see what–"

"I've been threatened by a lot worse than you," he sneered, "and for better reasons. Not because they wanted me and I let them get everything that they'd been dreaming of!"

Lina drew back her hand and swung it at Jae's cheek. He caught it just before it struck. "Legionnaire," he smiled so grimly at her. "You can't touch me. You're just an amateur – less than an amateur."

"And you are a cold-hearted bastard!" Lina hissed. "I never, ever wanted you. You just don't want to take the blame. You made a pass at me, maybe a couple, before last night and I may have been too stupid to recognize them as passes, but they were your passes and not mine! So don't blame me. Don't try to weasel out of your own cowardice behind your spoiled Legionnaire facade!

"You've always been too rich, too powerful, too beautiful. People god-damn worship you here, and you smile and take it. And it's sunk in. 'Oh, I'm Mr. Perfect Neutrino, the Last Holy Feithi. Everyone adores me, everyone looks the other way whenever I do anything wrong. And if I want to blame someone else for something I did, that's my prerogative.'" She sank into a deep curtsy. "Oh, do kick me again, your majesty!"

"Shut up!"

She looked up in triumph at him glaring down at her. "What's the matter, Jae?" she asked. "Is the only way you can have fun in bed anymore by switching from guys once in a while, just for the variety? By getting a friend flat-out drunk first so they don't realize what you're doing? Is your life so boring, Mr. Dangerous Legion-naire?"

"Shut up, shut up!" He whirled from her, but faced her in the mirror as she rose up behind him.

"Why don't you just play your trump card?" she smiled at him, her eyes slices of green fury. "'Oh, Stoan, she took over my mind. I couldn't help myself. She sure is one hell of a mind controller after all. Let's put her in jail and throw away the key!'"

Jae's fists opened and closed.

"'No, I've got a better idea, Stoan. Let's annul the marriage as well. Let's let Londo be a real Sarastoran Legionnaire again and–'"

"Shut up! Damn it, I'm in love with Londo!" Jae burst out. He turned, supporting himself on the sink behind him with shaking arms. "I'm in love with Londo and I've always been in love with him and goddam, now you two are *married*." His voice fell to a terrifying whisper. "Married!"

Were those tears? Lina couldn't move as she watched Jae squirm in his own agony.

"He knows. I told him years ago. And he still had me perform the ceremony." Jae's mouth worked. "He knew… He knew that would stop me from causing trouble later. He could point at me and say, 'But you presided, Jae. You have to approve.' God, he can be cruel!"

He pulled his hair down into his face. "I tried to hate you, I really did. But leave it to Londo to marry a version of himself. He's an egomaniac, you know. He'd do something like that. By the orb, you're just like him!"

"Me?" Lina squeaked.

The quick laugh was harsh and bitter. "Yes. You crazy Terran bastard barbarians! You're not afraid of anything, not down deep where it counts. You're not afraid to tell people exactly what they are. You show them how they're fooling themselves with all their pretentious shammery."

He wiped his hands slowly down his face as he met her eyes. "And you sing. You sing the sweetest love songs and you look into people's hearts and try to help. And last night…" He choked. "Last night I was crazy and you were barely dressed and so soft and warm and willing and…" His gaze fell on the floor now. "And it was my fault. All of it, every last bit."

Lina couldn't say anything, but a left-over sniff escaped her and Jae shook his head.

"If you only knew how sorry I am about last night, Lina. I–" His voice caught. He bit his lip, shook his head. "I don't want to hurt either you or Lon. Look, if you won't let me be the one to tell him, at least let's tell him together. So I can assure him that… that nothing really happened."

Nothing happened? "How much nothing?" Lina quickly asked.

"I – Great orb, I can't tell you what I want to tell you! Londo said – Damn! How can I convince you that Lon's not going to make as much of this as you think he will? You just don't understand. It's going to be all right for you. Me, Lon may never want to see again. I don't know. But I swear to you, I'll make it right. I don't want anything to mess up your marriage to Lon. Not in the least."

"I'm… sorry," was all Lina could think to say. How must it be for him? How long had he lived with this secret? That night that she'd thought that Londo was forevermore denied to her – She'd almost gone crazy. And yet Jae had had to live with that situation for years. He'd have the rest of his life to live with it. A lifetime without Londo.

"I don't want your pity." He stared at himself in the mirror. "It's so different from what I thought it would be. I thought I'd be jealous of you. I've been in love with Londo since… well, since we first met."

"But he does know?"

"Yes, yes, he knows. I told him a long time ago. But I've managed to be just… good friends with him for quite some time now. Has he… He hasn't told you any of this?"

"No." Lina stood quietly by the shower compartment. She could understand being in love with Londo.

"Londo is the love of my life." Jae hit the wall with his fist and let it remain there. "You might say I worship him, except that I know he's human. I know all his weaknesses and failings, but they're a part of him, and I love them for being a part of him. Do you understand that?"

Lina nodded.

"So I thought I'd be jealous when you came along. I *was* jealous when you came along, when those other women – He's told you about–?"

"I know there have been other women," Lina said, "poor Aiko especially. But you could never be intimate with Lon with his powers, Jae, no matter what he felt for you."

"No. Grigach, no."

"And then I came along. Where do I fit in in this?"

"By the orb itself, I don't know. All I know is that we've been holed up together, so close now for days. And every time I look at you, I know that you're Londo's, that you're a part of him. And last night… Things were crazy. Things were wonderful, and I went a little crazy. A lot crazy. I'm so sorry."

Lina's head hurt. "I understand. I think I do. But Lon and I are married. We took vows; you were the one who read them to us. Forsaking all others–"

"Wasn't in the vows." He smiled weakly at her in the mirror. "Feithi vows, different from Earth's. You haven't broken any promise."

"But it was implied in a marriage between two Terrans. Terran marriage means monogamy. It isn't a case of just vows. It's commitment, too. Trust."

"Lon doesn't trust anyone," Jae said.

"He trusts me."

They regarded each other.

Abruptly Jae frowned and straightened up, briskly brushing his hair out of his face with his hand. "But all that has nothing to do with now. What I need is cooperation," he said. "I've had one planet die on me, and it's not going to happen again. If I have to drug you up to make you into a player, I will and no one will charge me with anything afterwards. Can you do it, or do I order the drugs?"

"I… Yes, I can do it," Lina replied. She'd have to, wouldn't she? "But afterward–"

"Yes yes, afterward, whatever." Jae brushed it off like a mosquito. "What we have to worry about is now. We're fiancés, remember. We have to act that way. Happy, in love, glad to see the Aldierrans, fa la la. Wash your face; you're all blubbery."

Lina let the cold water revive her as Jae tutored her on his plan, which was different from what he'd been discussing with Wiley. Jae's was a little more daring – keep the enemy off balance, unprepared; use misdirection – and yet there was always the caution that the moment they thought any one of the enemy was becoming uncomfortable, they'd retreat back down to a safe level. Back them off, distract them, take them out on tangents, get them away from Sarastor. Nothing but nothing must endanger Sarastor!

Lina pinned her hair absently.

"Room service," Jae said to the bathroom ceiling. Two beeps. "Send up a large handful of flower petals."

After a pause, a human female voice asked, "Flower petals, sir?"

"Flower petals," Jae repeated. "Pink or white or a mixture. It doesn't matter what type."

Two beeps, and Jae smiled to himself. "I bet that's the first time they've gotten a request like that. You're not going to wear your hair that way."

Lina put her hand to the back of her head automatically. She'd worn a chignon today, hair up and out of the way. "What's the matter with it?"

"It's too efficient. Most of your job today is distraction. Hair down. Comb your fingers through it when we're with them. I don't know – shake it around a bit. Do you have any perfume here? Your hair doesn't smell like it usually does."

"Perfume?" Lina blinked. "That's not perfume, that's my shampoo. No perfume." She'd never owned any.

"Room service," Jae ordered. "A small bottle of perfume. With female pheromones and a masking light, floral scent." Two beeps.

"Jae, I'm not sure what it is you think I can do, but I've never–"

"You're going to today. Keep it subtle. Even one of us stupid males can see past an act if it's carried too far. But you'd be surprised what you can get away with."

"Should I sit in the admiral's lap?" Lina asked sarcastically.

"If it means saving four billion people, yes." Jae leaned back on the sink, studying her. "But I think if you are just as charming as you possibly can be, you'll have done your job very well."

Lina swallowed. How would Sofia Vergara do this? No, subtle. Keira Knightley. Maybe a little more than that. One of those horrible Bond girls. God. Angels, help her!

She stared at herself sickly in the mirror as Jae reminded her of where the seifer com tubes were kept, and that Lina would have to port them directly to him if he needed them.

Jae began fiddling with the bindings of Lina's costume. "Here," he said, and stretched them out. They were a webbing like his with decorative braids, that he pulled out from the coarse bands.

"Stop it!" Lina demanded. She slapped his hands away from her breasts.

"I was just adjusting."

"The hell you were. Just tell me how it goes and I'll do it."

Soon they were a matched pair, at least in general ambiance. Jae touched his earring and its color changed to match the grayish blue of his outfit. He watched Lina in the mirror.

"What?" she demanded.

"I'm wondering if we shouldn't get you something a little…" he waved his hands at her Feithi outfit, "less."

"And I'm beginning to think that the Feithi were not the paragons of virtue everyone thinks they were."

He leaned in close, giving her an evil grin. "Be happy I haven't told you to lose the tights," he said.

A soft tone sounded in the air. "Room service is here," Jae explained to her, and soon returned with a bowl of flower petals and a small black bottle. He spritzed it into the air and sniffed the fallout. "Not bad," he pronounced.

Lina paid attention to the mirror. She was trying for a mini-braid down one side of her hair, just to match the braids on the outfit. And to keep her nervous hands busy. "Why aren't you primping?" she asked.

"Because we're facing some macho straight types."

"Don't be too sure about that. Lieutenant Fadero seemed very interested in watching you last night, and not from a militaristic viewpoint."

"Fadero?" Jae looked into the mirror and reexamined his teeth. He decided to use the room's sonic toothbrush and regarded the result critically. "They all seem to be the type who'd be impressed with someone who wore a lot of weaponry. Too bad we come in peace." He ran a finger along the line of his arm above his flight wristband, and something about the gesture caught Lina's eye.

"You have a weapon," she accused him. Had he been smoothing down something just under his skin? Was the line of that muscle not quite right?

"Four billion people, Lie."

"Give me the damn petals," she said, and ported in more hair pins from home.

Jae helped her with them in back. "Wiggle a little every now and then," he told her. "Make it look natural. You've got the goods; you should let them jiggle. Think ice cubes. Hold their attention." He glanced into the mirror and saw her redden. "Blushing's good, too. The ol' virginal look gets 'em every time."

"They seemed to me to have been at sea a long time. They were–"

"Horny as hell," Jae grinned at her from behind. "So you're our ace in the hole."

"You want me to do more than sit on the admiral's lap."

He took her by the shoulders. "This is war. In war you use the weapons at your disposal. Our mission today is to distract, distract, and distract. We're buying time, looking for a loophole to come our way."

"I'm not a whore, Jae. No matter what you might think."

He dropped his hands immediately. "I never said you were. That never entered my mind."

"You want me to sleep with the admiral."

"I'm just mentioning it as a possibility."

She shook her head even as she began to tremble. "I can't do it. There's no way I can even come close."

"Lina…"

"I can't! Oh god, help me! I'm sorry, Jae. I'm so sorry–" She clapped her hands over her mouth.

He touched her shoulders again and rubbed. "That's okay, sweet. You can only do what you can."

"Don't you know any… women who would? You get some *pretty* women in that room and you wouldn't have any trouble at all."

"Even those stupid lieutenants would spot that trick," Jae told her. He turned her around so they faced each other. "Listen to me. Listen! If I have a minute, maybe two minutes, to work, I can kill them if it comes down to it, with no evidence left. If I have less than a minute, I have weapons hidden on me that can fry them to cinders. As soon as we step into their room, I'm activating communications that will keep us in constant contact with Sarastor Planetary Defense systems, so that if I do have to do anything, those systems can attack the fleet, ready or not." He shook her. "In war you do what you have to do. This is them against us. Their war fleet against four billion innocent civilians."

"So what does one person count for?" Lina asked weakly.

"Sometimes one person can change the balance of power, knock it for a loop."

"Have you ever had to knock anything for a loop?" She looked up at him.

He frowned. "You aren't supposed to ask things like that."

"Have you?"

"Yes. Yes, damn it. And I came through, and it worked, and I don't have to apologize for it!"

"It upset you."

"Of course it upset me. I wouldn't be human if it didn't."

"Oh." She turned away from him. It was normal to be upset. Not like in the movies, where people fell into bed with strangers and acted as if it were the most erotic experience of their lives, or else be completely untouched by it all. It was okay to be nervous, to not want to do it. "This is an absolute last-ditch gambit? I mean, I could port the admiral into one of Wiley's bomb rooms, and that would put him out of business without doing him any harm."

"Kidnapping," Jae nodded. "Good. That's a possibility."

She shook her head weakly. "Kidnapping. Well, there's always poisoning, too. Enough to make them sick. Rat poison in the banana pudding. We could say there were bad germs on Sarastor. It's hard to invade when you have the runs."

"You're tricky. I like that. Subtlety may be the best course here. Okay, if we have to resort to the poison, just tell me and I can adjust some of the food compounds. The poisons I'm carrying are too quick and lethal. We keep in touch the entire time, mentally. You can do that?"

She nodded as she checked the final hair petals, knowing she was pale.

"All right. We telepathically discuss possibilities before we carry them out, and we rely on trickery first if things get down to the wire." He paused. "And whatever you do, whatever you do, Lina – Don't tell Lon without me there. As soon as he gets back – No, I suppose not then. When you two come out and meet the world again, tell him that I have something to tell him, and we'll clear the air of this once and forever. Understand?"

"I'll think about it."

He leaned over her from the back, leaned so that he pressed against her most of the way down, dominating her. He glared into her eyes in the mirror. "I mean it. You're coming out of this unscathed, do you hear me?"

"You can say that all you want," she said softly, "but in the end, it'll be Lon's decision."

"He'll decide what I want him to decide."

"A little mind control?"

"If it comes down to it. Now hit the makeup kit. We need to go. Every minute we give them is another minute they have to come up with an alternate plan."

"Neutrino!" a man's voice came from mid-air.

"Neutrino here," Jae replied, shushing Lina. "I take it they're ready for us?"

"I just left them, sir. They're expecting you."

"We're on our way."

They hurried to the Aldierrans' room, slowing down for the last bend of thick-carpeted hallway. Jae held Lina's hand tightly, and her arm brushed up against his where those weapons had been secreted. It felt like normal skin to her.

*******That's because it's made from my skin,******* he told her. *******Here we are. By now they'll have some spy eyes outside their doors. They can see and hear us.*******

"I wonder if they're up," he said aloud.

"I'm sure they are," Lina replied, surprised her teeth weren't chattering. "It's such a lovely day. Who could sleep in? Or has everyone been bothering them all night and keeping them awake?"

"Wiley may have done just that, darling. You know how excited he was."

"Then they're probably sick of sitting around. Do you think they'd like to go for a walk while we talk? Oh, do you suppose they've had breakfast yet? I hear this hotel has wonderful tuddlies. Let's order tuddlies for them."

Jae's eyes narrowed ever so slightly at her, measuring the veracity of her performance when the doors to the Aldierran suite opened.

"Good morning!" Jae bowed to them all. The admiral sat next to Fadero on a plush couch while the others ate at a small dining table. A breakfast buffet had been set up for them away from the conversation seating. There was a larger conference table set in the suite's office or study space.

"It's so nice to see you all again." Lina smiled, hoping it looked genuine. "Did you get some tuddlies?"

After some small talk, they all moved to the conference area. The group of officers looked pleasant enough, but with grim undertones. Down to business at last, perhaps? Fresh tricks up their sleeves?

As the men took their seats around the conference table, Lina decided upon the role of French maid. That wasn't quite how Jae had explained it, but she'd seen it done enough on videos. Thank goodness they didn't have her in six-inch you-know-what-me heels. She bustled about serving hot drinks, offering breakfast add-on snacks as they talked. She silently conversed with each one's guides as she made her way around the table, relaying to Jae what she'd learned.

As she tried to remember the gist of the great heroine Olympia's last book on feminist goals for the modern millennium, Lina made sure she leaned over deeply whenever she served someone. She arched her back when she stood up, and paid attention to planting her feet directly in front of each other when she walked, causing her to swing. Men liked it when women walked funny.

Jae gave her silent prompts to complement the show he was presenting. At least he took most of the attention off her. Jae had been overly-blessed with the gift of gab and didn't mind rambling off on unrelated topics whenever they occurred to him.

It drew out the dialogue, but Jae kept his digressions humorous and entertaining before he would suddenly come back to topic. Typical Gemini: a real smooth talker who could make people feel at home. Someone who could talk you into doing anything. And his Piscean energy let him keep track of two different directions at once. Lina channeled from higher entities while he blathered, transmitting to him pieces of Aldierran information that he fit into the conversation.

Aldierra seemed to be a world already seething with war, of might makes right. It felt claustrophobic to her; did it have a high population? Maybe they were looking for more land to spread out.

She became aware of a small stab of alarm as Jae realized that the admiral and his men were paying most interest in a pattern of tours that, if taken by several crews, would set Aldierrans around some key Sarastoran military centers.

They hadn't called their invasion off. They had merely altered the plans for it.

After a while everyone took a break. She refreshed the drinks and brought in a new round of snacks, giving each of the Aldierrans their own special smile.

One of the lieutenants dropped a napkin. "Let me," she said and bent over from the waist to pick it up. She caught him sharing a smirk with the man behind her as she straightened up: a conspiracy at work. Gloria Steinem forgive her!

One of the officers didn't know how some of the snacks were eaten. Lina asked Jae silently, and then leaned over the lieutenant's arm to show him how you cracked it open first with a tiny sonic hammer instead of trying to bite into something too big. His arm brushed up against her breasts. "That's it," she cooed. "You have the hang of it now." And she was going to take a long, hot shower to wash him off her when this was over!

Easy, Lina, or I'm going to have to peel him off you.

So Jae was paying attention to her as well as the admiral. Jae was more adept than he seemed at times. Dangerous.

Lina found a chair to keep hostess watch from and perched on it with her legs crossed. That gave everyone a good view of her hip and legs.

She smiled at another of the officers. This one's name was Bartok, like the composer, mousy brown hair and gray eyes that almost never got up to her face. He asked about the population of Sarastor and she told him four billion as she tried to imagine the faces of those people. Ernst and everyone at the Terran Zone. ZoBois and her gang. Derainjt. Dari Signet and her little boy. The No-Talent Quartet. People who could be dead if she didn't play her part.

When Bartok put his hand on her knee, Lina didn't slap it off. Instead, she told him about the interesting customs of Sarastor, and how perhaps they should send cultural representatives to explain them to the crew of the Aldierrans' ships before they began shore leave, just so there'd be no unfortunate misunderstandings.

She recounted public beheadings by guillotine of men who had sexually harassed women. The women sat on the front row of the crowds and watched their harassers die while they knitted, laughing all the while.

"I'm afraid that some of us can be cruel at times, but only when provoked," Lina said in a very sorry voice, shaking her head sadly. "Of course, we would understand that the Aldierrans are new to our culture, and thus a little leeway could be allowed… to a point. I'll have Ms. Yency from Sarastor Protocol call on your people to explain, would that be allowed? Such a patient and understanding lady, Ms. Yency."

His hand stayed within the confines of his chair after that.

Another lieutenant came over and asked about the galactic geography of the AffSys, what some of the more interesting worlds were. This Aldierra must be very far away, Lina thought, for them not to be familiar with the AffSys. She tried to remember what she had learned from her study padd. Certainly that was general knowledge and wouldn't harm anything.

Unfortunately, she hadn't paid much attention about other planets and so began to tell them of the very interesting worlds of Qo'noS, the heart of the brutal but honor-bound Klingon race, and Vulcan, which was home to a people who believed only in logic. Gallifrey's populace liked to experiment with time itself, while the cold world of Darkover relied on a sword-based weaponry system because the world had been cut off from the AffSys for centuries. The Aldierrans seemed to be swallowing it all, so Lina told them about ancient, arid Mars with its almost-extinct three-legged aboriginal race and cute but prolific flatcats…

The talks wore on. No matter how they tried to divert the Aldierrans, they gravitated to tours of military installations. Jae acknowledged the admiral's hints but then led him back to parks, entertainment and recreation opportunities. His infopadd projected images of locations where young single women frequented. One seemed to be the pools at UNC where Jae had somehow captured some footage of those college girls in their bikinis. To balance that he also showed them the swim meet with the almost-naked men.

When Lina glanced over to Jae, he paused in talking to the admiral and the other aides and looked at her. He held her for a moment in his gaze, suspended alone within its endless blueness, before someone speaking her name snapped her back to greet workers bringing lunch.

The sheer volume of food set the invasion on hold all by itself. Lina wondered if Wiley had noticed, and thus ordered so much. These people seemed unable to step away from the table. They kept shoveling food into their mouths, even when they were talking.

Most were on the gaunt side. Had they been on short rations?

Lina thought that if she could steer them to enough simple carbs, they'd all pass out in a sugar coma. That would certainly put a crimp in their plans.

But three of the men clustered up around her at the service cart, their breaths on her neck and shoulders, their bodies rubbing up against hers. At least Aldierrans didn't tower over her, but someone had his hand on her ass! She felt the familiar white wall of panic starting to think about crashing down, felt her skin begin to recede. She felt so… whorish.

"How long have you been on your ships?" She tried to make the question light, even though her throat was constricting. It must have been ages for them if they were actually interested in her. She couldn't remember seeing any Sarastoran female officers.

"All too long," Capt. Liji said. "We would be pleased and honored if you would join Lieutenant Dayzen and me in my bedroom here for thirty minutes or so." He ran his thumb and forefinger down the seam on the side of her tunic, letting his knuckles rub her breasts. The third man, Lieutenant Fadero, had a sour look on his face, but Lina didn't think it was because of the public proposition. These men certainly wouldn't take "no" for an answer. She couldn't claim at being married because they thought she was only engaged to Jae. Would hiding behind a man be a good enough excuse for them?

"Ah, I think I should–"

"Forgive me, darling Lina." Jae came up to her from behind and slid his arm around her waist. He gently bumped Liji off her. Jae let his hand casually travel down to her hip to hold her there and she tried not to shiver. The other men backed off. "I'm beginning to feel a little jealous that you're paying so much attention to our guests."

"Don't be silly," she told him, thanking all the powers that be for his presence. "It's my pleasure to serve."

"And you're doing very well," Jae told her. "But I think the admiral feels neglected. Perhaps you could go cheer him up. He needs a refill on his tarn, too, if you would."

And what if he asks me to go into his bedroom?

Then do so, and stall, stall, stall. Redecorate the place. Call for room service. I'll see what I can do.

Saltpeter in the tarn.

That's a definite idea. But right now their minds are not on making war. Go charm the admiral, Lina. He thinks too much, unlike these louts.

The cunning admiral was indeed brooding, thinking, planning. He stood isolated on the other side of the room in front of one of the screens showing a world map.

She filled a cup with fresh tarn and took it to him, walking slowly, crossing her feet in front of each other to make sure she swung sufficiently, but careful not to slosh the cup. Behind her Jae was talking intensely to Lieutenant Fadero.

"So have you decided when your first crew will visit?" Lina asked, handing the tarn to the admiral. He took it and sat down in a plush chair built for lounging. "To tell you the truth, I'm going a little stir-crazy just being in this cramped old room for a little while. I can't imagine what your crew is going through."

He smiled, but not in his eyes. His mind was active on other thoughts. "They are used to being ship bound for long periods of time. Months."

"How horrible!" Lina let herself shiver for effect and his glance traveled down from her face. "Well, it's time they got out, don't you think? Think of us here as wanting to be your family away from home. Your wife, I believe, is about my age, isn't she?"

Bracken nodded. By now he'd be used to them knowing everything about them. Damn it, there weren't any other chairs over here. She sank to the rug on her knees next to him like a pet dog. God, she was going to go home after this and read Olympia's *The True Face of Woman* again to remind her of her feminist agenda! Oh my goodness, she was probably going to meet Olympia some day! If she lived through this day. She certainly wouldn't tell her about this.

Oh – Bracken was answering her. Time to reply. "Well, consider me to be in the same place of service as if she were here. What can I do for you? What would make you happy? Have you had enough to eat and drink? Perhaps you would like to take a walk through some of our parks? Or museums? To tour before you send your men down for shore leave?"

"Perhaps we could. Just to see what's here." He paused. "Tell me, Lina, how is it that everyone knows so much about us?"

"What do you mean?" She gave him her cutest, wide-eyed puzzled look.

"Everyone here knows about my family, about everyone else's family, about their jobs, about their lives... And no one seems to be looking at any kinds of notes. Telepaths can't do that, not that deeply, not that completely."

"Of course not," Lina agreed.

"Then how do you do it?"

Lina shook her head. *Little ol' ah jest don't understand...* "Why, we just know what we know, Admiral Bracken. Are your people so different then? I can't believe that. We seem so similar."

Lina became aware of a tickle in her mind. She had been channeling so much... There was definitely some kind of entity who wished to speak to her, but she couldn't bring it into focus. Ah well, if it were important it would come to her sooner or later.

The admiral had made a noncommittal answer. Now he swung his chair in a circle to survey the chamber, and she sat back on her heels to give him room. He was not pleased at all to be backed into a corner. Lina knew that corners made people do stupid things. Time to give him a door. What had Wiley and Jae said when they were discussing tactics?

"Let me ask you this," she said. "Perhaps while you're here we could work on providing closer ties with Aldierra. Promoting commerce, helping each other, making up for what the other doesn't have. What do you see as Aldierra's most pressing concern? Let us help. It's our greatest pleasure, to help others. Let's bring our people together. Family helps family."

Bracken looked up at her with a look of surprise. What, hadn't anyone else come out this directly to ask? she wondered. If she'd been in charge, this would have been the first thing she would have suggested last night, not all this fardling around and charm stuff. Point things in a positive direction and walk! Non-Sagittarians could be so obtuse at times. She supposed they couldn't help their natures.

He considered and spoke. "Perhaps that is the best approach for now. Let us talk. I have maps and information on my ship, if your people would like to visit."

Lina smiled at Jae, who was approaching with Fadero in tow like a puppy. "That would be wonderful. Jae, why don't you tell the others that we'll be going back to the admiral's ship?"

It might be dangerous.

But non-threatening.

"Would the rest of you like to return, or perhaps you would like to get some sleep, or take a tour?" Jae graciously offered as he bowed.

They decided that three of the officers would accompany them back, and both Lina and Jae would go with the admiral. Lina ported them to the ship's bridge. Bracken led them to a conference room from there.

The whisper grew in Lina's mind. She decided to tell Jae about it, let him hear it to see if he might know what it was. He shook his head at her. Not a clue.

The cramped room held a narrow metal table, strictly utilitarian, in keeping with the military purposes of the ship. Floating holoscreens showed them maps of Aldierra, charts of resources which Lina couldn't read at all because they were written in another language. She deferred to Jae, whom Bracken addressed anyway, and they began trade discussions. Most involved food. Aldierra seemed short on all kinds of food supplies.

Lina's attention was drawn to the one decorative element in the room: a globe of green material, perhaps malachite, but it looked like it contained some clear quartz, too. It was a good foot and a half across, and was displayed on a countertop upon a beautiful golden stand of human figures joyfully holding it in place.

The stand was a work of art, but what attracted her was the globe itself. The bands of patterning in the mineral formed continents, oceans… and she knew that it was entirely natural. Or manmade of natural materials, as if grown that way in a laboratory. It was very old, she knew that much.

The voice whispered and she could almost make out the words now. Someone was coming through this.

"Excuse me," she said, cutting into the trade talks. Jae raised his eyebrow at her, warning her not to interrupt. "I'm so sorry, but I simply must know about this." She stood by the globe, wanting to touch it but not daring to.

The admiral rose to stand beside her. "That's the Soul of Aldierra. It was lost for centuries until my great-great-something grandfather unearthed it years ago. It's been in my family ever since."

"It's spectacular," she breathed. "And… it's alive. No, it's not."

"Lina–" Jae warned.

Bracken was amused by her fascination. "They say it contains the soul of my world, if you can believe that," he laughed.

"Not contains. It's a focus. She's been whispering to me," Lina murmured. "May I touch it?"

"Of course. It's just stone; it won't break."

She let out her breath as she realized she had been holding it. As she did before touching any crystal, she centered herself, calling down the white light for protection.

Jae started out of his chair, crossing over to her. "Lina, I don't think you should…" **_Lina, don't touch it._**

She held her hands inches from the surface, and it was like feeling an etheric body radiating from a physical one. Before her it seemed the globe no longer consisted of mere stone, but rather continents, oceans, atmosphere…

You need more white light, a voice in her mind said.

Obediently she summoned the light, wondering what the voice was, who it could be. It felt like a friendly, loving presence, but one who was also angry. Not at her, though.

White light that no one else could see filled the room, showering down and through her. Protecting her and yet filling her with strength.

Jae took her by the arms, pulling her hands away from the globe. "Don't touch it," he ordered.

****_Let her,_**** three voices chorused in both of their minds. The admiral looked at them both curiously.

"Surely you don't believe in spirits residing in the stone," he said.

Lina shook off Jae to grasp the stone firmly on both sides. She gasped as she almost fell toward it, then held steady.

"I am the Speaker for Aldierra," she announced in a clear, ringing voice. Something sucked her mind in deeper and she lost herself, able to hear the words that came out of her but with no control over them. "I am Faun. I am Aldierra. Hear me now!"

19

Her mind raced outwards, past star systems, past hundreds of parsecs of distance, toward a place that resonated with this stone and the picture before her. This strange, familiar world. She was there now, and also in all the Aldierran ships that orbited Sarastor.

She stood within the mind of each individual native of Aldierra, wherever they were in the universe. Twenty billion people, and she addressed them individually so they could each hear her. She had not one iota of control over what she said.

"I am Aldierra," she repeated. "I am Faun, spirit of your world."

Jae saw the admiral freeze in place, the other men in the room do likewise, their expressions terrorized as if they beheld a personal spirit or demon. They were oblivious to him.

"Lina, release! Let go!" Jae hissed at her. He shifted to remove her hands physically from the globe, but when he touched her etheric field he abruptly heard the message.

He stayed where he was, not quite touching her, afraid to be caught up in the same paralysis the others had been. Keeping one hand above hers, he used the other to trigger his Legion ring to communication mode.

"Wiley!" he yelled into the ring, hoping that it would wake him up.

"Um, I'm here. What is it?"

"Get up here now. This minute. We're on the admiral's command ship. Use the transporter – follow the ring's signal. Hurry!"

Within moments Wiley was there, alert, looking around at the paralyzed people. Taking in Lina, bent over the globe.

"What's going on? There was no security shield around the ship. And this–"

"Get over here. Don't touch her; just put your hand close to her, like I'm doing."

Wiley did as he was told, but didn't hear anything.

"All right, then touch her. I'll take your hand off if you space out like them."

Wiley did so. Now he too could hear the message in its totality:

I am Aldierra. I am your mother, your nurturer, the source of your life. I have loved you for eons but you have tried to destroy me. No more! I will not take this abuse any longer!

I am an advanced being and I need to evolve. I can do this with you or without you. Make your choice. Stand by me; support me and love me, and I will continue to support you, too. You will receive my bounty in abundance. And in turn you will evolve, become more loving toward each other. Happiness will come within your grasp.

But continue to forsake me, to destroy me and the life that lives upon me without remorse, and I shall have to destroy you. Lovingly so, for you are my children. But I say I will not take this abuse any longer!

DECIDE! That word was seared into the brain. *You have three seasons to make your choice and act. Your deadline is the equinox.*

Please, my children, do not forsake me. I have enjoyed your presence until these last few centuries. I wished to be your home as you matured. But sometimes you have to cull the herd, thin the seedlings so that others may survive. I will do this if you force me to.

DECIDE. By the equinox after next!

Inform my Chosen and I will know.

The message ended and Lina slowly opened her eyes, swaying. The Aldierrans in the room stood paralyzed from the afterimage of the message. Her hands still gripped either side of the globe, but her head fell back and her knees buckled.

"Lina! Are you all right?" Jae demanded as he caught her. Wiley steadied the globe.

Lina regarded Jae with unfocused eyes endless as the green Feithi sky. "*Shalla dyem ta fal,*" she whispered, but it was not her voice.

Jae stared at her, his breath catching in his throat. "What?" he finally asked. "*Cha?!* What? Lina!"

But her eyes were focusing again. "Oooooh god. Um, yeah, I'm okay. I think. Dizzy, but fairly grounded. Oh, hi, Wiley. That was pure channeling, letting an entity talk directly through me. I've never done that before. Can I sit down?" She was wobbling in Jae's arms, and he set her in a chair anxiously.

Wiley got her a glass of water from a pitcher. The water sloshed from side to side as she drank it, but she was still able to note that Wiley had a large, faint scar that stretched across his midsection. He wore what looked like short pajama bottoms, with the matching shirt hanging open. Not very Legion Protocolish, shame on him. His hair was more scraggly than usual. He must have been summoned here in a hurry.

"What was all that?" Wiley asked her. He held a padd his hand. Did he sleep with the things? One of those camera eyes floated next to him.

"It was addressed to every human of Aldierran descent," Lina explained. "Over twenty billion of 'em. If you'd asked me while I was doing it, I could have named each and every one for you. Given you their life histories, their hopes and dreams, their most secret fears. That's gone now, thank goodness.

"She showed me what they'd done. Aldierra. Cities cover almost every square inch of land, even the ocean. Animals – mostly extinct. Smog. Terrible smog. She can't breathe because the trees are almost gone. Pollution – it's ghastly. And they've kept on doing it, more and more, worse and worse.

"The people, too – they hate each other, they hate themselves. Constant wars – It's a wonder that they got this fleet together. It's not a planetary government. It is, but it isn't. I don't – It's some kind of power struggle. The strongest are in charge, but it's not a country. Not land-defined. I don't understand any more. I did then. I did perfectly.

"They can't expand off their world because it's so isolated. They didn't have the means until just lately. Aldierra couldn't take it anymore. It's them or her. She's not a bad planet, she's just been driven to the brink. If she were human, she'd be in hysterics, but she's practically eternal. She sees the long run, the big picture. She's very sane."

Lina reached out and touched the globe tentatively again, knowing nothing would happen. "She arranged for the admiral to bring this along with him. He thought it was just an ornament. Apparently she needed someone to act as a channel for the message, and I just happened to be handy."

"Coincidence?" Jae asked, knowing what she'd automatically say. He rubbed her hand, hoping to see more color come to her face.

"There's no such thing… as coincidence." If that were so, then she was meant to do this. But why? How? Lina shook her head. "I could use a few days of sleep, starting right now."

"Do you feel all right otherwise?" Wiley asked as he scanned her.

"Yeah. I don't have any residual clogging energies, if that's what you mean. Aldierra's pretty advanced. All her energy's good stuff. I'm just tired. She's not used to working through a human. I think she pulled out without leaving me quite one hundred percent. I just need to rest, that's all."

The other people in the room were coming around, grabbing for something real to hang on to, blinking, holding their heads. Some slid to the floor in a daze.

"What was that?" Admiral Bracken asked.

"Weren't you paying attention?" Lina asked mildly.

Jae nudged her on the arm. **Be polite.**

"Aldierra. The spirit of Aldierra," the admiral said. "This must be some kind of trick."

"I suggest you contact the people of your world, Admiral," Lina said. "You'll find that everyone had the same experience you did. You have a decision to make."

"A decision." Bracken surveyed the room, his skin gone pale as death. "This is a trick. It has to be."

"Your people must not take any credence in psychic events," Wilder said.

"Of course not." The admiral didn't even blink at Wiley's sudden appearance or his state of undress.

"Well, you all just had one hell of an event, Admiral," Lina said. "I don't recall anything like that happening on Earth. Ever. How about other planets?" she looked at Jae and Wiley.

"Never on Feith," Jae said. "Nothing like this in Sarastor history."

"I don't believe there are any records of anything like this anywhere," Wilder said. His eyes darted around as if he were reviewing the histories of thousands of worlds in his minds.

Lina sighed and shrugged. "She's an angry planet. What can I say? Maybe no people in the history of the galaxy have mistreated a planet so badly that she had to take these steps."

"Check with your people," Jae urged Bracken. "See what their experience was. We'll be here to help. We want to help."

"She gave us three seasons…" the admiral said. He looked as if his mind were still parsecs away and not quite here, but then he snapped his fingers at one of his officers. "See how long a season is."

"You don't even know that?" Lina was shocked. "How can you be so separated from life?"

Wilder interrupted mildly. "If we average human-normal planetary orbits with a G1 sun," he told them, "that would be three-quarters of a year, or between 250 to 300 days, depending on… Well. You'll have time to stay here a few days, check in with your world, and tell us what you need in aid."

A brash buzzer sounded in the room, and the admiral hit a panel on the table in front of him. A screen slid down from the nothingness of the air, and on it was an angry, uniformed man, who demanded to know what was going on.

"Patriarch Lupoff," Bracken said with deference. "We have just had the most amazing–"

"*Her!*" The man pointed at Lina. "She's with you! In person! She's the one everyone saw!"

Wiley fumbled at his pajamas and produced a translator. It repeated the chairman's message into Panlingua in fits and starts, but enough to get his message across.

Lina looked at Jae. **So it wasn't just an audio message.**

"Exactly what did you see, Your Excellency?" Jae asked politely.

"Her! With the planet hovering… behind her, inside her, through her, I don't know. As if they were one. And she told us she would destroy us!"

"I didn't say that; Aldierra did. But only if you made the wrong decision, Your Excellency," Lina said. "Aldierra has given you two choices. Reward and happiness await you if you make one, and destruction if you make the other. It seems to me easy enough to figure out."

Oh god, Jae. I just realized…

What?!

Twenty billion people saw me in this outfit. I am so embarrassed.

She could feel him pause and then felt his shoulders shake with silent laughter.

"Perhaps we should leave so you can more easily communicate with your people, Admiral," Wiley said. "When you decide what your course of action will be, you know how to contact us. We will help in every way possible."

Bracken just looked at the three of them, looked at Lina, with the chairman scowling in the background. "How did you do it?" he finally asked.

"I've always talked to planets," she told him. "But I've never before encountered any that wanted to talk to all of her children at once."

"You said you were the Speaker for Aldierra."

"I can tell you what she says. If that makes me a Speaker, then so be it. If you want to ask her questions, I'll see what kinds of answers I can get you. I think though, that she's said her fill for today."

The chairman sat huffing to himself and life in general on the screen, rubbing his chin agitatedly. Admiral Bracken was fiddling with some communications controls, but it didn't seem as if he had any real purpose in mind. These men were still in shock.

"All of you need to sit down and figure how what happened affects you," Jae said. "We'll be getting back to Sarastor to give you your privacy."

"Thank you," the admiral said thoughtfully. "I do think you will hear from us soon."

"Until you contact us, then." Jae bowed as Lina ported them back to Wiley's lab.

"When in the world is Londo coming back?" Lina asked plaintively. She sagged into her special prison chair, so soft and comforting. Wiley moved quickly to his station, oblivious to his dishabille. Jae just stood where they'd ported in.

"They're still a day out," Wilder said without checking his board. He had a schedule of everything in one of his minds as small print screens slid down, connecting to Planetary Security command centers.

Wearily easing herself up on her elbows on the arms of the chair, Lina said, "Cover up, Wilder. Arms and everything else. I think I'll just go to sleep until Lon gets here. Permission to leave for quarters? Or do you want to listen to me snore?"

"Wait a minute!" Jae demanded. "Don't you want to see how it comes out? If they're going to decide to invade us or not?"

Lina regarded him blearily. "Jae, their own world has just threatened to wipe them out like bugs. Between preventing that and pulling off an invasion that they aren't sure any more they actually stand a chance in hell of winning, what do you think they'll do?

"They seem to be decent people underneath all their stuff. Let's hope that decency comes to the forefront for this. But I'm not going to help them make their decision. It's their free will. I'm going to bed. If I can't go back to quarters, speak now or forever hold your peace."

Wiley looked at Jae. "It is a rather obvious decision, unless they decide it was all a trick. Or unless they're the most stupid people I've ever met." He pulled a fresh lab smock from a cabinet, but it didn't close in the front, leaving his chest and legs bare.

Lina set her jaw as she sat straight up in her chair. "And the next time that you Legionnaires need someone to… to… Well, all I can say is, go hire yourselves some prostitutes! Apparently y'all have money enough. I'm not doing anything like that again."

"Prostitutes?" Wiley's eyes slid to Jae. "I don't recall anything about prostitution on the plan."

"There was no prostitution," Jae growled. "You wanted Lina to be charming. I just told her to go a little farther if needed."

"You? This was all your idea?" Lina asked. "Not the both of you? I stood there and let someone rub his hand on my ass and my… my… and it wasn't–"

Jae crossed his hands over his chest and gave her a level stare. "And it worked very well. If there was one thing those underlings weren't thinking of, Lina, it was making war. You should have seen her, Wiley. Three times subtler than Deegel and twice as effective. Add it to her list of parapowers."

Lina fumed. "You have so many strikes against you, Jaeson, that you aren't even in the league any more. You owe me. You owe me!"

"I'm sure I do."

Wiley made a note on his padd. "Lina, of all the Legionnaires, Jae is the one known to use people the most. Unless Londo has beaten him at that lately. Londo's only part-time, though."

"Wonderful."

"It makes them good team leaders. And it seems to have worked well today. We went from invasion to stall and confuse to… What is it we've come to? Apparently the Aldierrans are now on our side, or we're on their side, or something." Wiley scratched his head with one hand while the other tapped out a message on his board.

"We aren't enemies anymore," Lina said. They had managed a few things at that.

Jae sighed. "I can't change gears this fast. First we're stopping an invasion. Now we're stopping – genocide."

"Don't be silly, Jae," Lina said as she picked up her study padd from the table next to her chair. "They'll make the right choice, and then we won't be stopping anything. We'll be helping. I don't know about you, but I like helping people. Good night." She ported out and Wiley disarmed the alarm before it could sound.

"Lina?" Jae asked the air blankly.

Wiley checked the progress of the Coronasphere Line. It hadn't been finalized yet. There'd been unexpected conflict of programming commands. That was what he got for having a staff of single-minded assistants who all wanted to make an individual impression on the Legionnaire Dr. Mem-Bazer. No concept of teamwork down there. He'd have to run more training sessions with them.

Planetary defenses were organizing slowly but surely. Ten squads of Legionnaires were due to arrive within the next thirty hours from away missions.

Next he called up the Legion betting boards. He keyed in a new entry. "Two hundred credits that she's offered Legion membership within fifty days," Wiley said.

Jae looked at the screen sharply. "A thousand says she turns it down," he countered. The sub-wager took its place in print on the screen. "You want to counter?"

"Eh…" Wilder considered a moment. "No. I don't like the odds."

In the wee hours of the next morning as Wiley continued lone monitor duty from his lab station, a call came in from the Romaki Club on Sarastor. Non-emergency, it said. Ordinarily it would be automatically switched to L-PIC, but Wiley intercepted the call just to handle something besides planetary defenses. He was tired.

"Yes?" he prompted the bearded man on the screen. Records identified him as Ernst Holst, a Sarastoran of Terran descent. Holst's eyes went big; clearly he recognized the famous Dr. Wilder Mem-Bazer.

"Um. Eh hem. Sir. Dr. Mem-Bazer, I was wondering if I could speak to Starfleet."

"Starfleet? We have no member named Starfleet."

"Oh, um, she's not a member. Tall – well, you probably wouldn't think so – reddish-haired Terran female, a pretty thing, goes around in tee shirts and jeans. Neutrino's been with her for the past few nights here. He calls her Lina. I don't know the last name."

"Ah." Wilder nodded. He only needed one mind to handle this. "Lina O'Kelly. She's sleeping with a Do Not Disturb on her circuit. I'm afraid she's been through a lot today. Is this an emergency?"

Holst was hasty in waving Dr. Mem-Bazer off. "No, no, sir! I missed her when she came by the club last night. We've gotten used to having her stop by, and she left all suddenly. She didn't get sick or anything, did she? We were hoping she'd show up again tonight."

"I doubt she will. She was exhausted when she turned in some hours ago."

"Ah. Everyone here will be disappointed. Maybe she'll show up tomorrow?" the man asked hopefully, afraid to ask outright.

Wilder made a show of considering. Londo would be back. "I couldn't say for sure, but the odds would be against tomorrow night. The next one might be more favorable, but I don't wish to speak for her."

"Yes. Ah. Dr. Mem-Bazer sir, could I ask a question, then?"

"Go ahead."

"Since when does the Legion put up civilian personnel? Terrans at that?"

How many days had it been since Stoan had made his ridiculous proclamation of secrecy? It was to last for five days. Wiley checked a clock on his board and then replied, "Spouses of members are allowed use of their quarters."

There was a look of triumph on the man's face. "So she's married to Neutrino after all! And they said they weren't–"

"She is not married to Neutrino."

"Then who–?"

"Carolina O'Kelly is married to Valiant. He's on a mission right now, expected back this afternoon."

"Valiant?" The man's mouth dropped open. Wiley'd never seen a human jaw open to those proportions. Holst let out a little wheeze, then another. "Valiant? Valiant?! Married to–?!"

"That's correct. Good night. I will leave a record of your call to her attention." The screen cleared.

He really should have milked it more, Wiley mused. Sometimes Legion regs needed to be shaken. Too bad he didn't know Holst would take it… so entertainingly.

Tonight there were no language lessons as she slept, and her dreams were sound-free until a wisp of song filtered through. Lina relaxed in Londo's arms, and he sang to her with afterglow, his eyes sleepy and filled with love, his fingers tracing her body as if he were drawing it with charcoal.

She was Rose on *Titanic*, Rose on the sheet of paper wearing only the necklace as the hand moved, blurring the charcoal here and there with a touch of a finger. Someone tried to draw male genitalia on her and she said, "No!" and smeared them away with her own hand, drawing back the correct version of herself, and then let the artist continue with his drawing.

Jae looked up from his work to compare it to Lina lying on the couch, but she wasn't anywhere as fine as what he'd drawn. She was grossly imperfect. He came over to her to correct the lines of her body, drawing on her with his hands.

She felt her bones move to his command, her skin shift to his orders, and when his face lowered to hers, she met his lips with her own, as if she were Adam and he God on the Sistine Chapel ceiling, Adam reaching out to touch the Creator, except that this Creator had Londo lying nude on His back, whispering his instructions into His ear, pointing out Lina's imperfections to be corrected.

God became Ms. Yency, who shook her finger warningly at Lina and told her to shape up into a good little Legion wife as legions of winged baby cherubim gathered on the ceiling clutching their embryonic wine bags and shaking their fingers at her, too. Then they pointed out the bodies lying on the sand below, just mutilated rat food now. Zombie Dr. Menlo rose up to exhort at her in words she didn't understand.

She tried to run, but marching living bodies blocked her exit. They looked at her like they expected her to save them. More and more arrived, and she could see each and every one's orangish, pleading face, their arms outstretched to her. She couldn't move. There were so many.

A choir in the Sistine sang, "Bop shoo wop bop, bop shoo wop bop," all in their choir robes with strange symbols on them. They were putting a production of *Joseph and His Amazing Technicolor Dream Coat* on an empty stage, much to Ms. Yency's disapproval, and Jae was Joseph and Londo was a young Jacob so far away in Israel as Joseph was imprisoned in the tiny stage cell.

Lina walked down the stage stairs as… Pharaoh Elvis? But she wasn't dressed the part. Instead she wore a long, slinky burgundy gown of the heaviest velvet, so heavy it trapped her, and the crown on her head was the showgirl headpiece Lucy Ricardo wore down those long, winding stairs. Under its weight she kept tipping over the railing, lurching to regain her footing. But she wasn't the pharaoh, so that must make her the Narrator… or was that the Speaker?

Lina tried to touch Jae through the bars but someone pulled her away, only to have Lon's hand came out of the bars and grab her arm. It was a struggle between whoever was pulling her and Lon's strong arm, but the stranger was stronger. Now Jae's hand reached out from his cage, grasping for her, but all he caught was her heart. It slipped in its own blood as he brought it back to his cage, but Londo caught it before it could touch the ground and burst.

The chorus sang, "*Children of Israel are never alone.*" And the stranger in the Elvis mask and Egyptian royal kilt who was dragging her away from them laughed and shouted, "*Charrant!*" Whore. But it wasn't Dad.

The chorus of three voices kept repeating as if they were on a vinyl record with a scratch in it: "*For we have been promised… We have been promised…*" as the cage with Londo and Jae in it got farther and farther away, the only patch of light in the darkness, and Lina was being dragged to her doom.

Londo! Jae! Help me!

She screamed as her last hope faded away.

Lina sat straight up in bed in horror. Her heart pounded in her throat and she gasped around it.

It was just a dream. Just a nightmare. *Please God, don't let it be any kind of déjà vu.* She was lonely for Londo, that was it. Some kind of Freudian symbolism, or maybe Jungian. Lon was safe, he had to be.

She leaned back against the headboard and fought for breath, willing her heart-beat to slow from its frantic pace. The images of the dream remained. The sheer terror still shook her. Though she was absolutely exhausted from the doings of the day, it would be a long time before she could dare sleep again.

Next to her the dark bed lay empty.

If only Londo were here to hold her! She needed him to comfort her. To kiss away the fear and tell her she was safe.

She closed her eyes, and felt again that she was being dragged away from him. He was trying to get to her. He was trying to rescue–

A shadow against the hallway.

"Lina."

Jae's voice soft in the darkness.

"I'm here. You called me," he said.

"No. I was having a bad dream. If I called you, it was in the dream." She gathered the sheet around her even though she wore a chaste nightgown.

"It upset you."

"I've been upset before. It'll pass."

She could tell by the softest of shuffles in the carpeting that he'd come closer.

"As long as I'm here, I have a proposition for you," he said.

"No."

"Just give me one minute."

He sat down on the bed next to her. It was impossible to see him and just as impossible to ignore every other sense that revealed him to her.

"Go away. Please."

"One minute. A proposition."

She could feel his loneliness, too. Anyone could. It radiated from him like a howl across the face of the universe.

"You miss Londo," he said. "I miss Londo." He paused.

"Fifty-five seconds," she said.

"…What I'm saying is, is… Look." Suddenly he lay back next to her above the covers, up against the headboard just as she was. "Let's talk for a while. Nothing else. Pure and decorous with no recriminations. It'll calm you down. We don't even have to talk. I can make believe you're Londo and you pretend the same of me."

Lina didn't know what to say.

"We don't have to be lonely tonight," Jae urged. "We don't have to break any marriage vows, we don't have to betray Lon. Just talk. Or let me talk to you. Whatever you want."

He brushed a lock of hair out of her face, tucking it behind one ear. His hand remained lightly on her bared neck.

"You'll believe you're talking to Londo, is that right?" Lina asked him. He had to be able to feel her pulse drumming, but she didn't send him away. Right now any human contact was a welcome barrier between her and that dream.

"Yes. I'll pretend."

"And I'll pretend you're Londo." God, how she needed Lon here!

He snuggled to her and his finger and thumb began to rub little circles on her skin. "Right. I need to talk to someone." His thumb traced her jawline, then found her lower lip and outlined it.

"Do you always do this when you talk?"

"Do you always talk when Londo's lying next to you?" He turned in some way that his hair brushed against her cheek. "It's what I do when I imagine I'm talking to him. Just tell me I'm not alone. Tell me I'm not lost. Sing to me, sweet, sing me a song about Feith."

He needed her. As much as the people of the Terran Zone needed her to sing to them, so did Jae need her now.

"Please," he whispered.

Lina searched for an emotion to touch with song and what came to her was a Feithi lullaby. She sang softly and almost didn't realize when Jae began to stroke her arm in time with the music.

"That was beautiful," he told her when she finished. "I wish I'd recorded it."

What Jae needed was someone who could love him back both physically and emotionally. But what he'd come to her tonight for was mothering. Lina sighed to herself gratefully. That she could give. That was safe enough.

"When are you going to settle down?" she asked him as he nestled his head onto her shoulder.

"I'm settled," he said. "The Legion is my home."

"I mean with someone. For more than two weeks. Or is three your record?"

"Grigach, you've heard it too and you've only been here a few days."

"You have quite the reputation. A string of broken hearts in your wake. Some of them haven't healed."

Still he stroked her arm in long, calming touches. "I suppose there are some," he finally said. "You didn't have access to many people. Dellen?"

"She needs to move on if you're not interested."

"No." He shook his head against her. "Not interested. Nice for a time or four but not my type. Athletic." He gave the slightest of laughs at that. "Definitely a Legion-naire. We truly are the best, you know."

"Legends in your own minds."

"Legionnaires. She's a crack member, that Dellen. Knows her stuff. She's good to have covering you in a battle. She'll be on an alpha team before long. But I don't want her in my bed."

"Jae," Lina said quietly, "you're in my bed. I think it's time for you to go."

"Not for a while. Please."

He was like a little boy who thought bedtime came too soon. Maybe she could play mother for a few more minutes. If she was left alone, that nightmare might come back. She couldn't bear that possibility. Jae kept it at bay.

They lounged there for a long while, his hand so soothing on her arm. He spoke to her of Londo's kindnesses through the years and Lina could picture her wonderful

Londo doing such things to others. That's part of the reason why she treasured him. She told Jae of how Londo had protected her and kept her safe from her own fears. Jae said Lon had done the same for him.

Then he asked, "Is the nightmare gone now?"

"Mm. I'd almost forgotten it. Thank–" She stopped.

His hand had slid over to cup her breast.

"I want you to sleep well tonight," he whispered to her. His thumb rubbed her nipple under the flannel of her nightgown.

And then he kissed her neck. Lina found the hard muscles of his upper arm even as he kneaded her breast. Though she pushed, he didn't seem to be going anywhere except farther down her neck. She clamped down against a groan even as her body involuntarily rose up against Jae.

"Jae. Jae."

"Hmm?" He began to ease the shoulder of her gown down.

"Jae, are you thinking of Londo now?"

"Londo who?" he asked just before pressing his lips to the upper flesh of her breast.

"Get out. Get out now or I'll port you."

"Aw come on, sweet…"

"I mean it. You broke your promise."

He didn't leave, but at least he removed his hands from her. Somewhere in the darkness only he could see through, he shifted so he hovered over her, a hand on the mattress to either side of her.

"I did," he admitted. "I'll leave. Sweet dreams for the rest of the night."

He cupped her by the back of her neck so she couldn't squirm away while he kissed her hard.

And then he was gone, leaving her gasping again in the dark.

Since she hadn't gotten any sleep at all afterward, Lina spent most of her morning napping safely in Wiley's lab, waiting for the call to come in from the Aldierran fleet.

Jae had been summoned to the office of the Potentate of Sarastor, but now two squads of Legionnaires had reported in, their missions on other worlds complete. They were astonished when they found themselves back home instantly without having to endure a day of travel. From here they could signal their hyperspace ships to return home on automatic.

They were almost all of them very tall. Lina was used to that now. Here were eMage and Stain, Bolton and Shockwave, Stargust and Leenduk. At least they came in small groups so she could attempt to remember their names.

Wiley briefed each group as they arrived. They left hurriedly to clean up and then attend to the dozens of secret meetings that were taking place today all around the planet, all having to do with planetary security and the Aldierrans. The world was still bracing for a war… just in case.

The newly-arrived Legionnaires scrutinized her curiously on their way out and then back in, wondering why Wiley didn't send her away during these security briefings. She tried to look bored, as if these kinds of things happened every day. Then, bored with looking bored, she tried a shifty, criminal kind of look to fit in with her prisoner status. She hummed menacingly at one Legionnaire as he walked by, and noticed that from then on he gave her a wide berth.

Now some hyperspace ships that had been in transit for days began to arrive as well, combined with a shift change from one of the Outposts. Headquarters was beginning to fill up again, although due to the high sustained in-and-out activity Wiley's lab remained its command center.

When Jae finally came back, Lina ignored him, letting him do his Legionnaire business without the playful interruptions of day before yesterday. She didn't know how to feel about him anymore. Hate him, like him, or… or what?

He loved Londo.

That was the basic fact of the matter.

But then there was the night before last, and then when she thought they'd straightened things out, there was last night. She should be furious at Jae for what he'd done! What kind of person would do that?

And yet she could understand it. She was so lonely, longing for Londo after just these few days, and Jae had had to look at him from for years and years, not from afar but nearby. Knowing he could never have him, knowing that his feelings could never be returned the way he wanted them to be. It was some kind of simple transference, that was it. Poor Jae.

He masked things so well, commanding the Legionnaires who called him "sir" and the officials on the screens as they bowed to him. So in charge, and yet so out of control in his personal life. He cared for Sarastorans, absolutely determined that no harm would come to them or their world, and the other night he'd been desperate to find some way to help them out of the mess they'd dug themselves into, just like the Aldierran people must have. At least Sarastor wasn't screaming for her people's heads!

Sitting there ignoring him, Lina felt his eyes on her and shuffled around in her prisoner's chair so that all he'd see was the full of her back – her long-sleeved turtlenecked back. She was angry with him. And she was doubly angry at herself for having to remind herself of that.

Just because she was new to all this love and lust business didn't mean that she had to be stupid about it. After the fact had been when all the stories she had heard about guys "just wanting to lie down and talk" had come back to her. In person it had seemed natural, a nice thing to let him do. Afterwards she'd slapped her forehead hard for being such an idiot.

But all in all she thought the blame could be assigned to him and not her.

It was Legionnaires coming and going as usual, with only the volume of traffic and the number of Legionnaires increased. The only really interesting thing was a little machine Wiley'd rigged to scan all those library books into his system. He had to build a steampunk-ish device that could flip pages while a camera scanned the text to convert it to digital. But even watching that grew tiresome after a few chapters.

Frustrated with her conflicting emotions today, Lina actually volunteered for another spousal lesson from Ms. Yency.

Lina was tired of being a prisoner. Tired of her life being so out of control. Here she'd thought that by telling the White Puma about her legal problems that she had everything solved, but things were even worse.

Some things only Londo could make better. It would be up to him to decide what he was going to do with her after her faithless night with Jae. But dammit, it was time to fight back on the things she could have a say in. Time to show them she wouldn't be cowed.

After Yency signed off, Lina went to another section of her padd and signed up for a dozen abolitionist newsletters. Then she called up an art program and worked out a logotype design based on a souvenir she'd seen while waiting for a flight at the LA airport. She transferred it to a tee shirt template she made by holding one up to be scanned by puter systems. Trying to remember what Jae had told her about payment, she gave the final "buy" okay and had it sent to Lon's apartment. Within two minutes, it arrived there; better than FedEx. Good.

Checking it out in the lab's bathroom mirror, she was quite satisfied with the results. She'd had to whip up a snazzy font variant with the tiniest whiff of a serif to it. "OFFICIAL LEGION PRISONER" wrapped in a circle around the Legion symbol. She'd shove it down their throats, make 'em see she wasn't taking them seriously.

That hadn't taken much time. She searched the nets for something like the ACLU or Amnesty International and put her name on two lists there, knowing that she'd be cut off if she tried to do anything further.

That was a start.

Speaking of clothing… She was married now – she *was*! It was legal and binding and she'd been drunk in a good cause and Londo was going to have a fight on his hands if he tried to back out! And as much as the feminist in her loathed to admit it, she needed to take Lon's tastes into consideration when it came to what she wore.

He was constantly named to the Best-Dressed lists. A wife who lived in jeans and tee shirts just wasn't going to make it. What would he like? Cleavage and legs. Tight skirts and garter belts. Or was she relying on her Fifties view of marriage and a somewhat warped sense of men derived from work? She needed a new wardrobe, but it would be best to wait to consult with him on that.

Fashion choices reminded her that DragonCon would be coming up this fall in Atlanta. With an enervating burst of enthusiasm, she decided that she was going to attend as a cosplayer. It was on her list of personal goals, although she'd made it a C in hopes of getting out of it. Using clothing replicators, she could cheat. When used in ethical moderation, cheating was good.

Lina sketched a few ideas and settled on one design. It had a tasteful amount of cleavage. And oh yes, those wonderful soled tights they wore here. Definitely include those. She wound up with something that would look smart on a stage, maybe even win a prize if she accessorized it correctly. Purple body makeup? Wings? She saved the file for future work and changed her screen to scan the news.

But she began to daydream about the night ahead. In effect it would be their wedding night. Londo, Londo, Londo filled her thoughts, driving out the image of any other man. She pushed one face out of her mind. *Any other man!* she told it firmly, and relaxed when Londo again smiled at her.

Ohmigosh, she didn't have any kind of sexy nightgown to wear. That she wouldn't have to clear with Lon. She searched online. People here didn't mind bare anything with their nightwear, as long as they didn't have to worry about Legion Protocol doing a bed check.

There. Something that would do nicely. She touched the payment screen. According to the confirmation, it had already been delivered to Lon's apartment here in HQ. It was all so cool.

Oh well, as long as she had the screens up, she ordered more. Lon wouldn't want to see the same thing every night, would he? She didn't think she was spending too much.

Besides, sexy nightwear might make him overlook her night with Jae.

Once he got back she could drag him out to go shopping so she could get a handle on what he liked. Shopping with Londo. Walking with her arms around him in the sunlight. Free. She smiled to herself and sighed happily. Soon. Soon.

Nothing was going on, just Stain and Bolton in here now.

"Excuse me," she asked Stain, and the man? woman? startled. Lina hadn't been making any noise for so long, sitting there upside-down in her chair.

"I need to feed my cats sometime today. I missed it yesterday, and Fafhrd really needs her medicine. Is now a good time?"

After a discussion and check of previous trips, the shadowy Stain accompanied her to Earth for a few minutes. Lina wasn't allowed to play with the cats, since she was a prisoner. They ported back and Lina returned to her prisoner's chair.

She had nothing to do but think. What would she do if they ever allowed her and Lon to go home? Would she get a new art job at some horrible place in Wyoming? She'd think about that once they were settled. She just knew that she wasn't going to sit around and watch soap operas and clean house for Lon, even if he was Valiant.

Wiley finally returned for this busy day. His console buzzed and he put down whatever his latest experiment was to answer it. "Unauthorized package for you," he told Lina.

"Unauthorized?" She could have sworn that all those packages she had ordered had signaled that they'd already arrived, fully authorized.

"It's from the Romaki Club, Terran Zone," Wiley said.

She swung her legs down from the chair arm, hopping to the floor. "The Terran Zone?" she asked. "What could they want? Um, where do I get it?"

"Right here." Wiley had it materialize on his table.

It was a huge arrangement of something, bold and bright clusters of stiff petals that weren't flower petals, with a traditional Terran bridal couple figurine stuck in the middle of it. Tied to the bottom of the arrangement were two bottles of Coke.

Lina laughed to see it. She picked up the big card: "Congratulations to Starfleet and Valiant on your marriage," it said, and it was signed by about two hundred people. She recognized the largest signature: Ernst. He wrote next to his name: "Terra rules!"

"How did they find out?" she asked.

"Didn't you check your messages? They called last night. I told them."

"You did? Naughty boy. Since when do I get messages? And if I did, I have no idea how to check them."

Wiley took a minute to show her how to do it, and she ran the message on a small screen on the monitor table. She laughed at Ernst's shocked look at the end. "Looks like Ernst thinks that the Legion's going to start paying Earth some attention."

"Say again?"

She explained Ernst's point of view to Wiley.

"But Earth's not in the AffSys," he stated.

"Are all the planets the Legion helps in the AffSys? If Aldierra asks for the Legion's help, will they reject them?"

"No, there are exceptions for everything."

"Oh my, an exception to the rules. Can Sarastor stand it? Ah well, it's like I told Ernst; at least Earth has the ParaNet to take care of it. They've been able to handle things. So far. I hope that if they find they can't handle something someday, that the Legion will pop over and help out."

"It will depend on the situation."

Lina propped her head on her hand. "So tell me, how many members have actually visited Earth?"

"I don't think there's ever been any reason to. Besides Londo, and now the ones who've gone along with you – none."

"With megamega heroes like Maximus and Rico Carapella there?"

"Oh, they came here."

"What'd you do, like, summon them? Like for a royal audience? Did you have them wash behind their ears before they stepped into the grand meeting chamber? '*Yes, your majesty, no, your majesty, tell me how low to go, your majesty...*' Good golly, how in the world did Londo ever get in past your stringent standards?"

"As you might say, he is considered in the megamega hero range."

"Ah," Lina paused. "So it's a little like being a woman in a job on Earth. We've only gained some equality in this past century, you know."

"No, I didn't. I'm not that familiar with your history yet. I haven't had the time to research much."

"It's been said that for a woman to get a job equal with a man's, she has to be twice as good. I guess that's the way it is for Terran heroes, huh? I betcha Olympia or Bolt or... or Forte, or Maximus, whom you have already agreed is in the megamega hero range, would all make great Legionnaires. They could help a lot more people than they are. Of course, I don't know them, I don't know what their schedules are. But it just seems to me–"

"Hi, people. Any word yet?" Jae walked into the lab, unbuckling his cloak and flinging it onto a chair. Behind him were Stain, Bolton and Leenduk.

"Not yet. Lina and I were just discussing inequalities in Legion membership."

"Oh?" Jae looked around. "Narsaws," he observed, seeing the arrangement.

The word clicked in her mind. Narsaws were shells. Pretty.

"I believe they're congratulating Lina and Londo on their wedding," Wiley said.

Jae turned to her with that neutral mask of expression on his face, as if he were once again merely arresting officer and not the perpetrator of an ethical crime for two nights in a row. "Has the prisoner been spreading classified information?"

"The requisite five days was up," Wiley said. "I released the information to a friend of Lina's who called."

These narsaws looked out of place here. Lina gave a start. "Oh, sorry Wiley. I should have figured you wouldn't want them cluttering your lab." She ported them into Lon's apartment. Wiley gave her the tiniest of condescending bows of his head and she smiled at him, then turned her back on Jae and marched to her prisoner chair.

"Jae," Wiley said, "they originally thought that Lina was married to you."

Even from across the room Lina could feel Jae tense up within the group of Legionnaires. "Huh," was all he said.

Good; maybe he was feeling a little guilty about things. He should. Immediately Lina felt remorse for the thought. Everything had happened because of Jae's predicament. He shouldn't have to go around like this.

She had Londo arriving for her soon. She'd get over this… whatever it was she had for Jae that she kept pushing to the side. She couldn't even look at him directly any more. Well, good. Keep him out of the picture for a while, and she'd snap back to normal.

But poor Jae, going after anything nearby because he didn't have anyone. Maybe Lon and she could set him up with someone. Somewhere there had to be the perfect guy for Jae.

I've already met him, and he's yours.

What?

You were broadcasting. Try to be a little quieter, hm?

Since when are you a telepath?

Why do you say that? You've talked to me this way lots of times.

But I've always picked it up or instigated it. This time you did, quite on your own power, not borrowing anything from me. Ergo, you're a telepath.

Jae stared at her. ***What is going on around here? Powers popping up everywhere you look–***

"Message coming in from the Aldierran fleet," Wilder announced. All Legionnaires gathered around the screen. They made no pretense about presenting themselves as tourism promoters now. The Legion symbol stood out on the bottom of their transmission.

"Ah, I suspected as much," Admiral Bracken said as the communication screen lit up with his image. "Legionnaires. You played a very good game."

"But now the game has changed, Admiral," Jae said gravely. "We stand by ready to help you. Have your people decided anything?"

"Yes, Jae, we – I can't call you just Jae, can I? What is your name?"

"I'm known as Neutrino, Admiral."

Bracken squinted at him. "Neutrino is a myth. A Feithi. Everyone knows that Feith died."

"Not all, Admiral. I'm the last, and believe me, I'm quite real."

Bracken chewed on that a moment. "If that's true," he said, "forgive me for calling you Jae."

"That's my name as well. You're welcome to use it."

The admiral nodded in a way that looked more like a half-bow. "Where is the Speaker?" he asked.

Lina realized that he was talking about her. She stood up quickly and joined the Legionnaires before the screen. Bolton stepped back so she could go to the front of the group. "I'm here, Admiral Bracken," she said. "Do you have a message?"

"Of course we decide for survival. We will accede to Aldierra's wishes. We are informing the Speaker for Aldierra, as we were instructed."

She tried to tune into the essence that had taken her over yesterday, the mind of Aldierra. There she was. **They've agreed to help you,** she told the planet.

"She hears and says that she would like some active signs that you're actually going to mend your ways," Lina relayed, her eyes unfocusing as she channeled. "Before the equinox, with definite, continuing plans for the future. Large plans, not inconsequential tricks." Her eyes focused. "She's crafty, this planet."

Admiral Bracken nodded. "We will begin to formulate goals and plans of action. For this, though, we will need help. Help in figuring out where we are, in deciding where Aldierra wishes us to be, in actually getting there."

Jae smiled. "We are at your disposal – the people of Sarastor as well as the Legion. Let's set up some meetings and get some experts together, as long as you have ships here."

"Yes, that's a good idea," Bracken said tiredly.

"Admiral Bracken," Lina asked, "how long has it been since you've slept more than a few minutes?"

"About two days," he admitted.

"Then why don't you get some sleep now? By the time you wake up we'll be able to have some meetings and you'll be awake enough to take part in them. And you should have a decent meal, too."

He smiled at her. "Yes, I think I'll do that. Thank you, Speaker."

She smiled back. Underneath it all, he was a decent man. It was just his culture that stank as it tried to destroy one planet and take over another. "You're welcome."

CHAPTER

20

They arranged a time for talks the next day and the admiral signed off. The other Legionnaires moved to the communications screens along the wall to inform various points of Planetary Defense. Bolton took over at the main communications board. Jae and Wiley stood together talking near the break room, next to where Lina's chair sat.

"Well, music up to rousing finale and roll end credits," Lina declared to them. Her legs were hanging over the chair's arms. "Another job done in heroic style. Pretty damn fine stuff if you ask me."

"You mean, the real job's just beginning," Wilder said. "Now we have to find the experts, figure a preliminary plan of action–"

"As a Sagittarian," Lina announced, "I feel it's my duty to point out that Sags are much better at the big picture, the start of the action. For the finish work, the uninteresting work, you need–"

"Legionnaires." Jae laughed.

"You read my mind." **Telepath! I told you so!**

"So you're cutting out on us," Wilder said and Lina shrugged.

"Dumb ignorant Terrans... You know us barbarians." She considered. "Of course, you are going to include that plant woman on these talks, you know, the Legionnaire."

"You mean Nesh... Chloroplast?"

"Yeah. Any more of her at home?"

"Why?" Jae wanted to know.

"Because if there are, you send a couple of squadrons of them to Aldierra and tell them to find some nice spouses and settle down, have a few kids. Aldierra needs forests first and foremost; the poor planet can't breathe. Get those guys making forests.

"You'll need detox units so that the forests can grow well, in good clean soil and air. And educators. Eco-educators, because those people are good people, I truly believe that. I just don't think they realize what they're doing, much less how they can correct it. They've given up hope. And don't drill them with do's and don'ts; make it fun for them. People will work three times as hard as they would normally if you make it fun."

"Shouldn't you be writing this down?" Wilder suggested dryly.

"I've noticed that there seems to be a severe lack of paper on Sarastor."

"So use a note padd," Jae said, and picked up one. Wiley always had a dozen lying around, all interconnected. Jae transferred memory to the other note padds and cleared it before handing it to her.

"Um, I have no idea how to input on this," she said. It seemed like a study padd by its size, but its configuration was quite different. Its screen unfolded to the size of a sheet of regular paper, with the solidity of tough cardboard, but it had all kinds of displays down one side like a Mac's dock. The other side held a stylus clipped to it.

"Just write for the moment. I'll tell you later what all it can do."

"Hope it takes English. My written Lingua is slow."

Jae held his finger over one symbol on the left side of the padd. "English usage," he said, and removed the finger. "Go ahead."

She scrawled a test message on the padd: "Terra rules!" and was delighted when her handwriting transformed into New Century Schoolbook type. "Pretty cool. Okay, what did I just say?"

"Chloroplast, start reforesting efforts, detox units, eco-educators, fun," Wilder said.

"Got it. What else?" Lina gave an evil laugh and wrote something.

"What?" Jae peeked at her screen, squinting at the language.

"Get rid of weather control. Once I see how they do that on Aldierra, I can figure out how to get it done here. Sarastor really hates weather control. It's like… like having someone dictate to you when you can blink. Very uncomfortable and irritating."

The three of them spent an hour and a half coming up with a list of the people who needed to be at the preliminary meetings with their opinions, as well as contacting those people and arranging for them to attend. While the Legionnaires were busy using their considerable influence to persuade the experts, Lina sought a private communication screen and rang the Terran Zone. Ernst was there, and they called him to the screen.

"Starfleet!"

"Hi, Ernst. Thank you and everyone so much for the beautiful narsaws – and the Cokes. I know when Lon comes back, he'll appreciate the drinks at the very least."

"Starfleet – You married Valiant!"

"Uh huh." She grinned at him.

"I mean, Valiant!"

"You have a problem with that?"

"Not at all. But it's kind of like marrying God, isn't it?"

"The full Valiant image hasn't sunken in yet. I just really know him as Londo."

"Well, once you get back to Earth I suppose it'll hit you. I hope you're prepared."

"If he decides to announce it. We might keep this a private affair, you never know."

"Whatever you do, more power to you! And I mean that literally," Ernst said, winking at her. She laughed.

"Don't worry, I can handle him," she said.

He raised an eyebrow. How did Valiant…?

"Oh no, not that look again. I'm getting tired of it." She had to laugh again at his abashed face.

"So are you coming back to the Terran Zone? With your new husband?"

"I will certainly try to make it back with him in tow before we leave. Which won't be for a couple of days still. There'll be a funeral." The full import of that hit her. The Legionnaires would be coming back within hours, bringing news of Aiko's death to the worlds. "And after that's over, I don't know. I may have to stay around here for a while. I've gotten involved in… some stuff."

"Which was why you were so exhausted yesterday?"

"Yeah. I don't think I can talk about it at this point."

"Okay. I'll just consider it Legion business. Well, whenever you can make it with or without Valiant, just consider the Terran Zone your home away from home."

"Thanks, Ernst. Thank you very much; I will. Take it easy."

"Bye, Starfleet." The screen cleared.

They ate a late lunch in the main cafeteria, Jae and Lina and Wiley, whose reluctant attendance Jae had enlisted.

A chaperone, Lina thought. Good. They were snapping out of this. They'd be snapped all the way by the time Lon got back. Drunk, drugged and crazy; maybe he'd understand. He had to! Cold fear clutched her heart every time she thought about it so she refused to do so.

She'd reviewed the memories of that evening so many times now, as much as she was able to face them. What they'd done was wrong, but it wasn't so very wrong, was it? She'd been drunk in a good cause. Out of her mind. People did forgivable things when they were drunk.

And Jae – For a few moments there, she'd become a Londo substitute in his eyes. They'd been so close for so long, of course Jae would get mixed up when things went crazy. That was it, things had been just crazy. But they were forgivable crazy. He was truly sorry for what he'd done and wanted to make amends.

Londo would understand!

Wiley yakked about Aldierra while Jae and she studiously ignored each other, pretending to pay attention to him.

Why the blazing orb are you wearing that? Jae finally blurted silently. **I don't think it's very funny.**

I do. She took a deliberate bite of the stibbing, just like Bette Davis and the breadstick in *All About Eve.* So there, Jae.

Everyone's staring at you.

That was certainly true. She'd stood in line to choose her order and people had stopped eating, stopped talking to stare open-mouthed. She'd turned around casually, flipping her braid over her shoulder so they could get a good view from either side. The PRISONER logo was on the front, but on the back it said, "I'm a prisoner at beautiful LEGION HEADQUARTERS, Lirravon, Sarastor," in rubber-stamp type, all in Panlingua – a blatantly souvenir design with a panoramic Legion Headquarters pictured behind it all.

She'd caved in and made the shirt long-sleeved so she wouldn't have to cover it up with a sweater. As a final touch, she'd designed a ping of a holographic highlight that moved constantly in a circle around the type – very snazzy and quite eye-catching.

Can I help it if I'm a good designer?

Stoan will be back today. He won't like it.

Stoan can bite me.

Jae shook his head at that and went back to not listening raptly to Wiley.

A few minutes later as Wiley had produced his own note padd to compare with Lina's, a teenaged boy slunk up to their table.

"Um," the kid said. "Ah…"

"Hi, Troy," Jae said with a friendly smile, leaning back in his chair. "Anything we can help you with?"

"Um… That shirt, Mrs. Valiant," Troy finally managed to say to Lina. He scratched his ear. "Where'd you get it? I mean, it's not official issue, is it? It's a joke, right?"

"This little ol' thing?" Lina beamed at him. She gave Jae an evil grin.

That made Wiley look over and do a double-take. "What the blaze do you have on?" he asked. He hadn't noticed.

She stretched the front so he could read it and then turned in her chair so he could see the design on back.

"Great orb," Wiley groaned.

"The first product for our souvenir stand," Lina declared.

"I think it's cool," Troy said shyly. "Please, where'd you get it? I've never seen that one before."

"That's because I just made it up this morning," Lina purred at the boy. "Here, here's the program for it." She showed him her note padd screen.

"Can I have it?"

"Sure. Do whatever you have to do."

The boy grabbed her padd and ran his fingers over the screen, moving them almost faster than her eyes could make out. A para, of course.

"Great," he said seconds later. Apparently he'd ordered one for himself. He glanced back at his table, where some more kids looked at him anxiously. "Um, can I–?"

"Sure, give it to them, too." Lina smiled. "We'll have all kinds of prisoners running around. I used to design tee shirts. Maybe I should go back into it?"

He concentrated on what he was doing and didn't answer. "Thanks," he finally said, giving her back the padd. "Thanks a lot, Mrs. Valiant."

"Stoan is not going to like this," Jae muttered, and Wiley grunted agreement.

"Good," Lina declared with satisfaction. As long as they were going to force her to be here, she might as well start fomenting a little revolution.

Things were busy with newly-arrived Legionnaires being filled in with the news and then talking with planetary defense units and high-ranking politicos, too busy to switch communications stations over to the real thing now when so many Legionnaires streamed through Wiley's lab. Chairs were filling up with paraheroes.

Lina made a sign and taped it to the wall next to her chair: "Reserved for Official Legion Prisoners" with one of those three-dot arrows they had here. And she made sure she was never sitting quite straight in the chair whenever anyone glanced her way.

While quietly twirling her braid in her fingers from her corner of the room, Lina tried to watch it all: real paras operating on a huge scale, utilizing their many-layered organization to its limits. So many new people; so many to look up on her Legion rolls and try to memorize names for.

Her eyes kept sliding to Jae in front of his screens. He directed the actions of military groups, persuaded politicians into conforming with the Legion's plans. He was so confident, standing straight and sure, and those he spoke to listened closely, nodding their heads deferentially.

"Yes, Neutrino, sir," they'd say, and sometimes one would bow their head as if Jae were a king. He certainly looked like a prince at least, the kind you saw in movies, not in real life. The last Feithi; one of the preeminent Legionnaires.

He was grace and ancient power. He was embodied starlight that walked the worlds. And yet he'd held her, made love with her, and he'd felt very real. She could remember the way his hot flesh gave under the pressure of her fingers and arms the other night, the way it tasted. He'd had an other-worldly smell to him, fresh and open, like alien skies. His breath had–

Jae cleared a com screen and she quickly shifted to study her own padd screen, only to glance up to find him looking at her. He held her gaze with his own before he turned away to call his next contact.

Jae reached for the larex within the replicator but froze when he heard Lina's voice behind him. "We need to talk," she said.

"I told you," he said without turning around, "I'd tell him." He gestured for a privacy curtain for the break room.

It was easier to talk to his back. "Look, I don't know what's going on here. I'm all confused and I know it's because I miss Londo and because I'm new at all this and mostly because I'm so damned stupid. But the fact of the matter is that I'm married, and there's nothing more important than Londo."

He shook his head. "No, nothing's more important than Londo," he said softly.

"I love my husband."

He turned to face her. "So do I."

She gave him a frown and averted her eyes. "You should know that he needs someone who can provide a source of absolute stability in his life, someone he can trust to be there whenever he needs them."

She swallowed. Why couldn't she have been loyal sober or drunk to Londo? "Jae, I know you're his best friend. And I know that I've come to like you very much as a friend over these past few days. Is there any way we can forget any of this? Just wipe it out of existence? I want us to be friends, good platonic friends."

"The friends speech." He gave a bitter laugh. "I've only gotten this once before."

"No, really," she said desperately. She had to look at him for this. "Next to Londo you're the most terrific person I've ever met. You're funny, you're caring, you're smart. And you play music wonderfully." And your mouth was so persuasive, your arms so strong around me, she thought and colored. She pushed that out of her mind, hoping that he hadn't caught it. "I don't want to lose that. I need all the friends I can get."

"Friends."

"Yes. Let's let this cool down. Wait for Londo to come back. Get a little distance between us again. You'll see. This is just a case of bad circumstances. Please, Jae-Jae."

He straightened suddenly. "What did you call me?"

"Jae."

"No, you said 'Jae-Jae.' Is that a common Terran nickname?"

What was bothering him so about this when they were trying to sort through things? "Not really," she assured him. "What's the matter?"

"That's what Lon calls me. Sometimes."

They looked at each other, puzzled, as Lina's mind raced. "Then maybe when Lon and I were sharing minds I picked it up from him. Maybe I even picked up some of his feelings for you that I've misread or turned around."

He regarded her for a moment. "So. You were drunk, and they weren't even your own feelings."

That was it, Lina decided. That had to be it. She was a victim of scrambled neurons.

"Bullshit," Jae said so low that she almost didn't hear him.

She gritted her teeth. "Let's just get this one thing straight. I. Am. Married. I don't know how they do things Out Here, but on Earth a wife is faithful in body and mind to her husband, and vice versa. I owe Lon my life; I owe him my very soul, and he's the center of my universe, not you."

"I never claimed to be that."

"Well, you're not. So this thing is ended, finished, done." She couldn't look him straight in the eyes when her insides were smoldering like this. Damn, he was so beautiful. No – sensuous. He awoke her senses just being near. If she could just forget how his – "I wanted to make that clear. I will bring this matter up with Londo just as soon as I can."

"Not right away, Lina. Give him that much. Give yourself time to step away from it."

She nodded and clutched her stomach. She wanted to throw up. This was not the authoritative end that she had planned this talk to be.

Jae said quietly, "He won't be in good shape when he returns. He'll need you. The funeral will probably be in two or three days." He looked down at his larex and back up at her. "I don't normally act like this either. I choose whom I'm with, and I'm very careful in my choices. Or at least I make my choices for my own reasons. But you awakened my telepathy. I was a telepath when I was young, did you know? We all were."

Frowning slightly, he said, "So I am one again. I forgot how open it makes you, how you can react to subtle things as if they were grand overtures. Once I find my balance with this I'll be fine. I want Londo to be happy, and he's happy with you. That's the way it's going to be and I can get used to that."

"Yes. It's all brain sloshing," she finally said. "Spillage. It was–"

"A mistake," Jae said evenly, setting down his drink. "A huge mistake on my part. I forgot that you were new to touch, to the emotions that come with touching people. I should have been thinking of you as a child and I wasn't."

"I am not a child."

"You are in this case." He put his finger under her chin, pulling up her face. "Look at me. You can't even look at me anymore."

Her eyes were still averted. "I…" Helplessness flooded her features. "Perhaps I am a child. But I'll get over my childishness."

"Look at me, Lie."

"I can't." She brushed his finger away and he took her hand in his. "Don't do that. You underestimate yourself. No you don't; you hide behind the facial hair and the scratching and, and some of the craziness. You know what an impact you have on people. I've seen it in the others' eyes. Those people who bow to you, even the Legionnaires put you on a pedestal–"

"I am Feithi," Jae said simply, softly.

"And Londo is Valiant. I suppose that makes him your equal, definitely not mine."

"Londo is Londo, and that's what makes him special. And he doesn't fawn over me; I value that. I also value honesty – that's what I get from you. But sometimes honesty can go too far. We have an option of never telling Lon. Sometimes you have to keep secrets to preserve what it is you already have."

She nodded miserably. "I understand that. But Londo and I share minds. You can't keep secrets that way."

"Are you sure about that?"

"Not a secret this fresh, this… raw." She shook her head violently. "I'll tell him. I don't know how, but I will. Is that why you did that? So he'd reject me when he found out?"

"I swear, I didn't–"

"Get someone else to guard me, Jae." Now she did meet his eyes quickly and then away. "Find an excuse so it won't embarrass anyone or be bad for your record, and make the change. I don't think I should be alone with you for a while. Please go away and leave me alone and don't look at me. I need time… to get over my childishness. I don't mean to be such a baby. Usually I'm… I'm really quite…" She blinked hard.

"It was my fault," Jae told her again. "I'm so sorry. Here we were on our way to being the best of friends and I screwed things up royally. I get impatient. I do really stupid things. Ask around and people will give you lists of the stupid things I've done." He watched to see if she'd smile, and she tried. "Forgive me? Please?"

"I can't get mad at you, Jae-Jae," she said without realizing what she'd called him. "I told you, you're just too good a man for me to get mad at."

"Then we can get over this eventually?"

She took a breath. "Whatever Lon decides is what I'll go with."

"Whatever he decides?" Was Jae smiling? Lina looked up to him; he was making fun of her!

"I am not some kind of Stepford," she declared. "And I don't plan to be, ever! But this is Lon's call. I'm the one who betrayed him, so he should be able to name the terms afterward. In this case."

"That's another thing I like about you." His eyes crinkled a little like Lon's when he smiled. "You'll stand up to anyone, even Valiant. I think Londo gets a real kick out of that." Coming closer, he smoothed her hair away from her face. "He'll understand. He'll stand by you. He doesn't want to lose you, I can tell you that for a fact."

"Do you really think so?" She couldn't lose Londo, she couldn't!

"One thing Londo is not is stupid," Jae told her. "Only a very stupid man would let you go. You're too fine a woman. Much too fine–"

An inch away from each other, the warm currents of air swirled around them. Then his heart was beating rapidly against her own chest. Her knees went weak and she reached to support herself on his encircling arms. He had such wonderful, strong arms, and she ran her hands up them to feel more, just as he caressed her back, pressing her against him.

They were caught up in each other's eyes, his breath pulsing on her cheek. The faintest smell of sweat lent him an alluring musk. His fingers sank into her hair, pulling her head back to open her to him. His mouth softened. He was going to kiss her. She trembled with anticipation.

No! She shoved him away.

Like lightning, he released her, shock and shame flooding his face. She fell back against the table, supporting herself on the edge of it as she felt the blood drain from her head.

"I'm sorry," he managed to mutter. "Grigach, I'm an idiot! I…" Taking a breath, it was he who turned away from her this time. "You always look like you need to be kissed. I'm sorry, Lina. I–"

"This is not good." Lina backed away as far as she could in the room. "Not good at all." What to do? "Three weeks. No, make it a month away from you, Jae."

"No. A month is too long."

"You can see Londo whenever you want."

"That's not whom I'm talking about."

"Make it two months, then. Three."

"We have a lunch date the day after Londo comes back."

The lunch with just the three of them where Jae was supposed to tell her all the reasons she shouldn't have married Londo. "That's when I'll tell him," Lina decided. "I'll tell him first off. No, we'll eat first and then I'll tell him. No, I'll tell him first."

"I will tell him," Jae said in a low, dangerous voice. He shook his finger at her, stepping in to her. "No compromise on this. I'll be the one. Trust me, I'll–"

"Why should I trust you?!" Lina slammed her fist down on the table by her side. "I will tell you what we're going to do, and by god you'll do it my way. This stupid Legion has tried to take my life over since day one, and I tell you, I'm not having it! I refuse to have someone else control me!"

She stood tiptoe so she could be almost nose-to-nose with Jae. Well, nose to chin. "Mind control, eh? You haven't seen Lina O'Kelly take control of a situation. I don't need no stinkin' mind control to get things done."

She poked him in the chest. "You are going to keep your mouth shut around Londo about this until I – I! – bring it to his attention in my own way, my own time. Probably before our little luncheon, but maybe it'll be there. I haven't decided yet."

"I really–"

"Be quiet! You are going to turn me over to someone else's watch. I refuse to be under your command, and I'll make that refusal official and quite public without any explanation if you force me to. Let people draw their own conclusions about what-ever. You're off my case, Jae."

He was silent.

"And three months. Maybe longer, depending on how things go. We do not see each other. If you visit Earth, I'll find a reason to be gone while you're with Londo. I'm sure that after I tell him, he'll understand my not wanting to be in your presence."

"Do I frighten you that much?" Jae murmured. "Or do I tempt you that much?"

"Don't press your luck, Legionnaire. You are out of my life as of five minutes ago. Finito. End of story, adios. Good luck with your friendship with Londo and with all this Legion stuff, in case I never see you again. It's been… Well, it was fun up to that naked part, but then it kinda went sour. Shit, someone's coming."

Jae grabbed his drink and leaned casually against the counter while Lina scrambled to sit on the banquette's bench.

"Who's got this privacy curtain on?" Leenduk grumbled loudly as he eased through the shining translucency of the doorway.

Jae asked innocently, "Privacy curtain? I didn't even notice. Lina, the signal for privacy curtain is this," he made the signal in the air, "and the way to delete it is this."

Lina mimicked him, coming out of the daze of anger. "Like this. Maybe I did it accidentally."

"Well, watch it in the future, Mrs. Valiant," Leenduk said good-naturedly as he headed towards the replicator. "Some of us are dying of thirst. What were you two talking about in here behind a privacy curtain?" He wiggled his eyebrows as if to insinuate something going on, a sign that he had no idea.

"I was just explaining to Lina that I was going to have to make some other kind of arrangements for her confinement," Jae easily replied. "What with the Aldierran situation going on, well, I'm the one who's talked the most with Bracken and his people. I can't waste my time hanging around Headquarters on prisoner duty just because the commander's got a buzzer up his ass about Lina."

Leenduk nodded his approval of the plan.

"A rotating supervision," Jae said. "Puter, record that I'm transferring Lina O'Kelly's confinement to rotating supervision due to the Aldierran crisis."

Lina crossed her arms in front of herself and tried not to look like she was fleeing the room when she left as quickly as she could.

Now there were phone calls to the various ambassadors to set up meeting times, a call to the Aldierran fleet to confirm, and then there was nothing to do but wait for the main company of Legionnaires to return.

Ms. Yency tried to call through, but Wiley informed her that priorities had changed and Ms. O'Kelly should not be bothered for the rest of the day. Lina gave a relieved sigh at that and wondered what kind of gift she could get Wiley in return, but then he made her fill out a long debriefing form about the message from Aldierra.

After her report had finally been accepted by the system (it took three tries), she decided to put her wait time to the best use by meditating and then channeling Aldierra to see what the planet thought she needed the most. After all, if she didn't know, who would?

Aldierra could tell her what was wrong, but didn't know how to correct it on a human scale. She needed help. Lina wrote it all down in her padd, surprised that they had come very close in their own ideas in many areas.

Thank you for listening, Speaker, Aldierra told her. Funny; come to think of it, Sarastor had called her Speaker also. Lina was about to ask about that when Aldierra added, **You should go now. The Chosen you've waited for has arrived.**

Lina's eyes popped open, but she remembered to thank the planet. He's arrived? She ran to Wiley's console. He was doodling, it seemed, on some note padd, not really paying attention to anything but what was computing in his own mind.

"Aldierra said… Are they back yet?" Lina asked, bringing him out of his stupor.

"Not yet. They'll probably be… There they are now," he said as the signal came in. "I hope that the news about Aiko will–"

A screen materialized in the air above them, with Stoan filling the screen. "We're back," he said tiredly. "We're en route to deliver the victims to hospital facilities. It should take about an hour. And Wilder… we've had a fatality."

"Aiko." Wiley sighed.

Stoan stared at him. "How did you know?"

"We've known since you left. I'll fill you in later."

Lina could see Londo in the background sitting with the others, holding his head. Such joy flooded over her! Londo was back! Lon was alive! His presence filled that empty spot in her mind once more.

Londo love, are you all right?

Lina. Yes, I'm okay. The reentry from hyperspace just caught me off guard – suddenly getting all these telepathic impressions again. It's going away. How are you, chérie?

I'm fine now. She sent him a pure feeling of love, and she could see him smile a little on the screen. He was tight with anxiety and misery, but now she could feel him begin to loosen up and relax, and she realized that it was because she was here for him.

He wore her chain necklace around his neck.

Give us an hour, Lina.

One hour. Then I come looking for you. She could hear him laugh at that. **I love you. I've missed you so much.**

Baby, one hour and then I can show you how much I've missed you.

An hour! What was she going to do for an hour? Jae and Wiley were already firming up the funeral plans now that they were definite, a mournful air around both of them. The others here stood in shock; they hadn't had time to warn them. Bolton began to argue with Jae, wanting to know how the hell had they known? What had happened?

Lina felt guilty because she felt like celebrating. The last thing these people needed was her sitting around and singing.

"I'd like to go to Lon's room, please," she requested quietly. Wiley nodded his head, and she ported. There she took a shower and made sure her hair was perfect with a narsaw blossom in it. She ported on clean clothes. The pareo might remind Lon of tropical islands. Made sure the apartment was perfectly straight, clean sheets on the bed. She put the CDs on full blast and sang along with them in celebration.

As the hour wound up, she ported back to the lab to stand behind Jae. "I am going to greet my husband now," she announced.

Slowly he turned around in his chair. He took in the dress and jacket and nodded. "Computer," he said, "record end of house arrest for Lina O'Kelly. I'm handing full custody of her over to Valiant." He summoned up a smile. "Lina…" He started to say something and stopped. "I'm glad for you that he's back."

"Thanks, Jae," she said softly. "Goodbye."

She left her tracking and prisoner bracelets behind on the console next to him, and ported next to the main cafeteria, which was a fairly central location. From there she used the computer to guide her to the jetsons tube and then down long hallways until she came to a darkened hall next to the primary corridor that led to the hyperspace bay. That corridor was restricted access, but this one wasn't, and it suited her well.

After a few minutes, the doors to the corridor opened and through it she could see costumed people starting to file into Legion Headquarters. Some slowly and silently, others at a faster clip and laughing, happy or at least relieved to be home.

Lina?

She relayed her position to him, hopping in place as she felt him nearer and nearer. The hell with her jacket – She ported it away just as he emerged from the bay, walking calmly.

He looked healthy: black leather, honey-brown skin, powerful build. He unobtrusively split off from the main crowd to head down the dark hall, and when he'd gone about ten steps, he dropped his duffel and sped up, swooping to scoop her into his arms. They hugged fiercely and then covered each other's face with kisses, laughing and hugging.

Oh Londo, you're back, you're back… She wanted to cry with happiness. She couldn't hold him tight enough. He was here, he was alive, he was unhurt! Her universe, split apart for so many days, knitted itself back together in an instant. Her heart touched his again at last.

They stood there, their arms wrapped around each other, reassuring themselves of the other's reality. Nothing had the strength or the safety that his arms afforded. His fingers explored her flesh. Kneading, rubbing, exciting her as no one else in the universe could. Her head spun with exultation, with lust. This was what she'd pledged the rest of her life to: this man. Wherever he went was her true home.

Chérie, *I missed you so much,* Londo began when a buzzer sounded on his ring and in the walls of Headquarters.

"Debriefing in five minutes, main meeting room," Stoan's voice announced. "All members."

"No. That wasn't aimed at you," Lina whispered.

Lon sighed. "Uh huh. This may be a long one, maybe more than an hour. I'm sorry, *chérie.* I have to attend this."

"That's all right. You're back now. I can take it." She kissed him and smoothed his vest down from where it had rumpled. "Just don't go out with the boys afterward."

That made him laugh. He kissed her deeply, letting his hands travel over her. "I think that you can count on me being home promptly, ma'am. I plan on being a most dutiful husband."

"You better be." She pecked him on the cheek and gave him a pat on the butt. "Now get out of here before I make you late."

He turned to go, but then turned back and they kissed a long, long time before he let go and flew back down the hallway toward what Lina supposed was the main meeting room.

She heaved a frustrated sigh. Hurry up and wait. Get her all revved up and leave her hanging. She picked up his duffel and swung its bulk over her back, stumbling at the weight. Well, maybe it was over now, although a small voice on one side of her brain told her that it might always be like this. And the logical voice on the other side reminded her that she'd married a parahero. A megamegaparahero. Valiant himself.

At least he was home. Give her some time and her emotions would straighten out to normalcy, to propriety. The world was solid under her feet again. Londo's presence was once more a primary, living section in her mind. This was the way it was supposed to be.

Follow your heart, Sarastor whispered to her.

Follow your heart, she heard Earth and Aldierra echo. There was an even fainter voice there, hardly words, but a soft breeze across her mind: ***Shalla dyem,*** it said.

Lina told them all, "My heart is here now."

It was time to put her fantasized emotions aside. Londo was her reality. Londo was the center of her universe. There was no such thing as woulda, coulda or shoulda. She had made promises that were her joy to keep; she had set her own future. She was in control again. The road she was on was only wide enough for two, and she looked forward to walking it hand in hand with the one man she loved.

Lina set her shoulders and strode confidently back down the corridor toward her new home.

Illustration by Colleen Doran. Copyright the artist.

Don't miss the next chapter in the Three Worlds saga…

Stalemate

Three Worlds vol. 3

by Carol A. Strickland

He paused in the entryway to his apartment here in Affiliated Systems Mega-Force Legion Headquarters. Yullowei and Mix conspired in the dimmed corridor outside, having followed him. "GoooodNIGHT, Londo," they chorused. It had been days since anyone had laughed, but they did so now.

Londo Rand lifted his chin. "Puter," he instructed the air for their benefit though he didn't even glance at them, "lock my quarters behind me. No access, no interruptions." The door sealed behind him with a satisfying hiss, shutting out the raucous laughter.

Lights were on. His apartment felt somehow different though everything looked the same. It didn't seem as empty as it had always been. "Lina?" he called softly.

Londo's sharp hearing made out the sound of even breaths and he crossed to the center couch of the living room. His bride lay asleep, surrounded by study tablets and a notepadd. Her hair spilled all around her in a cloud of auburn curls. The smooth, inviting line of her leg peeked out from under the gauzy skirt of her night-gown.

He knelt next to her. "Lina…" he said softly, but she was already coming awake. Her green eyes came open to his. "Hi, honey, I'm home."

She threw her arms around him. There was nothing now but her, but him; the world stilled everywhere else for their reunion.

Somehow their embrace ended up in the neighboring chair, Lina in Londo's lap, hugging him tightly. "Don't you ever do that to me again!" she demanded.

"Do what?"

"Go off and leave me for days like that!" She held him at arm's length so she could look at his face again. She ran her fingertips over the line of his cheek and through his straight, dark hair. "Oh, Lon, I missed you so much. I was so lonely! You've been messing with my mind," she accused him. "Making me fall in love with the most wonderful man in the universe, talking me into a wedding, of all things – and then you run out on me!"

"I dreamed of you, *chérie*," Londo whispered to her. "Every time I went to sleep. You're more beautiful than I remembered, sweet Lina…"

They frenziedly kissed, and his tongue sought to penetrate her the same way the rest of him wanted to.

He tried to push her dress down, but it wouldn't go. Puzzled, Lon backed away to examine the situation. The gown was a laced-up satin leotard with a sheer skirt. Her neckline scooped very low, her full breasts straining at what material there was, enticing him. The slit skirt left one long, bare leg free for his hand to slide up, to find the soft warmth of her ass to massage. But he couldn't even get his fingers under the material much less push it aside. He frowned at it.

"I had a little accident with some glue." Lina's eyes were merry.

"Very funny." He looked for an easy way in, but the complicated lacing on the front prevented it, and that went all the way down the leotard. At least the skirt came off easily.

Londo pretended a pout. "You're making me work for this, aren't you?"

"Uh huh. You went out with the boys tonight. You must be punished."

So he began the happy task of unlacing her. "Did not. The meeting just went on for a long time. And afterward we had to have a press conference, and then they wanted me for individual interviews, dozens of 'em. You gave up on me." He grunted at the lacing. Even though he had it undone it a few inches, the material still wouldn't budge. "What the hell is this?"

"It doesn't come off until it's all unlaced. I was wondering why a woman would want to wear something like this, but about an hour and a half ago I figured it out: to teach her husband a lesson."

All he had to say was "I'm sorry," in any of three languages and the sound-activated material would slip off her like water, but Lina was not going to tell him that. Not yet.

"I've had a few days to think about this marriage," she said instead. "I don't know about you, but I've started to make plans. Legion Protocol certainly has its own rules of just what we can or cannot do. Did they have anything to do with all your interviews? They don't approve of me at all. Terran, you know." She made a sour-milk face at him, hoping that she'd caught Ms. Yency's expression to best effect.

Lon leaned so his mouth was right next to her ear. "Damn everyone in Protocol and let me in, *chérie*." He licked her in back of her ear and squeezed her next to her lacing. "C'mon, Lina. C'mon, baby."

"Um." She pushed him away from herself. "And I didn't give up on you; I just fell asleep." She brushed her hair back with her fingers. "Here I'd spent an hour trying to look just right for you. Now I'm all rumpled. Lon, let me brush my hair at least."

"*Non, non, non.*" He smiled at her and stood up. "I have plans to rumple you up some more tonight. You're going to be very, very rumpled." He lifted her into his arms without any effort as she caught her breath. "You can straighten up in... oh, two or three days, when we come up for air."

Flying quickly – very quickly – into the bedroom, he laid her down on the mattress and crawled in, hovering over her.

"Only two days?" She wrapped her arms around him.

A buzzer went off from his Legion ring. "Damn!" He hit a button on the nightstand. "What?!"

It was Legion Commander Magnos – Stoan Kinrol's – voice that came out of the air. "Valiant, you're scheduled for communications duty."

Londo paused a second in incredulity. "You must be joking. Refused. Not tonight. You can find someone to take my place."

"Can't do that. Everyone's in official mourning, Legionnaire, and procedures must be followed."

"There are exceptions to everything, Commander. I have tonight off. Period. Rand out."

He stared at the comm button for a second. "Damn."

"What?" Lina gazed at him. That famous frown had appeared on his forehead.

He grimaced in apology. "It's Stoan. He seems to have doubts about us. About you, really. It's–"

"Mind control of Valiant," Lina said. "Some strange telepathic woman comes out of nowhere and suddenly marries the great and powerful Valiant. Well, who wouldn't think that? He'll get over it. He'd better."

"*Eh bien*, he's being a royal pain in the ass in the meantime. He spent the entire mission harping about it. And the thing is, he's a really great guy, somebody you could trust your life to if you needed. He's the commander of the Legion for a reason. Now he's running this campaign against you – And he has followers. You heard about... about Aiko..."

"We've known for days. *They* told me when it actually happened. Oh, Lon, I'm sorry. I'm so sorry!"

He nodded, not looking at her, licking his lips. She had those spirit guides that told her *things*. "Maybe it's Aiko's death that's making Stoan so edgy. She was a good friend of his, too. As commander, he has a responsibility to his people, so he holds himself at fault."

Lina sat up on the pillows and smoothed Londo's hair. "If you want, I can take us home tonight. I've been practicing teleporting. Biofilter in place," she tapped her head. "No quarantine needed in either direction any more. There's no reason we can't go home now that you're back. Return to Earth and get away from this for a while."

He sighed as he pulled her to him. "No. If we run I'll just give those people more ammunition against you. We'll stay here tonight. The funeral will be in four days. Can you stand staying here until then?"

"Four days; that's fine. I know you must be taking this very hard, love. How are you doing through all of this?"

He closed his eyes with the pain. "I… Not well at all."

Lina hugged him to her and he laid his head on her shoulder, squeezing her hard. She stroked his hair, rubbed his back.

They were silent for long minutes. "Oh god," he whispered, wiping his eyes. "I thought I'd gotten it all out on the trip back."

"Tell me about her," Lina said. "Tell me about the good times."

"This is our wedding night." Londo anguished. "I'm not supposed to be thinking about old lovers."

Suddenly the door buzzer sounded and sounded again. "Intercom on," Lon directed to the air, and Stoan's voice again came to them. "Londo, open up!"

"God. Stoan." Lon's shoulders dropped. "Leave us in peace. Go away."

A creak from the direction of the apartment door told Lina that something was happening. The door let out a groan and she heard it scrape open.

"*Skurn* him!" Lon muttered. He moved forward on the bed to position himself in front of Lina.

Stoan entered the room, his face a little bluer with anger than usual, followed by the woman Lina recognized as Nurunori, aka Andri – parastrength for a power, she remembered, like Forte back home. She was subcommander of the Legion. Very tall, taller than Londo, and lithe; short pink hair. But Stoan was even taller. His parapower had to do with electromagnetism, with the emphasis on magnets. He was in full costume tonight.

"My door better be fixed by the morning, Stoan," Londo warned.

The tall man stared him down. "You've refused comm duty–" Stoan started.

"Comm duty is not the most pressing duty a team leader pulls," Lon growled. "I was called away from my wedding for an important mission, knowing it would last for days, and I went. Now I'm back and I'd like to have at least a few hours alone with my wife. My *wife*," he repeated. "I think that rules can bend for that. I've seen them bend for much less before. For people who didn't want to miss a rockerball tournament. For those who had distant cousins visiting. Stoan, this is my wedding night."

"We've been too slack in the past. It's time we got back on track. Communications duty, Valiant."

"If... if Lon goes on duty," Lina thought quickly, trying to spare Lon from getting in trouble, "could I go with him? That way we could at least talk."

"A prisoner sharing Legion comm duty?" Stoan's eyes on her were scathing. He could see now that the laces on her gown were half-undone. Lon had always liked well-endowed women, and he'd apparently been about to really enjoy himself here. "I don't think so," he said sarcastically.

"Prisoner?" Lon asked. "Since when?"

"Jae told me that was over," Lina told Stoan.

"Jae was wrong."

"What?!" Lon demanded. "What's this about Lina being a prisoner?" He turned to her. "How long? What happened?"

Stoan spoke before Lina could. "She's been under arrest for the past five days. I assigned Jae to watch her."

Lon couldn't speak for a few seconds. His face flushed red. "And... and you didn't bother to *tell* me this little detail?!"

"You never told him?" Andri gasped at Stoan.

"We needed Lon's full attention on the matter at hand," Stoan growled back at his deputy. "Apparently she wasn't kept in a cell. I need to speak to Jae about that."

"Instead I've been keeping people on communications duty company," Lina declared. "And, ah, three times I caught something that never showed up on the monitors."

Lon tried to catch his breath, tried to calm down. What was that she'd said? "Three times?"

She nodded to him. "So it's not like keeping you company at the monitors would mean I was totally useless."

"No," Londo said. "Don't worry about it, Lina. I'm not going on comm duty tonight." He turned to Stoan, his eyes narrowing, brows coming together again to form that frown. "There's no reason, there's no precedent, and I'm plain not doing it."

"Londo, be reasonable," Andri began. She had a remarkably soft voice for such a powerful woman. "This could mean a huge strike against your record."

"For not pulling an easily-substitutable duty on my wedding night? I don't think so. I think it might backfire against whoever tried to put something on that record."

Stoan raised splayed hands toward the Legion's most powerful member. "Work with us here. I'm doing this for you. There are too many questions about this so-called marriage that need to be cleared up. Who knows if there will be an annulment, whatever, before an investigation concludes?"

"Wait a minute," Lina said, angry in spite of her resolution not to be. From the very start, before she'd done the first thing here on Sarastor, Stoan had accused her of being a mind controller, something they seemed to have big problems with Out Here. The only evidence he'd had was that his friend, Valiant, had fallen in love with another Terran, and apparently to Stoan Terrans were the waxy yellow buildup of the universe. Except for Londo.

Lon raised an eyebrow as he realized that his wife was speaking Panlingua without the translator. That would explain the study tablets.

Lina continued, "Who do you think you are, to threaten annulment?"

"I am commander of the Legion," Stoan glared at her, "and I'm calling for an official investigation."

You can pick the format and store you want to buy from here:
www.CarolAStricklandBooks.com

ABOUT THE AUTHOR

When you think of strong women and strange worlds, think Carol A. Strickland.

Although born in a small town in Illinois noted for its Nineteenth Century demonic possession cases, Carol claims that all those voices inside her head are a result of having stories to tell and books to write. Even so, her strange devotion to and study of Wonder Woman would seem to indicate an abby-normal brain.

A one-time comics letterhack and outspoken member of various comics message boards, Carol has found herself the basis for two comic book villains (at times her opinions have not been taken well by the books' creators) (both villains were soundly thrashed) (and both, for some perverse reason, were male) and had one superhero wear her costume design. (Light Lass!)

Carol has also become an award-winning painter. Along with her writing, she exercises this skill in her secondary hours (both of them) as she waits for the lottery to free her 9-to-5 time to more fulfilling pursuits.

All product names, logos, and brands are property of their respective owners. All company, product, and service names used in this book are for identification purposes only. Use of these names, logos, and brands does not imply endorsement.